The Seven Year Itch

KATE MORRIS

PENGUIN BOOKS

PENGUIN BOOKS

Published by the Penguin Group
Penguin Books Ltd, 80 Strand, London WC2R ORL, England
Penguin Group (USA) Inc., 375 Hudson Street, New York, New York 10014, USA
Penguin Group (Canada), 90 Eglinton Avenue East, Suite 700, Toronto, Ontario, Canada M4P 2Y3
(a division of Pearson Penguin Canada Inc.)
Penguin Ireland, 25 St Stephen's Green, Dublin 2, Ireland (a division of Penguin Books Ltd)
Penguin Group (Australia), 250 Camberwell Road, Camberwell, Victoria 3124, Australia
(a division of Pearson Australia Group Pty Ltd)
Penguin Books India Pvt Ltd, 11 Community Centre, Panchsheel Park, New Delhi – 110 017, India
Penguin Group (NZ), 67 Apollo Drive, Rosedale, North Shore 0632, New Zealand
(a division of Pearson New Zealand Ltd)
Penguin Books (South Africa) (Pty) Ltd, 24 Sturdee Avenue,
Rosebank, Johannesburg 2196, South Africa

Penguin Books Ltd, Registered Offices: 80 Strand, London WC2R ORL, England

www.penguin.com

First published 2009

2

Copyright © Kate Morris, 2009
All rights reserved

Extract from *Albert le Blanc* © 2003 Nick Butterworth.
Reprinted by permission of HarperCollins UK.

Set in Monotype Garamond
Typeset by Rowland Phototypesetting Ltd, Bury St Edmunds, Suffolk
Printed in England by Clays Ltd, St Ives plc

ISBN: 978-0-141-03403-4

www.greenpenguin.co.uk

For Jude and Belle

I

It was early Friday morning when I murdered my husband. He was standing on the edge of a white cliff looking out to sea. It was a tiny, tentative push but he lost his balance and fell, shouting, 'Why, Ellie? Why?' The seagulls squawked and screamed overhead, swooping down menacingly towards me. My head rushed with a dizzying wave of adrenalin. The strange fizzing and frothing sensation reminded me of when I was a child and had dared myself to do something dangerous like walking across the road with my eyes half closed.

After he had crashed on to the rocks below, my six-year-old son ran towards me screaming, 'I HATE YOU, MUMMY,' while my little girl turned puce and sat on the grass shouting, 'I WANT MY DADDY!' I woke with a shudder, panicked and stricken with grief and remorse. He was sitting naked on his side of the bed, pulling on his boxer shorts. It was such a relief that he was alive that I made a vow never to take him for granted again. My heartbeat slowed but I was still shaking.

'What's the matter, angel?' he asked tenderly. 'You look sad and pale.'

'Awful dream,' I croaked, not wanting to admit the truth while he was being so kind. 'Jed fell off a cliff. I just couldn't get to him in time.'

'That's very dark, Ellie.' He was humouring me; as though I were a wife in Victorian England and all I needed to do to put myself right was to inhale some vapours. 'That's terrible. Who was with him?' Jack was pulling on his trousers; his bum looked a little flabby.

'You, I think,' I said, stretching my toes under the duvet.

'Oh, so you're blaming me, even in your dreams. Don't you see you're blaming me for everything in our life at the moment?'

'I'm not blaming you; you just asked who was with him. To say that I blame you for everything in our life is paranoid psychobabble.'

Jack left the room; I could hear him turning the taps on in the bathroom. The water gushed out, pounding savagely against the basin. I pulled on my once-white dressing gown that had lost its belt and needed a wash and pushed open the door.

'Jack, I'm very glad that you're still here,' I mumbled. He was looking in the mirror. Jack was a good-looking man. He had dark-blond hair that was greying at the sides, very bright blue eyes and a kind but mischievous face. He usually wore cashmere polo-neck jumpers through the winter and Ralph Lauren T-shirts in summer. He was neither tall nor short. When he was at home, he wore glasses that made him look more serious than he really was. He was a vibrant man who found it hard to sit still and he liked to laugh. About twice a year he would lose his temper and we would cower in corners around the house until he had calmed down.

I was a little taller than him, and my body shape was slimmer. I had long dark-blonde hair that was slightly frizzy and never looked neat and my skin was pale, whereas his was darker. His eyes were wide and trusting, but mine were narrow and almond-shaped, coloured brown.

'It was actually you who fell off the cliff in the dream.'

'What?' He was shaving; the water was still cascading into the basin.

'You don't have to leave the water running like that,' I shouted, 'it's not very ecological.'

'What?'

'Oh, nothing.' He turned the taps off. 'Sorry if you thought I was blaming you. I'm just feeling fearful.'

'Really ... what does that mean exactly? I mean what are you fearful of?'

'Just everything. Maybe I'm worried about you dying.'

'Me dying? I thought it was Jed who died in your dream.'

'Yes, well, dying in general and also flying. I'm fearful of flying.'

'We need to cheer you up. I think we should have dinner together at that little place on the river. An early anniversary celebration.' Jack returned to his shaving while I sat on the loo and flicked through a generic toy catalogue.

Little place by the river. Did he mean the River Café? The Italian restaurant that we used to go to so casually for a sea bass carpaccio on a Sunday, or an impromptu guinea fowl when the mood took us, before Jack lost the part of Dr Granger in *Country Matters*. Jack carried on spending as if he were still earning £3,000 a week and it was my job to curb the spending. Jack was not modest about anything. He always ordered wine by the glass, psyching himself into the idea that he was drinking less that way, and he usually chose the most expensive item on the menu – the lobster with caviar or the pasta with truffle.

Jack was patting his face with a towel. 'Don't worry, darling,' I said, 'we don't have to go there to eat. I really shouldn't eat starchy food at the moment and, anyway, Petra is going to a new-wave rave.'

'That girl,' he yawned and I caught a whiff of his slightly stale breath, 'makes me feel tired.' He gave me a quick kiss. 'We'll celebrate on Saturday as you planned. At the Chinese place.'

'Jack, you know I'd rather go to the River Café, it's just . . .'

'Oh, I wasn't even thinking of the River Café, I was thinking of the pub . . . what's it called?'

'Oh,' I said. 'OK, I was worried.'

'Yes, I know, nothing to worry about now.'

'Just Petra babysitting on a Saturday night. It's her big night out.'

'Um . . .' Jack had lost interest in domestic arrangements.

'Her life is exhausting . . .' I said. 'I'd hate it.'

'Whose life?'

'Petra's,' I snapped, annoyed that he was not paying attention.

'Yes, that's what I said. By the way, I'm going into town to have lunch with Eden.'

'Lunch? It's only seven fifteen in the morning.'

'Yes, well. I'm going to a small audition first.'

'Audition?'

'Yes, voice-over for Dog Delight.'

'Dog Delight?'

'Dog food. It's an advert.'

'What kind of advert?'

'Oh, nothing special. Television.'

'Please tell me,' I pleaded.

Jack – his real name is Guy Boore (God knows why he didn't change the Boore bit too) – and I had been arguing on and off for about ten days and it was beginning to wear me out. We argued in cycles, every few months or so, but ten days was a record. Tensions were running high because Jack was at home and unused to not working and our debts were mounting. When he was feeling anxious he would complain and say things like, 'Ellie, can you tidy up your toothbrush?' Sometimes when the children were out of the house we would resort to shouting and door-slamming – well, I would door-slam and then refuse to talk, like a silent, sulky child. I began to have fantasies about leaving him. On the seventh day of rowing, in desperation, I had called my friend Annie, who had been with her partner Marco for thirteen years.

'I don't know what to do,' I whispered, even though Jack was out of the house. 'My marriage is stifling me. We argue the whole time about everything. We even argue about what to watch on television.'

'Sometimes,' she counselled, 'Marco and I don't talk for about a week and then it just passes and I like him again.'

'But how? How does it pass?'

'He just makes me laugh,' she says. 'Suddenly one of us will say something completely absurd and we will collapse with giggles and be friends again.'

Jack was not in the mood for laughing that morning after I pushed him to his death. He couldn't find a pair of dark socks. He muttered under his breath about being unable to find dark ones to go with a dark pair of trousers. 'Why don't you look up your bottom?' Absolutely no response. I flopped back on to the bed and curled up on my side, as our new au pair Petra had offered to get up with the children on the mornings she didn't go to language school. He started swearing and in exasperation I climbed out of bed and found some of my own black socks. He called me a lazy cow and an incompetent wife. It was true. I had become lazy and incompetent, boring and tired. When I was working full time, I used to run everywhere as I was always in a hurry. But now I moved slowly and sluggishly, like a fat slug, and it took me a week to write a thank you letter, whereas it used to take me at the very most five minutes. I shouted, 'I'LL BUY YOU SOME BLOODY SOCKS!' and Petra raced up the stairs and asked, 'Are you all right, Mrs Boore?'

'Oh, call me Ellie, please.' She hadn't quite got the

hang of things. The day before, for example, I had found her giving the children toast and jam for supper.

'Toast and jam. But they can't have toast and jam,' I wailed, throwing my arms around, overreacting, slightly hysterical.

'They wanted it,' she protested, hunching her shoulders and raising her eyebrows.

'But they are only six and two years old, they need to eat, they need vegetables and fruit and protein and carbo-hydrate and minerals . . . and fish oils.' I sounded a bit mad – definitely a woman on the edge.

She looked at me with undisguised disdain and poss-ibly a hint of pity. I could see that in her eyes I was deeply boring and a desperate, mundane housewife. She was twenty-five but looked nineteen and I was nearly forty. I was so far out of her orbit with her cute pigtails and skinny jeans. My friends wondered how I could put up with having a girl who looked like Petra living under the same roof as me. She was six foot one with brown, slim limbs and long, sleek hair. Her face was small and cat-like and she had an infectious laugh. But at the time I appreciated a bit of razzmatazz at the breakfast table. It cheered me up. I also enjoyed her saucy single-girl stories. At the end of week one, she told me that she had hailed an out-of-service bus because she was lost and needed directions. The bus driver not only stopped but invited her on to the bus and drove her all the way to the tube station she was trying to find. How depressing, I thought later, that I could hardly hail a cab, even one looking for work.

Jack disappeared downstairs and I emerged from the warm folds of my bed to face the day. I ran a bath and pulled my hair into a tight ponytail because it made me feel fresher and somehow tauter, younger and more energized. I pulled on the green calf-length trousers that I had been wearing the night before and a tight top and a small jacket.

Petra was finishing her early-morning shift when I appeared. Jed was impersonating a helicopter and he had an unwashed face and no socks. Maud's face was covered in snot and she had porridge in her hair. I ran around trying to sort them out, cursing Petra under my breath. When I'd managed to force Jed's socks on he marched to the front door with his bicycle, shouting at me to hurry up. I thought of the calories that would burn away on the walk to school and how much greener it was to walk than drive. I praised myself, which was ridiculous really, as it was a seven-minute walk.

When Jack was starring in *Country Matters*, Jed went to a small, private nursery, where they had duck feather cushions to lie on and smoked salmon sandwiches cut into triangles and star shapes for snacks. Vivienne West-wood designed the divine little uniform. I'm exaggerating, of course; there was no uniform but it was very smart. Maud was still there, but since Jack was no longer Dr Graham, Jed – who had spent two happy years in a little private school where the boys wore navy blazers emblazoned in pink – was now at the local primary.

We trudged along the well-worn route to school. Jed bicycled ahead while I pushed Maud in her pushchair. We walked past the rows of houses and the small park where vandals had graffitied vicious squiggles over the benches, past the newsagent and finally through the gates of the school into the bleak grey playground. The school was a huge Victorian building, which looked more like a prison than a school. The playground swarmed with children, running, shouting and climbing the one wooden climbing frame. Jed had struggled when he had first arrived because he found the school loud and chaotic. He hated playtimes because there were a couple of older, stronger boys who taunted him with a rude song, and another thuggish boy who kicked and spat at him. When he told me what had happened at school, I would hug him and wait until we got home so that I could weep in the locked loo, sobbing into a flannel so he wouldn't hear me. Later I would relate what had happened to Jack and cry in a rather silly, melodramatic fashion and poor Jack would blame himself for the situation. But since the spring half-term, after Jack and I had gone to visit the Prada-suited headmaster about the boy who spat, playtimes became calmer. Partly I think because word had got out that Jed was the son of Jack Boore.

I was never quite sure how perfect mother Sarah managed to appear in full make-up and salon-style tresses at that hour in the morning, while her daughter Angelica always had perfect plaits that bounced gaily on her back and a gourmet lunch box. Sarah was chairperson of the parents' committee and occasionally approached me for help in fundraising. I never seemed to have time to stop and chat like the clique of other mothers because Maud needed dropping at nursery, so I hadn't had a chance to make friends.

Dr Graham had suffered a fatal heart attack swimming in a lake and although Jack had carried on appearing in the series for a short time after he'd finished filming, he hadn't been on television for six months. His agent, Eden, had a shrill tone to her voice when I answered the telephone to her. At first Jack had turned down three or four soap scripts with confident bravado – he was holding out for a feature film – but then a month slipped by when nothing came in and he had begun to fret, pacing around, bristling with nervous energy.

We had sailed through the years without saving, and spending nearly everything Jack and I earned (although I hadn't earned anything for at least a year) and we were very seriously considering downsizing to a smaller house in the area. We registered with agents and flicked through the particulars that were sent through the post. But I loved our house, perhaps more than Jack, and desperately wanted to stay. The house was part of me and I loved it because it was my first real home since childhood. Before meeting Jack I had always shared rented apartments with friends, or stayed a year or two with a boyfriend before moving on somewhere else. The thought of leaving my house distressed and saddened me.

We lived in Hampstead, near the heath, and we had a garden and a kitchen that glistened. Even though I couldn't cook that well, I just loved being in our kitchen and looking at all the granite surfaces and the shiny cooker and fridge where Jed's artwork and gold certificates for good work were stuck on with magnets. Jack liked to cook, particularly when friends came for supper when he would don a navy and white striped apron and a white chef's hat. He was a performance cook rather than a domestic cook. I loved Jack when we had people to dinner because he was fun and witty and absolutely charming to everybody, including me, and we would usually end up laughing uproariously or playing a silly game. He hardly ever bothered to make anything for the two of us, not now that we were seven years into marriage. And since money was tight, we had stopped having our fun lavish dinners, partly because we weren't really in the mood and couldn't raise our spirits enough to invite anyone and partly because we couldn't afford to.

When we were 'walking out' as my father would say, ten years before, Jack and I would go to restaurants. I had been to vegetarian and Indian places while studying at Exeter and the local Thai (which my father had great pleasure in pronouncing 'Thay' as a joke). But Jack took me to a whole new kind of restaurant – restaurants with glamorous interiors and celebrity diners. We ate in restaurants where paparazzi waited outside the door, and where it was almost impossible to book a table. He particularly loved restaurants like the Caprice, where he was greeted in a familiar manner and shown to 'his' table and served a cocktail called a Raving Bore that the barman had created just for him.

He did cook for me as well. I remember a particularly delicious risotto made with pea and Parmesan and on another occasion a chocolate and raspberry soufflé which years later he admitted he had had secretly delivered from a local restaurant before it had a chance to collapse. I'd never had boyfriends who cooked for themselves, let alone me before and so it was a real treat. My mother said one could not underestimate what a wonderful thing it was to find a man who cooked.

I had met Jack on the set of *Country Matters* when I was twenty-nine, working as a second assistant director. Jack was about thirty-six and at the pinnacle of his career; charming, successful and much in demand. He was very suave and sophisticated, and I was a little in awe of him. The rumour on the set was that he had broken the heart of a young actress who had appeared for a few weeks on the series. I was in the aftermath of a break-up from an abandoning man, so when Jack offered to get my lunch for me, I smiled and told him I was on a grapefruit diet. I was wary of him, imagining he was the kind of man who could hurt me. 'You look like a feather,' Jack had replied, 'one gust of wind and you would blow away.' The next day he brought me in a box of pink grapefruit and I had to go along with eating them even though I was ravenous with hunger. I wasn't used to being pursued by men and Jack pursued me; he said I needed to be fattened up and cherished and he was chivalrous in a quaint, endearing kind of way. He would open doors, and once when I was cold he stripped down to a T-shirt and gave me his jacket, while the cold wind whistled around us. He was the first man, apart from my father, who was really kind to me. We finally got together one freezing evening after he invited me back to his flat and made a real fire and fed me toast and Marmite.

He was on best behaviour, of course, but so was I. In the early days we spent a great deal of time in bed, laughing, fooling around, eating, drinking and lying in each other's arms. He was smitten after I'd arranged to have an old chair in his house reupholstered in a beautiful Indian material – sky blue with red flecks – that I'd found on sale. 'You must really love me,' he said when it was delivered, tears welling theatrically in his eyes. He talked incessantly, so there was never time to think or ponder or be sad. After seven years of marriage we could sit in brooding silence, neither making an effort to chat, but when Jack was in the mood he was a genius at making even the most mundane detail of his day into an amusing drama, keeping everything light.

'It was brilliant,' he would say, 'I was buying a paper and the man, the news-seller, funny little chap with a cap and fingerless gloves, called me Governor. "Have a good evening, Gov'ner,"' he impersonated the man's London accent. 'Ah, but wait for this bit, when the other paper-buyers went up to the stall he shouted out "*Standard!*" And handed the paper, folded in half, without comment. Made my day, you see, darling. Did you hear me? Made my day. He was like a character in a fifties' film. Darling? Do you think he knows who I am?'

'Not sure,' I replied. 'Maybe. I know the man you mean; he calls me "Miss" and I want to kiss him.'

I'm very good at listening to people who are funnier and wittier than I am, and I like to think I have a good sense of humour so I was a perfect match for Jack. In those days, Jack loved my ability to be spontaneous, but ten years on, if I suddenly suggested downsizing to Rome, rather than buying a smaller house in London, or taking a holiday in a caravan, he wasn't so charmed and accused me of being 'muddle-headed, and not thinking things through'. He was right; I wasn't thinking things through, just trying to be helpful. In the early days we took last-minute breaks in Paris or Rome. He seemed so urbane and unusual. On our last afternoon in Paris, he took me to the Île de la Cité because he wanted to show me a mausoleum dedicated to those who had died in concentration camps during the war. It didn't sound very joyful but it was beautiful. We crept down some stairs behind Notre-Dame at the end of a playground and entered an eerie other world where thousands of lit crystals illuminated the long, dark corridors. We clung to each other and Jack cried, because he said he had never seen his father after he left the family home and for all he knew he could be dead. I cried because he was crying and we sat down and hugged each other for a long, long time. Later I sketched a charcoal drawing of us huddled together in the mausoleum which Jack kept with him at all times.

I'm not a very good cook but I am practical, which Jack isn't. I know how to budget and make lists, change a fuse and get rid of a mouse. He admired my practical nature, because he said his mother could hardly switch the kettle on. It was only later, after the first romantic six months, that he discovered I was someone who cried a lot and threw things when I was angry and was neurotic about dust.

It was nearly ten when I returned from dropping off the children, and Jack was drinking a cup of coffee and eating shortbread biscuits.

'I thought you had an audition to get to,' I snapped. Jack would occasionally take Maud to nursery if he had the time, otherwise I would spend at least an hour walking them both to school.

'Yes, well I do.'

'So why couldn't you take Maud?'

'Well, I had to get ready, prepare myself.'

'Drinking coffee?' I was turning into a horrible, fish-wife harridan and it didn't suit me. If I wasn't careful Jack would leave me and he'd be right to.

'A man can have a cup of coffee and a biscuit before he faces the day, can't he?' Jack smiled at me, his actor smile – wide and charming, but not at all sincere. 'Come on, Ellie, sharpen up.'

'Yes,' I sighed, 'but it would be nice if I could occasionally stand staring into space drinking coffee, while you took the children to school.' I omitted saying, 'particularly now that you're not working, particularly now that we're in debt, with mountains of bills to pay and no money to buy a new boiler.'

'Ah,' he said, 'but potentially you could spend all day staring into space. It's not as if you're busy, are you?'

'Well, actually, yes I am. As you know, I'm starting up a business with Tilda.'

'Right,' he said, as if I'd just informed him that I was going to fly to the moon. 'Of course you are.'

The last long job I took on was as first assistant director on a Stephen Frears film; a period drama. It was something that I just couldn't turn down. Jed was only four months old and I hadn't stopped breastfeeding. I missed him desperately and when I had time to think I would be consumed with tearful wrenching sadness about weaning my boy and being away from him. I telephoned the poor New Zealand nanny, Donna, whenever I had more than thirty seconds free.

'He's doing fine,' she would insist, 'he's had his bottle, he's having a nap.'

'Is he missing me?'

'I can't really say, Ellie.'

'Did he have the bottle of my expressed milk? First? Before the formula?'

'Yes, Ellie, we discussed that this morning. Do you remember? There was very little expressed milk ...' She sounded mildly cross.

After desperately trying to express more milk in a damp temporary toilet structure, I would be back on set, which for most of the scenes was in a cramped town house in Regent's Park. It was my job to liaise with Stephen and direct the extras dressed up as guests in 1930s' evening wear for the party scenes. Some days I wouldn't be home until eleven and too tired to do anything but check on the slumbering Jed, so soft and gentle and lovely in his sleep. After about three weeks of filming I gave up expressing, as my milk seemed to have dried up.

As an assistant director I was on call pretty much all day and night and for several months at a time and I knew it was not a job I could pursue with young children. It was not a job I loved anyway; I regretted not having studied set design rather than working my way up to AD. So I made the decision not to take on any more feature-length films and struggled on, for nearly four years, taking shorter less glorious jobs assisting and occasionally actually directing advertisements about washing powders, badly lit corporate videos about staff training, anything that meant I could commit to short spurts of work. I hired nannies but then felt guilty that I was paying someone a small fortune to look after my children while I floated around the house between jobs. So I started hiring temporary nannies. But temporary nannies seemed to be quite random and impromptu – more into 'saving up to travel', rather than looking after children. Our last temp nanny, Tracy, was lovely but after a couple of weeks she informed me that she was pregnant and in a candid moment admitted that she had been having an affair with a married man. She left when she was eight months pregnant and Maud was just two and, not being able to face any more nannies, I stopped taking on any more work.

My friend Tilda and I were planning to buy a café together. There was a café near the nursery where we used to meet after she dropped off Frank and I dropped off Maud. I liked the man from Albania who smiled at us from behind the café counter. He was good-looking and smart and made a delicious frothy banana smoothie. He told us that the lease was up for sale and we planned to keep him on as manager. Tilda and I had written a business plan with the help of her husband Tom's accountant. We planned to borrow from a bank and our first meeting had not gone badly – at least we had got through without blundering or giggling from nerves.

I had been at home for a year and truthfully was relieved to be doing something again other than helping Jed with his homework, taking the children to the cranial osteopath/dentist/barber/doctor, making them packed lunches, tidying up, clearing away, ironing on name tapes, thinking of things to keep them amused. I was very, very happy to be planning a strategy, writing a business plan, flicking through suppliers' catalogues and meeting people who were not other mothers and children.

At first I had loved the novelty of being with the children, but in the previous seven months or so, since Jack had been out of work, it was more difficult. Even if Jack was home, smoking in the garden, he claimed he was busy thinking about future roles, or scripts he could write. He had lunches with actors and his agent and important research to do in libraries. Occasionally he would pick up Jed from school and lavish him with unsuitable snacks and fizzy drinks but later he would chastise me for not picking up Jed myself. We sold the silver Audi Estate, remortgaged the house and took out a loan that helped the situation and meant we didn't have to move straight away. I obsessed about working again but all my old contacts had moved on, so when Tilda suggested opening a café it seemed like perfect timing.

During my full-time mother job, nobody thanked me for being a good mother or reprimanded me for being a bad one, which made me feel truly invisible. Jack always slightly resented me for not earning, particularly when he wasn't and he would moan about my spending, which had been severely curtailed, even though he carried on having private squash lessons and buying gadgets. There were days when the only communication I would have with the outside world would be a chain text sent from a girlfriend:

> **The most used sexual**
> **position for married couples**
> **is the doggy position: the**
> **husband sits and begs for it**
> **while the wife rolls over and**
> **plays dead.**

Small domestic issues became huge. I resented Jack for the fact that he didn't ever pick up anything off the floor or contribute to the emotional welfare of the children. I had once left a sock near the sink as an experiment and three weeks later it was still there because I hadn't picked it up. The other depressing thing was that I got fatter at home with the children because I always ended up eating their leftovers.

*

Jack finally left and I went downstairs to fetch the post. Petra was skimping around wearing a square-inch hand towel, which was just big enough to wrap around her torso. Her hair was wet and she flopped down in the playroom to dry it with my hairdryer. She was getting ready for her language class. She had used my hairdryer ever since she had first arrived, three weeks before, yet she had never asked me if she could. I had meant to say something but hadn't and now it seemed too late. A small tight knot in my chest hardened as I saw that she was wearing Jack's slippers.

'What kind of acting does Jack do?' Petra asked brightly at teatime, pushing a pizza into the oven and then briskly taking it out five minutes later before it was cooked properly. That's the thing about girls who are as skinny as Petra; they all have weird eating habits.

'I'm so hungry,' she said, gulping it into her mouth.

'He was a television soap star.'

'What's this, soap?'

'It's like a daily story. He was in a series called *Country Matters*. He was the handsome doctor in the village who had an affair and left his wife.'

'He's very handsome,' she giggled.

As if on cue, Jack opened the front door. 'Just got a call from Eden,' he said, walking into the kitchen and laying a bag of groceries on the table.

'Oh yes?'

'Yes. They were very interested in me for the dog food gig that I went to today.'

'Great.'

'Eden has estimated that I'll be earning seven grand for a day's work. Well, including royalties.'

'The pudding dog food?'

'Yes, and apparently it's organic, biodegradable dog food, made with wholegrain harvested under a full moon or some kind of new age crap.'

'It's not crap,' I protested, 'it's a very good idea. Everything that we put in our mouths affects how we are ...'

'Yes, yes, darling. You sound tired, why don't you go and have a rest?'

'I'm not tired,' I yawned, 'just interested in nutrition.'

'Then you should learn to cook more.'

'Yes,' I bristled, not wanting to react in front of Petra, 'you're right.'

A few days later, Eden came over for supper. Well, she brought an Indian takeaway, lots of rice and chicken tikka. (I forgot to tell her that I never, ever, eat chicken without knowing its provenance. God forbid that it should come from a battery farm. Poor wretched creatures locked up in a cage, feathers and bone and unable to move. How could people eat chicken produced like that?)

She had come to persuade Jack to do the dog advert, but he'd already made up his mind. He had decided he would do it and that he was in good company because his friend Stephen Fry did voice-overs. But he always felt he should keep Eden on her toes, so he didn't want to acquiesce too easily. He said he was not sure he should do a voice-over. He worried that it was the kind of job that out-of-work actors resorted to. It was the thin end of the wedge, he said. He would accept that kind of work, he announced, striding from one side of the room to the other, and in two years' time he would be part of a crowd scene in some second-rate costume drama. He sat down. 'I may become a golf pro or open a scuba-diving school. My career is over.'

'Don't be absurd, Jack,' Eden cajoled in her crisp, posh voice, preferable to her shrill tone on the telephone. 'You're a name.' She blew out her cigarette smoke into his face. 'You're a star.' She stood up. She was a tall woman, with silvery grey hair which she wore pushed back with a black velvet hair band. She had lovely unblemished skin, and although she was about sixty she was hardly wrinkled at all.

'An out-of-work star.'

'You are taking a sabbatical after seventeen years' regular work. It's perfectly acceptable, the fans understand.'

'You mean Jean,' I snorted. Jean was Jack's most stalwart fan. She was about fifty, with bleached blonde hair and a fake tan. Occasionally she would wait outside the house and she always sent a Christmas and birthday card.

'No *fans*, Ellie. There are thousands of them.' Jack brushed his hand through his hair. The children billowed in from where they had been watching a DVD in their oversized white dressing gowns. I pulled Jed on to my lap and kissed him all over, kissing and sniffing his newly washed hair. Maud climbed on to me as well, taking prime position.

'I only smoke in the evening,' Jack said, lighting his fifth cigarette since the clock had struck six.

'But you make up for it, don't you, darling?' I ventured, sugary sweetly. 'You know that it's dreadful to smoke in front of the children.'

'Now, now,' Eden said soothingly, 'we're all going to die, may as well die from something we like doing.'

That's what's odd about Eden: her philosophy is quite dark. And she always sticks up for Jack, of course, but that's because he had been keeping her dogs in turkey breast dinner for the last seventeen years.

'There must be something else in the pipeline,' Jack said, standing up and exhaling smoke all over us.

'Well –' she glanced at her mobile – 'there is something I could put you up for. But it's another soap. And I know you were wanting to move away from that.'

'Still,' Jack said, 'I'd like to hear about it at least.'

'It's set in the sailing community. There's a part that may quite suit you. A banker who has taken early retirement to set up a restaurant.'

'Yes?' Jack was looking out of the French windows on to the wet patio. 'And . . . who is this banker? Is he very rich?' Jack rubbed his hands together in glee.

Eden shrugged and I sighed. We were like a grandmother and mother indulging a small, obnoxious child whom we both loved and adored.

'Only thing is,' she said, 'it's filmed somewhere down there . . . oh, you know, near to where your mother lives, near Southampton, five days a week.'

'Could be worse,' Jack said, 'could be worse.'

I imagined myself standing on a windswept beach looking out to sea under a grey, windy sky.

'Look into it, Eden, will you?'

Eden made some kind of note on her BlackBerry and promised that she would.

She left after a jasmine tea and Jack and I went to bed early, and fell asleep with our backs to each other. We didn't hug in bed as often as we used to and neither of us had said anything. We also had sex less regularly. It wasn't that we didn't enjoy sex; it was just that we couldn't quite be bothered. I was cold or tired or lazy and in the morning, when I would have been more receptive, he was not. When I asked Tilda how often she and her husband Tom had sex, she laughed, 'Sex, what's that?' Which made me feel better.

We were about to celebrate our seventh wedding anniversary. And weirdly, almost overnight, I had begun to be attracted to the oddest men – strangers, friends and other people's husbands. I became all stilted and fluttery in front of my son's headmaster, for example, although he couldn't have been more obviously gay. I knew that seven years into marriage was meant to be a pivotal moment; either you clung on to what was familiar or you glanced down new avenues. You could look, I thought, without actually going anywhere. Whenever my thoughts wandered off inappropriately, I remembered the priest who had married us. He was a distinguished, charming, intelligent man. His church in Chelsea had a vast congregation and hundreds of women vying to do the flowers, dust the pews and prop up the prayer books, etc.

The union of marriage, he had preached a couple of weeks before the wedding, is very precious. It's like a glass bowl that you are carrying in the wind. It's extremely fragile and can easily smash to pieces. Shoot down any distraction, anything that could potentially damage your relationship, with a *Star Wars*-type gun. You must never, he warned us, get into a situation where you have to lie to your husband or wife. My skin rose in little bumps. I treasured what he said and kept the words locked away inside me.

I read an article that said psychopharmacologists had learnt that lovers are high on drugs – natural hormones and chemicals that flood their bodies. During the attraction phase of a relationship the brain releases dopamine and norepinephrine, which gives that heady, floaty, filled-up feeling, when there is no need to eat or sleep. When young lovers trawled along the street entwined as one, I was envious. Sometimes Jack and I held hands but it was like holding hands with my best friend.

My nights were filled with dreams of one sort or another, mostly about liaisons with ex-boyfriends and occasionally the odd dark dream about murdering Jack. The ex-boyfriend who appeared most in my dreams was a man called Hal. He had not been so much a boyfriend as a short, absurd fling. I would wake with a sensation of excitement and guilt and feel disorientated and treacherous. He was a writer: broody, menacing and ugly attractive – his nose was twisted and large, and everything about him was too big. In one particular dream he seduced me, forcing me against a wall as he used to in real life. It seemed so real. It was almost as if I had been sleepwalking. All the way to Blackheath or wherever he lived. After one particularly riveting dream I wondered whether to track him down, but decided against it. He was a formidable character and didn't suffer fools. He was intellectually intimidating and extremely well read. He could quote Rimbaud in French, for example. He was sexy, but he scared me. I was afraid of appearing a fool, of twittering on in front of him about something inconsequential and for him to respond with a scathing smile.

'Something has got to give, something has to happen,' I muttered one morning after waking up from another disturbing dream.

'What?' Jack asked.

'Oh, nothing, just saying I'm lucky to live.'

'Good on you, girl,' he said, putting on his monster gold Rolex, given to him by the cast and crew of *Country Matters* when he left the series. 'That's the spirit.'

I was washing up on the morning of our anniversary dinner when, by chance, I heard Hal being interviewed about a biography he had written. It was the life of a Victorian poet named Arthur Munby, who had had a relationship with a maidservant, Hannah Cullwick.

As I scraped the porridge from the bottom of the saucepan, I remembered the evening Hal had accosted me at a bar. We had met on a few occasions, but had never really engaged in a conversation. 'Is that your lover?' he had asked gruffly, indicating the blond man

I was with. I giggled. 'Drop him and come with me now,' he commanded. It was scary and sexy at the same time. He was also with someone and I remember wondering vaguely whether the two dumped rejects would some-how manage to hook up, although it didn't come to that of course.

I was looking forward to dinner with Jack at the restaurant that evening and had even planned what I was going to eat. We hadn't been out to dinner alone for quite a few months and I was hoping we could just be happy for a while and have a drink and a chat. I knew he was looking forward to it too because I heard him talking to Eden on the telephone the evening before.

'No, no. I can't dog-sit, Eden. It's our anniversary dinner. Haven't you got anyone else who can look after Albert and Doggy on Saturday? What about Rafaella?'

So it was very disappointing when he announced that his mother would be joining us. Ruth had telephoned to say she was coming up to London on the evening of our anniversary and she wanted to invite us for dinner. She claimed not to have known it was our anniversary. I knew she knew, because she was the only person who ever sent us an anniversary card. She was lonely, she explained, and was missing her friend Nancy who had died the previous week. I was sure she was making mischief.

'Jack! How could you?'

'I know. I knew even as I was accepting that you wouldn't like it. But she's an old woman, she'll be dead soon.'

'But we could have dinner with her tomorrow.'

'Today is Nancy's birthday and it's an emotional day for her.'

'My seventh wedding anniversary is an emotional day for me.'

'I know, love.' He came towards me and we hugged. I allowed myself to relax into him and rested my head on his shoulder and revelled in being held and nurtured by him.

He had a thing about his mother though. He loved her and hated her too. It's possibly a Jewish thing. It kind of went two ways. He couldn't let her go, mostly based on guilt and worship, but he couldn't stand her either.

It was a small consolation that we went to one of my favourite London restaurants, the Royal China, which is near where Ruth used to live in Finchley Road before she moved down to Hampshire. She still had a tiny flat in a mansion block in St John's Wood that she used when she came up from the country, usually for a dentist appointment or to go to a funeral or see Jack. That evening she was wrapped in an ancient fur coat even though it was a mild April.

'You're late,' she said. 'I've been waiting all night.'

'Yes, Ma, good girl, now let me help you into the car.'

The Royal China serves delicious food: little pork and ginger dumplings and crispy seaweed and light noodles are a few of my favourites. Jack did what he always does and ordered the most expensive items on the menu, even though his mother is painfully frugal. On reflection that is probably his way of paying her back for not buying him what he needed when he was a child. She was the kind of woman who brought her own sandwiches to the theatre, wrapped in used silver foil that smelt of fish, and she refused to rinse her washing-up as it would mean wasting hot water.

While we were eating mango milk pudding I caught sight of Hal swaggering through the revolving doors. My heart whipped up into a frenzied thud. Actually, it was an uncanny lookalike and my heart returned to its usual dull beat. Ruth went through the bill, item by item, and then passed it to Jack to double-check. I resolved to buy Hal's book and somehow get him to sign it.

2

April. It was the month of birthdays, including mine and my friend Annie's and also my little girl Maud's, who would be turning three. The deluge of birthdays made me feel slightly weak; particularly mine, as I was going to be forty. I had read in a Sunday supplement that you are not really old until you are forty-nine. It was something of a relief but it made me wonder, who makes these pronouncements? Who decides that forty-nine is old and forty-eight isn't? Perhaps it was the journalist herself, pushing forty, who had decided to add an extra nine years on to her youth. Even when I was approaching thirty-five there were articles saying that I was then something called middle youth, which sounded so old, so much older somehow than middle age. Middle youth sounded almost medieval, like the fourth son of a family of eight children from the Parish of Whitstable circa 1340.

On the eve of Maud's third birthday I had got no further than wrapping the pass the parcel. I wasn't even sure I had done that properly because each of the little darlings was supposed to receive a present, which was the right and proper thing to do and all-inclusive and politically correct – not like my day when only one lucky child received a rubber ball in the middle. Tilda hadn't given in and still offered one present and a glass of orange squash and a bit of homemade cake to take home in a napkin. So brave! But after Natalie, a self-appointed super-mother, warned me that her son had had a spectacular tantrum when he didn't receive a pass-the-parcel present (it was more a threat than advice), I didn't quite dare. So I stuffed a few presents in the many layers of paper and hoped for the best. At ten p.m. I realized with a bolt to my stomach that there was nothing else for the children to do but open a parcel.

'Jack,' I said, 'Jack! There's nothing for the children to do at the party except sing happy birthday and open a parcel.'

'Can't they play musical bumps?'

'Yes, but that will take five minutes and they are so sophisticated – we need something else.'

Jack was watching a film on television about car chases and guns and men in leather communicating in swear words.

'They are only three years old,' he pointed out. 'Why worry? I mean, what did Jed do for his third birthday? Do you think he even remembers?'

'We were away,' I said. 'His birthday is in August.'

I telephoned my new best friend, Tilda, first but her answering machine clicked on. Then I tried my sister, because I couldn't think who else to call at ten o'clock at night – she was at a dinner party and doesn't even have children, but she suggested hiring a bouncy castle. She said her god-daughter had had one at her third birthday and the children bounced for the entire two hours. The mother was delighted. I flicked through the Yellow Pages and found the bouncy castle page and called about eleven numbers. No one answered, of course, they were all watching the car chase or down at the pub or asleep, but eventually I found a man on his mobile, who said it's very short notice, love, you're going to have to pay a premium, my love, to get the castle delivered next day, love. I was willing to pay anything at that point. I suddenly understood what it was like to be a junkie and finally have scored.

On the morning of her birthday Maud rushed into our room at 5.05 a.m. Jack completely ignored her and rolled back to sleep. He has the amazing ability of remaining asleep through fire alarms, police sirens, dustbin men and particularly the children.

Maud was a tiny, fearless anarchist. She was always jumping on the bed, rolling in mud, climbing up and down the banisters and running away. She was quite cool, even though she was only three, and she had a jaunty style of walking, swinging her arms when she was happy. Her hair fell across her face in a long fringe and was always messy and tangled no matter how many times we brushed it. She talked with a slight lisp and once when I asked her for a kiss she replied with a knowing grimace, 'If you cry I will give you a kiss.'

'Get up, Mummy,' she ordered fiercely. 'Go downstairs. I want my present.' So I rose from my bed at five thirty, wrapped in Jack's brown cashmere dressing gown. I tiptoed down the stairs, yawning, to find Maud standing in front of her biggest present. She loved the doll's house and stamped her small legs in glee, saying she wanted to dance. At eight when Petra appeared in a T-shirt and leggings I opened a can of Diet Coke, as the cup of coffee I had already gulped down didn't seem to be having much effect on lifting my exhaustion.

When Maud returned from her cute little nursery she took her lunch and sat on the bouncy castle (which fitted almost exactly into the paved part of our London garden without a centimetre to spare). She sat adrift in the middle, slightly bouncing until most of the baked beans, broccoli and potato bounced off her plate on to the shiny surface. I could feel my stress levels rising. I was sweating and panting and rushing around in circles, trying to tidy up. At 12.55 I left the house suddenly in a panic, knowing that I had to collect the miniature tables and chairs from Maud's nursery before one o'clock – in lieu I had to buy twelve 'beach balls' for the nursery playground.

At about two o'clock I remembered that I had a meeting with a surveyor for the café project and it would have to be cancelled. I asked Petra to make the sandwiches while I dallied around on the computer and made some telephone calls. She took to the task with gusto, even though she has issues with food. She spread thin wedges of butter on the bread and tiny splodges of ham.

'More,' I said to her, interfering and controlling, 'more food. Children are hungry.' I found that I had this weird habit of talking to her in pidgin English even though her English was quite good.

'Not good?'

'Good but more. More ham.'

We carried on making sandwiches and jelly and

blowing up balloons until Tilda telephoned to say that she and Frank wouldn't be able to come as he had a high temperature. 'He is the only child I know,' Tilda stage-whispered, 'who refuses to take Calpol. I mean, all children like Calpol. I think they put some addictive kind of sugar in it, but Frank will not even have a sip. I've tried everything, including mixing it with high berry jelly.'

I got off the telephone with a stab of disappointment and sent Petra to fetch Jed. 'I feel a little faint,' she said, putting on her tiny fur-lined jacket. 'I think it must be the balloon blowing.'

'You must drink,' I said, handing her a glass of water. 'Drink. Now.'

At 3.30 p.m. precisely a wave of mothers and push-chairs swept into the hall. The mothers (an obligatory fixture at toddler parties) piled their coats up on the banister and moved towards the table where they un-animously refused the bottle of chilled Cava. One jolly mother laughed that she'd be on the floor after even one sip. Wretched woman. I was trying to find the paper cups with the fairies on them because all the mugs appeared to be dirty and I was also trying to stop Maud ripping open all her presents. I wanted her to open them at an orderly pace, so that I could write down who all the dollies and gaudy games were from and then thank them with a perky note. What was I thinking?

Jack had not yet appeared. He had left the house at ten and had promised to be back at two at the latest to help. My fury was beginning to show, as I tripped up and dropped glasses and made far too much tea. Jed arrived back from school and tried to hug his sister but she was overexcited and wasn't interested. Petra went upstairs and came down in what can only be described as an ice-skating costume. The skirt was so short it barely covered her pants. But she got into the spirit of the party immediately and hurled herself into the pile of screaming children on the castle. They clambered all over her and she squealed and turned over on to her stomach and let them all sit on her.

I looked at Jed sitting in a corner, sharing his sweets with a child who was too shy to join the others on the castle. Jed was small and caught cold easily and liked to hold my hand. There were moments, perhaps once a month, when I imagined him grown up and leaving home. It made me feel desperately sad and bereft. I could even make myself cry. I had read somewhere – probably another Sunday supplement – that Italian mothers were possessive and passionate about their sons, and that is why Italian men – so used to being loved, worshipped and cared for – lived with their parents until they were about forty-five. The mothers also behaved strangely with their daughters-in-law. Some were sexually jealous. Maybe I had Italian blood; I was already envious of Jed's future wife. Not in a sexual way, but he was just such good company and so funny and sweet.

Ruth was driven over by Mike, the owner of her local mini-cab firm, from her pied-à-terre in St John's Wood. She had come up to London ostensibly to attend the birthday party, but I knew that it was really an excuse to see her beloved son Jack. She had somehow befriended

Mike and managed to procure him rather than anyone else to drive her around. She hovered over the sandwiches, picking them up and sniffing them.

'Do the children like these?' she asked. 'What is the smell?'

'Cheese.'

'Do the children like cheese?'

'Yes, most children like cheese.'

'Guy never liked cheese when he was a child.' (Ruth always insisted on calling Jack Guy, even though he'd been Jack for years.)

'Yes, well, Jack isn't everybody,' I said, 'even if he thinks he is.'

'What was that, dear?'

'Nothing. Do you want a cup of tea?'

She wanted a cup of very weak tea. 'Just dip the teabag into the cup,' she said. 'You know I like it extremely weak.'

'Yes, I know.'

'And could I have a biscuit?'

I handed her a plate of gingerbread men.

'I've got something for Maud,' she said, rummaging around in her bag and producing a filthy colouring book covered in dust and dirt and half wrapped in some well-crinkled tissue paper. 'Here it is.'

'Thank you,' I said, taking it and placing it on the counter.

'Won't she want to look at it?'

'She will later, very generous of you,' I added.

'What was that, dear?'

'Nothing, nothing, must dash, I can see some mothers with empty teacups.'

'Granny has given Maud a second-hand colouring book,' I whispered to Annie in the study. 'You would think that she could afford something a little bit more extravagant. It's not as if she's broke, she goes everywhere in a chauffeured mini cab. Sometimes she gets poor Mike to wait for her for hours on end while she flusters around Tesco.'

'My aunt is the same. Don't forget, not many of that generation embrace karma and spirituality – what goes around comes around. She's probably in some kind of financial fear – you know it goes back generations.'

'Yes, although Jack is the opposite – he's had a reaction to her thrifty ways and can't stop spending. Lovely really, he's very generous. But where the hell is he?'

The children had been bouncing for nearly an hour and a couple of boys had started pushing and hitting each other with balloons. The mothers were being very apologetic and coercing the tiny horrors to apologize to each other, but it was definitely time to move the party on. I was cajoling the little tinkers off the castle with the promise of a game when the doorbell rang. It must be Jack, I thought, running across the double sitting room, which was now strewn with wrapping paper and spilt drinks, and I clashed into Petra who was scooping jelly into paper bowls.

Unfortunately it wasn't Jack but my sister-in-law, Annie, who's married to Jack's younger brother, Graham. 'Sorry I'm late,' she said, blustering through the door, kissing me on both cheeks, 'but, as you know, my brood are at big school.'

'Oh, there you are,' Ruth said, beckoning her over. 'I don't know where Guy is.'

They kissed and her son Simon, who was seven and already very good at everything, including the violin, gave Granny Ruth a handmade card. The other two children stood neatly and politely behind.

'Where is Guy?' Ruth asked after she'd kissed them all hello.

'I don't know,' I said, dropping a paper plate of gingerbread men. 'But I've got to get the children off the bouncy castle before it bursts or someone is killed.'

'What was that, dear?'

'Just saying I think someone may be ill over there.'

'Ill? Who's ill?' she called after me.

Annie sat beside Ruth on the sofa, like a lady-in-waiting. The two of them were scrutinizing me. In my sleep-deprived hysteria I was convinced that they wanted me to make a mistake. Wait till they see the cake in the shape of a fairy, I thought. It had been ordered from Konditor & Cook and half our weekly food budget had been blown on it.

Finally, moments before it was time to light the candles on the cake, Jack arrived in a suit with a rolled up *Financial Times* under his arm. He never wore suits. He was even wearing a tie. He was talking on a mobile. 'Yes,' he said, 'if you shift over six and take nine from the Geneva account . . .' He was pacing up and down the room as Ruth tried to catch his attention.

'Guy,' she called, 'Guy. The cake.'

He ignored her and went to the window to carry on his conversation.

'What are you doing?' I stage-whispered to Jack as he passed me. He waved me away.

'I'm in a meeting,' he announced into his phone. 'Call you back in forty minutes.'

Jack immediately snatched the limelight by taking the cake in the shape of a fairy, with three pink candles, into the playroom where eleven children were banging their cups on the school tables and shouting, 'We want the cake, we want the cake.'

'Happy birthday to you, Happy birthday to you. You look like a monkey and you smell like one too!' Maud shouted louder than anyone else. All the miniature terrors joined in.

'I love my cake, Mummy,' Maud proclaimed as she stood on her little chair to blow out the candles. 'No cake for grown-ups,' she added.

'Who were you talking to?' I asked Jack.

'A banker at Merrill Lynch.'

Merrill Lynch? The bankers? Had Jack made money? 'Have we made money?' My excitement knew no bounds. Perhaps we wouldn't have to downsize to a smaller house with no utility room in NW10.

'To be honest, I'm not talking to anyone.'

For a moment I really thought he'd lost it. Was he mad?

'Method acting,' he explained. 'The banker. You know ... *We Are Sailing*, the TV show. Eden has arranged an audition.'

'But he's a retired banker,' I said with more anger than I intended, spoiling everything for him. 'He's retiring to the country. He's been a banker. He just wants to relax. He isn't pacing around the room at his daughter's birthday. His children have left home and gone away.'

'Yes, yes, but why do you have to be so literal? You're missing the point. I am trying to evoke the spirit of what it's like to be a banker. Just to know, to understand the stress.'

'If you need a bit of stress just look at our bank statements and your tax return and the pink indelible ink stain on our white finest cotton sheets.'

Jack was about to say something when a particularly large mother asked if she could have a glass of Cava. 'Let's go mad,' she said, flinging her handbag on to the sofa and smiling at Jack. She was the kind of mother who said things like, 'We're getting better,' when referring to her child's chickenpox. The mothers loved Jack; I was aware that it was quite a thrill to have him around. He was the only well-known face at Maud's school. As I was pouring her a glass, the self-appointed super-mum came to find me. I poured a glass for myself and took a sip.

'I think,' she said, 'that the children need some supervised play. What about a game? Have you got anything organized? They seem a bit bored.'

'Um ... yes.' I looked at Jack and noticed that my hands were sweating.

'Right,' Jack said, ignoring Natalie the super-mother. 'Where is the birthday girl?' He strolled over to the bouncy castle and growled at all the children, who screamed with delight and terror.

'My daddy,' Maud said proudly, kissing him.

'My boss,' said Petra, winking at Jack and doing a double somersault off the castle.

'Saucy slapper,' I hissed to Annie.

She didn't really somersault off, but given half the chance she would have done.

The children were running amok and all the mothers were now holding glasses of Cava. The mood was finally loose and jolly and slightly crazed. Even Granny was drinking and Annie was smoking, standing at the French windows, the cigarette smoke gusting into the bouncy castle. Petra was stuffing herself with cake and jelly. The children were buzzing; even though I'd put out carrots and cucumber and free-range mini sausages they had somehow managed to eat nothing but the biscuits and crisps and chocolate Rice Krispie cakes.

Jack was a hero. He dressed up as a wizard and made the children hide all over the house. He tickled and tortured them and told silly jokes. After everyone had gone home, Jack and I had the briefest of hugs.

'Well done, darling,' he said, 'that was a great party.'

'Thank you,' I said, 'for being such a good monster.'

I sat back and surveyed the scene – the trailing wrapping paper, the smeared glasses, the dirty teacups and the new toys, some of which were already broken – and I remembered the days when a hug between Jack and I would sometimes lead to sex. We'd had really good sex after Jed's first birthday, after drinking a bottle of champagne. It had just happened because we were so thrilled to celebrate our son's first birthday. We were so happy that he had made it to one, that he hadn't been swept away from us. No such romping now that Maud was three.

I curled back into my corner, wishing that I could wave a wand and find Jack attractive again or that he would seduce me with the right mixture of tenderness and determination. Annie had confided that her boyfriend, Marco, did not let her get away with not having sex and there was something sexy about that. I still loved the smell of Jack – cut grass and basil – and I figured that as long as I wasn't put off the smell of him, things were salvageable. That night, however, I dreamt I stood at Jack's grave. Friends commiserated, hugging and kissing me, but inside I didn't care. I didn't care that Jack was dead.

The next birthday was my friend Annie's. She was going to be thirty-eight so a whole two years younger than me. It had been a long and slightly dreary week and I was in the mood to be out of my shiny, glaring kitchen and the detritus of children's mess. I had lost a small amount of weight, partly by drinking vegetable juice for breakfast and partly because I was about to borrow a huge amount of money to open the café and stress suited my metabolism. And the final incentive was Petra; it was hard to avoid the fact that her clothes were two or three sizes smaller than mine. It made me absurdly happy that I could squeeze into some black trousers that I hadn't worn for five years and a transparent Temperley top with divine little sequins sewn all over it.

Jack complained that he was tired and didn't want to go and we had an argument as I said it was too late to cancel. He knocked back a glass of wine and smoked at least five cigarettes in the car on the way to the party. He also had a loud conversation with Eden about the dog food advertisement, which he had got – a huge relief to our finances.

We arrived with a bag of Jo Malone bath oils. As Annie was thanking me, a man who had come along at the last minute with Marco's friend Patrick introduced himself. Rick. Oh God, what a loser, I thought. How can you crash a dinner for eight intimate friends? You sad, single misfit. Annie's flat was very small and we squashed around the table in the kitchen. He ended up sitting next to me and we had a joke fight over the last bit of crackling. From my point of view the last bit of crackling was not a joke and with forced *joie de vivre* I snatched it from his hand.

We talked about our respective jobs. He was a scriptwriter and droned on about his latest project – the plot sounded completely implausible but he had a certain energy and in the subdued lighting was not bad-looking. Admittedly my standards had fallen low, but for a few foolish seconds I imagined slipping away with him to some hidden corner. We would kiss, I thought, and he would stroke my hair and we would arrange to meet for lunch the following day.

'What are you thinking?' he asked.

'Nothing much, nothing worth repeating.'

'Now I'm curious. Sure you're not thinking about me?'

'You?'

'Yes.'

'No, not really.'

'Sure?'

'Yes . . .' I was blushing as my face was suddenly, quite unexpectedly, very warm. 'I have to go,' I said, pulling my jacket on.

'Great to meet you.' He stood up and kissed me on both cheeks. 'Wait, before you go, would you like an extra portion?' He pushed a bowl of fruit salad over to me and then burst out laughing.

'What's so funny?' I asked.

'Sorry. Extra portion is an innuendo; it means do you want some on the side?'

'You what?' I stared at him blankly, not knowing what he meant.

'It's rhyming Cockney or something, means having some on the side. Like having an affair.'

He's a creep, I was thinking as I laughed at the joke.

I found Jack loitering in the freezing cold garden with a dusky not unattractive woman and at the first opportunity rushed over, suddenly desperate to leave. I had never wanted to disappear so quickly. How could I have contemplated a grope with such a slimeball, I wondered, as I got into the car.

'You're driving,' Jack said, throwing me the keys.

'I hate driving in these shoes,' I moaned, climbing into the seat but not wanting our exchange to develop into a row in case the story about the scriptwriter spilt out. Jack made no effort at conversation either. 'The food was delicious,' I said after ten minutes of silence. 'Marco cooks like a Michelin star chef.'

'Yup,' said Jack, putting a CD in the stereo. 'He's very good. A little rich for my taste though. Don't know how he manages to cook an egg in a kitchen that small.'

Hmm, I thought, he just can't bear the competition.

All night long I twisted and turned, wondering what on earth was wrong with me. I had never been one of those women who go out to score men. I was not a wayward wench who flirted with other people's husbands and partners. Jack had reached out for me and conked out. I sighed and stayed awake and thought about Hal, before drifting off into an uneasy, fitful sleep. I woke now and then to hear a pig beside me grunting and snoring and heaving around the sweaty bed-sty.

I was exhausted. Ever since Jack had been method acting the part of the banker, he had been putting on his alarm for five thirty in order to get to his 'desk' in the city by six forty-five. The alarm would go off and he would dress in a suit, then take the tube three or four stops before returning home.

It was maddening. Our new routine was to flop from the television to the bedroom and be asleep by ten o'clock. On one of those evenings when Jack was going over a scene he would have to read for the audition, I wanted to scream. I felt as though Jack was suffocating me, squashing down on me, with his overbearing reading aloud and method acting and invading my sleep with his early rising and terrible snoring.

'It will be great if you get the part,' I said to Jack, as we sat side by side on the sofa, 'really great. I know it's a soap, but with Danny Jones directing it should be really good.'

'Ellie, Ellie, leave it will you. I haven't even got the bloody part.'

'But we know it's a done deal.'

'No, we don't. I happen to know that Hugh Grant is going up for it as well.'

'You're joking.'

'Half joking. He was sent the script but turned it down. Hugh Grant has no reason, financial or otherwise, to accept a part in a soap.' Jack sighed. He looked a little crumpled so with a huge amount of effort I made him a herbal tea and rubbed his shoulders. 'Very good, darling,' he said, 'that's excellent, you are so clever. Thank you.'

When we got to bed it was ten fifteen, lights out ten thirty, Jack snoring by ten forty. I was still awake at two, plotting how to get in touch with Hal and run away with him to Blackheath or wherever he lived.

'What shall we do for your birthday?' Jack asked at breakfast the following day.

'Oh nothing, please, nothing.'

'But you're going to be the big forty, you've got to do something.'

'No, nothing. I mean it, Jack.'

It was partly because I knew he'd go over the top and hire the Ivy, or the London Zoo or the Natural History

Museum or something else that we really couldn't afford.

A week passed and Jack didn't mention my birthday again. The night before, he still hadn't said anything and I began to feel a little gloomy and forgotten and childlike.

At five thirty in the morning Jack woke me up and kissed me. 'Happy birthday, darling.'

'Hi, Jack.'

'Happy birthday, forty-year-old woman.'

'Go away. It's too early.'

When I woke again at seven, Jack had gone, but there was a bunch of flowers waiting for me and a card with a heart. 'I love you,' it said simply. I was overtired and a little emotional and burst into tears.

'What's the matter, Mummy?' Jed asked when he and Maud bounced in for their morning hug.

'It's my birthday and I'm too old.'

'You are beautiful, Mummy,' he said, 'the best mummy in the world. I love you more than all the stars.'

I hugged him, trying to stifle my sobs.

'What's the matter, Mummy?' Maud asked. 'Have you been crying?'

'No, I haven't,' I said, smiling.

'Yes, you have,' they both teased me. 'Mummy's crying, Mummy's crying.'

'Mummy is a cry-baby,' Maud announced with terrifying finality.

Petra ran upstairs in her nightie. 'Come on, you guys,' she said, tickling them under their arms. I have no idea where she picked up the American idiom but it seemed to suit her. 'Breakfast time.'

47

By the time I reached the kitchen Jack was back from his commute.

'Jack, this is beyond a joke. You have to stop this now. You haven't even got the part yet. What do you do on the tube?' One night, after Jed had woken from a bad dream, I couldn't get back to sleep and it had occurred to me that perhaps Jack was having an affair. I suspected that he was having what the French call a *cinq à sept*, an early evening affair, although astonishingly he was having one between five and seven in the morning. During the night I had tossed and turned, plagued with rather jealous thoughts that made me want to seduce my husband to show that I was still his girl. Now, looking at his grey shattered appearance, my fears were quelled.

'It's rather good,' he said. 'I watch people. Fascinating exercise. The light in the tube is particularly grim. Most people look so tired – like ghouls.'

'So you're not having an early morning affair?' I tried to sound witty and light.

'Good God, woman ... no.' He laughed though – despite everything, he had a good sense of humour.

'What's an affair?' Jed asked. Jack looked at me and I looked at him.

'It's a beautiful day today,' I said.

Jack was making porridge for the children, tipping the milk and whisking a little water with huge flourish into a saucepan. We were all drinking tea when he said he was taking me out for a surprise that night and I had to wear something special.

'Jack, nothing extravagant I hope. Promise.'

'No, nothing extravagant. I promise. What would you like as a present?'

'Well, there is this book I want.'

'What's that?'

I knew I was about to be tactless but I couldn't stop. 'It's by Hal White . . . biography about a Victorian poet.'

'Hal White. Hal White . . . that name rings a bell. Wasn't he a boyfriend of yours?'

'Just for a minute, you know, not even a minute, more like a second.'

'I'll see what I can do.'

Later that evening when it was time to get ready, I couldn't find anything to wear. 'How smart do I have to be?' I asked Jack, who was in the bath reading a magazine.

'As smart as you feel. I would like you to dress as though you were going to a party.'

'But I'm not, am I?'

'No, no . . . not at all . . .'

I surveyed the clothes hanging in my cupboard but nothing seemed to go with anything else and because I had lost weight everything was slightly too big. I flung the clothes on the bed and ended up wearing what I always wear: a black wrap dress. None of my shoes were right somehow. Some were too high and tight; some were too low and dowdy. In a moment of madness I asked Petra if I could borrow her black suede boots. 'Of course,' she said, 'of course you can.'

I smudged dark blue eyeshadow on to the corners of my eyes and sprayed myself with scent. As we were leaving, Petra asked if she could watch the television in our room as it had the free-view box. Normally I would have said no – how dare she – but now that she had lent me the boots I had no choice but to say yes.

'Well,' said Jack, 'I don't really think it's a good idea. I mean, the bed is a mess. Ellie's clothes are strewn everywhere.'

'No, it's OK.' I gave him a look.

'Yes,' said Petra, 'and if it is good tonight, we can do it another night.'

I smiled at her.

'Ellie, you look much younger like that,' Petra said as we left – I had straightened my hair.

'God, how old did I look before?' I muttered to Jack as we climbed into the car.

'I didn't get the book,' Jack said. 'I got you this instead.' He handed me a soft package. It was a small silk pouch and inside some little pearl earrings that would suit a very old lady.

'Thank you, Jack,' I said, kissing him on the side of his face.

'Here we are,' he said as we pulled up outside Tilda's house. She was a ten-minute walk away but we had taken the car.

'I thought we were going out to dinner.'

'We are.'

'At Tilda's?'

'Yes.'

'She never mentioned it.'

'No.' He was striding towards the door.

50

Tilda answered with an apron strung tight around her waist; she was wiry and had the figure of a teenager. Her hair was long and loose down her back; her cheeks were flushed and her apron was crooked. She gave me a kiss and huge hug. Then Jack propelled me by the arm towards the kitchen. The room was in darkness but then, suddenly, the lights were turned on and . . .

'Surprise!' A small crowd of party guests shouted and sang 'Happy Birthday'. Jack whistled through his fingers. I stood blushing and laughing until a young and very good-looking man handed me a glass of champagne.

I glanced around the kitchen and caught sight of Annie and Marco and Tilda's husband, Tom. Tom was a self-made businessman, balding, with a creative and restless energy about him. I wasn't entirely sure what he did, but it was something to do with microchips and he was the director of the company. He was the kind of man, a bit like Jack, who couldn't sit still. Eden was standing near the open French windows with my young beauty editor friend, Harriet. Eden gave me an arch little wave. She was wearing a purple Biba dress with silver bangles clanking up and down one arm. Ruth had obviously come up from the country for the occasion and sat on a large dining-room chair with armrests.

There were a couple of Jack's actor friends too and my favourite, the well-loved actor William Eade. He was camp and tall and made me laugh but he was also sensitive and kind and remembered our children's birthdays. Jack and William had appeared in a play when they were at Cambridge together and had remained friends ever since. Eileen, who was a young actress from *Country Matters,* flung her arms around me and kissed me.

'Happy birthday, darling,' she gushed. 'We all really miss Jack.'

I'm sure you do, I thought, eyeing up her jiggling breasts.

I smiled at Ruth and she patted an empty seat next to her, beckoning me over. I mouthed that I was going to the loo, not that pleased to see her at my intimate surprise birthday party.

'Where are you going?' she called out.

'To the loo.'

'What, dear?'

'Loo,' I mouthed and made a flushing motion with my hand.

'Haven't you just been?'

'No, I've just arrived.'

'You're leaving already?' she asked as I backed out of the kitchen.

Jack had disappeared. I found him having a lengthy conversation at the front door with a man who had arrived too late for the surprise.

'Come and meet my wife,' Jack said. The man was tall and good-looking with floppy dark-blond hair. He wore a loose linen suit. He was in his early forties. He had a surprisingly squeaky voice. 'This is Bill,' Jack said. 'He's the producer on *We Are Sailing,* the TV programme.'

'Oh, good to meet you,' I said, wondering what on earth he was doing at my fortieth party, particularly as Jack was not yet signed up for the part. 'We are really excited about the project,' I added with my most charming smile. 'Couldn't be more excited.'

They carried on talking and I lingered for a moment before moving on. Harriet handed me an enormous present, which turned out to be a small Japanese vegetable knife in a huge box. We went back into the kitchen, which was full of smoke and steam and far too hot. Everyone was crowded around the table of food, hustling and jostling for plates and fish pie.

I opened the door to the garden and sat down on one of the white fold-out chairs. Tilda came to find me. She had taken her apron off.

'I'm so hot.' She waved her face, 'I spent the early part of the evening heating up fish pies.'

'You're a darling. Did Jack force you into this?'

'No, not *force*. It was his idea though.'

'So embarrassing, I mean we hardly know each other,' I joked.

'I know, I know, the cheek of your husband.' We laughed. 'But you know I fancy him.'

'Do you really?'

'Just a tiny bit.' We laughed again; I didn't mind if Tilda really did fancy Jack, in fact I was pleased.

'Where did all these young gorgeous waiters come from?' I asked her as one came outside and offered me a prawn ball on a stick.

'Jack found them. I think they are mainly resting actors and boys on gap years. Shall we go indoors, it's a little cold?' I followed her back into the kitchen. 'I particularly like that one over there.' She pointed to the oven. A sultry, sexy boy was reaching up for some glasses. He turned round. He was dark-haired, with a hooked nose. He was young and unsmiling.

'Yes, I see what you mean,' I said. 'I used to have a boyfriend who looked like that. Tony Windhorn.'

'Tony Windhorn?' She sounded amazed.

'Yes, do you know him?'

'Well, yes, years ago, we hung out a bit. Just friends. He called me the other day. He's been living in France.'

'Yes, I know.' My heartbeat had quickened at the mention of his name.

'He said he'd call again.'

I'd heard that he had several children, dotted around the world. I imagined the children lived with forlorn women who he visited once or twice a year. He was the ultimate commitment-phobic, a man who I had seen casually for a couple of years. We had passionate, slightly kinky sex, until his deceptive ways and disruptive need to lie had begun to bore me.

'Oh, I'd like to see him,' I said, but when Tilda asked if she should give him my number, I replied a little too emphatically perhaps, 'God, NO!' And then more to convince myself than her, I added, 'He's so dark and I don' t mean black-haired, although he is that too.'

Ruth was hovering nearer and nearer.

'Could you show me where the cloakroom is, dear?' she asked me.

'I've got to find Jack,' I said, diving back into the hall-way and into the tiny dark loo. I locked the door and sat in the dark on the lid of the loo and then decided I was being ridiculous and turned the light on again and looked in the mirror.

'Hello, hello, is someone locked in there?'

I recognized William's voice booming outside. 'It's me,' I said. 'Birthday girl.'

'Birthday girl. Are you doing something v. v. naughty?'

'No, no ... I was just wishing I was.' I opened the door.

'Do I detect a woman who's running away from her own party?'

'No, it's just ... well, it feels more Jack's party than mine and everywhere I go his mother seems to be three steps behind. I don't want to get cornered by her for the whole evening. She just wants to complain – about Jack, about anything, and she's got a selective deaf problem, which is so annoying.'

'I sympathize,' he said, taking my hand. 'It must be awful to be surrounded by actors and agents and tiny deaf mothers. Absolute nightmare for you. Dear Jack, I think he's feeling lost and restless about resting. You know how us actors are.'

'Well, yes ...'

'That's why he's asked a few friends from the industry. To give himself a little boost. Dear girl, please have fun celebrating your birthday.'

'I'm far too old to celebrate my birthday.'

'You, old! That makes me positively ancient.'

We laughed in the corridor and made our way towards the sitting room. We fell back on an empty red sofa. 'So tell me about your friend, Tilda,' William said, glancing around the room. The floorboards were painted black and there was a large kilim in front of a real fire. There were two chairs with wooden arms that would not have looked out of place in colonial Africa and the walls were painted dark red. There was a skull of some animal on the mantelpiece and red cushions everywhere. It was a warm house, a welcoming house. My house was a bit stark – a bit white and hard around the edges.

'Tilda's a great mix: laid-back but organized, chic and cool too, intelligent but fun.'

'Mm . . . and not bad-looking,' William said. 'I imagine she's broken a few hearts in her time.'

'Oh yes, she's still breaking hearts,' I said proudly. I admired Tilda. There was something about her. All the mothers at the nursery longed to be her friend and it was hard to pinpoint exactly why. She was thin and zany, not exactly beautiful but very attractive. She had a purposeful, almost posh voice and an attractive energy, vital but not nervous or neurotic. She had worked in catering in her twenties and in her thirties had published two cookery books – one for children and one for students – but, like me, she hadn't worked for a while and we'd bonded as stay-at-home mothers who wanted to (and in my case needed to) do something else.

He escorted me back to the kitchen where Annie dipped a carrot in hummus and stuffed it into my mouth. 'I feel *slightly* bad,' she laughed, 'that it wasn't me who gave you a party.'

'Don't worry,' I said, 'I think Jack forced her into it.'

'He could have forced me,' she joked indignantly. It

sounded like a joke, but I knew she was probably a little put out, particularly as Tilda was a new friend.

I thought of Annie's flat, tiny and messy, with a huge overgrown garden. I loved it, loved it like an aunt loves a niece, loved to see it, but didn't want to live with it. I loved the quirky paintings and photographs, and the coat-stand made from neon perspex antlers and the bathroom painted pale yellow with a Victorian roll-top bath. 'Oh, Annie, darling Annie, please can I have my next party at yours?'

'Well,' she paused, and laughed again, 'we could fit you and Jack and about four others!'

Minicab Mike came to pick up Ruth and after she'd left I drank a glass of champagne and rolled myself a cigarette. I never usually smoked, and found myself feeling rather heady and loose and liberated.

My sister and brother-in-law arrived. They had been to the theatre. I adore my sister, Nicky; she's only eighteen months younger than me. She's married to a boy-man who writes music for films and jingles for advertisements. Nicky is a researcher and consultant for the history pro-grammes. Sam, my brother-in-law, is about five years younger than me but looks ten years younger because of his jet-black hair and unwrinkled face and hip way of dressing.

My sister gave me a beautiful brooch in the shape of a butterfly.

'I tried to get Mum and Dad to come,' she said, 'but you know what they're like, so reclusive. Dad said he couldn't get out of a seminar this evening and Mum said she has someone from a rebirthing group coming for dinner.'

'I'm seeing them at the weekend,' I said. 'Mum rang to say happy birthday.'

My parents live in Dulwich. Our father, Peter, is the head of history at a local college and my mother runs an Internet company selling spiritual baubles, gemstones, chimes and yoga mats. Her yoga mats are made in Peru and come in vivid colours and after a short piece about her in a Saturday magazine she'd had hundreds of orders.

'Mum's made quite a lot of money this year,' Nicky said.

'Oh good, maybe she can keep Jack and me,' I replied blithely.

Nicky laughed. 'Um . . . not the kind of money you and Jack are used to.'

'What do you mean?'

'Well, all those designer dresses, weekends at the Colombe d'Or, caviar dinners and new cars. Mum's cash won't stretch to that.'

I knew she was half joking, but I suddenly felt spoilt and useless and idle, the kind of person that presumed money could make you happy. 'But we're not like that any more,' I protested, wanting to confide in her. 'We were never that bad – maybe we were a little spoilt but we still had problems like everybody else. Our marriage was cracking before Jack lost the part and our financial situation changed. You know what he's like, so overbearing, so large in every way.'

She gave me a wry look and put an arm round my shoulder. 'I know you and Jack have problems sometimes;

all relationships go through hell,' she assured me, 'it's just that people don't talk about what really goes on in a marriage. It's one of those taboo subjects that is only really touched on.'

'Do you and Sam have problems?' Nicky is very private and doesn't usually discuss these kinds of issues so I was surprised we were even having the conversation.

'Of course. He usually gets his way about things, and I just sit there and take it and feel resentful. It was him who wanted us to live in a one-bed flat in Notting Hill. I would have preferred a two-bed or three-bed anywhere else.'

A waiter who was passing around a tray of mini sausages interrupted us.

'Anyway,' she said, 'it's your birthday party and we shouldn't be scrutinizing our marriage problems.'

The sullen-eyed, hooked-nose boy handed me a sausage on a stick and I tried to catch his eye, but he barely acknowledged me.

There was dancing in the conservatory and I joined the throng a little reluctantly with my brother-in-law, Sam. Jack was wearing a green suit with a tartan tie. He was dancing with Eileen, the piece of crumpet from *Country Matters*. Jackie Radcliffe played Jack's daughter in the series and I noticed he was whispering something into her ear and had his arms draped around her and she was laughing. I pretended not to care but I did care very much. It was humiliating to be hurtled into the spotlight at a surprise party and then to have your husband grope the most obvious woman in the room.

I went back to the kitchen and sat at a corner of the kitchen table and ate some fish pie with Harriet. We were stuffing ourselves with raspberries and ice cream when Jack finally emerged, sweating and puffing, from the dance floor. I didn't leap up and fling my arms around him. He could see that I was a little upset, so with an immense amount of charm and flattery he persuaded me on to the dance floor for a final whirl. The music buoyed me up and I was spinning, and light and slightly drunk. Jack stopped to talk to Eden so Tilda and I danced together and Jack wandered off. We sang loudly to the chorus of Sister Sledge like teenagers and everybody joined in and there was lots of hugging and kissing. We finally said goodbye at midnight after Tilda swore that I didn't have to help her clean up. It was my latest night of the year.

'But I wasn't groping,' Jack protested in the car on the way home. 'Nothing like a grope.'

'What do you call placing hands all over someone's bottom?' I wondered what I was turning into – a dreadful, petty, suspicious spouse.

'Did you enjoy the surprise?' he asked me, swiftly changing the subject.

'Yes,' I said, 'very much. It was lovely of you to arrange it. It's just that crumpet, she annoyed me.'

'You didn't like the party,' Jack said, changing tactic, 'I can tell.'

'I did, Jack,' I said. 'I loved the cake and the dancing and talking to William. I got a bit depressed when Nicky said how spoilt we were and how much money we needed to survive.'

'Oh, come on,' Jack said, 'just because she likes to dress in Oxfam and read second-hand books. I can tell you for nothing that Sam makes a lot of money and he's not giving it all away to Unicef. They somehow think it's dignified not to spend money.'

It was late when we arrived home. Petra had moved from our bedroom but was still up watching a movie on our television in the minimalist sitting room with the large, white, child-unfriendly sofas and the exquisite paintings in bold colours that hung on the walls.

Jack poured himself a large glass of water and went to bed. The film finished and Petra stood up and yawned.

'Happy birthday,' she said, waving at me as she backed out of the door.

'Thank you.'

'You look so sad,' she said, pausing for a moment. 'What's wrong?'

'Nothing. Nothing. Just feel so old.'

'You're not so old,' she said. 'You're not so young either,' she laughed, 'but not old. You have a lot of life with lovely children and a good husband. You must live more and do your own things.'

She trawled up the stairs to bed. Maybe she was right; the thing to do was to loosen up a bit and be more determined to find my own life again, rather than tagging behind Jack's. Whatever happened, I promised myself I would not abandon the café project in London. I went to bed, thanked Jack for the party and stayed awake worrying about anything that popped into my head. I worried about how small Jed was, about whether Petra was trying to steal my husband away and, finally, about the café. Why had I agreed to open a café? I couldn't even make a cappuccino.

3

Three weeks after my birthday, Jack did the recording for the biodegradable dog food advert.

'Just my bloody luck,' he said, 'that I've ended up making an ad about dogs. At least there was one consolation.'

'What's that?'

'No hair and make-up. And Eden assured me that they had asked for me personally. They like my gravelly, sexy voice. Not such a bad way of earning a living. An hour of work. I had to read the script once for rehearsal, once for the recording and finally to shave a second off. Interestingly, it had to be eight point six seconds precisely.'

'Umm, really . . .' I was looking at my ragged nails.

'Bloody dogs,' he muttered, opening a can of beer.

Jack was not really a dog person. His mother had kept a Labrador called Sally who lived to be 102 in dog years and as a child Jack was expected to take it for a morning and evening walk. The dog smelt of cabbage and carrots and made Jack wheeze. There had been a time, after we arrived in Hampstead, when we used to find dog turds up and down the pavement outside the house. Jack was completely incensed and telephoned the council to insist on prohibitive signs being installed with threats of huge fines. He also demanded CCTV cameras. One night he stayed up until two to see if he could catch the turd-laying dog but to his dismay had no luck.

I remembered the day after he stayed up all night watching for the dog, a photograph had appeared in a newspaper diary showing Jack and a two-bit actress from the Midlands having dinner. We had rowed and shouted and I had vowed to leave him. But the same day I reversed the car into a skip and momentarily forgot all about the bint.

Jack was so happy to have worked that he made a Bloody Mary to celebrate and danced a little jig. Then he sat down and played an Erik Satie piece on the piano which I loved because it was so mellow and mysterious. The next day, though, he was mumbling and chain-smoking and chain-eating toast, three signs that something was wrong. After a bit of probing I discovered that the audition for the soap, *We Are Sailing*, had been postponed because the producer had been called on to another project. Jack made a decision, there and then, to stop getting up in the early morning and stressing himself out, and travelling on tubes at unearthly hours. He would no longer method act the part of the banker. He swore a great deal and drank coffee and sat staring at his computer in the sloping office in the attic. He had decided to write his own script – he would have the starring role but he hadn't quite figured the plot.

'My life is over,' he announced once morning. 'I am jinxed; nothing works any more. Everything I touch is doomed.'

'Oh, don't be ridiculous,' I scoffed. 'You're just not used to being idle. Go to the gym. Or take a course in photography.'

'Now you're being ridiculous,' he said. 'I just wish Eden would stop inviting me to lunch.'

'She's only trying to jolly you along.'

'I'm not Father Christmas.'

'No,' I agreed, 'you're certainly not.' Poor Jack. He was like a grumpy teddy bear, particularly with his little pot-belly.

A few days later, Tilda and I lost the property that we had coveted in Queen's Park after the vendor had accepted our offer. At the last moment, literally days before we were expecting to exchange contracts, someone else offered £20,000 more than us. I suspected that Mick, the estate agent, had been a bit underhand and shown it to other people after promising to take it off the market, but he hotly denied it. 'Come on,' he said to me when I asked if he'd been showing other people, 'would I do a thing like that?' He called to tell me the news while I was on the school run and annoyingly he sounded rather pleased with himself. I chivvied Jed into his year group line and bustled Maud on to her scooter. I nearly wept. Suddenly the whole project was over, or that's how it seemed at that moment. I could almost hear Jack saying, 'It's not a joke starting up a café, you know, it takes hard work and commitment.'

'I don't want to go to school,' Maud said when we reached the pavement.

'Well, you are going today,' I said. 'You have to because all your friends are expecting you.'

'I don't like my friends.'

'Well, they like you.' I pulled her scooter along while she kept both feet firmly on the base.

After dropping Maud I had a little cry and, feeling heavy and sorry for myself, I called Tilda, as I'd missed her at school. 'Are you still near?' I asked.

'Yes. Are you OK?'

'Bad news,' I said. 'Must meet.'

'You sound like a text. Café? Five mins?'

'See you there.'

'The thing is,' I said to Tilda, sipping a hasty cup of takeaway tea on the pavement, 'that café was perfect for us: good position, affordable, just right. Maybe it was too perfect. Maybe it was jinxed.'

'Maybe it was haunted,' Tilda said. 'Maybe someone was murdered there.'

'Eek, maybe we'd have found chopped-up body parts in the freezer.'

'Yes, it was all wrong,' she carried on, 'all wrong, and I swear – and I'm not just saying this – there was definitely an odd atmosphere in there. Kind of creepy.'

'I think we should start looking for other properties straight away.'

'Definitely,' she said. 'Something better will come up.' She sounded confident, as though I'd be mad to doubt for a second that we'd find something else.

During the next few days we searched for another

66

café. We walked and drove around the streets making enquiries, we searched property sites on the Internet and telephoned estate agents, but there was nothing available that met our demands. We knew what we were looking for: it had to be a café with potential. We were searching for a rundown café, selling really mediocre food; a working man's caff with a bad smell. After weeks of discussion we had decided that our aim was to buy a café business from the leaseholder with a fifteen- to twenty-year lease and we wanted to pay about £15,000 a year in rent, which was almost impossible to find in our area of London. Our plan was to make the café a two-year project; after two years we hoped to sell the business for a large profit. We wanted to source really good organic food that we would use in the café and have a deli counter and we planned to cater for children's tea parties.

While I was out Jack would call me three or four times on my mobile. He would ask where the brown sugar was or inform me that there was dust on his bedside table, moan that the flowers in the vase had wilted or tell me to pick up green peppers when he could easily have gone to the corner shop himself.

We became obsessed with our quest and I began to pay Petra extra hours and missed my lunches with Maud and my afternoons with Jed. I would return home and Jed would run towards me for a hug, while Maud would refuse to come near me. I was so glad to see Jed's happy little face, and Maud's sulky one, that I would smother them both with kisses until they had to push me off.

Tilda and I carried on driving around the city looking

for new locations and stopping at cafés in the name of research. Usually around lunchtime we would find a café and stop for a sandwich and a snoop. Because Jack and I were in debt I was more obviously worried than Tilda about the money we would have to borrow. Tilda was sensitive about my concerns and would often end up paying for lunch; even though I would give her money, she would slip it back. She also knew that I was strictly unable to buy clothes as I used to or have my hair coloured and cut, so one afternoon she treated me to a haircut at the salon where she had hers done. I tried to think of ways to help her out; I'd once done a weekend course in massage and offered to give her one but she brushed my efforts aside and said I could take her for a cocktail on her birthday.

One morning we were driving through Kensal Rise when Annie called. She had found out that her local café was for sale in Shepherd's Bush.

'It's a fifteen-year lease. Twelve thousand a year.'

'That's really good. What's he selling the business for?'

'I don't know.'

'What's it like?' I asked.

'It's perfectly OK, but not great. You know, baked potato that tastes as though it's been cooked in a micro-wave with bottled salad dressing and curly bits of salad, tired tomatoes and hard avocado. If you could get in there and offer Illy coffee and a delicious croissant, you would have people begging to be allowed in. We need a cup of decent coffee on the Askew Road. We're on the frontline down here.'

'Thanks, Annie darling, we'll be down to have a look.'

We debated whether to venture west; it was, after all, so far from home. The lease was substantially cheaper than the Queen's Park café but it was in a less salubrious street. Tilda and I talked about it and decided we had to at least go and see it. The café, when we found it, was in a corner position at the end of a row of shambolic shops: third-hand furniture that spilt on to the rubbish-strewn pavements, funeral parlours, betting shops, a small dentist and a newsagent. Steve's Café was painted a cheerful yellow but inside it was drab. The floor was dirty, it was draughty and there was a miserable amount of food available to make into sandwiches: a couple of wrinkled sausages, a sad pink pile of gloopy tuna with bits of corn stuck into it, shreds of dry chicken and thin, processed slices of cheese were displayed behind the steamy glass counter. Despite the grotty food, the tables were full: a group of sharply dressed young businessmen poring over architectural drawings, a middle-aged man studiously eating a cooked breakfast and an Afro-Caribbean man talking on his mobile. I ordered an avocado sandwich but the avocado was tasteless and hard.

We both agreed that the site was the right size. The owner, Steve, a balding man with a white pasty face, was selling the business for £35,000 and emigrating, as he said, 'to open a bar in Cadiz'. We left the café and sat in the car for a while round the corner.

'So what do you think?' Tilda asked.

'I think we should make an offer.'

'Well, it was crowded with locals and that's with the grey and soulless food.'

'We will make it good.'

'It could be good.'

'It could be good.'

We kept repeating this one line over and over. We ummed and ahhed and made inane remarks.

'We have to telephone Annie; she's the only connection I have with Shepherd's Bush.'

I telephoned Annie and she suggested that we visit her for half an hour while she was having beetroot and carrot soup for lunch. She answered the door, mid-mouthful, and led us to her kitchen. She spoke very fast in between slurps of soup.

'I just know it would be a good idea,' she said. 'Trust me. It's already full most of the time. How could you go wrong?'

'Believe me, we could go wrong,' Tilda said.

'Yes, we could overspend.'

'Or underspend.'

'Or fall out with suppliers.'

'Or never make any money.'

'Or be closed down by Health and Safety.'

'Or talk each other out of doing it at all.'

On the way home Tilda and I discussed the terms of the offer and agreed that if we could get the lease extended by one year and the price reduced by two thousand we would take the café. We decided that we would make an offer the next day after talking to our respective husbands and that we would somehow lure the good-looking Albanian manager over from Hampstead.

'It is miles from us,' Tilda sighed unexpectedly after we'd finished discussing the rent.

'Yes, but it's liberating to be so far from home. We can reinvent ourselves. Can you imagine if we were at a café in Hampstead? We'd have Jack coming in and out all day making silly remarks.'

'Yes, that would be a bore.'

'Jack Boore – The Café Bore.'

'The customer from hell. The one who buys a coffee and stays for an hour, flirting with the waitresses.'

'Steady on.'

That evening, while Jack was watching himself on a film that was showing on television, I told him that we had found a café. 'We're going to offer thirty-three thousand for the business,' I said to Jack, 'two thousand less than what he's asking. What do you think?'

Jack was so engrossed in staring at himself that he just nodded and said, 'Well done, darling.'

'So you think it's all right?'

'Yes, I do. Where is this café?'

'Well, that's the thing – it's in Shepherd's Bush.'

'Shepherd's Bush?' Jack spluttered in horror, momentarily tearing himself away from the film. 'Land of shoot-outs and crack houses!'

'Shoot-outs – you make it sound like something from the Wild West.'

'It is. That's exactly what it is. Don't you remember there was a shoot-out in a restaurant in the Uxbridge Road, and a man died, and a car crashed into Winkworth estate agents?'

'I do vaguely remember, yes, but Annie and Marco haven't been shot at.'

'No, but it's much safer around here. And it's too far to travel there.'

'Stop being so controlling. We've made our decision.'

'Well . . .'

'There's no well about it. That's what we're going to do. We can't afford a café around here anyway. And we need you to help.'

'Me? What can I do?'

'You can help us promote it. You're Jack Boore and I'm Ellie, wife of Jack Boore.'

At first Steve refused our offer. We were ostensibly cool and left it on the table but behind the scenes we fretted through sleepless nights. We knew that we were not going to find anything else that we could afford. We had given up hope and were thinking of offering the full amount for the business when he called Tilda and said he would agree to our terms.

That evening Tilda came round to have a celebratory supper while Jack was taking his mother out to the theatre. I had been inspired by Annie's soup-making and had made my own version. 'Just peel vegetables, put them in a pot and leave them to cook,' she had instructed me, 'then add rice or barley or something.' We sipped the soup and drank not one but one and a half bottles of wine, and were giggling uproariously when Jack returned from the theatre.

'What's so funny?' he asked.

'You!' Tilda screamed. 'You're wearing sunglasses at night.'

'Ah,' said Jack, with a little hop, 'that's so my fans don't pester me for autographs.' He went over to the piano and opened the lid. Then he sat down and began to play the music from the film score of *The Sting*.

'Are you serious?' Tilda asked over the music.

'Well there's always one, isn't there? Ask Ellie.'

'Usually a little old lady, or a couple of little old ladies …' I said, but I had stopped laughing. It was so lovely to listen to Jack play. Jack was the man of my dreams when he played the piano. When Jack played the piano, I was in no doubt of my love for him.

A week later we sent round our surveyor and he came back to us with a worrying report. The roof was leaking and it would cost about ten thousand pounds to fix it. We sent the report on to the freeholder and for several weeks there was silence. While we were waiting we carried on looking, but found nothing. Meantime our lawyers called his lawyer and finally, just as we had really given up hope, there was word that our landlord was going to fix the roof. He asked for more money, but we refused to budge. Another week passed and he relented and agreed to do the work; our offer stood and was accepted.

We had decided a little genuinely but also quite ruthlessly that we should have an angle to pull in customers and procure some press interest. The café would be as eco-friendly as possible. Although we were not exactly eco warriors, we were eco foot soldiers. We recycled and endlessly tried to cajole our reluctant husbands to do the same. We bought our children organic carrots and spurned vegetables from Kenya, we switched off lights and anything on standby, we tried to avoid shops that sold suspiciously cheap clothes (although it was hard to resist the £3-packs of children's pyjamas from Primark). We were also aware that you had to have a certain amount of money to be selective about what you ate unless you chose to live off the land, which was of course highly unlikely.

But once we started investigating the organic café idea, we quickly realized that we wouldn't be able to describe ourselves as an organic café. We discovered that everything from the butter to the breadcrumbs would have to be organic, which was not economically possible. While planning the café we had grandly envisaged a wind turbine on the roof and a solar thermal heater, rubber crumb underlay made from recycled car tyres and recycled tablecloths. When we actually budgeted, we realized we couldn't afford to have it all. So we made compromises. We would use sustainable packaging and eco lighting. We were going to use organic frozen croissants instead of fresh because they would last longer.

I called William Eade and he promised he would give us an endorsement. 'Something along the lines that your café is the best in West London. What's it called?'

'Not sure,' I said. 'At the moment it's called Steve's Caff.'

'I rather like that,' William said.

'Café Blue!' Jack scorned our new name. 'I can't do publicity for a café called Café Blue.'

'Oh, go on, Jack,' I pleaded, 'you're an actor. Actors love publicity.'

'I'm beyond publicity,' he wailed. 'I'm looking into buying a golf course in Spain.'

'Any publicity is good publicity.'

'But this is publicity for you, not me.'

'So I'm your wife – it's a business. To earn money.'

'It's just a hobby job,' he said harshly. 'It's just something to do – you can't expect to make money on a café. You'll lose interest.'

'Jack . . . you bastard . . .' I imagined shooting him in the foot or swinging a punch into his balls or dropping our crystal chandelier from Venice on to his head from a great height. 'How could you say something like that? How could you? Just because you're out of work, you can't bear to watch someone else involved in a project.'

I left the room wanting to slam the door but instead I took refuge in the garden. Most of the garden area behind the small patio was embedded with a labyrinth made from raised stones. I walked along the labyrinth path breathing deeply. Finally I sat in an old deckchair and Jack brought me a cup of tea. He stood over me while I waited for an apology. None came. He seemed to

75

be pulling out some weeds when I heard the smallest 'sorry'.

Later that day, Tilda and I went to talk to the Albanian manager, Dionysus, who worked in the café we had lost. We sat down and waited for him to finish making a smoothie.

'What can I do for you ladies?' he asked, coming towards us with an alluring smile.

'We were wondering,' Tilda said, 'whether you would like to come and work for us? We're opening a café and we would love you to be our manager.'

He laughed. 'Where is this café?'

'Shepherd's Bush.'

'My girlfriend is au pair there. Nice area. But I like this café, I know the customers. They know me. We are like family. This is my home.'

Just at that moment, to prove his point, a large woman came in, wiped her brow with an oversized handkerchief, wheezed a little and asked how he was.

'Mary, hello, love, sit down, wait for me. One minute. I'm sorry, girls. Thank you for asking me.'

'OK. OK ...' I was basking in being described as a girl, letting it waft over me.

'Can I give you my card?' Tilda asked. 'Just in case you change your mind. Or in case the café is hit by a tornado or something and you need another job.'

'Tornado?'

'Big wind,' I said. 'Out of control wind.'

He laughed again. 'You are funny ladies.'

'Damn,' I said to Tilda in the car. 'And he's so sexy.'

'He's very attractive,' she agreed. Her mobile was ringing. 'Can you get it for me?' she asked.

'Hello, Tilda's phone.'

'It's me, Dionysus.'

'Oh, hello.'

'I have idea. My cousin is coming next week. He will need a job. He doesn't speak good English but he will learn.'

'We'd like to meet him.'

'Good. I will tell him to call you.'

'Who's he sending over to see us?'

'His cousin.'

'Everyone who comes to work in London seems to have a cousin who comes too.'

'Do they?'

'Yes, in my experience they do.'

'Well, if he looks like Dionysus ...'

'Exactly,' Tilda agreed. 'We're on to a winner.'

4

The following morning Eden spoke to Jack about an audition for a Sherlock Holmes TV series. It was a small part but two good actors were attached. It was rumoured that Kevin Spacey was considering a role and that HBO in America were collaborating. Jack put the phone down and immediately said he wouldn't mind if the house was photographed for an interiors article – he had refused only the week before. Then he wished me luck for the café and finally he took some mince from the freezer and began to cook.

Jack was better, but I was really tiring of Petra and her skimpy, flirty, coquettish ways. She had become far too familiar and treated the house as if it was hers. It was disconcerting to find her curled up on one of our white sofas when we returned in the evenings, watching our television and eating an extraordinary brand of low-fat nuts. She had an escort, a dark-haired Middle Eastern man who chauffeured her around. One day he drove Petra and her Norwegian friend to Brighton so that they could see the sea and do some shopping.

The friend was a little blonde thing. I imagined them giggling behind his back and cajoling him into paying for their cocktails and afternoon tea and little black dresses and faux gems. Maybe he gave them cash, which they spent later on their boyfriends. The possibilities were endless.

Petra's tiny clothes, sinewy figure and obvious sex appeal made me fraught. I was no longer skimpy and sexy and young. I wasn't someone who could stop buses like Petra, or dance all night, or get men to drive me to Brighton for the hell of it. Nor would I want to, but I wanted to be attractive again – before it was too late.

I scrutinized myself in the mirror one morning. I was still a good-looking woman but fraying around the edges. As I was going through my clothes I found a tiny pair of trousers that I had worn in my single days when I lived on carrots dipped in Marmite and pieces of celery covered in cream cheese. My face was now saggy and my hair a bit limp and my lips somehow thinner than they had been. When I pulled the trousers on I could see that I had gained at least four inches around the waist.

We had arranged to do a couple of photo shoots as publicity for the café and we were keenly aware that we needed to get ourselves into shape. I wanted to be edgy and thin and alluring, rather than cloudy and dull and flabby, so I was pleased that I had already lost weight due to stress, financial stress. The café was costing us more than we had envisaged – we'd been quoted a public liability cost of £1,200 a year which we had forgotten to budget for.

I tried walking around the park swinging my arms and later made a hair appointment. Tilda went one step further and had a series of anti-ageing facials using electronic pulses and a body-contouring treatment.

I was scheduled to meet a magazine journalist in a local Thai restaurant. She had asked if she could come to the house, but I had made excuses about building dust. Journalists had an uncanny knack of snooping around houses and bringing unfortunate snippets of domestic life into their articles.

When I arrived at the restaurant there was only one person there, eating alone, a man reading an evening paper. I chose a table by the window and dipped in and out of my London A to Z map book as it was the only thing apart from the menu (which I already knew by heart) that I had to read. I was becoming incensed that Mandy Rudd, feature writer, was twenty minutes late when a black taxi drew up outside on the kerb. A woman of about my age with dark hair and a black-belted jacket, a twenty-five-inch waist and dark sunglasses emerged.

'So sorry,' she said as she came through the door. 'The traffic,' she continued, glancing at her watch. 'This is nice.' She didn't sound at all convinced. It was obvious that she would rather have been at the Caprice. 'What do you recommend?' she asked, glancing at the menu, taking off her dark glasses. She was groomed immaculately, well made-up; pretty but hard-looking, and her skeletal body and face were a little ageing.

'Pad Thai is good.'

'I'm off carbs at the moment.'

'Tofu salad? It's a little spicy.'

'Spice upsets my stomach.'

'Rice?'

'Perhaps a bowl of rice and some clear soup.'

High maintenance. I imagined that this woman was single. No sane man would put up with her.

'I'll take notes, if that's OK.' She retrieved a gold pen from a dainty bag. 'I don't usually use a tape recorder, a lot of people find it off-putting.' She opened her notebook to a blank page and then looked at me expectantly. 'Tell me about your café – the press release says you are green and eco-aware. Do you live a green life? I mean, do you drive a car with low emissions, own a bicycle, etc?'

'Yes, I own a bicycle.' (I omitted to say I didn't actually use it.)

'Um, yes, I've thought about a bicycle myself. You see, cars can release twice as much carbon as flying.'

'Really?' I took a sip of the hot jasmine tea. 'I didn't know that.'

'Of course, some people are a little sceptical about this whole green thing. Me included. My father, for example, made a compost heap in the garden, but days later it was covered in rats. People find it hard being green and ethical; it can be time-consuming and expensive. What I'm saying is, what is the point of a green café?'

'Well, we are just a café, trying to offer good quality food ...' Before I'd had a moment to consider her questions and finish my answers, she bombarded me again.

'How far do you go in this café? Are your fridges and dishwashers rated A for energy and efficiency?'

'Yes,' I replied with relief. We had replaced both the fridge and the dishwasher, as they were old and not big enough. 'And we will use organic ingredients wherever possible ... because we like good quality food. We will also have low-energy lighting.'

'Great.' She leant back in her chair and studied me. 'That's really great.'

My vegetable Pad Thai and her bowl of sad rice appeared. My Pad Thai was steaming with tofu and cashew nuts and noodles. I stuck in one of my chopsticks and twirled it into my mouth. She left her rice untouched, which made me feel clumsy and greedy.

'And how is Jack? I interviewed him once years ago.'

'Did you?'

'Yes, we had tea at the Dorchester Hotel.' She smiled in a slightly sly, secretive way, as though she and Jack shared some fabulous secret. 'What's he doing next?'

'He's got lots of projects on the go.'

'Anything we should be looking forward to?'

'Yes, but nothing that I can talk about.'

She wrote something in her notebook, which was rather disconcerting. I had the impression she didn't like me. She took a spoonful of soup and then one more tiny sip. She asked me if Jack was missing *Country Matters*. I sighed and answered that he wasn't particularly.

'I'm surprised.' She wiped the corner of her mouth with the large linen napkin. 'After all those years, he must be missing something about it.'

'You'll have to ask him.' I scooped a large mouthful of noodles into my mouth, suddenly not caring whether I appeared greedy or not. Then she explained that the magazine was doing a men's fashion page for the November issue. She asked me if Jack had any bespoke clothes.

'Would you rather interview Jack than me?' I asked, trying not to sound too cross. 'He would be more able to answer these questions. You see, I can only suppose what he would say.'

'Well, no,' she retorted with a brief smile and a curt stab at her napkin with a knife, 'but you are the wife of a well-known actor. Readers are interested. You know how we are all fascinated by celebrity.'

'Are we? Or is it a myth perpetuated by magazine editors? Can I give you some advice? Some readers are bored. Yes, bored. People I know. My friends say that they are bored of reading about actresses' and models' dieting tips and which skin cream they use. It fascinates me that this celebrity junket is so relentless. I keep thinking the mood will change. We're all interested in someone who is globally recognized as being a genius, but really ... these actresses who ...' I stopped myself before I descended into a tirade about the bint from Birmingham.

'Um ...' she said, 'I do realize that Jack Boore is not a global name and I understand what you're saying, but we wouldn't do it if the magazines didn't sell. And they do. And you're buying into the frenzy by agreeing to do this article. It works two ways. You get publicity and we get Jack. We're interested in you too, of course.' She blushed. 'The concept of an eco café is good copy and a photograph of two attractive women running it helps too.'

It was true then: without Jack I was an insignificant nobody. And in the great scheme of things, Jack was not that important either. She asked me a few more formulaic questions about the café and then when we finished she asked for the bill. We said goodbye quite formally. I had the most uncomfortable feeling that somehow she had won, which made me more determined than ever that the café would be a success.

There was no going back now. Dionysus' cousin, Felipe, was going to be our manager. He was young and hardly spoke English but he'd worked at a university bar in Rome, so he knew how to make delicious coffee. We were expecting a couple of stories in magazines; one article in an ecology magazine was about how we would be using local produce, as far as that was possible in London. We had met a woman who kept honey hives in Ealing and Tilda had heard of a man who had an allotment near the café that could provide Belle de Fontenay potatoes. But the majority of our food was going to be delivered from a farm in Wiltshire. I had been to see the man who ran the farm, a kind of gentleman farmer who actually wore tweed plus fours and who kept pigs and geese and chickens, and also ran a farm shop where you could buy quaint-looking yellow tomatoes and every type of green leafy vegetable, some I had never heard of. He was enterprising and leased out his stables to a riding school; he had apple orchards and row upon row of vegetables; and he hired out his barn for parties. We would take deliveries twice a week to start and he gave us a competitive delivery rate charge, unlike other companies we had approached. A few weeks later we exchanged contracts on the café and every morning when I woke up my heart began to palpitate.

Jack had the interview for the Sherlock Holmes series but it turned out that if the production went ahead it would be only two days' work. He barely spoke to the children or me and I spent a morning working out how to cut down on our outgoings; anything that wasn't absolutely necessary would have to go. After one particularly depressing weekend when Jack would only communicate in grunts I went upstairs to the bedroom and began to cry. Jed found me and put his arms around me. 'I love you, Mummy, even when you're sad.' Maud joined us, demanding that I read her a book.

'If you don't read to me now,' she said, 'I won't kiss you goodnight.'

Eden telephoned me one morning on my mobile when I was having an onsite meeting at the café.

'Ellie. Eden. We've got to do something about Jack.'

'Yes, I agree,' I said, walking towards the door. 'He's depressed and depressing. It's just that I'm busy right now. Can we do something later perhaps?'

'He's absolutely impossible to get hold of. You would have thought he'd pick up the phone to me, after all . . . I mean, I am . . .'

'He's very low.'

'Tell him from me that we have a pencil for the *We Are Sailing* audition but it's not yet confirmed. They definitely want him though. The meeting is just a formality. It'll be very good money, enough to pay off all his debts – including what he owes me.' She laughed.

'You?'

'Oh, I'm sorry,' she said. 'Didn't he tell you? I lent him some money, just a little something to tide him over.'

'No, he didn't tell me.'

'Oh, he's a dear. How quaint and old-fashioned to keep it all from you.'

'I have to go, Eden – so sorry. Lovely to talk.'

'Lovely,' she repeated.

How much exactly had Jack borrowed? She had said a 'little something' but what did that mean? Was it a couple of hundred or £20,000? More debt. My head was already spinning with figures as we'd had a meeting with an accountant who had asked us to write a more detailed business plan for the café. I climbed into the car and decided to telephone Jack and confront him. Then a policeman approached to tell me I was parked on a double yellow line.

When I returned home, Petra was running around with yellow washing-up gloves on. She was screeching at Maud and Jed. They were covered in paint and looked like children starring in an ad for washing powder.

'What happened?'

'I don't know, I can't do everything at once.'

'My God, Petra, Jed's hair is purple. Were you watching them?'

'Of course,' she said. 'I just went to the bathroom for one moment and . . .' She sighed and pulled off her gloves, then flounced off upstairs leaving behind a riot of mess. Tea not tidied up, unironed clothes spreading over the tables and chairs, Maud in tired tears lying on the floor and Jed jumping on and off the white sofas, leaving cloudy paint marks on the covers.

I followed Petra to her room, where she was lying on her bed.

'What's the matter?'

'Nothing.' She exploded into a sob.

'Yes, what is it?'

'I don't know,' she said. 'Sometimes very difficult living with family – no private.'

'Maybe you should go home for a week. Take time out.'

'That would be good,' she decided. 'Maybe I should stay home and study.'

'Mmmm,' I mused, half hoping she would take her tiny skirts and bare midriff and pierced navel home and half dreading she would. It was hard to find someone both nice and willing, who could speak English and had an authentic reference.

The rest of the day passed slowly. The house had recently been photographed for the interiors magazine, one of a handful of magazines that had called us after we had sent out a batch of press releases. The photographs would show a gleaming, shiny family home. The photographer had been interested in the Tracey Emin bedcover that Jack had once bid for in a frenzied and competitive state of drunkenness at a charity auction. She also loved the labyrinth that I had designed with the help of an eminent landscape gardener who had once won the Chelsea Flower Show and the pin-board above Jack's desk that was covered in photographs of well-known faces, notes on napkins, newspaper clippings and posters of films that he acted in before he was signed up to *Country Matters*.

In the magazine we would be portrayed as a successful, happy couple, with two beautiful children. No one knew that our marriage was bleak, our debts were spiralling out of control and by the time the magazine was published the bedcover would have been auctioned at Christie's. My sister had often remarked that no one, under any circumstances, had the perfect life. We were all flawed in some way and no relationship really worked on every level. Tilda, for example, looked as though she had everything, but I knew that her sex life was nominal and that her husband was obsessed with his company. He worked weekends and could never relax on holidays (he absolutely needed to make a list of things to do which would always include some sport like hanging upside down from an aeroplane).

That evening, as Jack and I sat down for dinner, after some probing from me he admitted that he had borrowed money from Eden.

'How much?'

'Ten, fifteen, twenty thousand . . .'

'Jack.'

'I had to pay my mother back; she lost a significant amount gambling on the horses.'

'Pay her back for what?'

'Cash she lent me when I was at RADA and for the deposit on my first flat.'

'I never knew that.'

'Well, now you know. But once the new soap is in place, everything will come together.'

'Will it?'

'Yes, it will.'

'Eden thinks it's a done deal.'

'It is.'

'Are you sure?'

'Ninety-nine per cent.'

'Well done, Jack, well done.'

'Don't congratulate me yet. Not till it's one hundred per cent.'

My heart raced with pleasure, because at least Jack would be happy again; well, relatively happy – he would have preferred to star in a film. The soap was a compromise; he needed to earn. At least we would be able to keep the house. Or would we? I had noticed that he had begun to grumble a bit about living in London and filming for the soap would be in Hampshire, near to where his mother lived. He had been mumbling about wanting to go back to his country roots. He wanted 'views' he said and 'a large garden where I can fork a fat bit of beef on a barbecue.' Then something else had happened that made him more determined than ever to move out of London. Our neighbour, the ebullient Alex, who lived across the road, was mugged at three o'clock in the afternoon in front of her children as she walked to the post office. Two hooded men snatched her watch and handbag and ran away. A week later her house was on the market and a week after that there were two offers.

One offer she received was well over the asking price.

'So sad she's going,' Jack declared (though they had never exchanged more than a few words), 'forced out by crime. I want to live somewhere where I can walk without the fear of being mugged. What do you think about moving away, Ellie?'

How could he be serious? I thought. He knew that we had just exchanged contracts on the café property.

'Lovely to hear your opinions but, as you know, I can't move anywhere. Not right now. I could have moved a year ago, even six months ago, but not now.'

He looked at me with a puzzled expression. I sighed.

'Oh yes, because of your business thing with Tilda.'

'It's more than a *thing*, Jack. We've exchanged contracts and signed a lease. We've bought a business. We've done interviews in magazines. We're getting builders in.' My voice sounded just the tiniest bit hysterical, high-pitched and whiny. It was the harridan, the horrible alter ego that emerged when Jack was belittling me.

'Calm down, calm down. I'm just thinking about the children and, well, of course, me. I don't want to commute from Hampshire.'

'No, I can see that, but please don't bring the children into it.'

'All children love living in the country. They should be living in tree houses and playing outside from dawn till dusk.'

I wanted to throw something at Jack, but Pauline next door had once told me that if you feel like hitting your partner you should leave the room. I went to the garden door, but couldn't find the key. I looked out at the magpie strutting on the patio. I turned round.

'Well, Jack, let's have a serious conversation about this very big issue after you've found out if you're definitely going to get the part.'

I caught a glimpse of my new neighbour the day he moved in. A monstrous moving truck that was parked outside three houses seemed to take up most of our street. Uniformed men were running in and out of the house all day, moving trussed-up packages, long sofas and beds. He waved at me as he climbed off a motorbike. He wore black leather and when he took his helmet off I noticed he was blond.

One rainy Saturday afternoon in late June, a few days later, the children hovered and buzzed, eating my toast, climbing all over me and talking in high-pitched screeches. We had just taken over the premises of the café and my body ached with fatigue. We were committed to opening the following week but we had found that the coffee machine was broken and there was a typo error in the 500 menus we had printed. Felipe, the manager, could barely speak English and on a trial run of breakfast we discovered the chef, who was from Newcastle, overcooked the scrambled egg and burnt the bacon.

'I'm going mad,' I said out loud. 'I need a break.'

Jack offered to take the children for a swim at his health club.

Bliss: three whole hours to myself – to dream, to potter and languish idly on the floor pretending to be single.

I longed and longed to be alone. In retrospect, my single life had taken on a glamorous filmic quality, which it definitely didn't deserve. I recalled endless slim suppers and high-heeled shoes, manicures and massages, long nights and idle days. I remembered cocktails and parties and edgy affairs. Hadn't it been fun? All that sex and intrigue? I was musing on it all when the doorbell rang.

'Oh no!' I muttered, what hell, they must have changed their minds about swimming. I opened the door with a sigh to find the man who had moved in a few days before.

'Hello,' he said, 'I'm Mark Brandon, your new neighbour. I waved the other day.'

'Oh great, yes, I do remember,' I garbled and then added pointlessly, 'So you're not exactly my neighbour; you've moved opposite. We were wondering who would come,' I continued in an absurd suburban housewife manner.

'Me.' He waved his hands about in a razzmatazz joke fashion.

I laughed in a silly high-pitched giggle.

'I'm so sorry to intrude,' he smiled – he certainly had charm – 'but I've got a favour to ask. My television hasn't arrived yet. Can I watch the football on yours?'

'Of course. Come in. Why did you choose me?' I asked coquettishly.

'I like the colour of your door.' He squeezed past me in the narrow corridor. 'Actually, I did try both my immediate neighbours but there was no reply.'

I loathed football: the clothes, the oiks, the songs, the

92

hysteria, the car flags, the mindless running up and down a pitch chasing a ball. Jack was indifferent to football too, but it suddenly seemed like a really manly sport. Mark had an easy, engaging manner and it made me want to please him and make him smile. What was I doing flirting with a man I hardly knew? Obviously taking the 'being single' fantasy a step too far. He had something of a lost-boy look about him that I found very appealing. He told me that his wife and child were arriving the following week from America where his wife was visiting her sister.

We sat side by side and I feigned interest in the game. He had brought a couple of cans of beer and he offered me one. Beer is not really my thing, but I accepted one anyway. The children returned all too soon, there was some shaking of hands, anecdotes about the area and he was gone. After he left, I sunk back into the sofa and laid my head on a pink pillow.

'Strange man,' Jack said later. 'Not sure about him at all. I found him a bit slimy . . . where's his wife?'

'She's coming,' I said. 'She's visiting her sister in Kentucky.'

'Really?'

'Yes.'

'Well, at least he's got a job.'

'We didn't discuss his job. Any news on Sherlock Holmes?'

'Not sure,' he said. 'I think they are still trying to raise money. They just wanted some actors to attach to the project.'

'Oh right.'

'Yes,' he sighed, 'I told you, that's my life.'

It was difficult to ignore Jack when he was low, because his energy was either sluggish or manic. He made huge, messy sandwiches of cucumber, Marmite, gherkins, Cheddar cheese and anchovy paste that he ate over the sink, then he would write fifty emails and finally collapse on a deckchair.

I was composing an email to my sister saying that Jack was depressing me when Maud interrupted me. 'If you don't cook cake with me,' she said, 'I won't eat lunch.' She always called supper lunch.

'Oh, please,' I begged.

'No,' she said, 'no, I won't eat anything, Mama, not one thing.'

That evening, Petra told me that she would be going home at the weekend for a week.

'This weekend?'

'Yes, two days' time.'

'Two days' time?'

'Yes,' she said. 'You said take a break and so I take a break.'

'But this is such short notice,' I wailed. 'I need every minute at the café; we're opening next week.'

'My cousin is getting married. She cannot put off.'

'But you could have told me.'

'I did tell you but you forget.'

I wondered briefly whether I was going mad. 'Don't come back then,' I muttered to myself.

'What?'

'Oh, nothing, Petra. That's fine then. Have a great time.'

Later, when I told Jack that he would have to help with the children while Petra was away, he raised his eyebrows and said he'd get his mother to look after them.

'Granny! Are you mad? She can't watch an egg.'

'Well, she looked after me.'

'Barely. That was fifty years ago.'

'I'm only good with the children in periodic spurts,' he said. 'Honestly, you know that. And I want to write my script.'

'This is an emergency, Jack. I'm working again now. You have to get used to that. I have a business. Neither you nor Petra seem to understand.'

'I'll get some help,' he said, 'to help.'

'So I'll leave it to you.'

'Yes, leave it to me.'

'Thank you, but honestly, they are your children. You could spend time with them.'

'Now get some rest.' He was ignoring me. He gave me a kiss then turned to the sudoku page. 'I'll be up in a while.'

There was no point reasoning with Jack; sometimes it was better to back away. I climbed the stairs to our room. I fell asleep immediately but woke as he trundled in beside me, harping on about the state of British television. 'All those bloody documentaries about women with no breasts, and children who have to look after obese parents. It's like a modern-day Colosseum: victims being ripped apart by savage producers, while we are herded in, compelled to watch, even imagine we like watching . . . it's all so sick.' Within five minutes he was asleep, while I lay awake and spiralled into dark memories: I remembered the slattern from Birmingham and Mandy Rudd's knowing smile when she mentioned that she knew Jack. He was snoring, lying on his back. I gently pushed him to his side like a big baby.

5

It was a Sunday morning in July, already warm at nine o'clock.

'Maud needs to blow her nose,' Jack shouted as I was grinding coffee beans.

'Yes, well, you've got a hand.'

'But it's very happy spooning Crunchy Nut into my mouth.'

'Jack, have you forgotten? It's the brunch party today for the opening of our café. You should be offering me cups of coffee and lots of soothing reassurances.'

'Sorry. Forgive me. Can I squeeze you an orange?'

'An orange?'

'Yes, it's a round fruit, acidic, orange in colour, filled with vitamin C.'

'I need calcium and magnesium,' I wailed, 'for stress.'

'What shall I wear?' he asked me ten minutes later as I was ironing a T-shirt.

'I don't know. What about a pair of shorts?' I had a sip from the quarter of a glass of orange juice that he had given me. I inhaled deeply to stop myself screaming.

'Shorts! Are you sure? Have I got the legs?' he asked in a brilliant imitation of a camp television host.

'Oh, for God's sake, Jack.' I was too nervous to laugh

or to say anything much; I just longed for him to ask me if I was all right, or if I needed any help.

'I think I should wear my black linen. Be a darling and iron them for me while you're doing yours?'

'Sorry, I haven't time. Tilda will be here in ten minutes. Anyway, it's high summer, black is not really appropriate.'

'What do you want me to wear ... yellow? Orange? Light blue?'

'No, just something normal – brown, or cream or . . .'

'Something autumnal then?'

'Jack . . .'

'Did you invite Eden?'

'Yes, but she can't come. She's visiting her brother in Wales.'

'Shame. Are you going like that?' he joked for the benefit of the children as I ran around in my knickers and T-shirt.

'Yup.'

'Fatty tummy,' Maud called out.

'Fat tummy!' both the children shrieked.

'When shall we join you?'

'Jack!' I was about to lose it. 'Jack, I've told you about fifty times, the invitation is from twelve till two, but you and the children are welcome to come and support me and arrive earlier. In fact, that would be nice. That would be a good thing; you could help.'

'Won't get there much earlier,' Jack said. 'I've got to shower and shave and . . .'

'Fine, fine ... See you when I see you.'

I was zipping up my jeans and panicking because I knew Tilda would be arriving any minute, when Maud went to the loo and screamed at me to wipe her bottom. 'Jack! Jack!' I called to him – he was immersed in the paper – 'Your child, your daughter, can you go?'

'Go where?'

'Maud's bottom.'

'Must I?' He looked up with a horrified expression on his face. 'Really?'

'PLEASE, JACK, I'VE GOT TO GO.'

'Oh, OK,' he stood up, 'but you really don't have to cause such a scene.'

'Don't argue,' Jed said, 'please don't argue. I hate it when you do.'

'Sorry, darling; sorry, darling.' I kissed the top of his head, too rushed to stop and hug him.

'Where are you going?' Maud asked when she came back from the bathroom.

'To the café.'

'Can I come wid you?'

'No, you come later with Daddy.'

She lay on the floor of the hall and wailed, while Jed skulked in the doorway. I heard Tilda hooting the horn of her car. 'Bye, everyone!' I waved at them.

'Bye, darling.' Jack hardly looked up from the paper.

'Good luck, Mummy,' Jed called out just as I was opening the door.

'Absolutely no support from my family,' I said to Tilda, sliding into her car. 'Well, except from Jed. Darling Jed.'

'I know the feeling,' Tilda sighed. Her eyes were watery-red as though she had been crying.

'What's up?'

'Tom is so absent. This morning, he went for a jog at six. He was talking to Japan at eight and working on a spreadsheet of impossibly difficult figures while we ate breakfast. Under much duress he's agreed to take Frankie to the playground before the opening, but still . . . Are all men like him? Or do I have a strange husband? He hasn't got home from the office before eleven any day this week.'

'He's probably very stressed at work,' I soothed.

'But he's always stressed.'

'There are different types,' I continued, feeling slightly brighter that it wasn't only me who had a difficult husband. 'At one end of the scale is the career-obsessed like Tom and way, way down at the other is the freelance creative like my friend Lucy's husband, Dan. He's an illustrator and when he's at home, which is most days, he helps with the children. The downside is that they are always broke, juggling money between accounts, selling paintings, remortgaging and borrowing. Anyway, Dan apparently gets up in the morning, forages around in the kitchen for food and – wait for this – he usually gives the children breakfast butt-naked. It can't be that sexy. What must the children think? What will they think in retrospect when they're older?'

'Uh, no,' Tilda stage-whispered, 'not at that time in the morning. Do you think it's some kind of statement? Some kind of post-hippy, anti-establishment, back-to-nature kind of thing?' She had cheered up a little.

'I've no idea. Maybe he enjoys the freedom. Maybe he takes holidays on nudist beaches. Maybe that's his thing. Or maybe he doesn't have to be anywhere and he's just lazy.'

'It's potentially quite creepy.'

'You're right.'

'I'd rather Tom in his shirts and suits eating his blueberries and cornflakes.'

'Me too. Rather Jack in his Ralph Lauren. Hate it when he's home all the time.'

'I've never had that experience. I've never had Tom at home during the week before. Don't know what I'd do with him.'

We drove in silence for a while. 'Do you think I look smart enough?' I asked Tilda. I was wearing a pair of jeans and red short-sleeve T-shirt and a badge that Maud insisted I wear which said '3 Today'.

'Yes,' she said, giving me a quick glance, 'you look great. Maybe you could just pin up your hair at one side,' she added sweetly, 'so we could see more of your face.'

She looked far more chic than I did. She wore a summer sleeveless dress, in pistachio-coloured chiffon, with a band below the breasts and a big bow. She looked beautiful and serene, like a turn-of-the century hostess at a garden party.

'OH MY GOD,' Tilda screamed out as we neared the café, 'I'M SO NERVOUS.'

'Me too.' I clutched her arm. 'Me too.'

'What if no one turns up?' Tilda turned to me with a mock-horrified expression on her face.

'What if it's only Tom and Frank and Jack and the children?' I joined in.

'Maybe they won't come either and it will be just us and Andy and Felipe.'

'And we have an orgy and . . .'

'You get pregnant with Felipe's child, leave Jack, move out and go and live in the flat above the café, while Andy and I elope to Argentina and open a steak joint.'

Tilda parked the car and we walked towards the café. 'Here we are again,' she said.

'It looks fabulous,' I said, glancing at the gleaming windows. We had spent hours the afternoon before, just polishing and cleaning the windows and glasses and preparing for the party.

Felipe was moving tables with Magdalena, one of the part-time waitresses from Poland. Tilda went downstairs to the kitchen to talk to the new chef, Andy, whom we had recruited after the boy from Newcastle burnt the bacon on the trial run. (We had had thirty applicants for the job and whittled down to a shortlist of four, who all had to cook us a trial breakfast. Andy was the one with the best eggs.) I began to dust the shelves like some feverish housewife strung out on speed and then began to blow up the heart-shaped balloons but failed miserably to find my breath and had to hand them over to Felipe. I then began to arrange the lilies and other flowers into black pots that we had covered with silver foil the night before. We had bought the flowers dirt cheap from a girl who owned the flower shop nearby and had already used them for a wedding.

Tilda appeared, eating a piece of smoked salmon.

'Wow, you clever Martha Stewart-type person. Those flowers look beautiful. Well done.'

'Why, thank you. Did I tell you that my friend Harriet, the beauty editor, asked if she could send a photographer to take pictures of the party for the magazine party page?'

'Oh, really? No, you didn't tell me. Who are they expecting to photograph?'

'Well, Jack, I suppose, and William is coming, and Annie wants to bring a girl who's modelled for her and who is now the face of something and her friend, an eco designer.'

'Yes, well, that's at least three photographs.' We laughed.

'I suppose we could get Jack to change his outfit so he could be photographed twice.'

'They'll have to resort to photographing us, I suppose,' Tilda said.

'Lucky them.'

Over fifty people came to celebrate the opening of Café Blue. We served organic scrambled egg and wild smoked salmon, pink champagne and miniature frozen yoghurt cones. The atmosphere was relaxed, probably because it was a Sunday. Michel, a Venezuelan with a full moustache, greased-back longish hair and a cowboy hat was playing his saxophone and singing. Jack had stopped to listen to him at Hyde Park Corner underpass the day before, decided he was good, and had offered him one hundred pounds to play at the party.

While the frozen yoghurts were being passed round, Petra (who had strangely decided not to go to her cousin's 'wedding' when she heard I was having a party) stood up and wiggled her hips – soon, she was doing her version of a full-blown belly dance. 'Harlot hussy,' I whispered to Annie. Petra's little blonde Norwegian friend clapped enthusiastically, then somebody else joined in and soon there were ten or so people gathered around Petra in a loose circle, whistling, clapping and urging her on. Felipe came over to see what was happening. He immediately threw off his apron and grabbed Petra by the waist. He twirled her around and the small crowd cheered. He wore a white vest and blue jeans which showed off his taut, muscular physique, of which he was obviously proud, perhaps compensating for the fact that he was a short man; a good three inches smaller than Petra. The pair then attempted a kind of dramatic tango.

Jack and William Eade were chatting at one of the tables outside. I went over to join them, brandishing a tray of macaroons. They were talking about Beckett, one of Jack's favourite subjects.

'He was way ahead of the game, completely misunderstood at the time. Only now has literature caught up with him ...'

'Why is it,' William asked, 'that Beckett inspires such devotion in people? My father had a friend who used to hang out outside his front door in Paris in the hope that he would bump into him.'

'Good question. Well, of course ...'

They sounded a little stilted and William laughed a little

too hard, the way people do when they are being photo-graphed. The photographer, a weary-looking grey-haired man, abandoned them when he caught sight of an un-canny Tyler Williams lookalike, complete with tufts of hair appearing out of the neck of his T-shirt, coming through the café door.

'Have you seen that man who looks exactly like Tyler Williams?' I asked Harriet when she came over to say hello.

'That *is* Tyler Williams.' It was a great line and Harriet obviously relished saying it.

'Tyler Williams, American film actor?'

'Yes.'

Harriet the beauty editor looked beautiful as always. She was a gamine girl, like a French film star, with a short wispy haircut and long curling brown lashes over the biggest brown eyes. She was one of the only women I'd ever met who could wear light-blue eyeshadow and still look classy. We had met on a yoga retreat in Tuscany, where we had shared a bedroom. At the time she had just broken up with a boyfriend and she was sad and tearful. We talked into the early hours all four nights we were away and had remained friends in the way that a married woman can be friends with a single girl, ten years younger, who lives in another part of town.

'Are you sure? My God, what's he doing here? At a Shepherd's Bush café? Tyler Williams at our opening? Could it be true?'

She laughed. 'Sorry, sorry, I'm responsible. He's here making a film and we interviewed him on Friday and he

asked the stylist if anything was happening at the weekend. He doesn't know anyone in London apparently.
Anyway, she was going to Paris and asked me to take care
of him, so I suggested that he should come here. I should
have warned you. Actually, come to think of it, I'm sure
I did leave you a message. Did I?' she asked herself
vaguely. The photographer was beckoning her over and
she wandered off.

'Have you seen who's here?' Jack lurched at me. 'Tyler
Bloody Williams.'

'Yes, I know,' I said with affected nonchalance. 'It's
great, isn't it?'

'Yes,' he said, 'bloody marvellous. He's probably
lunching with Spielberg the day he gets back and I really
should say hello.'

Harriet sloped back.

'Harriet, you are looking particularly beautiful today,'
Jack said. 'Will you introduce me to Mr Tyler? I've always
wanted to meet him. I'm a huge fan.'

'Yes, Jack darling, of course I will. Don't you worry.
And can I say,' she continued, 'that you look more and
more like a younger version of Bill Nighy every day. He's
so sexy.'

Jack smiled like a man who had just acted out a long-
standing sexual fantasy. 'Thank you, thank you. And,
Harriet, don't forget about Tyler. It has to be soon, before
he realizes he's at a café next to a crack den, comes to his
senses and decides to leave.'

'Yes,' she said soothingly, fumbling around in the
latest, most fashionable, most expensive, impossible-to-

actually-buy bag, to retrieve a shiny mobile telephone that was singing out a Frank Sinatra song as its ringtone.

Mandy Rudd, the waspish features editor, who surprisingly had written a very straight and rather flattering piece about the café, came over to say hello.

'I see that despite your tirade against celebrities there are a couple here today.' She looked me up and down, taking in the '3 Today' badge which seemed particularly silly and childish under the scrutiny of her gaze.

'Nothing to do with me. William is a great friend of ours and someone brought Tyler Williams along as he's filming here.'

'Is he?'

'Apparently.'

'I must go and introduce myself.' She was so petite and polished that she made me feel slovenly. Her hair was shiny and pulled back, her eyebrows groomed in an exacting arch, her foundation perfect, her lips shiny, her hands smooth, her nail polish perfectly applied and unchipped. 'Well, good luck,' she said. 'I have a feeling this café will be a huge success.'

'Thank you.' She left me and I noticed that my hands were tightly clenched, the nails pressing into the flesh.

'Tyler would love to meet you.' Harriet dragged over Tyler Williams by the hand. He was much smaller than I had imagined, even more hirsute, and dressed in a truly terrible sweatshirt adorned with something that looked a bit like an alien on the front.

'Listen, darling,' Harriet said to Tyler as though he were a small child, 'I'm going to have to leave you with my lovely friend because the photographer needs me.'

'Great,' he said, shaking my hand, 'so great. What an amazing occasion. Love it.'

Jack was waving at me from the other side of the room and mouthing something. I tried to ignore him. It was only later that I discovered that I had a thick moustache of white frozen yoghurt coated above my lip and he had been trying to warn me.

'Who's that waving man?' Tyler asked, glancing over at Jack. 'Is he a politician?'

'That's Jack. Don't say anything rude. He's my husband.'

'Husband? Husband? Are you a wife with children? But you don't look a day over twenty-one, particularly with that ice cream all over your face.'

We laughed. He laughed louder until people began to turn around.

Jack could not resist coming over and introducing himself.

'Oh, so you're the husband,' Tyler said in an absurd English accent. 'Hello, husband.'

'Jack Boore,' Jack said with a flourish, waiting for a flicker of recognition.

'Interesting name,' Tyler said. 'Is that name for real? Are you a stand-up comic?'

'Actually, I'm an actor,' Jack declared, offering his hand.

'Of course you are.' Tyler was shaking Jack's hand up and down, pumping it and wringing it in an exaggerated fashion like a scene from a silent slapstick film. Jack made a desperate plea for him to let go and pulled away, waving his hand around in exaggerated pain.

'Good God, man? Are you trying to kill me?'

'Not yet, not yet.' Tyler smiled.

Harriet reappeared looking a little flushed and shiny-eyed. 'Tyler, let me introduce you to William,' she said. 'He's a great, great friend of Jack and Ellie's.'

'William Eade?'

'Yes. Look, he's standing over there by the window. He seems a bit lost and alone.'

'William Eade, the great comic genius? A man of wit and style?'

'Well, yes. That's the one.'

Jack was put out by Tyler's enthusiastic response to the idea of meeting William – when he so obviously hadn't heard of Jack – and went outside to smoke a cigarette. Then he came back in, complained of a headache and knocked back a glass of champagne.

'Are you all right?' I asked.

'Fine, fine . . . bloody Williams.'

'He's obviously mad.'

'Clinically insane.'

The grey-haired photographer wanted to take a photograph of Jack and me. Jack said he would be delighted and ran his hands through his hair. We stood together side by side. The photographer asked for a photograph of Tilda and me, so we draped arms round each other and laughed. It was really exciting to look around at the room full of people and I laughed and smiled with satisfaction. The room was buzzing, people were laughing and seemed to be enjoying the food. We had done it: we had bought the café. We were serving food in our new café and I was genuinely thrilled and proud.

Tilda and I were standing side by side, discussing whether to bring out some more food, when Jack suddenly shouted out, 'SPEECH.'

'No, Jack,' I hissed. 'Stop it. We're not quite ready.'

'SPEEECH,' he called out louder.

'Shall I do it?' Tilda turned to me.

'Yes, you do it,' I said.

Tilda paused. 'Well, maybe we should both say something.'

'Oh, come on, girls.' Jack put a hearty arm around each of us. 'Which one of you is going to do it?' We looked at each other and before I'd had a chance to protest, he was standing up on a chair muttering that someone had to say something. A few people wound up their conversations in anticipation but most of the guests didn't notice that Jack Boore, actor, was about to make a speech. Jack cleared his throat and struck a biro against a glass. 'Silence!' he boomed.

'Jesus!' I muttered under my breath.

'We are gathered here today,' he began in his famous, gravelly, sexy voice, 'to celebrate with my dear wife, Ellie, and her equally dear friend, the wonderful Tilda ... Tilda, yes, Tilda, she has always reminded me of the American actress Anne Hathaway ...' and so he went on and on, diverging into different subjects. At one point he was talking about global warming and how the ice age would return and how apt it was that we were doing our bit for the environment. The captive audience began to shift and cough, becoming more and more distracted while Jack, oblivious to the mood, became more and more magnanimous and emotional, as though he were accepting an Oscar. 'Well done, girls,' he raised his glass, 'for all your hard work and determination. The food is delicious and the café looks great. Girls, I'm proud.'

We all cheered when he'd finished, partly from relief that it was over. After the speech he offered to help pass around the coffee, and Michel the busker really made the party swing. In an exultant mood, I hugged Jack and thanked him for making the speech, though later, long after the party had finished, I wondered why I had allowed him to do it on our behalf. It was the story of our marriage, and the dynamic had to change.

'It was a fabuloza party,' Tyler said, 'Fabutastic. Loved the girls, those pale-faced models, the food, the heat ... your speech,' he turned to Jack, 'was sooo long!'

'Dad,' Jed had an insistent tone and was pulling Jack by the hand, 'we really would like to go home now.'

Tyler put his hand behind Jed's ear and produced a one-pound coin.

'This boy is raining money,' he shouted out. 'Come, everyone, gather round. We have a human boy who rains money.'

Jed began to laugh.

'Do it to me,' Maud demanded, 'do it to me.'

'Ahoy, pretty lady,' Tyler said. 'Come hither and thither, and I will show you a good time.'

The children were delighted. They screeched and

clustered around him before Jack asked me if he could take them home and left 'nursing' a bad headache and telling me to hurry. By five most of the guests had gone, but there was a hard core of about ten people who were still milling around. Tilda and I began to tidy and put things away, stopping short of actually telling people to go. It was five forty-five when we began to put chairs on top of tables, giggling and snorting at the blatant absurdity of it.

Annie was the last to leave and after she'd gone we sat down, sighing and whooping. I flopped down and Tilda stretched her arms above her head and yawned. 'Exhausting but fun.'

I sat up. 'I'm so proud of us.'

Andy came upstairs holding a glass of champagne. 'Quite a few bottles of plonk left.'

'Well done, Andy. Take some home.'

'Thanks, mate. Well, I'll be off.'

'I think it went really well,' Tilda said. 'I'm so proud of us too.' Her chiffon dress was slightly wrinkled and her hair a little askew.

'Yes, it was much better than I had expected,' I agreed. 'We did really well; though Jack was a little over the top in the speech.'

'He did go on a bit,' she admitted, 'but I'm sure no one noticed apart from us. Tom stayed at least forty minutes, which is almost a record for him. He's usually looking at his watch thirty minutes after we reach a party. Everything was eaten, every last scrap, every morsel. There were queues of people telling me how delicious the food was. And there was a journalist from the *Evening Standard* who I spoke to briefly.'

'That's great; a mention in the *Evening Standard* would be brilliant.'

'We've done so well, Ellie, and it's going to be a success. You do realize that.'

'Oh yes, I do. Of course I do. I'm very pleased. Jack doesn't take it that seriously but I have a feeling we're going to make money.'

'Definitely, yes,' Tilda said.

We said goodbye to Felipe and the girls and congratulated everybody. On the drive home we talked a little more about the party, and particularly about Tyler Williams.

'Was he actually there,' I asked Tilda, 'or was that an impersonator? Do you think Harriet hired an impersonator as a joke?'

'Um . . . possibly.'

'How weird. He seemed so real.'

'Maybe he was a wax model robot?'

'Creepy.'

'Very creepy.'

Home again. The kitchen surfaces were slightly cloudy as there hadn't been time to wipe them shiny and glistening, as I like them, after breakfast. One of the sofa cushions was on the floor; Sunday newspapers were spread across the kitchen table. Petra, of course, had made no effort to lift a finger to tidy up after she woke up late. I leant over to pick things up off the floor and was struck with a strange inertia, weightiness; a body stuffed with salmon blini and a champagne head and an overall feeling of dread.

'How was it?' I asked Jack.

'What?'

'The party – the launch.'

'Well done. Quite a spread.'

There was something in his tone that reminded me of a maths tutor I'd had at school: Mr Clark, with his greased-back white-grey hair, stale tobacco breath and hard, yellow fingers. He looked harmless enough, but he was patronizing and preoccupied – and teaching maths to eleven-year-olds was not what he enjoyed.

'Was it really?'

'Really. I mean Tyler Williams was there, what more could you ask for?'

'Alan Bennett. Alan Bennett would have made my day. If Alan Bennett had been there, I would be a happy woman now.'

'Why Alan Bennett?'

'He's so funny. Sweet and sharp. I would have liked his opinion on how the café could be improved.'

We sank back on the sofas and were watching a programme about elephants trampling tourists to death when there was a knock on the door. Jack made no move to get up and neither did I. 'Can you go, Jack? I have a full, fat tummy. I can't move.'

'I'll go,' Jed offered.

'No, I'll go!' Maud screamed.

'I'll go with you,' Jack said. 'Wait for me.' I heard Jack

say hello. A woman with an American accent was introducing herself.

'I'm Lorrie, Mark's wife. The new neighbour. Your wife met Mark the other day. I know you've had a busy day ... I just wanted ...'

'Come in, come in.'

She followed Jack into the sitting room. This was the woman married to the sexy man, who had made me flutter and giggle and drink beer. She was a similar height to me, although younger, with wide eyes and cascading hair. She looked like a woman in a portrait by one of the British Pre-Raphaelites; pale face, crinkly hair and slim wrists. She was even wearing a kind of smock with a William Morris-type pattern on it. In fact, I realized with an eerie sense of shock, she looked very familiar, almost like my sister.

'I just came to apologize for not making the opening party today,' she said.

I stood up slowly, my back aching with the effort.

'I was up between one and six in the morning with the baby and so grouchy. Mark didn't dare come near me,' she laughed, 'and he didn't quite dare leave me either.'

Jack and I laughed because we felt we should.

'Anyway, I've slept now, so I'm feeling better and we were wondering whether you'd like us to bring over a take-out later and a bottle of wine? You probably don't feel like cooking.'

'That sounds wonderful,' Jack declared.

It was very thoughtful of her, but I imagined Mark coming over to find me lounging around like a tired, beached whale with the vague remains of the ice-cream moustache and I decided the plan would have to be halted.

'That's so kind of you, so thoughtful and sweet, but you see I'm exhausted, and the children have had quite a boring day. Could we ... would you mind if we postponed the drink for another night?'

'Of course, of course, sorry,' she said, 'so full on of me. What was I thinking? I've been watching too many episodes of *Desperate Housewives*. You know the way they turn up at each other's houses with fruit pies and baskets of muffins?'

'It's so kind,' I repeated as we walked to the door. 'We must do it another time.'

'What about coffee tomorrow?' she asked.

I nodded, yes, mumbling about checking my diary.

'Well, she's quite a formidable woman.' Jack shut the door. 'I'd like to give her a good slapping on her behind.'

'Jack! That comment about how Mark was too scared to go near her or leave her. That was something else. I think to be on the wrong side of her would be terrifying.'

'She left us champagne,' Jack said. 'Shall we just open it?'

'Oh, why not? I can't get much drunker or fatter.'

It was that time of day. The dreaded bath and bedtime. I had many women friends who needed a drink to get them through it. Occasionally when I was tired and the children splashed water on the walls and hit each other and left their clothes in muddy clumps, I found it hard to laugh at their jokes and raced through their bedtime stories, desperate for it all to be over. When I'd really had enough, the story would be vetoed in favour of a DVD. That evening I took a glass of champagne up with me, looking forward to having another, but by the time the children were bathed and dressed in their white dressing gowns, with flushed cheeks and wet hair, Jack had nearly finished the bottle. He roused them up and tickled them, making them scream with excitement. I shouted at them all to calm down and Jack managed to get them up to bed by suggesting a race up the stairs.

When the children were finally asleep, Jack sat down and asked how much the party had cost. I rather smugly told him we had hardly spent anything as most of the food had been provided free, negotiated by eager press relations officers who represented organic food suppliers. 'Didn't you notice the sponsors on the invitations?'

'No.'

'I can't believe you missed it, Jack. Did you even look at an invitation?'

'Of course I did. But anyway, free food is good news,' Jack said. 'I thought I would have to pay for all of this out of my first pay cheque.' He opened his arms, spreading them wide and knocked over a cup of coffee.

'What do you mean? Your first pay cheque?'

'I got the bloody job,' he said.

'What bloody job?'

'The bloody TV soap job.'

'Jack, you got the television job? You mean the *Sailing Fuck* thing?' I was obviously a little drunk too.

'I presume you mean the *We Are Sailing* soap?'

'Why didn't you tell me?' I asked.

'I'm telling you. I went for the audition and I got the bloody job. And a bloody salary.'

'Great.'

'You don't sound pleased.'

'It's wonderful.'

'Do you honestly think I want this bloody job? TV soap? Twelve hours a day on the set. No, I don't, but we've got debts and a bloody monstrous mortgage. And your café is marvellous, darling, really fine, but it's not going to help with our bills.'

'Jack, I'm not opening a café for fun you know. I want to make money to help pay for all our debts. I may not be earning huge amounts for the first few months, but I will, Jack, I really will.'

'I'm sure you will. Sorry to explode.'

'I'm really pleased for you. Well done. That method acting must have helped.'

'Yes, I'll have to go back to it.'

I laughed.

'No, really. It's a good discipline.'

I saw years stretching ahead of me, with Jack playing a retired businessman, a widower and a magnet for the lovely ladies of the sailing community. Big Jean, his most stalwart fan, would go back to her weekly letters, which would be enclosed with snippets of information about her family, photographs of her pets and grandchildren. Jack would be photographed for second rate 'celebrity magazines'. He would be tied in for the next twenty years and we would be old and tired by the time he was finished. We would be dressed in beige slacks and comfortable cardigans and in the summer Jack would be wearing a flat, white cap. It didn't bear thinking about.

The next day there was a paragraph about the café in the *Evening Standard* diary. Jack and Tyler and William Eade were mentioned and there was a quote from William saying he would travel from south of the river just to sample our almond cakes. Tilda had said that instead of selling bottled water we would be offering customers filtered tap water and would not be charging them for it.

I telephoned Tilda. 'Hey, have you seen us in the *Evening Standard*? Isn't it brilliant? But what's this about filtered water?'

'I don't know what came over me,' she replied. 'I just read that another organic café was offering filtered water and thought we should be competitive.'

'But we don't have a filtering system.'

'I know. But we could.'

'What if someone comes in for a filtered water experience?'

'We'll think of something. Decant a bottle of mineral?'

6

On the first official morning at the café we were busy and ran out of croissants and orange juice before ten o'clock. We had taken a gamble with the croissants and at the last minute had decided against the frozen ones and gone for freshly baked, from a local patisserie, which we had to buy for sixty pence and sell for £1.50. I was concerned that people wouldn't want to pay that much for them but they were far superior to any others that we had tasted. You could buy really cheap, nasty croissants from a basic catalogue for seventeen pence. God knows what they were made with, stale bread?

After the croissants finished we decided to offer organic toasted cheese and tomato sandwiches. One woman, a bossy English type with an unflattering sunhat and a fraught, regal voice had heard about the filtered water and asked for a glass. When we said the system was on order, she accused us of being misleading, but sat down with her coffee and carrot cake anyway.

I was pleased to see that the local coterie of business-men, mothers with toddlers, sharp architect types, Afro-Caribbeans and lone men still came for their usual breakfast, post-breakfast coffees, lunch, snacks and tea. My face ached with smiling. We were so busy that Tilda and I had to take it in turns to have ten-minute coffee breaks. It was good to be moving, shifting calories, and not so good stuffing them back in with the odd chocolate croissant or irresistible piece of carrot cake with the creamy icing.

Later that afternoon, Jack telephoned to say he would start filming the soap in two months' time and that we should put our house on the market and drive down to Hampshire to search for properties.

'Jesus, Jack, this is my first real day at the café and you're telling me that we have to put our beloved house with the granite kitchen surfaces on the market and move to the *country*?'

'I'm sorry to call you when you're so busy –' he was eating something like toast, which resounded like the crunch of gravel in my ear – 'I'm just excited.'

'Yes, sorry, darling, just a bit stressed here, first day and all. We'll talk about it later.' He was trying to wind me up.

'You wouldn't have to commute, darling. Maybe you could rent a small pied-à-terre near the café?'

'In the land of crack houses and shoot-outs?' I laughed.

'Well, yes. It's expensive running two houses. You won't be able to rent in Hampstead.'

'We'll talk later.'

'Yes, we will. Goodbye.'

When I finally returned home, far later than I needed to, Jack was beaming and smiling, offering me a drink.

'Sorry, darling, so selfish of me to call you at work, your first day.' He led me by the hand to one of the white sofas and we sat down next to each other. 'Why don't we just drive down there this weekend and take a look? Imagine: wild ponies, coastal living, children with happy, beaming rounded red faces.'

'Jack! Please. You sound like Enid Blyton.'

'Like I said this morning, maybe you could rent a flat near the café. You could do Tuesday and Wednesday and leave Thursday and Tilda could do Monday, Friday and Saturday.'

'I see you have it all worked out. But we can't afford a little flat. And what about the children? I can't leave the children. And Tilda can't do Saturdays by herself.'

Jack moved closer to me. 'No, but you could get a part-time girl to do the Saturdays and we will be able to rent a pied-à-terre and the children will be fine. Really, Ellie, you have to think about it. You will have better times with the children than you do now.'

Neither of us spoke. He was trying to be nice to me.

'Sorry, Jack.' I broke the silence. 'I will think about it. It's just so hard to imagine moving away when I'm on day one at the café. Tilda and I are working really hard. We're really proud. I want to be near the children and near the café. I have a real chance.'

'You would thrive in the country.'

'You're not listening. I don't want to live in the country. Not yet, not now. I'm too young.'

Jack laughed. 'May I remind you you're not that young?'

'Well, I'm younger than you.'

'I do realize,' he said, 'that you've just started a project . . .'

'It's more than a project; you make it sound like something temporary. Like something I'm doing at school, that will be handed in and marked out of ten and forgotten about . . .'

'Yes, yes, sorry . . .' Jack looked a bit alarmed. 'We can work something out. Maybe I'll go down and stay with my mother for a bit and commute up at weekends. It will be long days and early starts. I'll be tired, but very rich.'

'Ummm.' I began to feel guilty.

'Let's see how it goes,' Jack said. 'Let's discuss it again soon.'

'The children are happy in their schools.'

'But we could find a much nicer school for Jed.'

It was true, we could find a better school for Jed.

I stood up and Petra sidled past me to say she was going out. Then Jack announced that he was going to the off-licence to buy some wine. He put on his jacket. I sat down in the garden and watched the swifts with their scythe-shaped wings, diving and swooping and wheeling above me. I was already in mourning for the house with my stone labyrinth and my kitchen with the absurdly expensive granite surfaces and even for Maud's little school with the soft cushions. What would I do? Live somewhere I didn't want to live? Stay with the children in London? Let Tilda buy me out? Find someone else to take over? I went inside and made myself a sandwich of Marmite and cucumber. Whatever happened, I couldn't let the café go. It had only just started and it would be scandalous to let Tilda and myself down.

There was the issue of Jed's school with the grim

playground. He probably would be happier at a small country school, with a packed lunch of homemade bread and local cheese. I had no idea who would be making bread, but it was just a thought. He'd been begging us for a pet. In the country he could have a menagerie of animals – his own private zoo. Maybe, I thought, Tilda and I could come to some agreement whereby we job-shared, with perhaps one shared day together on a Wednesday, but that would still mean at least two or three days away from the children a week.

When Jack returned from the off-licence, he was whistling. 'I've been thinking that the best thing to do in September is nothing. Keep the children where they are. I'll stay with my mother. That way I can give my rather generous living expenses to our rather healthy mortgage.'

'Thank you, but she'll probably want you to pay her rent. You know what she's like.'

Jack laughed.

'Oh, Jack.' Now that he had capitulated, I was beginning to feel guilty and selfish. 'I wonder what will happen?'

'It will be fine,' he said, patting me on the back, reminding me of Mr Clark, the maths teacher, again. 'I talked to Eden,' he went on, 'and I get all my weekend travel paid. First-class train ticket. You can stay here, in your wonderful house and keep the café.'

'Thank you. That is so kind. But you're going to be lonely.'

'Well, there's a whole community on the set every day. Ninety of us.'

'Oh, Jack!'

'Yes, well, I would prefer to live with my family, of course. I do think it's something you should consider. The children will miss me. Despite what you think about me, I do like being a father.'

We talked until quite late, past my usual bedtime of ten thirty. Jack chain-smoked and drank wine. I waved my hands around, trying to blow the smoke away and sipped herbal tea. Jack was being kind, but the more he drank, the more I realized he was playing a game with me. He knew me well enough to know that if he looked as though he was giving in to me, I would backtrack and give in to him. I double-bluffed him though and stood my ground, never actually saying that I would leave the café but feeling guilty and distraught that I had to make a choice.

Was it my imagination? Or did Jack really believe that his life was far more important than mine? It was as though he had worked out that if he went along with my whimsical idea of owning a café I would soon get bored of it and come to my senses. I would realize that the children were missing out on a fabulous way of life down by the sea and that to keep them in London was selfish and silly of me. These kinds of thoughts kept me alert most of the night until I concluded that I was silly, selfish and ridiculous and that our marriage couldn't go on, as you do at three or four in the morning. Jack slumbered on, snoring and heavily content. I finally slept at about five o'clock, only to be woken by Jack at six thirty complaining that he couldn't find his watch.

*

That morning, just after Jack had gone off to buy a paper and before I was leaving for the café, Mark came over to borrow some sugar. I was dressed in baggy grey yoga trousers, which were truly hideous, and a maroon T-shirt, which was besmirched with breakfast stains. I looked unbelievably awful, my hair limp and my face unmade-up.

'Hello,' he said. He was so sexy, better than ever. He wore a dark suit, mauve shirt and silver cufflinks. He was swinging a briefcase and held a cup of tea in his hand. 'Can't stop to chat, although I'd really like to. I've got a very, very heavy day today.'

I went to fetch the sugar and quickly brushed my hair at the same time, cursing my yoga trousers. But I managed to drape a scarf around my stained top.

I stirred the sugar into his cup.

'Thank you. Lorrie doesn't take sugar with anything and always forgets to buy it.' He smiled at me. I smiled back, lost for words. Poor uncared for man. We stared at each other, for a moment, before I looked away.

'You look very well,' he said. 'But have you got a sore throat? The scarf?'

'Um,' I mumbled, 'kind of. But are you sure I look well even with my stained top and baggy yoga trousers?'

'I wasn't so much looking at your baggy trousers and stained top, more at your face.'

'Thank you.'

'Well, see you soon. You must both come over; bring the children.'

'OK. Thanks, see you soon.'

My heart was beating as I turned round and literally bumped into Petra who was on her way to school.

'Who is that man? He looks good. Very handsome.'

'Oh!' I blushed. 'Just new neighbour.'

'More than that,' she laughed.

'Petra, what do you mean?'

She giggled and ran out of the door.

Both come over, I repeated to myself. It didn't sound exactly like a come-on, not at all. He couldn't find me at all attractive, especially now that he'd seen me in those clothes and I'd drawn attention to them. But I couldn't help giggling and when I drove to the café that morning I sang loudly to myself and out of tune.

Later that day, after the café closed at four, I returned home to find Lorrie unpacking her car. The baby, whose name I still did not know, had been plonked in her car seat on the pavement. 'Come in,' she said. 'Come in,' she repeated, 'and have that coffee we've been talking about.' I had never been inside their house and the offer to have a look was quite tempting. Petra would be arriving back soon from the park and there were a few minutes to spare.

The house was still but unsettled. There were boxes lined up in the narrow hall, suitcases piled up in the sitting room and baby clothes strewn around the washing machine. I shuddered at the memory of baby life and wondered how we had got through it. It was all so totally consuming, miraculous, frightening, depressing and re-lentless and – ultimately – made life worthwhile. Some days when the children were young I used to wonder what I did with all those luxurious spare hours before they were born. Of course there was work, but what about weekends, holidays? What did I do? Did I sleep? Eat? Read? Have sex? All the things I no longer had time for.

Jack had been thrilled when I found out I was pregnant with Jed and then later with Maud, but he was not one of those fathers who mucked in to the extent of wiping bums or feeding them. Occasionally he would mash some potatoes for the children or change a nappy, but very rarely.

I remembered staring at Jed when he was born. He was a miracle. I just couldn't believe he had been inside me. It was a wonder that I'd managed to get through the birth. The lowest point came after I'd been pushing for more than two hours and felt as though a watermelon was ripping through me. The pain was savage, unforgiving and intense; never forgotten. I squatted down, screaming, shouting and demanding a caesarean. I had to be re-strained by not one but two midwives. Jack, however, had actually managed to sleep through most of my labour, curled up and snoring on a yoga mat.

'How could you sleep?' I asked him afterwards, feeling tired and happy but still resentful. 'How could you sleep through all that noise?'

'Just so worried about you,' he said tenderly. 'I couldn't bear to be awake and watch you in so much pain.'

I had managed to laugh. Jack held the unnamed Jed and I had never loved him so much. But then a young nurse came in to unswaddle the baby and weigh him and the magical moment of pure happiness dripped away.

Lorrie's baby, a girl named Alice, was six months old and not quite sitting up on her own. I'd already forgotten what a six-month-old baby looked like and had made a random guess – three months? Lorrie had put me right and I worried that perhaps she was upset because I'd underestimated the age of her baby, so I made far too much of an issue of how I always got babies' ages wrong.

To my relief her house was not severely cleaned and polished. Although I am a tidy person and I like to dust, very organized women make me anxious. I worry about putting the glass down on the wrong table and leaving a rim. I am conscious that my hair is uncombed and my clothes slightly strange – jeans mostly, but occasionally I would venture into a vintage skirt or one of Annie's recyclable jumpers.

When Lorrie realized that she didn't actually have coffee or tea she offered me warm milk, which we drank like big babies. It was surprisingly good and I suddenly relaxed; she wasn't one of those domestic goddesses who shop for store cupboard items and have them ready in case of a spontaneous supper party or a nuclear disaster – twenty-five cans of tomatoes, sixty cans of baked beans, forty-four bottles of anchovies. Lorrie kept tripping up over baby things and then sitting down and sighing. 'I used to be so dynamic,' she said, 'before this, before all of this.' She indicated Alice, who was sitting up in a baby chair, chewing her finger. The baby looked tired and unhappy. I asked Lorrie if I could pick her up.

'Go ahead,' she said, and handed me a white muslin cloth. 'I should change the diaper,' she added. 'It's probably covered in poo.'

Alice smelt slightly stale, not like babies usually do, with their rose-blossom skin.

I couldn't decide whether I felt sorry for Lorrie. I wasn't even sure if she was hard and brittle or just very tired. She didn't strike me as a person who had accepted the idea that she had a baby and her life was now different. She seemed frustrated and trapped, and not quite genuine, but perhaps my judgements were biased in favour of myself to justify the fact that I was attracted to her husband. Was I looking out for things not to like about her? Or did I genuinely not like her? I wasn't sure.

'I was a reporter,' she said, 'and I wrote travel stories. I travelled and shot photographs and I was a person with a byline.'

There were photographs of her around the house, in what looked like war-torn deserts and in front of crumbling buildings and laughing with a group of soldiers. She showed me a pile of framed photographs shot by her. There were desert cities and vivid sunsets and a witty photograph of Japanese tourists having a group exercise class in a swimming pool, and about four or five portraits of Alice. Her photographs were mostly black and white, moments caught rather than posed and not at all sentimental.

'I'm taking iron but I feel so tired and apathetic and not myself. Poor Mark, he married a completely different woman. I used to have so much energy.'

'I was lighter in every sense, and possibly less serious, and more up for a laugh. And I definitely went to bed later. But having children has softened me and brought out a side of myself I really like,' I said. She wasn't listening to me though; she was heating up a bottle for Alice.

'Do you and Jack generally get on?' she asked bluntly as she was giving Alice the bottle. 'I sensed a little friction in the house the other day.'

'Did you? But you were only there for three minutes.'

'Yes, well, I'm quite intuitive. Sometimes I sense stuff.'

How dare she? I hardly knew her. I wanted to make some excuse and leave, but couldn't think of anything that sounded true, so I replied, 'Everything is fine, up and down like most marriages. How is yours?'

'The thing is, we've taken on so much; we've had a baby, moved country, and Mark has changed jobs, so we're really stressed and we don't seem to get any sleep.' She sounded angry and I wasn't sure how to respond. Eventually I suggested that perhaps she should have a massage treatment, which would calm and soothe her.

I went to their bathroom, gathering my courage to leave. I felt like a fly caught in a web; it seemed so hard to extricate myself from her clutches. The bathroom was next to the baby's room, with a window that backed on to the garden. There was a changing mat and piles and piles of nappies, nappy cream, baby shampoo, and squeezed between her make-up, toiletries, hairdryer and cosmetics and the baby's paraphernalia was a small sign that Mark lived there too – a razor and aftershave lotion were positioned on a tiny slot on a shelf.

There was a photograph of Mark with a group of university friends. They were clad in scarves and wore their hair long. Mark looked lush and rebellious and gorgeous. I thought about taking a photograph of the photograph with my mobile. I considered putting a note inside his dressing gown pocket but decided, quite wisely, against it. What would I have said? I fancy you?

'Are you all right in there?' she asked after a few minutes.

'Fine, fine, just coming. Actually, I must get home,' I said as I emerged from the bathroom.

'Oh no,' she protested, 'you've only just arrived.'

'Jed will be back from school. I must go.'

'OK, well great to meet you properly at last.'

'You too. You must both come round for dinner one night.'

'Oh wait,' she said as I was opening the door, 'I have my diary right here. Why don't we make a date now and then I can organize a babysitter.'

'I don't have my diary,' I said, 'but I'll let you know.'

She took my number and I waited around on the doorstep while she tapped it into her mobile, which she didn't quite know how to use and had to keep re-doing, while I waited and waited until she had finally managed.

She rang me three hours later as I was putting the children to bed and asked me if we could come over on Saturday. I was reading Jed a story and really shouldn't have answered.

'Can I let you know tomorrow? I have to ask Jack.'

'Could you let me know just as soon as you possibly can?'

I said that I would.

'My God,' I said to Jack later, 'she doesn't understand the etiquette of a vague dinner invitation. She's so intense and obviously a little lonely. It can't be easy moving country and having a baby, but she overwhelms me. I think if we became friends she'd be popping over all the time, twenty-four seven.'

Jack asked me to go to the off-licence to find some particular red wine he fancied. He claimed he couldn't move as he was waiting for a call from Eden. She was going through his contract and he needed to be near his desk to answer the telephone call.

It was really warm that evening, balmy and sultry. I put some make-up on and brushed my hair, preparing myself for the unlikely possibility that Mark would stop off at the off-licence on his way home from work. I was wearing a pretty white sleeveless dress with a navy cardigan. Jack commented that I looked like a nurse.

I was dawdling in the off-licence for about twenty minutes, picking up bottles and putting them back. Finally, when I couldn't waste any more time hoping to see him, I went to the counter to pay. Mark opened the door and my heart began to thud against my chest and my face heated up. He was carrying a sports bag.

'Hello.' I was flustering in my wallet, trying to find the right debit card, hoping – no praying – that I was no longer red with embarrassment.

'Oh, hello. I was just thinking about you.'

'Really?' I smiled with joy at the possibility he had been thinking of me at exactly the same time as I had been thinking of him.

'Well, Lorrie said she'd invited you both for dinner on Saturday and I was wondering if you were going to come. You see, there is this beef dish I've been wanting to cook.'

We were standing really close in front of the till and I dropped my wallet. We both leant down to pick it up, my hand touched his and tingled with a surprising force. He helped me up and handed me the wallet.

'Yes,' I said, trying to pull myself together, trying not to show that I loved him already and wanted to embrace him, 'of course we would love to come for dinner; I just have to check with Petra. She's our au pair and Saturday is her big night out.'

He waited for me to pay and I almost wished that he would just walk on and leave me to be flustered and gauche on my own. He opened the door for me. As we walked down the street together I had a moment of reality, when it struck me that I was being silly. He was a married man and I was being childish to even consider that he might be interested in me.

'Love the frock. Are you going somewhere?'

'Well, yes,' I lied, embarrassed that he had noticed my effort. 'I may go to a birthday party. Haven't decided yet.'

He was wearing tennis shorts and running shoes. His body was tanned and his calves and thighs lean and a little muscular. He was so much taller than Jack. I really liked the way he called my dress a frock.

'Are you going to play tennis?'

'Just been.' I wondered for a moment whether he was lying. Perhaps he'd dressed up in tennis gear because he'd known he might bump into me. Very doubtful, of course; men didn't usually go to such extremes.

A police siren wailed by and I told him the story about Alex, the previous owner of his house, who had been mugged. It was a deeply inappropriate anecdote to mention to someone who had just moved in, but he didn't seem to mind although he did say that he wouldn't tell Lorrie. He slowed down on the corner of our road. 'We must do this again some time.'

'What about tomorrow?' I nearly blurted out, but thankfully held myself back, only to ask something even more absurd. 'What must we do?'

'Well ...' he paused, 'chat, bump into each other in the off-licence.' He suddenly seemed anxious to finish the conversation with me.

'Oh, yes.' I reddened. What had I expected?

He opened his door. I wanted to rewind the last few weeks and erase the part where I found Mark attractive. How could I be a woman who fancied another woman's husband? And particularly the husband of a woman who quite possibly was inflicted with post-natal depression? I had always wondered how women could go after married men and here I was, a total hypocrite and a predator. On the other hand, I thought as I opened my door, Mark was interested in me too. Or was he? Maybe he was just a flirtatious man. Maybe he treated all women with a vague sense of interest.

Jack was watching one of his violent American cop programmes. The volume was up far too high. He seemed to be spread over most of the sofa and he was drinking beer and eating some of Petra's nuts. He didn't look up as I drifted in and through to the kitchen. I was making some pasta sauce and thinking how lovely it would have been if Jack had prepared me one of his gourmet dinners as he used to, rather than waiting for me to struggle on with my basic cooking skills.

We ate the pasta on our laps, and then Jack drank coffee and chain-smoked and I thought: there must be more to life than this. There must be more to life than cooking pasta and slumping down beside a partner who was so familiar that they didn't even notice your entries and exits. A life of safe and predictable routine, a life of lifeless sex, of going through the motions, playing a role, pretending that everything was fine. I missed the life that we'd had together. I missed pleasing Jack and him trying to please me. I missed cuddling him and I missed his delicious dinners.

'Do you think we should see someone?' I asked Jack as one man shot another on the TV. He didn't reply and I asked the question again.

'Who?'

'I mean like a therapist.'

'Why?'

'Well, we don't seem to be in love any more. We just sit and watch television and barely talk to each other.'

'I love you. Silly girl,' he said. 'And you love me.'

*

That night I went to sleep and dreamt of Mark. We met in the street and went off to the park and chatted and then, after a while, as the sun was setting, he put his arms around me. I was just sitting there basking in the last of the rays, when I was woken by a huge grunt. Jack was lying on his back with his mouth open and he was snoring. Great torrents of snores and grunts came out of his mouth; he reminded me of a wild boar, the kind that men in lederhosen with Bavarian hats hunt in Austria and Germany.

I tossed and turned, trying to fall asleep again, trying to return to the blissful dream, but it was impossible. I was thinking about how it used to be with Jack, so long ago. He had wanted to marry me three months after we had met, but I hadn't been sure. I was still very much aware of his reputation as a philanderer; a man who had caused a young woman to have a nervous breakdown. I was almost sure that we were destined to be together, but I wanted to keep him interested; I wanted him to chase me a little more because I felt that if I gave in too easily, he would tire of me.

He used to bring me flowers nearly every day and surprise me with beautiful necklaces; some were expensive, others were just trinkets. My favourite was made of coloured seeds from an Indian fruit. He had found it in a market and I had worn it every day until it broke. He gave me long massages. He would chat to me while I was in the bath, and we would walk entwined and hold hands over dinner. We would discuss art and literature, politics and film. After the children had come along things changed. We began to talk about schools and budgets and property and au pairs. We talked diaries and schedules and what was on television. The problem was I couldn't remember what it had been like to really be in love with Jack.

7

My friend Annie came for a drink a few days later, and
we sat in the garden while Jack gave the children a bath.
Jack facilitating bathtime was a once-a-week ritual, and
almost not worth the twenty minutes of peace. After a
Jack bath-night, the floor and towels would be sodden.
The murky bath water would be left in with the toys floating on top of a thin layer of scummy soap. The children's
clothes were abandoned wherever they had happened to
drop them and strips of soggy loo paper would be strewn
across the floor.

Often Jack would miss bath-night altogether, as he
would drive down to Hampshire to see his mother. Sometimes when he disappeared to Hampshire, I would make
him promise to do another night and then, when it came
to it, he would only half do it. He would run the bath and
undress the children and then wander downstairs where
he would get involved in a telephone conversation with
Eden or his mother and leave me to finish.

But that night, Jack was giving the children a bath, and
Annie and I were drinking vodka and cranberry juice.
Annie always looked stylish, no matter what, whether
she was at home working or at a party, even in the coldest
winter when she was wrapped in several layers, she managed to look original and unique. She wore clothes that

she had designed and rolled her own cigarettes and didn't have children, which meant that she looked young and seemed younger than me even though we were nearly the same age. I, on the other hand, had to make more of an effort and was in the habit of resorting to jeans.

Annie had been struggling for years designing re-cyclable clothes, but recently her company had taken off and she had orders from Japan and Italy, as well as a couple of shops in the UK. We had known each other since we were four years old and had gone to school together but had lost touch until we met again at Heathrow on the eve of Jack's fortieth birthday, which we were celebrating with a weekend away in Venice.

When I confided that I sometimes wondered whether Jack was the man I wanted to spend the rest of my life with, she commented, 'But you used to be so happy. You were so in love.'

'Was I?' I asked. 'Really?'

'Yes, so in love. So happy. Don't you remember how Jack proposed?'

'Yes, up a mountain.'

'That's right, and you told me that you both cried and hugged and he had brought the ring all the way up the mountain on a tiny purple cushion. Or something like that.'

'True. I'll never forget the light when he asked me to marry him. It was beautiful: matt and still and golden, poised at that moment between day and evening.'

'You sound like one of those ladies from an amateur poetry club.'

I laughed. 'Remind me what we were like.'

'You used to laugh together. I have photographs of you both looking so in love.'

'Are you still in love with Marco?'

'Yes, but we have lots of time and space for each other because of me being in Italy or Poland so much for work.'

'Umm, maybe that's a possible explanation.'

'You were really in love with Jack; remember that and somewhere deep down, you probably still are. You just need to rekindle your affection for him.'

'It feels as though being in love with Jack was in another lifetime,' I said. 'Things are different. So complicated. I have a crush . . .'

Jack joined us in the garden followed by the children, who looked more dishevelled after their bath than they had done before it. Maud's hair was drenched and she hadn't washed her face. Jed was dressed in the same clothes he had been wearing before. He looked furious.

'What's the matter, Jed?'

'Everything,' Jed shouted. His face was pale and the circles under his eyes looked very black. He was on the verge of tears. 'I don't want a bath with Maud any more. She's a girl.'

'Yes, um, Jed decided he didn't want a bath tonight,' Jack said, sitting down on one of the garden chairs. 'Fair dos,' he continued. 'A man doesn't need a bath every night.'

'No, but it's funny that it should be on your night that he chooses not to have a bath.'

'Yes, yes, well ... that may be.' Jack was lighting a cigarette. He'd lost interest in bathtime, children and me.

'First fag of the day, best one.' He turned to Annie.

'Jack, you've already had one in your study. I smelt it,' I said.

'That was just a taster of good things to come.' He winked at Annie; she laughed, which annoyed me.

'Annie. Annie, Annie, lovely Annie,' he said, 'what have you two been discussing?'

'Oh, world events,' Annie said, 'sex with strangers ... that kind of thing.'

'Yes,' I agreed breezily, 'that kind of thing.'

'Wish I'd been here,' Jack said, 'sounds interesting.'

'Mum,' Jed said, 'can I watch television?'

'Yes, do, do,' I said, 'but wouldn't you rather do some painting or drawing or something? Or cutting out?'

'Uh no, no, I wouldn't.'

'Or what about a jigsaw? Or sticking something?'

'Mum, I'm six years old.'

'OK, OK. It's just there must be something else you could do rather than watch television.'

'Can I play a game on your computer?' he asked.

'Um,' I hated to say no to him, 'not now, darling, I'm in the middle of something on my computer.'

'What about your mobile then?'

'OK.' I handed it to him. 'Are you sure you wouldn't rather do some Lego or something?'

'NO.'

'Can I do some computer?' Maud asked. Annie had Maud on her lap. Annie was Maud's godmother and

Maud loved her and always sat on her lap, whereas she only very rarely sat on mine, usually when she had hurt herself or was frightened. Annie had promised to read her a story. 'But I'm about to tell you a story,' Annie said.

'OK,' Maud said, 'go on then. Go on, Annie.'

Annie opened the book. It was the same story that Maud liked to be read every night, about a sad bear called Albert Le Blanc.

'"This is Albert Le Blanc. Even from the back he looks sad. His head hangs low. His shoulders are hunched. His arms flop loosely by his side."'

I dragged Jed on to my lap while he played a game on my mobile and Jack talked to his mother on the telephone. When the story had finished, Annie took Maud to bed and then came down and put her jacket on.

'Better go,' she said, 'while I'm still somewhat sober.' We walked towards the door and as I opened it, Mark was parking his bike.

'That's the man,' I whispered, 'that I have a crush on. There.'

'Where?' Annie asked.

'Shssh,' I giggled. 'Hi, Mark!' I called out.

He turned round, squinted at us and called out hello.

'He's absolutely gorgeous,' Annie said. 'Where did you find him?'

'He's my new neighbour.'

At that precise moment my immediate neighbour, the lovely Pauline, was letting one of her three cats out. 'Have you met him then?' she asked, following our adoring gazes. 'Our new addition?'

'Yes, I've met him and his wife. They're really nice.'

'We should meet up for a drink soon.'

'Yes, that would be lovely.'

She thought for a moment. 'Come to ours. I'll talk to John and we can fix a date.'

Annie left after giving me a kiss. Jack and I were alone together, eating soup on our laps, when I suggested that we should have a date night, like Annie and Marco.

'Date night?' Jack spat. 'What the hell is that?'

'It's when you make a special day of the week, like Thursday, to go out.'

'I'm not sure,' he said. 'It sounds a bit processed, a bit predictable.'

'But, Jack! It would give us a chance to talk.'

'We talk all the time. We're talking now for example.'

'But we never talk about anything interesting or amusing. We talk timetables.'

'What do you want to talk about?'

'You shouldn't have to ask.'

'Give me a clue,' Jack said.

'Don't worry; don't bother.'

'By the way,' he said, 'tonight is poker night. Remember? I'm going over to Simon's.'

'Are you?'

'Yes, you know I am.'

'Oh, I'd forgotten.'

Jack went to poker night about once a month and the following day was always a wipe-out, as he'd be hungover and bad-tempered.

He had a shave, smoked a cigarette, knocked back a glass of wine and left the house. I went to bed at my usual time, drifted off to sleep over a novel and woke suddenly at three in the morning. Jack wasn't back. I tiptoed down to the kitchen to see if he was there, but he wasn't. I resisted calling him for five minutes, then another five, but finally I gave in and called. I left a message, yawning, asking where he was.

I stayed awake until four. I woke at five to hear him singing downstairs. He was a parody of a drunk man, slurping and singing his way to bed. He crashed out with all his clothes on, stinking of cigarettes and alcohol – the sight of a full-grown man, my husband, reduced to a drunken slob, made me first angry and stirred up, and then sad and tearful.

Saturday morning. Jack was lying in. Jack rarely, if ever, got up with the children. He would reluctantly get up on my birthday and he once made me breakfast in bed on Mother's Day. After one of these gestures there would be a lot of talk about the effort he had made – the cards the children had drawn, the egg that he had boiled – and there was so much debriefing about how great he had been that it almost obliterated the actual favour.

Jack refused to rouse himself that Saturday morning after poker night, even though I was due in at the café. He used a trick of pretending that he couldn't hear me. He moaned that he was hungover and I told him that he was deservedly hungover because at our age you couldn't stay up until five in the morning and then expect to feel alert. I was about to leave but all was not well. The children were running amok and hitting each other with Jack's tennis racket so I shouted at Jack to get up. He thumped up to Petra's room and I heard him knocking on her door.

'Petra,' he cleared his throat, 'it's Jack. Can I offer you thirty pounds for two hours' work?'

'OK, OK,' I heard her saying hoarsely. 'I will do it. Nice price.'

'Thanks, Petra,' Jack said gruffly, 'you're a good girl.'

Saturday mornings at the café were frenzied and more stressful than Maud's birthday party and a long day on a film set. Harried, bleary-eyed parents would arrive with their frenetic, runny-nosed children. Lone fathers would hype up their offspring to screeching point on hot chocolate and Coca-Cola. Health-conscious mothers would ask for rice milk and non-wheat bread and jam with no sugar. Cool, languid couples who had spent the night together would also arrive, wanting poached eggs, fruit smoothies and cups of coffee. It was hard to find a balance. The slim, single women were not that enamoured with the clambering toddlers and snotty-nosed kids but these same women, fixated on love, did not spend money on hearty breakfasts.

We served coffee, tea and organic sausages and tomatoes, bacon and beans, and endless rounds of toast. We didn't offer anything fried, luckily, as the public liability insurance went up to £1,300 a year if a café had a fryer. We did serve baked chips but we lost money on them as they were expensive to buy. Some Saturdays people would queue, which was aggravating for both us and the customers who were sitting at tables trying to relax. We literally ran from the kitchen to the tables. Felipe manned the coffee and smoothies, while Tilda and I served the food and made simple salads and sandwiches. We worked on alternate Saturday mornings. I rushed everywhere, tripped up often, forgot what people had ordered and, on my first morning, spilt a glass of orange juice on a small child and a plate of chips on a man's lap. We realized quite soon that we could only offer one local speciality a day – a tomato tart or cheese omelette. We posted our two reviews up on a board and after an initial rush of interest there were days when we barely broke even. But we were determined to make the café a success. In any spare moment we had, we trawled through catalogues choosing suppliers, and making arrangements to sample food and visit food fairs. I began to dream of food; I could smell it in my hair.

When I finished at the café that Saturday afternoon, I went for an appointment with Alistair the priest. He had made a big impression on me seven years before when he talked to us about the value and sanctity of marriage. I had been meaning to see him since killing Jack in my dream and because I felt like an adulterer. In my dreams I certainly was one. There were days when I found any man attractive. Not literally anyone, of course, certainly not Steve the plumber who must have weighed thirty stone and came to install the new boiler. Mark was different though; he was the first man I'd met since marrying Jack that I actually, truly, felt drawn to.

Alistair and I met for half an hour, which was very generous of him as he was a busy man and extremely popular with the women of his parish. There was one pale blonde woman who answered his telephone and showed you into his office, and others who hung around his church and had important things to discuss with him like the altar arrangement for the Harvest Festival. So I felt rather privileged to be whisked into his quiet, orderly office, away from the hordes of other women who would have given so much for a few minutes alone with Alistair. Alistair was tall, with thick white hair and an easy laugh. He looked and had the air of an erudite headmaster. He stood up when I came in to his book-lined study and towered over me. He shook my hand and looked me directly in the eye. He asked me to sit down.

'Very good to see you, Mrs Boore.'

'Oh, call me Ellie, please. Do you remember me?'

'Yes, of course I do, and your husband the actor, Boore, one couldn't forget. I remember him as being rather an impatient man. What can I do for you?'

I didn't know how to begin. 'Well ... I was very struck by our conversation before we were married and, well ...'

'Take your time,' he prompted me.

'My mind is wandering off my marriage. I'm finding it hard to stay focused on my husband. I'm afraid ... I ... I find that I am interested in other men.'

He paused for a moment, looking at me over his reading glasses, and I squirmed in my seat like a child.

'A long time ago,' he confided, 'I was a little foolish.' He picked up a large glass paperweight which had some coloured patterns floating around inside. He gently bounced it in one hand before changing to his other. 'I ... well.' He paused. 'It doesn't matter. Suffice to say that the Lord saw fit to save my marriage. But,' he added gravely, 'be careful. Do you really want to lose all that you have now? The union is a spiritual thing and needs to be held and cherished like a glass bowl that you are carrying in a treacherous wind. It's precious and you will take exactly the same frustrations into any other relationship. Don't take risks. Shoot down any distractions with a *Star Wars* type gun.'

He'd said almost exactly the same words to us seven years before, only now I could really relate. I had to start shooting. Fast. Of course, it was so easy. All I had to do was picture Mark and then shoot him down with a *Star Wars* gun. Alistair was so wise. So attractive. I imagined the vicar and I discussing theology and world religions over a ham baguette in a café in Budapest. Despite the fact that he was a man of the cloth he had nearly swayed from the path once before and perhaps he would find me irresistible.

'So, my dear ...' He was standing up, indicating that it was time to go. I shook myself out of my reverie and thanked Alistair and he said I could telephone him at any time.

*

I joined Jack and the children in the park. I wanted to run into Jack's arms and tell him how much I loved him but he was holding his head and moaning. Maud sat straddled over his chest, bumping up and down, while Jed climbed a tree nearby. As soon as I had sat down on the grass next to him he announced that he was too hungover to have dinner with Mark and Lorrie.

'It's far too late to cancel,' I snapped, hating myself for sounding so ridiculously cross and for breaking the spell cast on me by Alistair the vicar.

'I can't come,' he moaned. 'My head feels as though it's about to crack open.'

'But it would be so boring for them to just have me. Please don't make me go on my own. Lorrie probably went to Billingsgate at five this morning to select four succulent monkfish, or to the butcher for sirloin steaks. Maybe she's marinating something – oh, Jack, you have to come with me; they'll be so disappointed if I arrive on my own.'

Even as I was telling him I had no desire to go alone, there was part of me that quite liked the idea. Sometimes when Jack was in the right mood, he would hold the table and tell everybody amusing anecdotes. His stories would usually involve a monster name drop and some wild fabrication. 'When I was in Africa during the wildebeest migration, drinking at one of those colonial clubs with Peter O'Toole, he told me that Elizabeth Taylor liked to chain-smoke cigars ...' The more people laughed and applauded him, the more invisible I felt in his presence. So sometimes, when he wasn't with me, it was rather

enjoyable to be my own person, rather than feel super-
fluous, as though I was only there at that dining table
because he was.

'You'll have to call that weird Lorrie and explain.'

'Can't you do it, please?' Jack pleaded with me.

'Jack ...' He was beginning to infuriate me. 'No, you
do it.'

'They're your friends. I never wanted to go.'

'What do you mean, you never wanted to go? You
were gagging for them to bring a takeaway over the other
night.'

'Don't argue,' Jed pleaded. 'It's horrible. You argue
too much.'

'Sorry, Jed.' I kissed him. 'Sorry, but you know how
it is. Sometimes you and Maud argue, don't you?'

'But parents shouldn't argue.'

'They can't be perfect all the time but we'll try not to,
won't we, Jack?'

'Absolutely.' He stood up and came towards me
and hugged me. 'I love and adore your mummy. Always
have, always will.'

'Thank you.'

Maud was whining for an ice cream. I'd been very
careful with Jed and his nutrition. During weekends or
rare days off I had puréed him organic carrots and
made them into frozen cubes, and squeezed real juice for
him to drink and limited his intake of wheat and sugar
and ice cream, but by the time Maud came along I was
less organized. Jed had wandered off to play football
with some boys who were far, far bigger than he was. I

watched him for a moment and worried because he was running after the ball but never actually kicking it. Jack was propped up on his elbows moaning and holding his head until a couple of elderly women came up to him and asked for an autograph. He immediately transformed from a hopeless hungover bore to a charming celebrity and signed their well-worn notebooks.

I took Maud's hot little hand and drifted away from Jack towards the ducks. Damn Jack. I decided that the best thing to do would be to turn up at dinner and just announce that Jack was feeling ill. I sent a text to Petra to say she didn't need to babysit. She texted back straight away – HURRAY.

We reached the duck pond where I caught sight of a woman reading Hal's biography, and immediately decided to go and buy the book for myself, once and for all. So I returned to where Jack lay on a rug and bribed the children to come with me with an offer of ice cream for supper. Jed climbed on to his bicycle. I pushed the buggy while Jed sped ahead. There were quite a few men on weekend duty in the park pushing prams. I always noticed that women pushed with two hands, whereas men, including Jack, liked to push with one hand. My theory was that it was their way of remaining literally half detached from the whole scenario of child-rearing.

By the time we reached the bookshop, the children were bored, hot and annoyed and refused to come in with me. I ordered them to stay by the door and rushed to buy the book, which I put straight into my bag. I was aware that my behaviour was strange and compulsive, and that I was swinging in my fantasyland from admiring and wanting Mark to remembering the attraction I had felt for Hal. It seemed that almost any man but Jack would do.

When we got home, Jack was in the bath; but had kindly prepared a supper for the children, cooked mince. All I had to do was boil the pasta. Sometimes I even managed to get that wrong and either undercooked it or overcooked it, depending. The children whirled around me, slipping and sliding on the shiny floor. I drained the pasta and forced them into their chairs and presented them with pasta, mince and peas with lumps of cheese as the grater had gone missing.

'Not again,' Jed moaned. 'We had pasta, mince and peas yesterday.'

'Did you?'

'Yes. Petra made it.'

'Sorry, darling.'

'That's all right, Mum.' He was so charming, my boy. If anything happened to him . . . it didn't bear thinking about.

When they went to join Jack in the bath, I curled into one of the white sofas with Hal's book. I turned immediately to the photograph of Hal at the back and the brief author biography. My heart pounded and fluttered as I read that he lived in North London with his wife and children. Hal, married? Hal being married had not figured in my plans. Why was I so surprised? He was, after all, an attractive, intelligent man in his late thirties. It was shocking to me because in my lurid dreams, he was eternally available, willing and able to pull me against a wall and fuck me.

I flicked through a few pages of the book and settled on a chapter about Arthur Munby's infatuation with a Victorian maid, Hannah Cullwick. I knew a little bit about Hannah as I had once read her diaries. She had worked sixteen-hour days with one afternoon off a week, but always said that she took pride in her job. She'd had a chaste but charged relationship for twenty years with Arthur, a middle-class poet and barrister whom she'd eventually married in secret. She had called him Massa, like a slave to her master, and on her one afternoon off she would clean his flat and wash his feet. I wondered if she had scrubbed his feet out of a genuine desire to please him, and because she thought it her duty to do so, reinforcing her humble background and their class differences, or whether it gave her a kind of masochistic sexual thrill to be so enslaved to him. Probably both, I concluded, and wondered briefly whether I should offer to be a sex slave to Jack. The problem was, I couldn't imagine that washing his hairy-toed feet would turn me on at all.

The photographs in the book showed a lump of a woman with a healthy, not unpleasant, face. Her arms were huge and sturdy; her hands looked large and lumpy. She complained that after she was married she couldn't squeeze her raw, red hands into the white gloves that she was expected to wear. I read an extract from one of her letters to Arthur describing how she had stripped off and climbed the kitchen chimney to clean it when she was a maid of all work. She explained in exacting detail how she had been covered from head to foot in dirt and how she had enjoyed the filthy hard work. She had obviously written the description because she knew it would please him. I wondered whether Jack and I would have a more successful relationship if I didn't feel pressurized to have a career, to have it all. Would our relationship work better if I had lived a hundred years before and trudged along as traditional wife, who stayed at home and gave myself to my family and spent time and effort thinking of ingenious ways to please him?

Arthur and Hannah never had children. Jack and I argued about childcare all the time. If I was brutally honest, our relationship had deteriorated since we'd had children. Usually we would have the same kind of dialogue:

'You never help with childcare,' I would protest after Jack refused, as usual, to give the children their baths.

'What about the other week,' he would ask, 'when I took Maud for the whole day and gave her a bath?'

'Jack! That was at least two months ago!'

Hannah and Arthur didn't have sex until twenty years after they met. Our sex life after seven years of marriage was already stale. It did occur to me that perhaps I should buy something sexy to wear and a selection of sex toys but the thought just seemed so tiring, embarrassing and contrived. I imagined that if I dressed up in a leather corset and came downstairs brandishing a whip Jack would laugh at me. The humiliation didn't bear thinking about.

Jack came into the room, smoking a cigarette. 'I feel better,' he said, 'and I'm going to come to dinner.'

'You'll have to call Petra. She's not going to be happy when we announce at seven o'clock on Saturday night that she's going to babysit, when I told her at five o'clock that she no longer had to.'

'I'll talk to her,' Jack said, as though just the sound of his voice and immense charm would win her over.

'She'll probably ask for more money or something, but . . .'

'I know what to say.'

At that very moment, she returned from wherever she had been in time to change for her big night out. Jack took her aside and I heard her protest, 'Oh no!'

She was sighing and shrugging as she came into the kitchen. 'It's too much,' she said, 'that you change plans all the time.' She sounded very angry. She opened the fridge and then shut it again.

'I agree with you,' I said, feeling a mixture of fury and guilt that she should be talking to me in that tone. 'I'm sorry, Petra. It's Jack. He thought he was ill and now he's not, but I've still got you the fish and frozen yoghurt and there's a bottle of champagne. You can have that too.' I regretted offering the champagne; that really was overcompensating in a most absurd, out-of-control way.

She gave me a sulky smile and said, 'OK. I have Felipe coming over and we will go out when you come back.'

'Felipe?'

'Yes, he's coming to see me.'

'Right. That's fine,' I said, but I was already feeling

slightly annoyed that Felipe was befriending my au pair and at the pressure not to be late as they were going out. I wouldn't even know where to go at midnight, except bed.

I climbed upstairs feeling anxious and also remorseful about messing Petra around and offering her champagne. I ran myself a bath and thought about ringing Mark and Lorrie and calling dinner off. How ludicrous, I mused as I undressed, that I should be considering flirtation with a man who was not my husband. How arrogant, I decided, surveying my body with all its ripples and lumps and sags, even to imagine that a handsome man like Mark would be attracted to me.

But as I lay in the bath, soaped my limbs, submerged myself under the water and washed my hair, I began to relax. I looked out of the window at the tops of the trees swaying in the breeze. I rose from the bath and a little trickle of excitement flickered through me.

We knocked on their door and I heard Lorrie shout, 'Mark! They're here!' We heard footsteps approaching and then he opened the door.

'Hello.' He leant forward to kiss me and smiled at me. He shook Jack's hand. 'How was the journey?' he joked.

'Good, good,' Jack laughed.

We were ushered into their sitting room, which had been cleared of all the piles of books and stacks of boxes. Whereas our house was all glistening and granite and white, theirs was more rustic and embroidered and book-lined. Their kitchen was smaller as they had not done their side return, and they had mismatched pieces of free-standing wooden furniture and a country kitchen table with four rickety chairs. Their house was like a cosy country cottage, probably more welcoming than ours. I gave Mark some red tulips. He kissed me thank you and arranged them in a long glass and then Lorrie appeared in a vivid purple silk kaftan, clouding the atmosphere with her forced smile and changing the temperament of the room.

'Jack Boore.' She shook his hand. 'Delighted to see you again.' She was trying to be warm and open, but she seemed heavy and tired, and her eyes were puffy. Her face looked thinner and pointier and she had dark circles under her eyes.

'What can we offer you? Champagne? Vodka?' Mark asked.

'We have a treat,' Lorrie said, brightening a little. 'Our friends in Moscow have sent us some caviar.'

'*Dobro pozhalovat.*' Mark was holding a bottle of chilled vodka and pouring it into four small glasses. Lorrie flopped down in a red armchair by the fire while Mark went to check on his stew in the oven. Lorrie was picking at a tapestry, telling us how her mother loved to sew, when baby Alice began crying upstairs. She made no effort to move; in fact she sank deeper into her chair. Mark went, resigned to his child-caring duties.

I drank the ice-cold vodka in tiny tentative sips. Lorrie had turned to Jack and was questioning him about his acting career; she wanted to know where he had studied. I sat, still and quiet, looking around the room.

'Ellie?'

'Yes, yes, sorry, miles away.'

'Lorrie wants me to describe the *Country Matters* soap. What would you say?'

'Well, yes, it's . . . um, let me see . . . It's about a country doctor; well, it was until Jack was killed off. Now I don't know what's it's about . . . um . . .'

Mark poked his head round the door. 'Everything all right?'

'Yes.' Lorrie looked up briefly.

They carried on talking about Jack's favourite subject – himself. He was embellishing a story I had heard before about one weird female fan who once streaked naked across the set of *Country Matters*, waving a flag which said SUCK ME, DR GRANGER.

'I'll just go and see if Mark's all right.' I stood up.

'I'm sure he's just fine. He's very capable.' Lorrie laughed. 'He makes me feel useless in comparison. I'm not at all domestic.'

'No, nor am I.' Jack smiled. 'Well, I can cook. I need to cook. I like cooking. Ellie is not so keen. She's always having to follow me round, picking up my discarded clothes. Aren't you, darling?'

I raised my eyebrows at him, wondering if Lorrie presumed that Jack was permanently in a state of undress because he was a rampant sex maniac. 'I'll see if Mark needs help.'

Mark was putting some wine glasses on the table. I admired his hands and I was thrilled by the small crescent moon tattoo on his wrist. I wanted him to touch me.

'Come and taste some stew.' He was leaning over a steaming orange casserole dish.

I lifted the spoon that he offered me and sampled the hot and delicious meat, lush in its pool of thick, warm gravy. He not only looked good, but could take care of small children and he was a cook. What better combination in a man? Then, as I was swallowing, Alistair the vicar's words came back to me, like an ominous voice-over in a movie: 'Shoot down all potential distractions with a *Star Wars* type gun.'

I sat down at the table and waited until Mark had turned back to his stew, then I closed my eyes and imagined picking up a flashing gun and pointing it at him. But in my vision he held up his hands in mock horror and began to laugh. The gun was too toy-like and it didn't work.

'Ellie, are you all right?' Mark asked. 'You're sitting with your eyes closed. Are you meditating? Are you having a turn?'

'No!' I opened my eyes and burst out with embarrassed laughter. 'Sorry, I just, I . . . well, I was trying to budge my contact lens which seems to be stuck in my eye.'

'Oh, I see.'

The table was laid beautifully with napkins that had been folded in a complicated origami style and red gladioli in a glass vase. He had an artistic, attractive sensibility but he also gave the impression that he would protect you from lions on safari or bandits in a tribal region in some far-off land.

'Did you lay the table?'

'Chieko, a Japanese girlfriend, taught me.'

I picked a napkin up. 'It's beautiful. Can I help?'

'No, unless you want to help me stir the spoon.' Was he flirting with me? Or simply being a good host? I wasn't quite sure.

Lorrie came into the kitchen, ostensibly to fetch some ice, but I had the feeling she wanted to check up on us. 'Let me take that,' Mark said, relieving her of the bucket of ice and leaving the room.

Lorrie sat down heavily and sighed.

'Are you all right, Lorrie?'

'Not exactly. I'm going home tomorrow, to my parents in the States. Kentucky. They're going to help me with Alice. I need to get away, it's very difficult. There is just so much to do. Silly things like ... well, I can't think now. Just remembering everything that Alice needs ... there is so much. So much infant stuff.'

'I know. I always used to try and travel light, with a nappy and some wipes in my handbag, but it's hard.'

'Yeah.'

'Are you all going?' I finished my glass of wine.

'No, just Alice and me.' She was examining a loose strand of hair. There was a pause as she got up and then changed her mind and sat down again.

'How long are you going away for?'

'I just ... well, I don't know ... a few weeks, a month, two months? It's not like I imagined, being with Mark and having a baby. He's a great guy, I just don't know ... I feel very, very tired and I'm just so intolerant.' She sighed and leant back in her chair; then her eyes welled with the beginnings of tears.

'Would you prefer to have your last evening alone with Mark?'

'No, we'd probably just bicker. No, please stay, it's fine.'

When we sat down for supper I looked at Mark for signs that his marriage was on the brink of dissolving, a signal that his wife and child were about to leave him, but his smiling eyes and jovial manner gave nothing away. He saw me appraising him and when Lorrie stood up to fetch something and Jack was searching for his cigarettes, he winked at me.

We had lentils, warm slices of beef and sweet baked chicory. He was a serious cook and put Jack, who was a good cook, in the shade. Jack was telling some story about when he fluffed his lines in a production of *Macbeth* at the Oxford Playhouse. Lorrie was listening intently, but she seemed weirdly relaxed. At one point when she said she was allergic to wheat Mark rolled his eyes, and when Jack praised Mark on his culinary skills she pointedly yawned.

Jack, of course, was oblivious to the unravelling of their marriage and when I mentioned that we needed to get home as our au pair was anxious to go out, he blundered, 'We don't both have to leave. You stay, darling, and I'll go home.'

'No, you stay and have fun. I'll go. I'm tired anyway.'

'No, I insist. Why should you have to leave a perfectly lovely dinner?'

'Are you sure you don't want to stay?' I asked desperately, but keeping my tone light and easy.

'No. You stay.'

He sounded so insistent that it would have been rude to actually leave. So Jack left me at their house. Five minutes after he had gone, Lorrie stretched and yawned and announced that she was going to bed, leaving me alone with her handsome husband. She kissed me goodbye, thanked me for coming and yawned her way out of the room.

Mark offered me another glass of chilled vodka. 'Well, this is good news.' He smiled. 'Alone at last.' I loved the sound of his voice, soft and sensuous, not harsh and loud like Jack's. I liked his black T-shirt with the symmetrical black and white pattern. He stood up and put some music on.

'Actually,' I corrected him pointlessly, gulping down the vodka, 'we've been alone a few times.'

'Yeah, when I watched football at your house.'

'And when we walked back together,' I reminded him, instantly regretting admitting how precisely I remembered our moments together.

'Yes, of course; I will never forget that cute nurse thing you were wearing.'

There was no question now, he was openly flirting with me, and I was beginning to feel a little worried that he would actually pounce on me, in his marital home, with his wife sleeping upstairs. We sat together in silence for a few seconds, which felt like a few minutes ... I wondered whether I should just stand up, walk over and kiss him.

'I know about ...'

'About?'

'Lorrie leaving tomorrow.'

'Oh, yes. I'll be alone for a few weeks. I think she's depressed,' he said matter-of-factly. 'Maybe post-natal. To be honest I think she's had post-natal depression since the day she was born. It's been very difficult.'

I couldn't help sniggering at the post-natal joke, and realized I was being drawn in with him, distancing myself from Lorrie more and more.

'I think she needs a break from me. We are people who both led very independent lives before we married. It's her idea to go.'

I must go home, I said to myself, as he lounged back on to the sofa, uncrossing his long legs and stretching them out languidly in front of him.

'Don't go.'

He suddenly seemed a little drunk and I wanted to get away.

'You're going to have to look after me,' he said. 'Will you? Please?'

'Yes, well, I'll try.'

'Good,' he said, patting the empty space next to him on the sofa. 'Why don't you come and sit next to me?'

'I've got to go home,' I said, shifting myself to the edge of my chair.

'Won't you stay for a coffee? A small one?'

In my deluded head I was convinced that the coffee reference was an innuendo, another way of saying he wanted to wrench off my clothes and take me there and then on the living-room floor. I still blush in embarrassment recalling my reply: 'No, thank you, I've got my period.'

'What?'

'Nothing, nothing.' I would have run if I hadn't been paralysed with shame. 'I have to go,' I said, 'I'm really tired.'

'Must you?' he asked 'Period or not?'

'Yes.'

'OK – well, it was great to see you. You look lovely when you blush.'

'Thank you for dinner.'

'Thank you for coming.' He walked me to the door. I could feel him behind me and smell him – cool and suntanned. He placed his hands on my shoulders but this time there was no tingle; no sensation, nothing.

I walked on to our street and he watched me cross the road and waited for me to open my door. I closed the door behind me and leant against it. What had happened was so embarrassing and awful that potentially, in retrospect, I could see that it might be quite funny.

'How could you leave me like that?' I called out to Jack when I'd recovered. 'Didn't you realize what was going on?' I walked into our whiter than white sitting room to find Jack asleep in front of the television.

He woke up. 'What's up?'

'How could you leave me there?'

'I thought you'd like to stay.'

'Didn't you notice?'

'Notice what?'

'What was going on.'

'No.'

'They're separating.'

'Oh, so that was it. She seemed to yawn an awful lot and almost deliberately didn't eat her dinner. But how do you know?'

'She told me. She's going home. So awkward, I hardly know her. She's going home to the States tomorrow.'

'Really? Poor bloke.'

'I know, and he's so nice, he's so . . .' I checked myself before I lapsed into some embarrassing eulogy.

'Yes, he's all right. Well, guess what was happening when I got back?'

'What?'

'Petra was here with your manager. What's his name?'

'Felipe?'

'Yes. There's something going on between them. She said she was staying out; she'd be back tomorrow.'

'Couldn't be more blatant then.'

'Not really,' Jack said, 'not unless they appeared together for breakfast, Petra sprawled on his lap while he spoon-fed her grapes – that would be just the tiniest bit more brazen.'

'Or imagine if they stayed the night and he came down at three in the morning to ask you for a condom?'

We laughed. We could still make each other laugh.

When it actually came to it, I was scared of the madness, the uncertainty and the strangeness of a new life that would be the inevitable outcome of breaking up with Jack. But that night I dreamt that Mark and I lay in a bedroom, naked, making love, somewhere very warm, because there were shutters shading us from the early morning sun.

Sunday. It was meant to be my lie-in but Jack was snoring and I could hear Maud screaming downstairs.

'Could you go, Jack? It's my lie-in.'

'What?' He turned over and fell back to sleep.

I prodded him.

'What?' he spluttered, sitting up. 'Where am I? What's going on? Who am I?'

'YOU'RE A BORE IN BED!' I thought of Mark, laying the table, making dinner, running to his baby. 'JACK, WILL YOU DO SOMETHING OR I'M GOING TO LEAVE YOU.'

'You what?' he asked.

'Nothing. The children are screaming and it's meant to be my lie-in.'

'You go,' he said, 'please, I beg you.'

'It's just ridiculous,' I said to Annie later, 'that I have to threaten to leave Jack and still he won't climb out of bed on a Sunday morning.'

After my outburst, Jack was on best behaviour and as a very special treat made a roast lamb lunch with Yorkshire puddings, despite the fact that it was 28°C outside. The problem was that when Jack made lunch, he didn't clear up. He used nearly all the saucepans and different uten-sils, plates, whisks, gravy boats and glasses, and left everything for me to clean. It was annoying that he clearly thought he had tidied up just because he put all of it in the sink. As if that was enough.

We sat around the table, just the four of us, and I ate too many roast potatoes and then felt sick. Jack did his array of regional accents to amuse the children. But he lost his good humour when I asked him to take the children to the park. 'Just for an hour,' I pleaded, 'just one hour while I clear up.'

'But I've done all the cooking, I've made Yorkshire puddings. I don't want to go to the park. I hate the park.'

'Jack,' I said, 'if you don't go to the park, I'm going to leave you. Really and truly.' I realized that was the last time I could threaten to leave him; the next time I would really have to go.

He left reluctantly and I lay on the sofa with the Sunday papers. I flicked through the interior pages and spent a few minutes looking at one particularly real-looking fake wood gas fire (£15,000) that would have been perfect for our bedroom. Then I flicked through the travel pages and pondered over the desert hotel in Egypt. Finally, after half an hour of restless reading, I got up and began to lift a couple of plates away from the hazard that was Sunday lunch. I wondered if Lorrie had left for America and how Mark was. I wandered over to the sitting room bay window and peeked out to see if he was standing forlornly on his doorstep. The sun beat down on the road; the evergreen hedge that grew over the wall was brown and patchy. I went to fetch a watering can and watered the wretched hedge, very conscious of Mark living across the road; maybe he was watching me.

I passed the lunch mess and picked up one more plate and pushed it into the dishwasher, watching the gravy slide off into the bowels of the machine. I meant to clear all the plates, but it was so hot and humid that the action of lifting the plate and scraping off the congealing meat and shrivelled vegetables was tiring. I went to the garden and lay on the small patch of grass. I drifted off and woke to the sound of my doorbell ringing out. I stumbled towards the door, trying to focus because my eyes were adjusting to the darkness of the hall after the brightness of the summer day. It was Mark at the door and when I saw him my body responded with a shiver as I remembered making love to him in my dream.

'I'm so sorry to turn up again like this,' he coughed, 'but I don't have your telephone number.' He looked down at my raggedy shorts, torn T-shirt and muddy knees. 'I have a piece of mozzarella and a piece of avocado and I just wondered whether you have a tomato?'

'Come in, come in, I'm sure I must have a tomato.' I turned round and he followed me into the kitchen. 'Huge mess. Jack and the children went to the park. I'm meant to be tidying up.'

'I'm meant to be writing a report on the infrastructure of water pumps in African villages . . .'

'That sounds far more interesting. What do you actually do?'

'Oh, I'll explain another time. That looks good.' He was appraising the remnants of lunch, which now somehow looked horribly smug.

'Oh yes, you need to eat. Let me look for that tomato.' I was aware that I was kind of prancing around the room and talking rather fast. I offered him a beer. 'Look, I can't find that tomato, but would you like a sandwich?'

'Well, that sounds like a great offer.'

He sat down with his cold beer on the faded pink armchair in the playroom, overlooking the garden, while I cut some bread, spread it with butter and mustard and cut a thin slice of lamb. I gave it to him and he ate it greedily in two or three bites.

'Mmm . . . very good. Thank you.'

'When did you last eat?'

'I had a bowl of stale Frosties just after Lorrie left and half a banana.' He stared hard down at the floor.

There wasn't another chair to sit on in the playroom, so I leant against the doors that led to the garden and after a quick banter about the muggy weather, suggested we go outside. We lay on the grass and he looked up at the sky and squinted and he finally spoke.

'I already miss Alice.'

We were inches away from each other and it would have been so easy to take his hand and wrap myself around him; indeed, I was consumed with a physical pang, a sexual longing that started in my groin and swiftly spread throughout my body. It was an urge so powerful that it shocked me.

'I'm sorry.' He sat up. 'I shouldn't be burdening you

with all my problems; you hardly know me. I'm really sorry.'

'Don't worry. Maybe I'll be rushing over to you in three or four days after I've walked out on Jack.' Oh, why did I say that? I could feel myself turning red. 'Please feel free to come over and see us any time,' I garbled, hoping to cover up my absurd throwaway remark. 'What about some supper one day this week?'

He was stretching now, and he put on some wrap-around dark glasses. 'I've booked myself up this week, to keep my mind off things. It's just so strange being a father and a husband one moment and a bachelor the next. I've got a game of squash with my nephew, a movie with an ex and a work dinner. Then I'm going to my parents for the weekend. I don't know when or if Lorrie will be back.'

I wanted to ask him if Lorrie had actually left him, but it didn't seem right.

We were eating some chocolate biscuits when he asked me to show him the 'stone path' at the bottom of the garden. I worried that he would find it precious and silly.

'Is it a sculpture?' he asked me as he followed me towards it. 'It's rather beautiful.'

'It's a labyrinth, a place to walk and meditate.'

'Oh, really? My brother does a lot of meditation; he swears by it.'

'Well, you could try if you like. It has an interesting effect,' I added, 'on the soul.'

He didn't scoff and tease me as Jack had done after the labyrinth was built. 'What happens when you walk around it? Is it like a maze? Do you have to find your way out?' he asked

'No, it's not like a maze. But my labyrinth is so small, it would be hard to get lost anyway. You're travelling towards the centre, and I know it sounds a bit sort of strange, but you're meant to be travelling to your own centre at the same time. Grounding yourself. It has a decided path which will take you through and out again.'

'At this point I'll try anything.' He began to pace around. 'Is this right?' he asked. He walked with a self-conscious stance.

'It's best to try and let go of all thoughts.' I demonstrated, walking ahead of him, hoping that he wasn't finding me too off-beat and odd. It would be awful if he dined out weeks later on the story of his weird New Age neighbour, 'a rather whimsical woman – in the Middle Ages she would have been persecuted as a witch'.

We walked around in silence, but it was hard to focus with him walking right behind me. We stood side by side in the centre and I wondered what he was thinking.

'So how was it?' I asked a little anxiously.

'I'd like to try again.'

'Good. Well, I'll leave you this time, it will be easier to concentrate on your own.'

In the kitchen the mess was really overwhelming. I managed to take everything off the table and pile it near the sink. On my journey back to wipe the table down, I glanced outside the window and saw him plodding around, then backed away before he caught me staring. I pulled on the yellow rubber gloves and tackled the greasy baking tin. I had finished washing-up when he came through the door.

'At first nothing happened at all. It was like walking around and around a small path. But I have to admit after a while I fell into a kind of a trance,' he said. 'It was like watching myself in slow motion or being in a dream. I had the comforting thought that what's happened between Lorrie and me is happening for a good reason. Thank you for the sandwich and the beer. I should be going now. Got a report to finish by tomorrow.' He was leaving rather too abruptly; I wondered why.

We walked towards the door. I could sense his physicality and his smell, hear him padding in his bare feet. I wanted him in an almost involuntary way, as though my body were directing me.

'Can I kiss you?' he asked as I reached out to open the front door. 'I want to.' He pulled me towards him and I pushed the door closed with my foot. For a moment the thought crossed my mind that it was very wrong to kiss a man whose wife had just left, but the lure of the kiss was so powerful that I could no longer direct myself to rational thoughts.

Jack and I hadn't kissed properly for such a long time. Was it months? Years? Kissing is such an intimate embrace, but there are kisses and there are kisses: the sodden mealy-mouthed kiss, the fond, mildly stirring married kiss and the kiss with Mark, which after the first self-conscious, tremulous seconds was a mind-blowing, shivering, stomach-turning, groin-lurching kiss. Long, slow and electrifying. Slow, faster, faster, until nothing mattered, a long, long, heady kiss. We pulled away as I heard Jack and the children returning from the park, Jed's little voice shouting through the letterbox – 'HELLO! MUMMEE!!'

Jack and Mark said hello and goodbye in the hallway.

'Couldn't he just go to the shops to get his milk? Like everyone else?' Jack asked as soon as he'd gone.

'He didn't have any change.'

'Oh, I see. It's all very neighbourly.'

'Some people like the idea of neighbours.'

'Yes, I can see the point of neighbours: they take in your post and keep a key while you're away. It's just slightly lazy of him not to go and buy a pint.'

'Don't forget, his wife has just left.'

'Forget? I didn't even know. By the way, you're doing children's tea,' he announced, 'and I'm having a siesta.'

That was fine by me. The kiss had surged through me and I was still high. I sailed through teatime, beans on toast, no problem – even I could open a can and heat up the contents. I made the children faces with broccoli for hair, beans for eyes and bits of cut-out toast for nose and mouth. I calmly allowed ice cream for pudding, which usually sent me giddy with despair because of the sugar and the phlegm-inducing cream.

It was while watching them float underwater in their bath and hoping that they wouldn't drown, or that nothing awful would happen to my children, that I began to feel ashamed. I had gone too far and stepped over the line, coarsely flaunting the advice that the attractive vicar had given me. Was I mad? How could I be so weak? How could I, a woman who liked and admired other women (preferred them generally to men), kiss someone else's husband? I had condemned women who had behaved like me in the past. I dried Jed's hair a little too roughly with the towel and he burst into tears.

'You're so rough, Mummy. You're not concentrating. You're too quick. You're not thinking.'

'Sorry,' I said, hugging him. 'You're right. I was too harsh, too hurried, not thinking. Sorry, my love.'

'That's all right, Mummy,' he said. His large, long-lashed brown eyes looked up at me. He was such a poignant, innocent boy, the son of a treacherous, sullied mother.

Later, after the children had gone to bed, I telephoned Annie and whispered that I had kissed the neighbour, the gorgeous man who she had seen walking out of his house. She was riveted and wanted to know all the details, but just before we said goodbye, she advised me to be careful. 'One kiss could stay as a kiss,' she warned, 'or you could go further and watch your marriage unravel. Think about it.'

That night, lying awake listening to a drunken man singing a tuneless warble, I decided that I would not kiss Mark again. Ever. Shame.

8

It was the first day of the interminable summer holidays when Petra told me that she and Felipe were going to Ibiza for the summer. I had staggered down to breakfast to find her lying on the floor, wearing a pink leotard and teaching the children the down dog yoga stretch. She lifted herself nimbly out of the position – hand on the floor, bum lifted in the air – and asked to speak to me.

'Can it wait till I've had a cup of tea?'

'Yes, Ellie,' she said sweetly, 'it can wait.'

I ate my toast and honey and drank my tea. The children had tired of yoga and Jed was making a magnetic model while Maud created a huge mess with some paints. I had an inkling that what Petra was about to tell me was not going to thrill me.

'OK, Petra,' I called out to her, when I'd finished my toast.

She slinked into the sitting room, her legs so long, brown and slender, the cut of the leotard so high on the leg, that she really did resemble a star. I admired her appearance, forgave her erratic behaviour and weird eating habits, just because she was not exactly beautiful but thrillingly attractive. We sat opposite each other – she was perched on the ottoman while I sank into the white sofa.

'You will find this difficult, Ellie,' she said, looking uncharacteristically serious, 'and me too, I find difficult.'

'Oh God. What?' My immediate thought just then was that she was pregnant.

'Well, me and Felipe, we booked flight to Ibiza, to find work for the summer. We have to go soon to find this work.' She started biting her thumb nail, something I had never seen her do before.

'When?' I asked calmly, but feeling wild and turbulent.

'Next weekend.'

'Next weekend! Petra, are you mad? How could you? You have to give me notice.' A whole series of swear words very nearly erupted from my mouth. I thought about what to say while she sat in front of me coyly, staring at me with a mixture of sauce, arrogance and guilt. 'But how could you do this?' I asked her as she stretched out her legs and examined her nails. 'You look after my children and Felipe is my manager – how could you both give me four days' notice when I've employed you for four months? At the interview you said you could stay a minimum of six months.'

It was contemptible that she didn't show the children or me any loyalty, particularly when Maud seemed to really love her. I was overcome with giddiness and anger at the same time and had to stop myself asking her to leave straight away.

'Remember what it like to be young and in love?' She was twisting a little bit of material on her leotard. 'You did something crazy like this?'

'Petra, I don't know what to say to you. I can't think.

I do remember what it was like to be young and I do know what it's like to be in love —' I thought of Mark then and my heart pounded erratically against my ribs — 'but really . . .' (Why did she always have to bring references in to how young she was, in relation to how old I was?)

'I'm sorry. I'm sorry.'

'Let's talk later,' I said, 'when I've calmed down.'

'OK, OK.' She backed away from me. 'Will you still give me reference, Ellie? I can go maybe not at the weekend but weekend after. Ten days' notice?'

I nodded vaguely in reply. I couldn't bring myself to be nice to her quite yet.

On the familiar drive to the café, with all its bends and turns, roadworks and sneaky short cuts, I wondered what to do. My mind was in such turmoil that by the time I had parked I had to make a quick decision and conclude that it was a positive thing that Felipe was leaving. We couldn't really afford him and if Petra wanted to rave in Ibiza, that's what she wanted to do, and it would be a bore to have her slouching and sad around my children and resenting us because she had been forced to stay in London against her will. She was a young girl, trying to learn English, not a career nanny, and not a godmother to my children. Be careful what you wish for, I heard my mother's voice warning, and thought guiltily of all the times I'd half wished that Petra would just pack her bags and leave. I had to think about the nightmare in a positive way, as Mark would have done. It was true what Mark said: sometimes when you stood back, you saw that things, however awful, happened for a reason. What the reason was, I wasn't sure.

Where was Mark? Mark! I smiled at the sound of his name. We hadn't seen each other for eight days since the kiss and I'd had the feeling that he had been avoiding me. I'd made a decision not to kiss him again, or flirt with him, or confide in him, but I hadn't thought that he would back off too, and now that he had, I yearned to see him. I had left a message for the vicar, with one of the nice blonde ladies of the parish, and he'd called me back three days later for a ten-minute telephone appointment. Afterwards I had forced myself not to walk to the off-licence in full make-up, or loiter on my doorstep in a coquettish way at around the time Mark returned home. But my will was weakening, my longing for him gathering strength.

Felipe was writing up the menu on the blackboard when I arrived at the café. Tilda was serving a customer.

'I've heard you're leaving,' I said to Felipe as he passed me on the narrow stairs to the kitchen.

'Yes.' He smiled. 'I sorry, really. My friend has good job for me in Ibiza.'

'That's funny, because I have a good job for you here.'

'Better money,' he shrugged, 'and better more sun.' He laughed. 'He find job and I must go quick before someone else takes.'

'I think you should give us more notice – at least two weeks.'

'One week? I found a good ticket for this Saturday but I haven't buy. I can try Saturday after that?'

'That would be better.'

I carried on down the stairs as he went up.

A group of six women came in for what appeared to be some kind of celebration. They all wanted variations of what was actually on the menu and we were running up and down the stairs to the kitchen bringing up baked potatoes with salad (no cheese or butter), steamed vegetables, carrot cake with no icing, toast and Marmite without butter and other girly specials. Tilda and I were just about to have a coffee break, to discuss what to do, when Mark came through the door.

He was wearing a blue shirt that matched his eyes and he was more suntanned than I remembered. He smiled and I dropped some change that I was holding and blushed. 'All right, darling?' he whispered. I liked the way he called me darling, more thrilling and intimate than the way Jack said it. Jack called everybody 'darling', including Eden, the children and the motorbike courier. Sometimes I wished he would refer to other men as 'mate'.

'What can I get for you?' I asked, playing along, playing a charade. I had read a passage in Hal's book about how Arthur had playfully come to lodge in a seaside boarding house where Hannah was working as a maid, so that she could serve him without anyone knowing of their relationship; it must have turned them on. No doubt she also licked his boots when he left them outside his door to be cleaned. The secrecy was sexy, the clandestine affair so appealing, so fraught, so off-limits, that every emotion, every snatched minute spent together was precious and memorable.

I led Mark to one of the outdoor tables. He put on the wraparound dark glasses. The glasses accentuated his lips, so large and lush. I noticed he was still wearing his wedding ring. We sat down.

'How did you get off work?' I asked.

'I'm out at lunch – just a little delayed getting back. Listen, I have to talk to you.' He pushed the glasses up on to his head. 'I'm wondering if we could have dinner tonight? I'm going away in two days and I'll be gone for two weeks. I know we are both married; well, my wife is missing, but you're happily married and I don't know why I am sitting here asking you out to dinner, but I am.'

He was asking me out to dinner and not to discuss recipes or good schools. He wanted to have an affair with me. I felt as though I was about to tip over or be pushed into a giant cake mix. Be careful what you wish for. I blushed from my toes to the top of my head and he obviously noticed because he said, 'Don't worry, I shouldn't have asked. I've put you in a difficult situation and I'm sorry.'

I squinted because my sunglasses were in the car and I couldn't think what to reply.

'I can't come to dinner with you. Although I would really like to.' I wanted him to persuade me, but I couldn't willingly go out to dinner with a man I wanted to sleep with, however much I wanted to. 'Come out to dinner' was really a form of foreplay, a euphemism for *come to bed*. What would I have said to Jack?

'I understand,' he said. 'We'll leave it for another time, but before I go, can I just show you something in my car?'

He crooked his arm through mine and as soon as we were out of sight of the café and around the corner he very gently twisted me round and, before I'd time to even think, he kissed me and it didn't seem to matter that out of the corner of my eye I could see one of our café customers leading a dog.

His breath was warm and we kissed urgently and briefly. When we drew away, he hugged me tight.

'Where are you going?' I asked.

'New York and then on to Lagos.'

'How is Lorrie?'

'We haven't spoken. We've sent texts.'

'I should get back.'

'Yes, you should. Goodbye, Ellie, I . . . I'm sorry about dinner.'

'Goodbye. Don't worry about asking me to dinner. I'm sure we'll see each other soon.'

'Look, I know it's not an ideal situation,' he said, 'but if you need me, call me, and we can have that dinner when I'm back.' He gave me another, less tight hug and we kissed once more, briefly, exquisitely, on the lips.

He climbed into his car, pulled the seat belt across him, buzzed the window down, waved and was off. Off into the rest of his life, while I remained on the pavement, watching and waiting and hoping for the smallest of seconds that he might come back.

*

'Who was that?' Tilda asked as soon as I'd walked through the door.

'No one.'

'Ellie, what do you mean?' She laughed.

'Just a friend of Jack's.'

'Really? He looked so urgent, so intent on talking to you.'

'Yes, well, he's one of Jack's producers on the new show. I think they're worried that he's going to pull out. Eden mentioned that Jack had been offered a small but important part in a film and Jack wanted to pull out of the soap, but the problem is that he's already signed the contract.'

'Oh, I see,' she said, but she looked doubtful. I loathed myself for lying to my friend, but I was worried that she would disapprove and judge me.

'We have to talk,' she said, 'about the Felipe situation. Shall we have a meeting now? Are you all right?'

'Yes, why?'

'You look preoccupied.'

'I'm just worrying about the café, and my personal life. Everything feels a bit out of control.'

A couple of men pushed through the door. I wiped my eyes with the apron I was wearing and busied myself with restocking the food display cabinets while Tilda took their orders. Felipe, who had been helping in the kitchen, returned upstairs with a tray of salads. Tilda served the men their takeaway coffees and we sat down at a corner table.

'Are you sure you're all right?' Tilda asked kindly.

'Yes, yes, I'm fine. Sometimes ... Jack is so difficult, so wrapped up and I fantasize about what it would be like to go off with someone else.'

'We all do that,' she said reassuringly, 'and at times we all hate our husbands, but you have to focus on you – what is going to be different if you go off with someone else? You'll still be bringing all your stuff into the next relationship. Remember that bad days with Jack will pass. God, I sound so wise and evangelical, but I'm not really at all wise.'

I sniffed. 'We do get through it, but we have longer and longer stretches of bad times, not even bad, just boring. We don't really communicate. We sit on the white sofas every evening, watching television with food on our laps, mostly inedible food cooked by me. We discuss when he should do his cartilege operation and how I should book my hernia operation like a couple of ageing queens. I find endless excuses to go out in the evenings. There must be more to life than that.'

'Well, is there? I'm not sure. You see, there's no one sitting on my sofa. Tom is never home and it can be lonely night after night. What I'm trying to say is, does anyone have a perfect life?'

'There must be marriages where people are happy.'

'I think there are more marriages where people are not unhappy.'

We ate some carrot cake and I drank two coffees, and then we talked about Felipe and Petra leaving and I wondered out loud how I was going to cope with the rest of the summer holidays.

'Well, don't forget I have Lily to help with Frank,' said Tilda, 'and she could take Jed and Maud some days, while you sort yourself out. And now we're up and running we could probably manage without Felipe. Do you think we could?'

'We can't really afford to replace him and we only employed him because we thought his cousin was sexy and made good banana smoothies. But without him we're going to have to be here full time and now that Petra is leaving, that just isn't going to work.'

'We could try getting someone part time, so that we don't have to both be here all the time.'

'OK, let's think about that. We can put a notice up here, ask Andy, ask Magdalena and the other part-time staff. Shall we say lunchtimes and Saturday mornings?'

'Good plan.'

There was some familiar music playing on our sound system, Neil Young.

'I love that song.'

'I wrote that song,' Tilda announced.

'Really? Well, that's interesting, because I composed the music when I was still at school.'

'Really? Because I wrote the lyrics and I still get royalties.'

'Isn't that the weirdest coincidence?'

'Really weird. When did you last see Neil?'

'Not for a while.'

'Me neither.'

Driving home that evening, to another night on the white sofa, I mulled over the idea of crossing the road and ringing Mark's bell to tell him I had changed my mind about dinner. But Big Jean, Jack's most resilient fan, was waiting behind our dying hedge with a parcel.

'Hello, love.'

'Hello, Jean.'

'I've got something for Jack, didn't want to disturb, could you give it him?'

'Thank you, Jean, that's very kind.'

'I won't stop,' she said, 'must get on.'

'He'll really appreciate it, Jean. Thank you.'

I took the parcel and suddenly remembered. It was Jack's birthday and I hadn't even given him a card. It was the first time in seven years of marriage that I had simply forgotten. What a shameful, shallow wife.

I unlocked the front door. Petra ran down the stairs to greet me and showed me a whole series of artwork, amazing collages made with old cartons and buttons and pieces of glass, some pressed flowers and coloured gems, that she and the children had made together, plus a pink cake for Jack and some muffins.

'How did you know it was Jack's birthday?' I asked.

'Well,' she explained, 'he told me.'

Now, of course, just as she was leaving, she was turning into the perfect Mary Poppins, all-singing au pair. It would be a terrible wrench to lose her.

Jack was sitting in the white living room with Eden. They were drinking glasses of champagne.

'Oh, there she is, my lovely wife. How are you? You look stressed.'

'Hello, my dear,' Eden greeted me with a peck on my cheek. 'It's true you do look tired.'

'Well, thank you. Thank you both. Happy birthday, darling.' I handed over Jean's present. 'That by the way is from Jean, not me,' I added as he ripped open the silver paper to find a blue crocheted strip.

'Any ideas?' He held up the dark-blue piece of holey wool.

'Isn't that touching?' Eden peered over Jack's shoulder. 'It could be a tie.'

'Or a very small belt,' I said.

'It's a willy-warmer,' Jack concluded.

Eden laughed the loudest. When she'd calmed down she turned to me. 'We're celebrating with a couple of bottles of champagne, unless you have something in mind?'

'I, er . . . sorry, Jack, I haven't arranged anything.'

'Did you forget me?' he asked in a little-boy voice.

'I had some stressful news this morning and, of course, well, we'll celebrate at the weekend, before Petra leaves.'

'Petra leaves?' Jack repeated.

'Yes, Petra and Felipe are leaving to look for work in Ibiza. She told me this morning.'

'Not if I have anything to do with it.' Jack stood up. 'Just have to double her salary and she'll stay.'

'Well, you would have to double Felipe's as well.'

'Don't you worry. I'm going to talk to her later.'

Eden's dogs were lying at her feet and she had spread her bags over two chairs.

'Isn't it wonderful that Jack has got the soap?'

'Yes, yes, fantastic.'

'He's done very well. It's going to be very big. Very big. They have a huge budget and it's going to be scheduled for prime time.'

'It's great news.'

'And I hear you may be living apart?' She looked at me, waiting for confirmation.

'God, Eden, you make it sound like we're breaking up. We're just doing what many working couples do, spending some time apart in the week.'

'Don't forget that Jack was voted second sexiest man in *Woman's World Weekly* in the over thirty-five category, second to the gorgeous Bill Nighy.' She licked her lips.

'You don't need to remind me that Jack is sexy,' I said, accepting the glass of champagne that Jack offered me. 'To you, darling,' I raised my glass, 'and all your fans!'

The children came in demanding to watch television and Eden stood up and then toppled backwards on to her chair. 'Getting old,' she said as Jack helped her up. I walked her to the door and worried as she limped towards her car.

Later, after the children had gone to bed, Jack and I ate some smoked salmon, a gift from Eden, and huge slices of pink birthday cake. We listened to Johnnie Cash. Jack loved the music but I was a little indifferent. I was very reluctant to dance, partly because it was difficult music to dance to and also because I didn't feel like being near Jack. But I had been so impossibly remiss about his birthday that I forced myself to stand up and he took me by the waist and whirled me round, faster and faster, and I remembered our wedding party, when we'd danced for several hours and what fun that had been, and the time we had danced in a Greek restaurant, spinning around in a huge circle with Annie and Marco and a couple of other friends and laughing so much that I had cried. Jack was a very good dancer and as he guided me round I began to relax and laugh because it was quite fun and slightly odd to be dancing around the sitting room on a Tuesday night. He pulled me towards him and out again, like a yo-yo, and we collapsed laughing on to the sofa.

'Best fun I've had all year,' Jack said sweetly, 'better than any birthday present.' He mopped his brow with his pressed handkerchief and undid the buttons on his shirt. 'Elle,' he said, pulling me towards him for a hug, 'I have to tell you something.'

'What's that?'

'The thing is, I think it's a bit cavalier to say the least to just totally forget my birthday. There is the new café and there's the Petra problem, but still, it's a bit ... I know I'm an old fart, too old for birthdays perhaps ... You seem very detached at the moment. As though you are not really here. Is anything wrong?'

'Jack, Jack, I'm so sorry.' I buried myself into his chest and breathed him in and to my relief was still drawn to his warm, woody, lime smell. It was, however, a little unsettling being so close to two men in one day.

'It's all right,' he said, kissing the top of my head. 'It doesn't really matter a fig.'

'No, it does matter.' I swayed in front of him. The

champagne was making me feel good. 'It was dreadful of me to forget and dreadful not to make a plan, but let me make it up to you. I can be very spontaneous,' I said, leading him by the hand. 'Come on, let's go to bed.'

The following evening we were invited to our neighbours', Pauline and John, for a drink. She was in her fifties and lived with a man who was five years younger and they had been together for more than twenty years. She was a director of her own public relations company and always looked well put together, and did things that mothers of small children couldn't do: she went jogging every evening in Juicy Couture tracksuits, and had her teeth lasered, and took time out to go on mini-breaks with John. She was quite petite and always slim, and her hair was dyed a natural-looking reddish brown. Pauline would never be seen without her mascara, even to rush to the shops, and her silver window box put ours to shame. She spent hours planting it with seasonal flowers and uprooted the plants at the end of every season to replace with new ones. We, on the other hand, had had the same shocking display of depressing dead or dying daisies for over two years.

They lived in an immaculate ground floor and first floor garden flat, where everything was highly polished. On the ground floor there was a spotless sitting room and kitchen. From the kitchen there were steps that led down to the trimmed garden complete with tubs of herbs. Their bedroom had an en suite bathroom. There were photographs of them everywhere: stuck into mirrors, framed on the walls, on top of the flat screen. John and

Pauline getting married, on a beach, kissing in front of Ayers Rock, sunbathing topless, all displayed in silver frames.

John was small and lithe and permanently tanned. At weekends he liked to relocate to his allotment, where he would set up camp outside his shed, with deckchairs and a barbecue and a small, portable, wind-up radio. Jack and I had once been invited for an alfresco early summer lunch and John, dressed in black briefs and nothing else, had served us asparagus. Didn't know where to look, Jack joked afterwards, in one of his particularly funny camp voices.

John was a chef at a river café in Ham and sometimes he would drop round a box of potatoes or some carrots or other surplus food from the café or the allotment. In return Jack would give him out-of-date signed photographs of himself (he was far too vain to give photographs of what he actually looked like) and John would auction them for a local boys' sports charity that he was involved in.

I imagined that John and Pauline were the kind of childless couple who cooked together by candlelight and then made reckless love on the kitchen floor. She probably kept her spindly high heels on and wore a G-string and a corset to delight John. She would almost certainly understand Hannah's thrill when she licked Arthur's shoes.

We'd been over to each other's houses a few times over the six years that we had lived in the street and we'd often chatted on our doorsteps about neighbourly topics such as the pigeon's nest that Sam Taylor, the man who lived opposite Pauline, had ripped out of some ivy growing on his house, or the dog poo that Jack hated so much, or the stray cat with an injured paw that we once found cowering behind a rubbish bin. We had often bonded over animal rights issues and were really concerned for the pigeons after their nest was exposed to the harsh summer light.

That evening, John wanted to show Jack a script he was working on in his spare time. Pauline handed me a plate of crisps and nuts and poured me a warm glass of wine. 'So how are you? What's up?'

'Nothing much. Just work. Come and visit the café, it's not far.'

'Yes, I will. We were so sorry to miss the party; we went to John's mum. I'm sure I read something somewhere. Where was it?'

'*Evening Standard*? Saturday *Telegraph*?'

'Can't remember, but,' she patted her hips, 'at my age I have to avoid cafés – just one whiff of carbohydrate and my thighs dimple. One spoonful of sugar or bite of croissant and the pounds just seem to appear that very same evening round my waist.'

I looked at her in mock surprise.

'God's truth, wait till you hit fifty, you'll see.' She screwed up her small nose and cackled. She had a surprisingly dirty laugh, which reminded me of Barbara Windsor in the *Carry On* films. She poured me another glass of wine. 'Can't complain though. I've just found myself another new account, representing a facial reflexologist and a teeth-whitening system.'

'That's great. Well done you.'

'What about you? Are you enjoying the café?'

'Yes, it's hard work but I love it. I love having something to do again. The problem is that Jack is probably moving out of London and I don't want to give up on the business just as it's starting.'

'I understand that.'

'What would you do?'

'I don't know. I'd be wary of letting John loose on a film set without me being there to welcome him home in the evenings, if you know what I mean.' She gave me a wink and another of her dirty *Carry On* laughs.

'Um . . . well, there is that issue as well but I don't want to move down there just to be a chaperone.'

'Jack seems like a sensible man. Sure he wouldn't want to put his marriage at risk.'

We heard the men laughing heartily downstairs. Even the sound of Jack's laugh annoyed me – it seemed so insincere.

'Jack doesn't seem to understand that now I've got the café, I can't always be at home. I forgot his birthday and that pretty much sums up our marriage. I'm not sure what to do.'

She handed me a cheese straw which she said she had made that afternoon and I nibbled off the top and it crumbled and flaked over my trousers. I brushed the crumbs into my hand and she handed me a tissue to put them in and took them from me, like a mother would do to a child.

'You have to put some zest back in your relationship.

You must talk, even if it's only twenty minutes a day. Talk about books or movies or something neutral. Don't talk about the children or the weather or how much you've spent on the tax bill and, God forbid, don't talk about cellulite or send him off to the chemist's to buy hair-removing strips! You have to be a bit mysterious.'

I laughed, partly because that was exactly what I had done the previous weekend.

'We do talk but he doesn't really listen. It's so frustrating. He only really likes to talk about himself.'

'I suppose that's what actors do,' she said. 'I've heard that before. Well, you have to keep romance alive. Go on dates. Oh, Johnnie and me had such a beautiful night on my birthday last week. He arranged everything. Took me to the café down at Ham, sent out a cake and candles. Beautiful cake, carrot cake it was, with thick, white icing. You two should go out on a lovely date.'

I sighed as I thought about the effort of making Jack take me out to dinner.

She took my hands. 'My last two rules of romance might be pertinent considering Jack is moving to the country. Number one is welcome change and number two is spend a little time apart.'

'Oh, I'm so glad you said that.' I finished my fourth glass of wine just as the men were returning from the study.

We said goodbye quite a bit later after I had decided I wanted to go home. I had drunk too much and eaten too little and I was tired and my head was spinning. It was a really warm night and after we arrived back I flung open the doors to the garden and walked towards the labyrinth. As I walked round and reached the middle, I was imbued with the sense that as Jack and I were going to spend some time apart, it would be beneficial to take some time together without the children. It would be one last effort to rekindle our marriage.

We used to go away and laugh, relax and fool around in extra-large beds. We used to have so much fun on our little breaks. I was almost sure a mini holiday would breathe a surge of energy and renewed optimism into our marriage. And we would have to go very soon as Felipe and Petra were leaving.

'Jack,' I began as I was rubbing cream into the heels of my cracked feet later that evening, 'the thing is, why don't we have a late celebration of your birthday and go away together for a couple of nights before Petra leaves?'

'Just us?'

'Yes, we'd have to go next week.'

'Um ... very short notice but it's not a bad idea. I would have to juggle a couple of things, but in principle I like it. Anyway, Petra is not going to leave. I'm going to go and talk to her now.'

I lay on the bed and waited for him to return. I picked up a magazine from the floor and flicked through it, stopping to peer again at an article about adopted children who had traced their parents. I'd already read it two or three times before. I put it down as Jack returned.

'She says she's definitely leaving.' Jack was frowning. He looked as though he was about to have one of his rare outbursts, the frightening kind, when he would turn a shade of dark pink and shout. He sat down heavily on the bed and I leant forward and rubbed his back. He turned round. 'But the good news,' he said, recovering a little, 'the good news is that she said she would take the children for two or three days if we want to go somewhere. She demanded fifty pounds extra a day, plus expenses. You've got to admire the cheek of the girl. Ah!' He rubbed his hands together. 'Wonder where we should go? Mmm . . . Ha ha,' he said, 'this is going to be a surprise.' He paused. 'I've got it,' he announced, 'I'm going to take you somewhere I've always wanted to go.'

Somewhere he's always wanted to go, I mused, as I pulled my weary body up from the bed. I looked at myself in the long, white eighteenth-century mirror that leant against the wall. Maybe he'd take me bullfighting in Seville or Granada. Jack quite fancied himself as a bit of a Hemingway character. He liked to play poker and occasionally go to bullfights and drink whisky late into the night. Sometimes I quite liked his beefy male side, it made me feel light, and breezy and feminine. I wouldn't have to actually go to the bullfight, I could shop and lounge at a café, or in bed. We only had a short time so I knew we wouldn't be going anywhere too far. Maybe we would go to Paris; Jack liked to eat in Paris. The possibilities were endless.

We were eating a late dinner, grilled squid and salad made by Jack, when Petra came in looking quite simply stunning. I noticed that Jack sat up and looked at her with a keen and lavish interest. It was disconcerting and slightly depressing to know that I would never, ever look that good again.

'Bye!' She waved the way she always did and said, 'It's OK. I can watch the children two or three nights. But I think good idea if Felipe stay with me. I could be scared?'

'Ha ha,' Jack said, 'so you would like to have your man friend to stay? I see, I see . . . I see.'

'Yes. Yes. Last time you away weekend, I saw mice in the kitchen and fox in garden and everything noise and banging. I was very scared.'

'Really?'

'Yes. It was horrible.'

'Where will he sleep?' I asked, struggling with the idea of Petra and Felipe in my bed.

'He will sleep with me in my room.'

'In your bed! It's too small.'

'Or maybe he sleep down on rug next to me.'

'Like a dog?' Jack sniggered.

'No,' she said crossly, 'he's not like dog.'

'I am joking,' Jack said with a big smile. 'Please don't be angry, Petra.'

'You laugh at me,' she said half sulkily, half pleased.

'Would I ever laugh at you?' Jack said. 'In England we have an expression – I don't laugh at you, I laugh with you. There is a difference.'

Petra, I decided, was fickle, self-interested and the ultimate opportunist. She looked amazing, she was flirting with my husband and we were paying her a fortune to go away for two nights so that she could stay in our house and have sex with her boyfriend. How did she get away with it? But I also knew I was really going to miss her. I had got used to her perky, paradoxically uplifting but insulting pep talks and her generally sunny nature.

For the next few days before we left on the trip I spent any spare time that I had on the Internet and talking to agencies, trying to find a replacement for Petra and also a part-time help for the café. One of the au pair agencies said that I would be able to interview a couple of girls when I returned from our trip, but they didn't sound that promising – one had no experience with young children and the other barely spoke English. I also put up a note in the café and hoped for the best. It didn't seem very professional, taking off on holiday with a café to run, but Tilda and I had agreed that it was probably best to take a couple of days off each before Felipe left for good.

9

'Port Appin!' I exclaimed to Jack when he announced our destination. 'Where's that?'

'West of Scotland, the perfect antidote to this heat.'

'West of Scotland,' I repeated aimlessly and a little ungraciously. 'Why?'

'I used to go there as a child.' He raised his eyebrows. 'Happy memories, happy memories. Fishing with Billy the gillie, salty picnics, beautiful scenery, and I had a good friend, can't remember the boy's name. Wallace something. Ma loved it there, you see; I think she and Pa had their honeymoon somewhere near.'

I tried to summon feelings of excitement as I packed some summer jumpers, rain kit and a few good books. I threw one slinky dress on to the pile of clothes on the bed to cheer myself up.

I wrote out pages of instructions for Petra. There were lists of things that the children liked to eat – chicken legs, sweet potatoes, rice pudding, pasta, shepherd's pie, pineapple, melon, etc., food that she already knew they liked or that I forced them to like. There were lists of numbers to contact us on, even though she had both our mobile numbers, and lists of people to contact in case of an emergency. At least I stopped short of leaving a letter about what to do if I died, unlike my mother, who used to leave one pinned to the fridge every time she went away somewhere.

We planned to leave very early on the Tuesday, before the children were up. We had barely left enough time, because that was the way Jack liked to travel – at the last minute, wearing dark glasses (I think it made him feel more like a film star) – but punctuality was something, apart from dusting, that I was neurotic about. Jack won, of course, and set his alarm clock for six a.m. The plane left at seven forty-five. We crept out of the house, yawning, and slid into the car. (Jack had decided that he wanted to use airport parking because he worried that it would be vandalized if he left it lingering outside our house. Highly unlikely the car would be vandalized just because we were away, but Jack refused to listen.) We had driven for about five minutes through the empty streets in silence when Jack announced that he'd forgotten his mobile phone.

'Oh God! Jack.' I was already tense and nervous about being late. 'Do you really need it?'

'Yes, of course I do.'

'But we'll be late. We'll miss the plane and they're non-refundable tickets.'

'We won't be late,' Jack assured me, doing a rather flamboyant three-point turn in the middle of the narrow road. 'How do you expect me to operate without a telephone?'

He double-parked the car outside our front door and spent what seemed like ten minutes inside. He eventually returned, followed by Jed waving at me and blowing a kiss and making a sad face. Petra had her hands on his shoulders and a just-out-of-bed look.

'Oh dear,' I said to Jack as he climbed back inside the car, 'look at Jed. He seems so sad.'

'He's just putting it on. Honestly, he knows how to pull your strings.'

'He's only six. He's sad that his parents are going.'

'You're projecting all of that stuff on him because your mother took off to the ashram and Greenham Common and all that.'

Jack drummed his fingers on the wheel, crossing lanes whenever the traffic (which there wasn't much of at that time in the morning) built up. We sped along the motorway, with Jack now singing and banging the wheel of the car. As we turned into the airport entrance, there were thirty-five minutes to go before the flight to Glasgow took off.

Jack dropped me at the departure entrance. I dashed through the circular doors and scurried with rasping breath, pushing our overloaded trolley to the check-in desk. I queued up behind a flurry of short, fat businessmen. When I reached the head of the queue I triumphantly produced my ticket and suitcase; there was now twenty-five minutes till departure. The uniformed woman behind the desk, aged about forty-five, surveyed my ticket and asked where Jack was.

'He's just parking the car, he won't be long. I'd like to check in on his behalf.'

'Oh no, you can't do that. Security issues. We have

to see him in person. And the gate will be closing now.'

'Please,' I begged.

'Flight's closing,' she repeated rather severely. 'Sorry.' She gave me a boarding pass.

'We're going on a romantic holiday, the two of us, there is absolutely no point going on my own.' I had embarrassingly begun to cry, seeing the disastrous start to our holiday as a metaphor for our whole relationship. No matter how much we tried, nothing seemed to make it better.

Jack ran up to the desk panting, bending over, making a scene. 'You won't believe what bloody happened.'

'What?'

'They've closed the parking for some kind of building works and bloody well moved it somewhere else to another bloody terminal. Then the bus didn't come.'

He extended his hand to the thin-nosed, thin-lipped woman behind the desk. 'Hello, pleased to meet you, my name is Jack Boore. You may have seen me on television.' Jack had absolutely no qualms about saying this kind of thing.

'Yes, Mr Boore? What seems to be the problem?' Jack was drumming his fingers on the counter. 'I'm afraid that you can't check in to BA 207 to Glasgow as the gate is closed and passengers about to board. Mrs Boore, may I suggest that you go to the gate now?'

'But what about my husband? What about Jack? If you checked him in now he could come with me to the gate.'

'Mr Boore will have to get the next flight. There will be a supplementary charge, but I can organize that for you.'

'My dear girl,' Jack said, 'this airport is accountable for the fact that I was not here twenty minutes ago. There was no information given to me about the change of airport parking facilities and I was not to know. Plus my wife has a terrible phobia about flying. It's really not a good idea to let her fly without me.'

It was actually Jack who was afraid of flying.

'I'm sorry, Mr Boore. The parking details and any changes to the parking facilities are published on our website.'

'Do you think I have time to peruse your website?' Jack banged his fist down on the counter. 'I shall be writing to the chairman. In the meantime, please issue my ticket. When does it arrive in Glasgow?'

'Ten thirty-five.'

'Darling,' he turned to me, 'don't forget your medication and breathing exercises. Ask the stewardess to help you through take-off and get her to warn the captain that you may faint and that he will have to make an emergency landing.'

'Yes, all right,' I said, playing along, 'I'll tell the captain.'

The seats were small and the legroom cramped. The flight was nearly full but luckily I had been allocated an aisle seat. The head steward, an auburn-haired Scotsman of indeterminate age, took pity on me. He asked me if everything was all right and I explained about my poor abandoned husband who had been unable to board the flight.

'We are meant to be having a special few days away,' I sniffed to emphasize the romantic aspect, the togetherness, of the holiday. 'You may have heard of him, he's an actor – Jack Boore.'

'Yesss, I think I have.' He frowned and put his finger on his chin and turned round to a flight attendant who was fussing over an orange juice carton. She had definitely heard of Jack, in fact she said *Country Matters* had been her favourite soap.

'I'm so sorry, Mrs Boore,' he said, with theatrical raised eyebrows and a meaningful, pitying look. 'Our apologies, Mrs Boore,' he continued, flicking imaginary dust off his lapel. 'How can I make it up to you?'

'I don't know,' I smiled sadly, 'but do call me Ellie.'

'I'll see what I can do, Ellie,' he said, turning on his heel.

I was dozing off, dreaming of sunny Seville, when he returned with a plastic bag. 'The captain would like to give you these complimentary drinks,' he said, handing the bag to me with a toothy smile. 'It's our way of saying sorry.'

'Thank you, that's very kind.' I had assumed that the captain was going to give me complimentary flights to Glasgow for life and was rather relieved to receive complimentary drinks instead.

Inside the bag there were about twenty miniature bottles of whisky and gin, my two least favourite alcoholic drinks.

'Hope it helps to cheer you up,' the steward beamed at me and I couldn't help but beam back.

'Um, yes. Yes, thank you.'

'Don't get too carried away now,' he joked before whizzing past me with a tray of bread rolls.

After a bumpy landing and a dreary wait for luggage, I read my book in the red tartan-patterned lounge area. I talked to Petra about what to give the children for tea, even though I'd already written sweet potato and tuna on her list (I had never really got over the incident when she had given them toast and jam for supper). Jack came through finally, a couple of hours later, chatting to a middle-aged lady with silver hair, and we marched off to the hire-car desk. 'It's going to be fine,' he said as we strode out together into the pouring grey rain to find our Toyota. 'We're going to go on the scenic route which will be beautiful.'

On the road to Port Appin the rain drenched the windscreen and the roads became more and more twisted and bendy. The more nauseous I felt, the more I resented Jack for bringing me to Scotland with its low-slung cloud and grey sky. After half an hour of climbing the endless roads I had to ask if we could stop the car so that I could actually be sick.

We stopped outside a rather ugly Victorian Gothic chapel and I stumbled into the pouring rain. Jack ran after me and dragged me by the arm towards the church door. We pulled and pushed and twisted the heavy door but it appeared to be shut. Jack ran towards it like a raging bull and fell through, landing on the floor where he writhed in agony, twisting and turning and moaning. I helped Jack to his feet and he limped towards a pew.

I knew that I was supposed to feel sorry for him; a normal wife would, but he'd always been a dreadful hypochondriac, so I didn't really take him that seriously. I was used to him complaining that a headache was a life-threatening tumour, or a stomach-upset would become liver cancer. I lowered my head into my arms and tried to block out his groans of agony. The church was dark and cool and restored my faith that our holiday could only get better – it couldn't possibly get worse – but my hopes were dashed when Jack demanded to be taken to hospital to have his ankle examined. 'We'll have to go back to Glasgow,' he said, 'right away.'

'Jack, are you quite sure you need to go to hospital?'

'Look at me,' he groaned, 'I can hardly walk. I could be damaging some nerve-endings as we speak, maybe I've fractured a bone. Oh, Ellie! I'm due to appear on tele-vision quite soon. They're not going to use me if I'm limping.'

He hobbled towards the car, leaning very heavily on me and breathing in gasps. He took five minutes to struggle into his seat, while I studied the map, wondering if there would be a hospital anywhere a bit nearer than Glasgow. Oban was definitely closer to our destination, but Jack said he would much prefer to go to Glasgow because that's where he would feel safe. 'Let me find out if there's a hospital in Oban,' I urged him, dreading the drive back down to Glasgow, negotiating the city in the pouring rain, but neither of our mobiles had signals.

'Drive,' he murmured, with a screwed-up, pained expression and closed eyes, 'please just drive to Glasgow.'

I settled into the driver's seat, adjusted the mirror and set off down the twisty, bendy roads, with Jack shouting 'Owwww' every time the car slid over a bump. He buzzed down the window of the tinny Japanese car and lit a cigarette. It wasn't long before feelings of nausea surfaced again and I had to open my window, so the driving cold rain flew across my face. As I drove, I fantasized about being transported out of my life into another life, with my children, but leaving Jack behind.

It took us three hours to manoeuvre from the chapel to the hospital. We drove slowly through the city, most of which I could barely see because of the rain which was almost sleet. Some of the buildings were beautiful and we made a detour, at my insistence, to see the Arts and Crafts Glasgow School of Art, designed by Mackintosh, but when we arrived there was nowhere to park and we had to move on. We got lost several times before we found the hospital. I dropped the invalid at the entrance and parked the car.

Jack was waiting for me at reception, leaning heavily on a crutch that he'd been given. He'd unequivocally refused to accept the wheelchair that he was offered. We trekked at a snail's pace through long corridors over well-worn, shiny, institutional floors covered in black scratch marks. Nurses, doctors, porters scurried along, too harassed and busy to notice us.

When we eventually found casualty, Jack took one look at the assorted mix of people waiting – which included a man with a bleeding hand, a sad woman with a droopy mouth, a skinhead with a weeping sore on his cheek and several other motley-looking characters – and he decided not to bother. He wouldn't listen to me and despite my pleading sensibly and then whining spitefully, he insisted on leaving right away.

'But, Jack,' I tried hard not to shout, 'we've driven – I've driven – three miserable hours to Glasgow because you wanted to be checked up in hospital.'

'I'm sorry, but the hospital is depressing.'

'Jack, really. A hospital is a hospital is a hospital.'

It was by then four o'clock and we hadn't had lunch. Jack said we should go to the best restaurant in Glasgow to make up for it all. Jack called Eden's assistant Karen and asked her if she could book us somewhere. 'Could you do me a huge favour? You see, I'm stuck in Glasgow and don't know where to go and eat.' While we were deciding what to do, I tried to quell my hunger pangs with a couple of packets of salt and vinegar crisps.

Jack vaguely remembered a fish and chip restaurant from when he was a boy and beseeched me to go and look for it. He was almost sure it had been on the River Clyde because he remembered seeing a man who looked like a pirate.

'Jack!' I was stuffing myself with some of Jed's Smarties that I had found at the bottom of my bag. 'It's way past lunch; all the restaurants will be closed. I'm sorry, but we're going to definitely, without a doubt, leave the city and head to Port Appin.'

'What do you expect me to eat?'

'We'll stop at a petrol station and buy some sand-wiches.'

'I didn't come all this way to eat in a petrol station,' Jack shouted at me.

'Fuck you, Jack.'

At that moment Karen telephoned to tell us she'd found two restaurants, the Willow Tea Rooms in Sauchiehall Street and Regano which, Jack relayed to me, 'serves seafood and has an original Art Deco interior'.

'Jack,' I said pointedly, looking at my watch, 'it's four thirty-five, we're not going to get lunch, we may as well carry on and at least find dinner.'

'Point taken,' he said. 'But we could just get a cup of tea and a scone' – he said scone in a Scottish accent – 'in the tearooms.'

'I just want to drive to our hotel. Sorry to be a bore, but it might be another hour before we find the café.'

'OK. Let's get there,' he said, grabbing a handful of my Smarties.

We arrived at Port Appin at seven in the evening instead of before lunch as we had planned; we had already missed an entire day of our holiday. Jack took several minutes to heave himself out of the car with the crutch that he had taken from the hospital.

'Wait here,' he instructed me, 'while I find a man to collect our luggage.'

A no-nonsense woman with big, bare, chunky arms and brown hair tied up in a loose ponytail said she would take us up to our room. The pub was meant to have the best food in Port Appin and my stomach gnawed and churned with hunger when I read the specials written upon the blackboard – Clam Chowder and Fisherman's Pie. 'How delicious.' I was following Jack up the stairs. He was hobbling and I was behind, bumping into him. 'I bet all the fish is fresh. I'm really looking forward to supper.'

The bare-armed woman led us up some narrow, twisting stairs. She made no attempt at any kind of conversation, but when Jack questioned her about the food she said the restaurant had a fine view of the loch and Castle Stalker. She climbed ahead of us while Jack hauled himself up, stopping every few steps to find his breath.

It was a room under the eaves, with a queen-size bed. Jack and I always avoided sleeping together in a queen-size bed as we were a couple who stretched out in our sleep and thrashed around. But I was too tired and hungry to suggest moving. I lay on the bed with all my clothes on and almost instantly fell asleep.

I woke an hour or two later to find Jack next to me on the bed wearing a towelling dressing gown and snacking on a club sandwich.

'Look, the thing is,' he said, with his mouth full, 'I booked here because this place is meant to have such good food. I asked for a double bed but perhaps I didn't use the word king. Stupid of me.' He kissed my forehead. 'I ordered a sandwich because I couldn't quite face going downstairs on my own and didn't want to wake you.' From somewhere below I could hear the sound of people in the pub, shouting and brawling and generally having a great time, no doubt eating seasoned clam chowder and creamy fisherman's pie.

'I hope pubs close at eleven in Scotland, like they do in England, otherwise I won't sleep with all that noise, but I have an awful feeling that they don't and that we'll be awake most of the night.'

'Ummm,' Jack said, slobbering over his sandwich, 'I think you're right.'

'How's your leg?'

'Better,' he said, patting it, 'much better.'

'Well, at least that's something.'

'Do you want to hop down to the restaurant?' he asked. 'Hop, as in I hop and you follow?' He didn't sound that enthusiastic. He took a huge bite of his club sandwich.

There was no such thing as room service at the pub so I went downstairs and ordered an omelette because they had run out of clam chowder and fisherman's pie, and I asked them to call me when it was ready. It was half an hour before someone called, after which I devoured everything that was in my food basket including the gherkins and crisps. Later I ran a bath. The hot water trickled out of the tap at a drip pace. By the time the bath was full, I had almost lost interest in it.

During my bath in the grey, windowless bathroom suite, I lay in synthetic smelling 'musk' bubbles and thought about Jack. We had outgrown each other and no longer enjoyed each other's company. The revelation, so final, made me weep silently into my flannel.

That night I spiralled into a whole series of inconsequential worries: What would happen if Petra kept the children up too late while we were away and didn't feed them properly? What would happen if Maud had one of her scenes, when nothing but a bribe of ice cream or chocolate would stop her from screaming? Sometimes even ice cream and chocolate would not quell her – she became so deranged on occasions that she would literally scratch her face and pull out her hair.

When I was away from Maud, I missed her with a gnawing desperation and worried that no one but me would be able to manage her moods. I missed Jed too of course, with a searing intensity, but he was more sensible and more adaptable; people loved him. Maud was more of an acquired taste. Even Jack didn't have much patience when she was in one of her moods.

I'd heard women, mothers in the know, confiding that generally little boys were nicer, easier, more pliant than girls. They admitted that there was a special mother–son bond that was difficult to put into words, perhaps because it was too shocking to admit that mothers had small spirals of sexual feelings for their sons, who as babies had sucked at their breasts. It sometimes felt thrilling but disloyal to agree with them, to nod my head, to offer a snippet. Did men have these feelings for their daughters? I suspected so. I suspected that these feelings came later when their daughters reached puberty.

The next morning we changed hotels to the only other hotel in a five-mile radius. The room we were shown to had a large double bed with a pink ribbed bedcover, floral curtains and a tea-making service. It was clean but uninspiring, the kind of hotel that had Bibles in the dusty drawers of the bedside tables.

Downstairs there was a chintzy sitting room stacked with out-of-date copies of *Country Life* that were piled on the central low-slung glass table. There were prints of thunderous seascapes by Turner on the walls and a vase displaying fake chrysanthemums made of silk. We went for a walk in the cold drizzle, back to the pub we had left that morning because we fancied a change of scene for lunch. The day stretched ahead and we both yawned.

We returned to the hotel in time for a cup of tea in the sitting room. We talked about the dreadful weather and drank our tea and started a worn puzzle of Edinburgh Castle, until a woman dressed in black came to clear away our tray and asked us what we would like for dinner. It was five o'clock and we were full from our plate of sandwiches and cake.

'Dinner!' Jack spluttered. 'But we've only just had tea. It's five o'clock. We'll order dinner when we sit down for dinner.'

'The chef likes to get the orders in before five thirty,' the brisk woman informed us. She was tall and broad-shouldered, middle-aged, with dark, shoulder-length hair and a pale, pinched face. She stood squarely in the door frame, holding the tray. Jack was on the verge of being very angry; he was about to have a fit that had been stirring in little flurries for twenty-four hours.

'Sorry,' he stared calmly, 'but what's your name?'

'Louise.'

'It's simply not civilized to be asking a man what he

wants for dinner three and a half hours before he eats it.'

The woman scurried away and Jack fumed silently. Ten minutes later there was a knock on the sitting-room door.

'Oh God,' I mumbled to Jack, 'we're about to be evicted.'

'You go,' Jack said. 'I can't walk.'

I opened the door to find a small, balding man in a dark suit who introduced himself as the manager, Rob Buckley.

'Mr Boore,' he said, 'we are honoured to have you here and I do hope you are being taken care of.'

'Well, my good man, this is my wife, Ellie,' Jack said as he stood up. He knew it rattled me when people only addressed themselves to him because he was famous, and I stood awkwardly by his side like a lemon. 'What can we do for you?' Jack continued.

'I just came to say sorry about the dinner arrangements, but the chef needs to know well in advance so that he is able to prepare the ingredients in time. We are a small restaurant and we like to use fresh food.'

Jack sighed and made a kind of exaggerated pout. 'We'll have the fish.' I tried not to laugh. The little manager checked his pad of paper.

'That's lucky,' he laughed weakly, 'because we do actually have fish on the menu, sea bream and mushrooms with a courgette sauce.'

The idea of the courgette sauce made me feel a little sick. 'What else do you have?'

'Ah ...' He stared at the pad again, squinting. 'Oh, I

can't seem to read chef's writing. I'll just go and check.'

Jack and I looked at each other and began to laugh.

'This is absurd, really,' Jack said. 'What does a man have to do around these parts to just sit down at dinner, order some food and go to bed?'

The manager returned. 'We have steak or stuffed peppers.'

At about eight we descended the stairs for the restaurant. It was completely empty except for a corner table, where two old ladies sat over a pudding and a couple of brandies.

'Lovely.' Jack's voice boomed through the room as the young, shy waitress showed us to a table. 'Well, this is fun,' he said, shaking out his napkin.

It wasn't at all what I had envisaged for our romantic interlude, our little break to rekindle the slump that was our marriage, but then it would have taken a miracle to convince me at that point that the marriage was worth fighting for. It would have been different if we'd just met and were really only interested in each other, and having sex was more important than what was for dinner, but not at our stage of marriage, seven years in. Everything that went wrong just seemed to confirm the idea that the marriage was over. We couldn't seem to make anything work, not even a three-day holiday.

The kippers at breakfast were over-cooked; the skin was so crispy it was, in fact, hard. The orange juice was advertised as fresh but it was obviously mixed with orange juice from a carton. Jack said his eggs were very good though and the tea was hot. My head hurt and I was so tired I had to go back to bed. Jack organized himself a fishing trip, and limped off into the swirling grey mist with a packed lunch provided by the hotel – probably more sandwiches. After he'd gone I spent a long time, perhaps half an hour, staring out at the glacial loch. It was such a relief to be absolutely on my own, away from everybody. I ate lunch by myself (in the rather formal dining room), and was waited on by two self-conscious young girls. That afternoon I went back to bed and slept, gathering my strength. I hadn't realized how tired I was: too tired to be romantic or loving, too tired for anything but rest.

The sun had just begun to glimmer from between the grey clouds as we walked down to the shore the next morning. We walked along the coastal path, admiring the silvery flat water, and got carried away with a fantasy about living in the beautiful whitewashed cottage we discovered on the peninsula. Jack had finally relaxed, he'd even left his mobile in the room, but I had developed a really bad cold.

We sat side by side, staring out on to the water.

'What are you thinking?' he asked me.

'Just thinking how lovely it is here,' I replied. 'You?'

'Me too, me too.'

While Jack sat there staring broodily into the swirling mist, subdued, there was a quiet dignity about him. He seemed sad and heavy and I wondered whether he too acknowledged that our marriage was beset with problems. He probably knew, he was probably sad about it like I was.

'Are you sad about us?' I asked.

'Sad? Not particularly.'

'Come on, Jack, we're not like we used to be.'

He put his arm around my shoulder. 'No, love, that's true. I wish it was easier. Maybe it will become easier. Maybe it's just a bad patch.' We walked back silently and with a surge of fond love for Jack, the man I had married, father of my children, I took his hand as we crossed the little road back to our hotel to pack our bags and pay our bill.

Later, as we were driving on the non-scenic route back to Glasgow, we both found we had mobile signals. I had a message from Sally at Aupair Plus who had fixed me up with a couple of interviews the day after we returned. There was also a message from a girl called Marie, who had left her number.

'Have you had any experience?' I shouted down the line.

'I've looked after . . .' We were cut off, the signal dead.

I called back at the airport and heard a few more details about Marie. She was a student who needed a temporary job, she had looked after her four-year-old niece and she lived near Bath. Best of all, she could speak fluent English. The only downside was that she wasn't returning to London for a couple of weeks and I couldn't interview her until then.

*

We arrived home on Friday to find that the fridge was bare and so was the freezer. From the amount of plates that were stacked up in the dishwasher it was obvious that Petra had invited several friends over. It was late and I was incensed that she had left us no food, not even milk to make a cup of tea. She was there to greet us, kissing me hello, charming as always, but not so charming was the fact that Felipe was with her, wearing a sleeveless T-shirt and drinking one of Jack's beers. The children were in bed she said, fast asleep, and she and Felipe were going out. 'So I go tomorrow,' she said.

'Yes,' I replied, 'you go tomorrow. Could you get some milk while you're out?' I wanted to make the point, but she just nodded that she would.

'So we go then.' Felipe sloped after her, humming and lighting a cigarette as he crossed the threshold.

'I'm glad they're going,' I said to Jack, 'really relieved, actually. It's just so thoughtless to leave nothing for us to eat.'

I looked over at Jack. He was asleep, his head tilted back; he was beginning to snore.

I tiptoed into Jed's room, climbed up the ladder to his top bunk and kissed his sweet pale face. As he grew older, he became more of a boy and sometimes growled and shouted and refused to let me kiss him, so this was a treat. A stolen kiss. I pushed open the door of Maud's room where she lay halfway down the bed, with all the covers off her. She was hot and sweaty. I kissed her too and she opened her eyes and stared at me, then closed them again.

I walked up a further flight of stairs, right up to the top

of the house, and pushed open the door of Petra's attic bedroom. I pushed it further and walked in, quietly like a guilty interloper. A suitcase was standing upright by her bed next to a box of shoes. Clothes were draped over the chair that lay on the floor and an ashtray was filled with cigarette butts. There were a couple of beer bottles in the rubbish bin, a photograph of Felipe blu-tacked to the wall above her bed and one of his jackets thrown casually over a chair. It touched me to see that there was a photograph of Jack and Maud stuck to the top of a notebook that lay on the small table at the side of her bed.

10

We were having Saturday breakfast – delicious, sweet-smelling chocolate croissants for Jack and the children and plain, boring fibre and bran cereal for me – when the first au pair, Mediha, arrived half an hour early for her interview. She was from Turkey and was accompanied by a friend. The friend, Soraya, embraced the children with gusto and asked to see their toys, while our potential au pair sat slumped and uncomfortable on the edge of the sofa. Soraya acted as translator, so the interview took an hour instead of half an hour, but I'd known within a few minutes that Mediha was not going to be right for us. It was all down to my shoe test. If the girls wore high, impractical heels and too much make-up like Mediha, it screamed at me – this girl's heart is not really in childcare.

Magda, who had the next appointment, was pretty and sweet and also came from Turkey. She wore modest make-up and trainers, but when we asked her what she could cook, she replied rice and omelette.

'Anything else?' Jack asked.

'No,' she shrugged and I wasn't sure if she'd understood.

'Can you make potatoes?' I asked. The reply was a resounding 'no'.

The last girl, Jesse from America, who had seen a sign at the café, wore sandals and no make-up but stated very clearly that she would be interested in more money than we were offering. Au pair wages were called pocket money, as if that made the paltry sum sound better. Jack shifted and coughed and asked her why she had come to our interview when she knew what we were offering as a salary.

She was very confident and sat very straight on the sofa and explained to us that she had lots of babysitting experience and good references, and was sure we'd be open to negotiation. She wanted to know if she would be able to drive my car and take long weekends to travel around Europe. When I told her about the attic bedroom, which was sweet with a lovely view of the garden, velux windows in a sloping roof and a comfortable armchair, she said she would prefer to have a double bed.

She left with a beaming smile and a kiss for each of the children. 'I think she would drive me mad,' Jack commented when she was only seconds away. 'She's just too perfect and too demanding, and too all-American. That blonde fringe is such a cliché. And what's with the double bed? Is she planning to have boyfriends over?'

'Don't know, Jack.'

'Is there anyone else?'

'Well, there is this girl Marie. We are meant to speak tomorrow and make a date.'

'Who is she?'

'She's the English one.'

When Petra finally roused herself that morning, bleary-eyed and pouty-lipped, Jack told her what a disaster the interviews had been.

'I'm sorry,' she said, boiling some water for an egg. 'It's my fault.'

'Yes, I have to agree with you, Petra, I'm afraid you have left us in the lurch.' Jack didn't sound cross, but humorously stern.

'Lurch? What is this?'

'Lurch –' he looked to the ceiling for inspiration – 'you have left us on a boat without a paddle, climbing up a mountain in a blizzard, ill-equipped for the conditions.'

'Oh, Jack,' she laughed, 'now I know you're joking.'

'Not exactly.' He laughed back. 'No, not really joking at all. This is quite a serious situation, Petra. You have let us down.'

'I'm sorry, much sorry.'

'Yes,' Jack said. 'Well, let's see how it all turns out. Life can be very interesting sometimes, with all its twists and turns. You never know what could happen.'

Felipe arrived to pick her up after lunch and we huddled into the corridor to wave her off. As she was finally leaving we hugged her and Jed looked as though he was going to cry. Maud refused to say goodbye and twisted her body round and hid her face when Petra tried to kiss her.

'I will write postcard and come visit when I'm back.'

'No, don't write,' Maud said firmly.

'OK, sweetie,' Petra said, tickling her, but Maud refused to laugh.

'When exactly are you back?' Jack asked. She shrugged. 'Maybe October, or even stay longer if it is good.'

Felipe shook my hand. 'Thank you for everything. I have a cousin,' he added, 'who . . .'

'No. Stop right there,' I laughed, waving them off. 'No more cousins,' I mumbled to Jack, 'and no more German au pair girls.'

The house was quiet after they left and Petra's room seemed bereft without her belongings. The bare walls were ripped of her posters, the orange silk cover gone from the plain white-stained chair. I was surprised by how much I already missed her. Jack and I sat for a while downstairs, barely talking, flicking through newspapers, trapped in our own thoughts, while the children hosed each other down in the garden.

Tilda and I were clumsy and awkward and inept without Felipe. We had our first argument when we were both stressed and tired, and Tilda was hungover after a night out with some girlfriends.

'Don't use so much fruit in the smoothies,' Tilda scolded me. 'It's all organic and we're going to lose money.' She took a giant swig of Coca-Cola.

'What else are we meant to use? I mean, they are fruit smoothies.'

'Apple juice, everybody else does. You know my friend Star, who had a café in Glastonbury? Well, she used to buy organic apple juice in cartons and fill up the smoothies with it.'

'That seems a little disingenuous.'

'No, it's definitely not. It's still organic and it's still juice.'

'Just not fresh juice. Though you're right, of course, we're here to make money.'

Tilda took another swig of Coke. 'Yes and have a life,' she said, washing her hands in the sink.

There were things about Tilda that I'd noticed since we had started the business. She was slightly odd about cleanliness; for example, she washed her hands at least once an hour and used antibacterial wipes on the loo seat. She also confessed that she didn't eat eggs unless she had cooked them herself and it was obvious that she found them hard to handle. She couldn't explain exactly what it was that she found difficult about eggs. When I questioned her she said that a tiny part of it was to do with the threat of salmonella, although I suspected there was something much deeper going on. I had always thought she was a very relaxed person until I'd discovered these quirks in her character. I had a feeling she was having a really difficult time at home because she had stopped talking about her husband, Tom, though I didn't think it would be right to ask her. I still really liked her, but was not so in awe of her now I realized her life was not perfect but as difficult as it was for all of us.

I wondered what Tilda had noticed about me. What weird and strange nuances of my character? She may have noticed that before Petra left, I spent a great deal of time texting her with instructions. And she'd probably observed that I always had a perfect manicure; if my nails chipped – which they were prone to in the café – I would panic and in my free time repaint the chipped nail with a bottle of varnish that I carried around with me. Paradoxically, I dressed haphazardly and my clothes clashed. She'd probably noted my dusting habit and my punctuality pattern and my habit of sneezing and of losing my sunglasses.

Andy the chef was on call to carry down the boxes of deliveries so Tilda was attempting to cook the eggs, bacon and other breakfast foods. The problem was that she couldn't seem to fry the eggs without the yolk running out of its smooth circle and I think this inability to deal with the eggs was because of her strange relationship with them. Whenever I had a minute I would nip down to the cramped, hot kitchen just to do the egg bit, but it was my job to make all the coffees and smoothies and there wasn't always time. My fruit smoothies, though, were becoming less lumpy, probably because half the glass was filled with apple juice.

By the beginning of August we were really busy because there had been an item in an online daily style email saying that Café Blue, on the Askew Road, in Shepherd's Bush, made the most delicious non-wheat almond cakes and fruit smoothies and that Tyler Williams, Jack Boore and William Eade were frequent clients. Not exactly true, of course, they had only been to the opening party, but we framed the story and displayed it in our window.

The almond cakes came from a recipe that Tilda had read about in a vintage Italian cookbook. All sorts of people now turned up at the café, young and old, and there were queues outside the door, particularly at lunch-times and Saturday mornings. The mothers in the area seemed to want our salad baps (we grew lettuce on the kitchen windowsills and I took some home to put in our already crowded garden). The office girls liked our light-weight sandwiches, and our new children's menu was very popular, particularly the macaroni cheese and our fruity mixed-colour sorbets. I was proud when I heard Jed boasting to some school friends that his mother had a really good café with games in a box on the floor.

At that time, just after Petra left and before I'd found someone new, my childcare arrangements were rather fraught and tenuous. Some days Tilda's nanny would have the children, but Jed found it very boring and even though we shared her hourly rate, I didn't want to take advantage and send them every day. A couple of times Jed went to a school friend and rashly I thought I should invite the family for a free lunch at the café, which Tilda wasn't too happy about. Jack agreed to have the children for one day and a couple of times I brought Jed in with me, but after colouring and eating croissants he wanted to go home. One morning, when I'd arranged for the children to go to Lily, Tilda's nanny, Tilda telephoned because Lily was ill and she was sending Frank to her mother's. I telephoned my mother and literally begged and bribed her to come over from Dulwich for the day.

Although Mum had toned down since I was a child, she was not reliable. She could take or leave the children, as she had taken or left us, and it didn't come naturally to me to look to her for help. When she came back from her various long sojourns away from us children, she would spend hours meditating and attending soul-searching workshops, yoga workshops, peace workshops and so on, and it was down to Dad, as usual, to look after us with the help of the Irish nanny. Then she would tire of meditating and find some other cause to follow. Every so often she would take a job as an art supply teacher and occasionally she would take elderly ladies on a watercolour course to the country.

In 1982, just six months after the first women settled at Greenham Common to campaign about the ninety-six cruise missiles that were sited there, my mother decided that she too must go to the peace camp. I was thirteen or fourteen and Nicky a year and a half younger. At first she was a weekend visitor, but then one day she made the decision to go to the camp full time. She said the other women didn't much respect the part-time peace campaigners. My father, knowing she was strong-willed, didn't object. I began to question Dad, asking why he let her go. But Dad was orphaned as a child and didn't want to lose my mother, so he tolerated more than he should have done. For a long part of my life I wrote him off as weak and didn't want a man like him for myself, but in my twenties I began to understand that he was a good man, a decent man, the kindest and most intelligent man that I knew.

We went to the women's peace camp for a visit and were shocked by how Mum was living. Her house was a piece of plastic tied to two trees and she bedded down on hay at night like an animal. They had 'shit-pits' as loos, and makeshift showers. I remember seeing a banner saying, 'We fear for the future of our children,' and asking Mum about it.

'You should fear for my future,' I said, 'because you are never home. Life is hard without a mother.'

'One day,' she said, 'you will understand why I did this.' But I became an adult and still didn't understand why she had left us, sacrificed her children for a cause. I don't think she was really that passionate about nuclear weapons, but just needed to do something with her life that she perceived was worthwhile. So there was this niggling rift of resentment that never really healed.

She sent us letters when she was away, scrawled on lined exercise book paper.

Darling Bunnies,

Missing you very much. A gang of local boys came to taunt us and called us slags. I was cold and it made me cry. Sometimes hard to know why I'm here. Yesterday we joined hands around the perimeter fence. As you know, we are non-violent protestors. Next month there is a plan to cut the fence – an operation called Black Cardigan. It's rather exciting, like something out of James Bond. Top secret and don't tell a soul. I will probably be arrested, but that is something I am prepared for – we all are.

How is school? Riding? Dad?

Please send loo paper urgent, c/o women's peace camp, Greenham Common etc.

All love always

Mum

Some days when I looked after the children full time, I would envy my mother having a cause that enabled her to be reckless enough to abandon her children. But I couldn't desert my children as she had done and sometimes overcompensated by being far too involved in their lives. In an ideal world I would have liked to have trusted someone like Petra to look after them without leaving a thousand instructions and interfering all the time, but I couldn't.

Jed and Maud were excited when I told them my mother was coming. They liked the way she gathered them up and told them weird and wonderful stories that she made up on the spur of the moment. They were dazzled by her rainbow-coloured jumpers, wooden bangles and her charm bracelet hung with little gems – skulls and arrows, a tiny treasure chest, a golden snake, a heart, a photograph of Dad in a miniature frame and a bow and arrow. She quite often brought a cake made with treacle instead of sugar, and semolina or some other kind of substitute for flour. Sometimes she would bring pizza bases made from spelt. When I was a child it had annoyed me that we ate weirdly, but after having children I understood the point.

She arrived half an hour later than she'd said she would, and she didn't have any change for the car-parking. She wanted me to root some out. Poor Mum. If a friend had asked me I wouldn't have minded, but I was infuriated that she'd come so ill-equipped. She said she wanted to take the children swimming but her arm was in a sling.

'How can you take them swimming with your arm in a sling?' I asked.

'Well, I don't have to actually go in with them.'

'Yes you do. Maud is three and the pool insists that an adult goes in with children who are under eight.'

'How ridiculous,' Mum said, sitting down and taking off her various layers of clothing; a thin wool shawl, a kind of sleeveless cardigan. Her hair was tied up but strands of it escaped from the brown clip at the back of her head. 'God, in my day you just threw the children in and let them get on with it.'

'Is that what you did with us?' I asked.

'Not exactly threw you in, but let you get on with it.'

'Well, please don't let my children get on with it. I don't think it's a good idea with your arm.'

'OK, OK.'

I gave her a cup of green tea and she asked me why I didn't live nearer to her in Dulwich, and I responded by asking why she didn't live closer to me in Hampstead and we went on bickering until I had to leave.

She called me halfway through the afternoon to say she had to get home as soon as possible, as she'd forgotten to arrange for someone to walk the dog, Miss Missy. I rather suspected that in fact she'd just had enough and who could blame her? She asked me if I wanted her to drop the children off and I said no, I would be home as quickly as I could. I ran around the café, trying to tidy and put away as much as I could, but poor Tilda was left with a kitchen awash with dirty plates and greasy pans.

I arrived home to find the white sofas stained with

coloured pen and toys strewn in lumps on the floor, going up the stairs and even in the bathroom. Mum seemed completely oblivious to the chaos and completely unapologetic. She kissed the children on the cheek and gave me one too.

'Thank you very much,' I said, accompanying her to the car.

'We had super fun,' she said. 'Look in the garden.'

Oh God, what had she done? I made my way through the overwhelming mess and opened the garden door. I couldn't see anything amiss and was pleased. 'What's in the garden?' I asked Jed. 'Granny said I should look.' He led me to the labyrinth, where I saw that Mum had made a beautiful, long daisy chain twirling along the paths. Mum was like that, I reflected; selfish but with moments of delightful surprises.

'You're never home with us,' Jed said when I was giving him a bath, 'and it's the holidays. You should be home.'

'Yes, I know I should and I'm sorry.' He broke my heart; he didn't sound demanding but just clear and hopeful, as if I had a right to be home. 'Darling, don't forget I've been home all year and we're going to spend some time together on holiday. It's just that, well, I'm starting something new. A new café to make us lots of money.'

'But you can get lots of money from the bank machine outside the post office.'

'Yes, darling,' I laughed, 'but that's my money. I have to earn that money.'

Later that evening I telephoned Marie, the student

who lived near Bath and who'd read my *Au Pair Wanted* note in the café. She was back from her holiday and said she could come for an interview the following evening.

'So what makes you think you'd be good for this job?' I asked, rather dreading the whole process of another interview. There was a long pause on the other end of the telephone and finally she replied, 'Dunno really, just think I'd be good.'

I checked my computer to see if Mark had discovered my email address, but there was nothing from him. My inbox was full of the usual array of messages from Viagra companies, penis enlargers and memos from the admin. office at Jed's school. I became used to the idea that Mark and I had kissed twice; two still-heightened points in a steady married life. Sometimes there would be a song on the radio that would make me think of him or I would see his car parked, which would unsettle me. About the time he was due back I looked out for him, but never saw him. He didn't leave a message for me or call me. I'd refused to have dinner with him and he'd given up.

We had arranged to see Marie at six fifteen. At six twenty she telephoned to say she was on a bus and would be there soon. She finally arrived looking quite bedraggled, with hair in her eyes, chipped vivid purple nails – which Maud loved – and a ripped maxi skirt. She said she really liked children, and it looked as though she loved her food. She was big, but she cuddled Jed and tried to hug Maud, and at least she spoke English.

'What do you like to do in your spare time?' Jack asked.

'Just chill.' I imagined her on the sofa, lounging and eating crisps and swigging from a Coca-Cola bottle.

'What do you want to do after college?' I said.

'Probably enrol at art school in London and look for a job.'

'What kind of job?' Jack asked.

'Just something, anything really that will pay me to carry on with my art.'

'So how did you see the note? If you don't live in London?' I suddenly wondered.

'My friend saw it and telephoned.'

'OK,' Jack said, 'well, give us a few minutes to think about it.'

'I've brought my suitcase.'

'Have you?'

'Yes.' She pointed to the large, pink PVC handbag she was carrying. 'I've got enough here for a couple of nights. Mum will send the rest later.'

I didn't like to imagine what she could be carrying in her PVC bag. Old knickers? Used chewing gum wrapped in paper? Some diet pills?

'Well, I admire your initiative; let me have a few minutes with Ellie.'

'My view,' Jack said to me as we huddled in the garden under a tree, because it was raining, 'is that at least she's keen. She's brought her suitcase. Plus I'm working tomorrow and can't go on being nanny. So shall we let her stay?'

'I suppose she can always go if it doesn't work out.'

'Yes, if you want to be negative about it.'

'I'm not being negative, just real.'

When we told Marie we were going to employ her, she managed to smile and said she was pleased. She moved in and filled the children's bathroom with her cheap products – dark shades of eyeshadow and lip gloss, hair dyes, henna kits and razors. I had never seen any evidence that Petra used the bathroom at all.

Over the following week, I noticed that Marie had the habit of washing her horrible G-strings, holey bras and footless tights by hand and leaving them to dry over the children's towels. It seemed a bit petty to ask her to move her underwear, but the sight of them made me think of brothels and students' digs. So I asked her in the nicest possible way, and she sighed and dragged them in a sodden heap into her bedroom.

She moved at half the pace of Petra and ate about three times as much. It literally took her twice as long to get out of the house. She was charmless and seemed indifferent and bored to mostly everything, except a rock group called Race Xtra. The clashing sounds reverberating from her room were like the worst possible mix of heavy metal and punk. She cooked for the children using too much butter and cream, and gave them my exclusive truffle sauce from Fortnum's on top of their tomato pasta, but she was good at art and spent a lot of time drawing great cumbersome charcoal pictures and encouraging the children to do the same. One morning I came down to breakfast to find that she and Jed were drawing skeletons, dripping blood and brandishing guns.

'Do you not think that subject matter is a bit grim for children?' I asked, scrutinizing Jed's drawing while he was cleaning his teeth.

'No, young children love skulls and bones and that kind of thing.'

'But I'm worried that they'll have nightmares.'

'I'm sure they won't. You don't need to protect them so much, honestly. Jed's a big boy.'

Was I overprotective? Maybe she was right. Would Jed turn out to be a little afraid of life? Like my father, a brilliant historian who had resigned himself to teaching at the local college? Or was Marie out of order? I didn't have time to debate the merits of drawing skulls or to reprimand her further for introducing my children to such dark subjects as I was late for the café. At the last minute Maud ran after me, pleading with me not to go. I picked her up and swung her little body on to my hip, and she clung to me and began gently patting me. It was too hard to say no to her; I was worried that Marie would start playing voodoo dolls with her or wacky witches.

Jack had started rehearsals for his new soap and we were frantic at the café, which was why I was reluctant to bring Maud with me. But the guilt that preyed on me about being away from the children was only mildly less troublesome than the guilt I was consumed with when Jed was a baby and I worked as an assistant director. But it would be impossible to return to the thankless role of stay-at-home mother. At least now my life had another dimension. At least I didn't go into Gap and hear myself saying things like, 'It's such a shame that you don't do those shirts with the teddy logo any more.'

Tilda was in the kitchen and I was arranging for Jed to have a swimming date with a friend from school when Mark walked through the café door. I waved at him coolly, as though a friend had just come in. But my heart lurched and my palms began to sweat. He was still beautifully handsome. He appraised me, delved into me with his green, slanting eyes, and then he smiled as though he'd never been away.

'Bye, Sally. I'll drop Jed around this afternoon, then pick him up from yours at six. Thank you. Bye.'

Mark was now standing inches away from me. He sat down next to me and his slim fingers touched my hand, which made me quiver. Suddenly my whole life took on a new technicolour quality that had been lacking for the previous two weeks. My energy surged. I pointed at Maud and he slipped his hand away. Maud was drawing a rainbow. Rainbows were her only drawing subject. I had managed to keep her relatively happy by feeding her a never-ending supply of chocolate croissants and juice.

'Hello, Mark.'

'Ellie, can we go outside for a moment?' he asked quietly.

'Why? Do you need to smoke?'

'No, I don't smoke, I just want to show you something.'

'I'll join you in five,' I said. 'Just go right out of the café and wait on the corner.'

He left immediately; I think he quite liked the covert nature of my instructions. After he'd gone I stared out of the window, wondering what to do. It would be wrong to see him, particularly with Maud, but I could just go and say goodbye. I could leave Maud for a few minutes to go and explain that I couldn't risk seeing him. But I knew that wouldn't work. The last time we had walked round the corner together he had kissed me. Maud would have to be my protection.

I waited for a good five minutes then told Tilda that I was taking Maud out for a little walk.

'What, in the rain?' She sounded suspicious.

'Yes, she needs some air. I'll go to the newsagent to buy a comic. Back really soon.'

'OK.'

We ran towards my car. He was standing there, leaning against it. 'Let's go and buy a comic,' I urged Maud.

'I don't want to buy a comic.'

'Yes you do,' I said, lifting her into her car seat and doing up her belt.

'I don't, I don't.'

'OK, we'll buy a chocolate.'

'What, now?'

'Yes, in a minute.'

I let Mark into the passenger seat.

'Who is that daddy?' Maud asked, straining at her belt.

'That's a friend,' I replied gaily.

Mark turned to Maud. 'I've been sent by Father

Christmas to find out what you want in your stocking this year.' Maud half smiled but then changed her mind and raised one of her shoulders into the side of her face and peered at him with undisguised sulkiness.

'Where shall I go?' I asked with an erotic sense of giddiness.

'Anywhere but here.' He turned in his seat. 'Where shall we go, Maud?' he asked.

'To get an ice cream.'

I drove towards the nearest park, Ravenscourt, and parked.

'Can we go in the park, Mummy?' Maud asked.

'No, darling, it's raining.'

'Where are we going, Mummy? Why are you parking near the park?'

'Mummy just has to chat to this man about my café.'

'But you said I could get an ice cream.' She was whining now.

Mark leant towards me and put his hand on my thigh, between my legs. *I can't stop thinking about you*, he wrote in hasty, almost indecipherable writing on the back of the box of tissues that he'd found on the seat.

'Me neither,' I mouthed, wanting so desperately to devour him. 'But I . . .'

'You are a poo and you smell like one too . . . poo poo,' Maud sang.

'Can you come to New York this weekend?' he whispered in my ear. 'I have to go for business.'

'Stinky poo. Stinky poo,' Maud chirruped in the back. 'Stop whispering,' she commanded.

'I have a secret for you too.' Mark whispered something in her ear and she laughed.

'No, you're stinky,' she screeched at him.

New York. He was asking me to New York, to consummate our relationship. New York. There were a thousand reasons why I should have said no and a thousand reasons why he shouldn't have asked me.

'Yes I can,' I said, without knowing how I would get away.

'Can what, Mummy?'

'Can do anything,' I laughed, but Maud stared back at me and shrugged.

'It's not funny, Mummy.'

I dropped Mark back at his car then stopped to buy Maud's chocolate and ice cream, and stumbled back to the café in a haze of confusion and desire. I couldn't concentrate and kept checking my mobile.

'Expecting a call?' Tilda asked.

'Well, no . . .'

'We saw a man in the car, Mummy's friend who is a daddy,' Maud chirped to Tilda.

'Really? Who was that?'

'Don't know. Who was it, Mummy?'

'Maud, I don't know what you're talking about.'

'Yes you do,' she screeched at me. 'The man in the car.' She frowned at me.

'Oh, that man, I said. 'That was a friend, who was walking along and happened to see me. Mike Straw, he was at university with me.'

'That man,' she repeated, and, 'he likes Mummy.'

'Well, she's a highly intelligent, very attractive woman,' Tilda said, lifting up Maud to kiss her. 'Your mummy has many admirers.'

'What's an admirer?'

I blushed. Did Tilda know? Did she suspect? She was whooshing Maud through the air, laughing.

By the time the baked beans were gently cooking on the hob, I'd changed my mind about New York. I had been shocked by how easily I had lied to Maud, my own little girl, and so ruthlessly to Tilda. If I went through with it, I'd have to lie to Jack. The Reverend Alistair had said that whatever happened in a marriage, you didn't want to end up lying to your spouse. Would Mark lie to Lorrie? I wondered, as I spooned the beans on to the cheerful plastic plates. Did he even speak to Lorrie? Had Lorrie really left him?

But then something happened, which helped me to change my mind again – although it didn't take much. Marie had gone out for the evening, and Jack and I were playing backgammon, without really talking, when my mobile rang. 'Hello?'

'It's me, Petra.'

'Petra?'

'Yes, me. I have a problem here.' I could hear she was near to tears. 'Can I come back?'

'She wants to come back,' I mouthed to Jack. Jack shrugged and raised his eyebrows to heaven. 'Petra, what a surprise. Are you all right? Are you in trouble?'

'I'm not in trouble, but I don't want to stay here in Ibiza.'

'I'll have to speak to Jack and get back to you.'

'Please ring my mobile. Felipe is not good to me.' She began to cry.

'It's all right, Petra, we'll sort something out. Don't worry.'

We said goodbye and I explained the situation to Jack.

'What!' Jack spluttered. 'She can't decide to leave and then change her mind and come back. What does she think this place is? A hotel?'

'But she's young,' I sighed, my mind flooding with relief at the idea of scatty, crazy, skinny Petra coming home. 'She's coming home!' I sung out. 'Yipadee do da, yipadee day!!'

'Well, you seem to have made your mind up.'

'Maybe she could take the children to your mother's next week. Your mother really likes her; she thinks she looks "classy".'

'Ah, yes,' Jack pondered the idea, 'that may work out.'

'I couldn't have sent Marie, not with her purple streaks and tattoos, pale skin and magenta lips.'

'What are we going to say to Marie? I mean, we can't just sack the poor girl.'

'We don't need to sack her, because she has to go home for a wedding anyway. We'll just say that the children are going away on holiday and that she doesn't need to come back after the wedding. She was only booked as a temp.'

'OK,' Jack said, 'but this is Petra's very last chance. I mean, honestly . . .'

'Jack . . . there's something else . . . I . . .' My heart was pounding in anticipation. 'I need to go to New York this weekend.'

'New York? Why?'

'It's a trade fair,' I lied spectacularly, falling into the deceit so easily and not knowing where the idea of a trade fair had come from, 'a trade fair that I need to be at, to buy equipment. It's all so much cheaper there.'

'But what about import tax?' Jack was more astute than I had given him credit for. 'You'll need to pay it. It all adds up.'

'Yes, well it still works out cheaper.'

'This is very sudden, very sudden indeed.'

'I know, Jack.'

'Well, if you must, you must. Who will look after the children?'

'You will.'

'Me?'

'Yes, you're the father.'

'Right,' he said, 'I suppose I am.' I was surprised he didn't ask me if he really was the father. Jack could go that far if he didn't feel like doing something.

I stood up and looked at myself in the mirror that hung on the wall opposite. It could all stop now. I could just pretend to check my diary and say I'd made a mistake. But I convinced myself that would sound so unprofessional and flaky. And a strange grip had taken hold of me. I knew that I was going to go to New York, no matter what. The

Reverend Alistair, Jack, the café, not even my children were going to stop me.

'Petra's coming back,' I said to Maud.

'Well, I don't want to see her.' Maud crossed her arms over her chest and frowned.

'Why not? I thought you loved Petra.'

'No, I don't love her.'

'Well, she's coming back anyway and guess what? She's going to go to Granny Ruth's with you.'

'And I don't want to go to Granny.'

'Why?' I asked, with exaggerated brightness of tone and spirit. 'It's fun there . . .'

'No it isn't.'

'And,' I said, taking her out of the bath, 'guess what?'

'What?' She looked up at me, all big eyes and mouth.

'Mummy is going away this weekend on an aeroplane.'

'Why?'

I am a lowlife, substandard mother, I thought, rubbing her back; but it would only be the once and that would be it. After the weekend I would never see him again.

'Please don't go, Mummy,' Jed implored me, as I kissed him goodnight.

'It's only for the weekend; not very long at all. Mummy has to have some time to do business.' Now I was lying to my trusting, loving son.

'But we're going to Granny next week. When will we see you?'

'I'm coming to Granny's the weekend after I get back.

I'll be there. Don't worry. You can pack your cricket bat and model clay and acrylic paint.'

He curled up in his bed, around his teddy bear. 'I'll miss you, Mummy. I won't see you all weekend and then not all next week.'

'But you'll have Daddy, won't you?'

'Yes, but it's not the same.'

'And you'll have Petra.'

'Yes, I like Petra. When is she coming?'

'Friday. It's not very long. Daddy is going to take you to Granny's for the weekend, while Petra helps Tilda in the café and then Petra is coming up to join you after the weekend. I'm going to miss you too. So much.' I had a tiny cry into the top of his head.

I read him a story about a Martian who landed in a supermarket car park and was rescued by a little girl who took him home in her jacket. I kissed him once more and turned off the light.

Petra arrived on Friday morning laden down with presents and shy with remorse. She had bought me some chocolates, a bottle of sherry for Jack, a rag doll for Maud and a water pistol for Jed. She was tanned but strained and sad-looking.

Marie had gone in a fug of patchouli the evening before, leaving behind a photograph of herself as a baby, framed in a blue velvet frame. She had also forgotten a red vest and a plastic bag filled with what I presumed were dirty clothes.

Petra came out of her bedroom waving both her hands. 'It smells in there,' she wailed, going back in with a pinched nose and using her available hand to open the windows. She then spent an hour vacuuming, dusting and rearranging the room. When she finished we drank tea together in the garden and I explained what to do in the café while I was in New York.

'Why you go to New York?'

'Just to buy some equipment for the shop.'

'OK.'

She seemed fairly confident because she said she'd worked as a waitress once in her home town. She was just turning round to go back in when I asked her what had happened with Felipe.

'Felipe promised that we had good jobs and some-where to live, but we arrive and no job and no house.'

'What did you do?'

She sat down on the step next to me, stretching her long legs in front of her and kicking off her flip-flops. 'His friend let us stay on the floor and in three days Felipe found a waiter job, but I could only find bar job at club. I work twelve till five in morning. There were so many drugs, so many old men. I think he found another girl. We had a big argument and I telephoned you.' She sank her head on to her lap. Poor Petra.

'I'm so sorry, Petra, that must have been horrible.'

She lifted her head to look at me. 'Yes . . . but at least now I'm with you and the children again.'

I leant back in the deckchair and raised my face to the sun. I guessed that now she was back with us, she would be meek and mild and loving, so grateful would she be to be away from the lecherous old men and the drugs. We chatted amiably about the children and the language course she was going to apply for.

I was not looking forward to telling Tilda about the weekend. I was sure that she would know that my trip to New York was to do with the blond stranger who had come to visit me in the café. She would guess that an assignation was imminent and that I was about to embark on an affair. She could probably tell that I had lost weight and that I was flushed and girl-like. She would probably think I was letting her down by disappearing without much notice and leaving her with zany Petra. But it was only a weekend, I reasoned, nobody was going to die. Couldn't a girl have a break? As I whirled headlong into the treachery, I justified the reasons that I was going. It was a one-off, it would never happen again and I deserved some fun. The weakest and most absurd excuse I came up with was that meeting Mark for a weekend would energize my own flailing marriage.

I arrived at the café for the breakfast shift and at about eleven Tilda and I sat down on the outside tables for our coffee break. We discussed the menu, and then she told me she was giving a dinner on Saturday night for Tom's birthday. I sat half listening, wondering at which point I should break in to tell her about the weekend.

'Tilda, there's something I have to tell you . . .'

'What?' She looked worried.

'It's like this,' I said, folding the foam of the cappuccino into the coffee. 'I told Jack that I wanted to go to a trade fair in New York to buy stuff for the café, but actually I just need a break, away from him, and there is a flat there I can use this coming weekend. I need time to think about our relationship and whether it can go on.' I took a sip. Mark had a friend who had an apartment on the top floor of some kind of industrial building in Tribeca and we were going to stay there.

'So you want to go all the way to New York?'

'Well, yes, because there is this empty flat.'

'But won't it take you at least four days to get over the jet lag?'

'No, I don't think so. I should be fine. It's just for the weekend. I know it's our busiest time but Petra has just got back from Ibiza and she's agreed to help in the café.'

'She returned?'

'Yes, it's a really long story, but there was some kind of fall-out with Felipe. You know, usual stuff, he's unreliable and I think he's gone off with someone else. But she's very good and I'm just away for the weekend,' I added anxiously, tearing at a croissant that I didn't really want.

'Will I have to spend all day teaching her? Or is she quite quick?'

'She's bright and willing. She has slight issues about food, in that she is quite odd about what she eats, but she moves quickly and she's reliable and she really owes me. She'll be on her best behaviour.'

'OK. That should be OK. If it's not, I'll just torture you slowly when you get back. Don't look so worried. I thought you were about to say that you wanted to sell your share of the café and that you were no longer interested.'

I could have kissed her. 'Thank you so much, Tilda, thank you, thank you.'

'But you could have told Jack you needed a break. I'm sure he would have understood.' She was walking through the door with her empty coffee cup.

'He's not like that. He would have made such a fuss. He would have gone on and on about how selfish I was being, how last minute it all was. How it was too late for him to make any arrangements for the children.'

'Yes, I understand,' she said. I was confused. Did she mean she understood Jack's point of view or mine?

*

Jack surprisingly offered to drive me to the airport, which was something he'd never done before on the rare occasions that I had needed to fly somewhere without him. I insisted that it would be better that he stayed with the children. He hovered around the bedroom in the early morning, just before it was time to leave. I longed for him to go away so that I could pack my red knickers and black bras. I wanted to take my slinky short skirt and my high, high shoes, but instead I had to pack my jeans and T-shirts and sensible skirts. In the bathroom I wanted to spend ages filling up my sponge bag and waxing my legs and bikini line. I hoped that he'd tire of hanging around with me but he was following me here and there, talking about the party he was planning for his mother's eightieth. So I went through the charade of shutting my case, zipping it up and letting him take it downstairs. Then I found my straw basket and smuggled some bras, lacy knickers and shoes into it and covered them with magazines and books.

I went downstairs, kissed the children then kissed and hugged Jack, perhaps more ardently than I would have done normally.

'It's a brief trip,' Jack said, standing by the door. 'I hope you don't suffer from jet lag.'

Jet lag? It was the least of my worries. I wasn't going to get much sleep anyway, I joked to myself. I climbed into the taxi cab and, as it drove away, cheered inside because of the sense of freedom that taking off in a taxi gave me. Then I hastily applied some make-up, eyeliner, foundation and blusher, and sat back with a jittering sensation spreading through my limbs and settling in an awkward and fluttery bump high in my chest.

He was already at the check-in desk; his back was turned from me. Even from behind, he was attractive – the golden-blond hair that curled over his collar, the well-cut suit; even the khaki green bag that was strung over his shoulder was just right, not too effeminate but practical and stylish. He was on his mobile. As I walked towards him it did cross my mind that I could turn round and leave before sinking in deeper. I could find a taxi, then text him to say I couldn't come. I would return to normal life, with the weekly shop at the supermarket, the pick-up and drop-offs at school, the gossip with Tilda at the café – but at the precise moment of doubting, he turned round. He smiled and waved and finished his telephone call. He laughed when he saw me, came towards me, kissed me, then took my bags and laughed again.

'You look great,' he said. 'How mad is this?'

'What?'

'Us! Here together at the airport, going away to New York. I mean, we barely know each other.'

I laughed too, and pushed my big Jackie O sunglasses up on my forehead and agreed that the situation was not only mad but insane. My sunglasses were far too big for me and kept slipping off my hair.

I wore a light-brown sleeveless shift dress and a short swing coat, trying to look fun and carefree, not a woman burdened down with a husband and a business and two children. He took my passport and dealt with the blonde, smiling airline woman, charmed her with his big and easy smile. She consulted her computer and tapped away on the keyboard. Consulted her computer and tapped away again.

'Mr Brandon,' she smiled at him, 'we are pleased to offer you and your . . . friend, an upgrade.'

'Good news.'

'You can wait in the business-class lounge,' she said. 'Just show them your boarding passes.'

We strolled hand in hand through security and pass-port control. The whole experience was so much more organized, exciting and civilized than the fiasco with Jack en route to Glasgow, which I couldn't help comparing as it had been my last trip to the airport.

'Why did she give you an upgrade? Do you think she fancied you?' I asked as we stood next to each other on the escalator.

'I think I must be on some kind of list, because occasionally I'm offered upgrades. No reason why I should be given one.' He squeezed my hand. His hand was long and narrow and fit snug with mine as though it was meant to.

We were walking into the business lounge when sud-denly, like some pivotal scene in a movie, Eden, with a glamorous pile of hair on top of her head, was coming towards us.

We huddled together in an awkward little crowd and I introduced Mark and Eden, and then Mark extracted himself and showed his pass to the receptionist at the desk. Eden carried a white leather handbag and she wore

dark glasses and a thin, chic shawl. She looked sophisticated and smart, like a revered editor of a distinguished
fashion magazine.

'Have I met him before?' she asked. 'Maybe at your
house?'

'No, I don't think so.' I laughed. 'Hardly know him
myself. He's my neighbour. Hardly know him,' I repeated
inanely. 'He and his wife moved in recently.'

'Good-looking man.'

I paused and looked puzzled as if the thought that
he was good-looking had never occurred to me. 'Yes, if
you're into that suave look, but he rather reminds me of
one of those models who advertise naff country-casual
looks for aspiring Sloane Rangers. You know the type.'

'Really, Ellie – he's better than that. By the way, where
are you off to?'

'New York JFK.'

'New York? Why?'

'I'm going to a trade fair, to pick up some ideas for the
café.'

'Is the neighbour going to New York too? Are we all
on the same flight?'

'British Airways,' I replied, only half answering the
question.

'Oh no,' she wailed, 'what a shame. Karen has booked
me on to some extraordinary airline that has women-
only loos. Can you imagine? Can't be very good for the
mile-high club. But they do fabulously generous air miles.
I've got an important meeting tomorrow with a casting
agent.'

We talked a little more about Jack before she left the business-class lounge and I entered it. Mark was sitting at a table reading a newspaper. He smiled at me as I sat down next to him.

'Of all the people that I could bump into! That was Jack's agent. She'll be on the phone to him right away.

'Oh no.' He laughed. 'I should probably meet you on the plane, just in case.'

'No, don't worry; she's going on a different airline and she's probably left by now.'

'Can I get you a drink? A cup of coffee?'

'A ginger ale would be great.'

While he was getting me the drink, I dialled Jack's number.

'Hi, Jack.'

'Hello, hello. Lovely to hear from you so soon.' I could hear Maud screaming in the background.

'Guess who I bumped into?'

'Rolf Harris?'

'No, that new neighbour. What's his name? Oh, can't remember. He's going to New York too.'

'Really? You called me to say that?'

'Well, yes.'

'Listen, love, I'm taking orders for lunch right now. One burger, one cheeseburger with bacon. Petra is having an omelette made just with egg white.'

'You're cooking lunch for Petra?'

'Yes, anything wrong in that?'

'No, I guess not.' Of course there was something wrong; why should he suddenly be cooking lunch for

Petra the minute I was out of the door? He had never cooked lunch for Petra before.

'Good, glad that's sorted. Anything else?'

'Yes, I bumped into Eden as well; really strange.'

'Good, good. Well, talk to you later. Bye.'

The news that Jack was cooking lunch for Petra unsettled me. Here I was marching through an airport and airily deceiving my husband, while my husband was at home about to deceive me. How did that feel? Here I was behaving badly, but Jack was probably capable of behaving badly too. Perhaps he suspected that I was going to New York to see a lover but he didn't mind because it meant he could seduce Petra. But he wouldn't go off with Petra, I reasoned. ACTOR LEAVES WIFE FOR NANNY. That really was a joke, but a possible joke. Actors had gone off with nannies before. I was about to tell Mark that I couldn't go to New York when he put his arm around my shoulder and told me how excited he was. It was too late to turn back now. I would just have to renew my marriage vows when I returned. This was just an exceptional weekend away. It didn't mean I couldn't still love Jack and be married to him.

I carried on through the airport, musing on how I was marooned in a delicious, steamy love bubble with Mark, while all around me life went on as normal. Children died from malnutrition, Jack made egg-white omelette for Petra, people ran to catch planes. While we rushed to the gate, I worried that Eden would pop up again, witnessing us running away together. I only relaxed when I got to the safety of my seat.

'We made it,' Mark whispered. 'Who will we bump into next? My mother-in-law?'

'Oh, don't,' I said, shuddering at the thought.

I sat looking out of the window while the aeroplane rose through the meadow of clouds.

'What exactly will you be doing in New York?' I asked him. 'Apart from seeing me?'

He was drinking a Virgin Mary with pepper and tabasco, which the flight attendant had spent an inordinately long time preparing. I thought of Jack then, who always drank too much alcohol on aeroplanes which, compounded with his jet lag, rendered him a very bad travelling companion.

'I'm giving a speech at a benefit dinner – a table for ten costs about forty thousand dollars. We're raising money for school children in developing countries. I'm a director of the Global Institute, and adviser to the government on poverty issues around the world.'

'Wow.' I looked at him in awe. 'That sounds so impressive. I had no idea you had such an important job.'

'Yes. I know it makes me sound so bloody good, so perfect in every way, but I'm not. I can't resist temptation.' He took my hand. 'I just can't think too hard about what we are really doing, what the implications are. I don't want to go there.'

'Me neither,' I smiled. But, actually, I wanted to talk it through. I wanted to discuss the craziness of eloping to America, the madness of embarking on an affair, because there was no one else I could talk about it to. But I didn't want to risk spoiling the two days we had together. After the weekend I wouldn't see him again.

We accepted little slices of smoked salmon wrapped around cream cheese. I loved that what he was doing seemed so worthwhile. I was so used to Jack thinking and talking about himself that to hear somebody thinking and talking about others was inspiring.

We sat in silence for a while then he leant over to me and said, 'I've arranged for you to have dinner on my table. I've said that you're my research assistant.'

'Research assistant? What if someone recognizes me as the wife of Jack Boore?'

'Are they likely to?'

I shook my head, no. It was very unlikely, I had to admit.

'Do you want to play hangman?' he asked.

We were spinning into Manhatten in a yellow cab. We kissed in the back of the car; the way you do, when you first spend time with someone you are attracted to. The most exciting part of being with Mark was the thrill of desiring him; all I wanted to do was touch him and lie naked with him. He took my hand and whispered into my hair.

We alighted in the East Village, because that was where he had once spent an entire summer and he said it would be a good place to find something to eat. It was very humid and sultry, romantic weather if you're in love, hell if not. There seemed to be a lot of groovy types walking big dogs, cool black boys rapping in cars and steam coming out of street ventilators. It was like walking on the set of a musical. There were guys and girls hanging out everywhere, eating pretzels and gooey pizza. We stopped to watch a man in a white vest strutting around like a peacock on some scaffolding, while down below his girlfriend clapped.

We wandered into a Japanese sushi bar and I sunk back into my seat almost too tired to eat.

'Come on,' Mark cajoled me, 'eat a little.' He asked the beautiful Japanese waitress for the bill in Japanese which really impressed me. Jack had always been hopeless at languages, but was confident enough to try speaking French or Spanish or Italian with an exaggerated and rather pompous English accent.

Mark had borrowed an apartment on the top floor of a huge industrial-type building in Tribeca from a cameraman friend of his, who was on an assignment in Afghanistan. We walked up five flights of stairs; on the fourth flight I had to stop to catch my breath. The apartment was vast – a huge open-plan space with a large stand-up fan dominating the sitting-room area. There was a big painting of the figure four in various configurations propped up against the exposed brick wall. At the other end of the apartment was a kitchen with a dishwasher that had a side missing and flaunted yellow insulation foam like some bold and sassy piece of conceptual art.

The bed was a plain wood four-poster in a bare room off the main living area. We both gravitated towards it and lay down next to each other. I wanted to know him for a few more hours before actually having sex with him and I was shy of exposing myself to a man other than Jack. My relationship with Mark had been so speeded up that I think we both wanted to slow it down. We lay for a while, chatting and listening to the whirr of the fan. Then he had a shower and came to bed in his boxer shorts. I went to clean my teeth, had a quick shower and then joined him wearing a long-sleeved Moroccan shirt. I climbed into bed and curled on to my side and he curled up beside me, hugging me from behind, so safe and warm. A few moments later I turned towards him and he kissed me in the dark and we made love, sighing and gasping but not speaking, and afterwards we were silent and slowly he slipped away to the other side of the bed. It was almost as though it hadn't happened; almost as though neither of us wanted to admit that it had.

I woke up early, at five, when the street was relatively quiet, although I could hear someone banging what sounded like the top of a rubbish bin. Mark was still asleep, the sheet tucked around his long thighs. His body was fit and young-looking. His stomach was lean. Mine was slightly wobbly and I was very self-conscious about it.

It was ten or eleven in the UK and I slipped out of bed to text Jack.

> **Arrived New York, very**
> **humid, very tired, ate**
> **Japanese. Love to children**
> **xxx Ellie**

He wrote back immediately:

Missing you very much.

Miss you too

I tapped into my phone automatically. Than I tucked my long shirt over my knees and drew them towards my chest. Poor Jack. What was I thinking? Of course he wasn't seducing Petra. And here I was in New York having made love to our neighbour. How could I do that to my poor husband? I sat for a few minutes longer, promising myself that I would not see Mark again when we returned to London. There was too much to lose. The children needed us; they needed two parents. I wanted to hug them and kiss their faces.

I slid back into bed with Mark. He stretched out for me, fondling my breasts, gently, slowly kissing me all over. We made love for the second time, but it was as though we had known each other forever – the love-making was so tender and gentle and easy. Loving and warm and right.

We got up around nine and headed downstairs. Mark wanted to try a café called Bubbly, which his friend Martin used every day for breakfast. We walked down the street filled with discount stores and takeaway food out-lets before turning a corner and finding the café on a quiet side street.

Mark ordered poached egg and bacon, and I ordered eggs Florentine (eggs with cream over spinach on a muffin) with a huge glass of orange juice and toasted poppy-seed bagels, then worried that he would think I was greedy and undisciplined. We didn't really say much as we ate our breakfast, but we sat very near to each other and it was just lovely to be with a man who wasn't talking loudly about himself.

Lorrie telephoned while we were having coffee. It had to be Lorrie, because Mark stood up and walked away from the table. I heard him say *must go now, yes, goodbye, goodbye, talk to you later.* He sat down, fiddled with the napkin, smiled at me and cut into the perfectly cooked poached egg.

'That was Lorrie,' he said, as the yellow yolk ran on to the cream-coloured plate.

'Yes, I guessed. What's happening with you two?'

'The latest is that she wants to come back to London and give it a go.'

A jolt struck through my body. It was not the kind of news that was welcomed after spending the night with a man that you could potentially fall in love with.

'Are you going to have her back?'

'Well, she is my wife, it would be churlish not to give it one more go.' He took my hand but it was hard to hide how crestfallen I felt. 'Don't let that news ruin our time together though. We're both married, having a weekend away. Nothing has changed.'

'No, no,' I smiled bravely. 'No, I know nothing has changed.' I nibbled on a piece of his bacon smothered in maple syrup.

I excused myself from our small table and locked myself in the loo, and because the bubble of romance had burst I let myself cry. The truth was, I was a married woman going through a mid-life crisis and having an affair with a neighbour. It was like the plot of a soap opera. But it wasn't a soap opera and we weren't going to leave our respective partners and elope together. I came out, straightened my skirt, splashed water on my face and looked in the mirror. After the crying, I looked exhausted. He was right: we were both grown-ups, I was fully conscious of what I was doing. What did I expect? A small part of me, a part that didn't quite dare even think the thought, had hoped that Mark and I would somehow, against the odds, end up together.

Later that day, after a long, lingering lunch, we went to the Union Square Greenmarket and bought some cherries and maple syrup candy and Mark presented me with a bunch of lilies. I tried to feel romantic as we walked along together, but truthfully I was nervous when he took my hand that someone would approach us and accuse us of being adulterers; the news about Lorrie had sadly sobered me. We walked in Central Park for about two hours, passed the tennis courts and people jogging, and watched a man standing and singing opera, before going back to the loft apartment. Mark made a few business calls while I put away our provisions and found a vase for the lilies. He came up behind me after his telephone call, kissing my neck, breathing into my hair, and even though part of me wanted him to stop, the part that was afraid to fall in love with him, I didn't want him to stop at all and eventually, against my better judgement, I succumbed to his kisses, because wasn't it better to be passionate briefly than not at all? I pulled off his T-shirt and he pulled off mine. We took a long shower together and made love standing against the wall, more rampantly than before, thrusting and urgent and sexy.

After the shower we lay around on the huge bed, wrapped in towels, lazing, reading and chatting. Too soon, it was time to get ready for the benefit night, which I was now dreading. I discovered that I hadn't been able to slip enough clothes into my basket to make up one whole outfit. I had forgotten the sheer gold tights that I needed to go with the sparkly gold shift dress, and in my haste I'd packed a black bra instead of the neutral-coloured one. There was no way I could wear the black bra under the gold dress because it would show, dark and ugly under the sheer silk. I sat on the bed in a complete panic, not wanting Mark to know. This was meant to be a romantic trip away, not a domestic crisis.

He came out of the bathroom, freshly shaved. 'Not ready yet?'

'Well, no, the thing is, I didn't have time to pack everything I needed. Jack was standing over me and so I panicked and packed all the wrong things.'

'I'm sure Martin's girlfriend, Pat, has left something you could borrow,' he said. 'She's cool; she'll have something in one of these cupboards.'

I opened a cupboard door to find a string of tiny, groovy outfits that would fit on to one of my legs. 'Oh no, she's the same size as my au pair, Petra – size minus ten.'

'There must be something,' he laughed at my admittedly not very good joke, flicking through the cupboard, bringing out a black skirt with an elastic waist. 'What about this?'

I tried it on and was able to fit into it if I kept my stomach taut and didn't breathe out too hard. Then we searched her drawers until we found a sparkly low-cut gold top that made me feel vulnerable and exposed.

'Well, this will have to do.' I turned to Mark.

'Stunning,' he said. 'Now let's go.'

'Are you sure?'

'You would look good in anything,' he assured me, doing up a cufflink on his shirt.

I knew I didn't look stunning at all. I looked like a middle-aged woman trying to be young.

'Middle-aged,' he scoffed. 'You don't look a day over thirty.'

'Thank you,' I purred with delight; he couldn't have said anything better.

We took a cab to a fancy hotel where the lobby looked like a bar. We were led to a huge ballroom where dinner was laid on twenty or so tables of ten, decorated in gold and silver; even the spoons had been sprayed gold. Mark introduced me to the charity committee as his research assistant and I was placed on his table. He sat between two well-polished women, with smooth foreheads and bulging eyes, while I was next to a gay accountant, Robbie, who specialized in working for well-known contemporary artists. On my other side was a retired senator.

During our first course, prawns on a bed of rice noodles, the gay accountant asked me rather pointedly, I felt, what Mark's wife was like. He was dark-haired with defined eyebrows and he wore a tiny silver stud in his left ear. He mentioned 'running numbers' and talked with a Brooklyn mafia boss accent.

'She's great. She's American and her name is Lorrie; she's a photographer. They have a six-month-old daughter.' I smiled at him, hoping to charm him.

'Where is the wife?' He searched me for clues.

'Well, I'm not entirely sure, you'll have to ask Mark. I don't really have anything to do with his private life.'

'He's a gorgeous man,' he said. 'I saw him on television a few months ago. He was being interviewed in some kind of documentary about children in developing countries other than Africa, or something like that. He must be fun to work with.'

'And what about you? What's your star sign?' My question seemed so clumsy and gauche, but I was keen to change the topic of conversation. I had no idea what to say about working with Mark and didn't want to become entrenched in more lies. He spooned the prawns into his small mouth and flowed into a long description of himself.

'I'm a Virgo, unromantic, sharp intellect, and "detached enough to break many hearts".'

'Wouldn't like to be in love with you,' I joked, 'sounds scary.'

'No worries,' he hooted, 'not a chance that you would be. Or I with you.' He laughed then looked disapproving as I helped myself to one of the thin pieces of toast and smothered it with butter. 'Eeugh . . .' he grimaced, snarling at the toast as it passed through my lips, 'all those carbs and fat, you should be careful, specially as you're over twenty.'

'But I'm only nineteen,' I garbled between mouthfuls. It was a really bad line and I cringed later when thinking about it. He attempted to laugh, but it was more of a titter.

'You have to think about it,' he advised me, 'if you want to go on wearing clothes like that.' He was looking at my gold top.

It was halfway through the main course, little lamb steaks wearing frilly chef's hats and perfectly cooked baby vegetables, when Mark stood up to make his speech. I was pleased to have a break from my deaf, retired senator and the gay accountant. The audience of well-groomed women, who were mostly wearing long, designer dresses, and the men in tuxedo jackets clapped their hands as he took to the platform.

He had the confidence to wait until there was absolute silence in the room, until every cough had subsided and every chair had stopped scraping on the floor. He smoothed his tie and cleared his throat.

'Children in developing countries die because they don't have a bed net or a dollar to buy medicine, antibiotics to treat a lower respiratory infection contracted from living in conditions where dung is burnt to cook meals. It's hard for us to imagine, sitting here eating our organic lamb and steamed asparagus, going home to laundered and pressed sheets, what extreme poverty tastes and feels like, what it actually smells like . . .'

I looked around at the audience, some of whom had abandoned their steamed asparagus to watch and listen to him. Others carried on eating and drinking, but the room was very still. He spoke beautifully and with passion. I was sure that the rich ladies must be falling in love with him and wanting to give him huge sums of money. It was hard to believe that the man I had run away to New York with, the man who made me laugh, the man who cooked stew, who fucked me in a loft apartment, the man who was married and father to baby Alice, was the same man who stood on the platform talking now. He looked so important; he was so erudite, so handsome and so worthy.

I was beginning to sweat under the tight gold top and I could hardly breath. When he was finished a few of the ladies stood up to clap, and more followed; soon the whole room was applauding Mark. I shuddered with pleasure and delight as I had done in the early days of being with Jack and watching him on stage or on television. When Mark jauntily stepped off the platform, a West African musician arrived to play a set. The music was sweet and light and beautiful, and the room hushed once more.

Later, between the main course and the pudding, I was struggling with a long-winded and rather difficult conversation with the deaf senator about contemporary Irish art. It was hard to be spontaneous when the poor man could hardly hear me. Mark was finishing the meal that he had left to make his speech. He glanced at my desperate face and when he had a chance he came over and leant down towards me. 'It's all right, babe,' he whispered, 'we'll be out of here soon.'

'We have to go,' he announced, just as the dessert course was being delivered to the table. The bulging-eyed women tried to restrain him with endearing comments – 'Don't leave us so soon', 'we never see you', 'you have to sample the white peaches from Italy with cream and mascarpone'.

'Where are you two going?' one long-haired woman demanded tetchily.

'Thank God that's over,' Mark said, whisking me through the double doors and into the elevator, which went so high it made my ears pop. We got off at the top floor and made for the small sofa with a view of Brooklyn Bridge. We sat for a while just looking and eating nuts and sipping ginger Martinis.

'Are you wearing knickers?'

'No.'

'Can I just film you walking towards me?' he asked, pulling out his phone. 'Look, I've got this mobile which has a really good quality video on it.'

'Are you sure you should?' I was thinking of Lorrie.

'Yes, I'm sure.'

The bar was pretty crowded and normally I would have been too shy. But I wanted to be filmed by Mark. I wanted to be scrutinized and consumed by him.

'Where shall I walk from and to?'

'Just walk as though you're coming to meet me.'

I stood up and left the bar. I waited outside for a

moment and went to the bathroom. My cheeks were flushed from the cocktails and my hair was tousled. I had grown fond of the sexy gold top.

I entered the bar and looked around, as though I was meeting someone. I was aware that a few men were looking at me and it was exciting to know that Mark was searching me out on the camera of his phone. Then, when I found him, I walked towards him trying to look cool and sexy and smouldering, but actually I tripped up over someone's bag and began to laugh.

After the drink on the rooftop bar we went to a basement club and listened to jazz. It was hot and I had drunk too much and I thought I could love him even though it wasn't right. I fell asleep on his lap as he stroked my hair.

It was late when we finally returned to the apartment on the top floor. We had a drink, talked about our respective lives and went to bed with the fan whirring in overdrive. I couldn't sleep that night, knowing that the next day I would be returning to my normal life, my real life.

On Sunday morning we went to a café in the Meatpacking District, where hip young parents were having brunch with their perfectly coiffed, adorable children.

'I'd like to stay here with you for at least another week,' he said.

'Me too.'

'I can't though. I have a diary full of meetings,' he added quickly, as though he was worried I would take him seriously.

'I have a café waiting to be run and a husband who thinks I'm at a trade fair, and I don't think I'll get by on another sleepless night.' I hoped I didn't sound too competitive.

'Do you still love Jack?'

'Yes, I do love Jack, but he's impossible. We've lost any sense of mystery or romance. We've said things that are too hurtful to repair, it's . . .'

'I understand,' he leant back on his chair, 'you don't need to say any more.'

We landed back at Heathrow very, very late on Sunday night and shared a cab. We asked the cab to stop at the end of the road and walked separately back to our houses. It all seemed so strained and difficult, so over and so final. Back in my cool house, I noticed first of all that everything was very quiet. There was a note from Jack on the kitchen table: 'Welcome Home.' I walked to the bay window that looked on to the street and saw a light on in Mark's bedroom. I pictured him lying on the bed with a towel draped over him, reading his mail. Then I went downstairs and made myself a cup of herbal tea and picked up the telephone to call Jack.

'Hello,' he said gruffly, 'you've woken me up.'

'Sorry, just wanted to check in with you.' I yawned. 'And I know you can fall easily back to sleep.'

'How was the flight?'

'Fine, really good, nothing much to report.'

'I've got a surprise,' he said, sounding alert. 'I've found a wing of a house to rent. I thought we could take it for a couple of weeks while the children are on holiday. Ma's house is really too cramped for us all.'

'That sounds great, Jack, but can we afford it?'

'Producers are paying. I'm needed here for a couple of rehearsals.'

'Oh good, OK. I can't wait to see it and I'm planning to join you and the children for at least a week. Did Petra arrive all right?'

'Yes, she got here this evening, picked her up at the station. Maud pretended not to know who she is, but Jed was pleased.'

'Were you pleased?' I asked with a silly stab of jealousy, remembering how Jack had cooked her lunch while I was on the way to the airport.

'Yes, nice girl, charming, but mad as a snake.'

'Well, listen, I'll see you at the weekend.' I was relieved to hear that Jack thought Petra was mad. 'The house sounds really lovely.' I doodled a heart on a small yellow pad, with an arrow going through it and the letters M and E at either end. 'Will you send my fondest love to Jed and Maud?'

I was just getting ready for bed when a text from Mark showed up on my mobile.

No one so much as you, ever again, ever

I read it a few times, wondering where the quote was from. Had he made it up? It sounded desperately romantic but, paradoxically, perhaps it meant our relationship was over. Did it mean he had loved me more than anyone else before or ever again? I read it twice more, savouring the urgency of the words. I texted back:

> **Loved our weekend. Have come home to an empty house.**

My text seemed normal, middle of the road and ineffectual compared to his, but I didn't want to encourage him when I knew that I would never be able to sleep with him again.

I climbed into the huge king-size bed I shared with Jack and threw the biscuit-coloured cashmere blanket on to the floor. The bed seemed huge with just me in it. I missed the children and Jack, and Mark. I turned over on my side and began to cry; I was so tired but so awake too, which reminded me of Jed. When he couldn't sleep he would creep downstairs and post a note under the door, saying, 'I can't sleep. What shall I do?' Then I'd find him sitting on the stairs and he'd say that he was too tired to sleep. I snuggled into the pillows and glanced at the photograph of Jack and me that had been placed in the large mirror above the Victorian fireplace. It was a photograph taken just after we'd got married and Jack had his arm draped around me. We looked happy.

I tried to sleep, but my mind was busy with questions. Could Jack and I ever be like Mark and I had been in New York? Having sex in the shower? Laughing at each other's jokes? Wanting to touch and kiss each other? Or was that loving, giving giddiness just a symptom of the early part of relationships? Was lust and feeling generous and excited by somebody destined not to last? Were some couples better at covering up general ennui and inertia than others? Were there couples who were still genuinely in love eight/eighteen years into marriage? Were Jack and I abnormal or normal? Was he quite simply the wrong man for me? If I left Jack for Mark were we destined to be in the same trouble seven or eight years down the line? Not that Mark was going to leave his wife for me, he'd made that clear when he said he wanted to give his marriage another go.

Before I'd met Jack, I'd never had a relationship that had lasted more than three years, and by that time, usually, the sex had grown tired. Jack and I had known each other for nine years – that was a record for me. A friend of mine had once told me that the secret to remaining in love with your husband or wife was to be a little bit in awe of them. The problem was, I had been in awe of Jack but no longer was. How could you remain in awe of somebody after you've seen them drunk and floundering up the stairs, or walked into the bathroom as they sat reading on the loo? How could Jack be in awe of me, after seeing me suffering a miscarriage or flossing my teeth or shaving my armpits once on a train from France to Italy?

Tilda looked fraught and thin. She radiated distress and was picking at a croissant and drinking a very small, strong coffee. She had obviously been crying. Her long brown hair, usually so lustrous and glossy, was dry and done up hastily with an office rubber band. She wore a grubby jean skirt and a red T-shirt. It was the first time I had seen her in such disarray but, even shattered and battered, she was still beautiful.

'You all right?' I sat down opposite her

She shook her head and let a tear or two trickle into her cup.

'What's the matter?'

Her mouth twisted into a grimace – 'Tom is having an affair.'

'Are you sure?'

'Yes, Saturday – it's all such a cliché.' She burst into tears. 'It's such a cliché that it's almost funny. But I don't have the energy to laugh.' She was chewing gum. I leant forward and took her hand.

'I was preparing dinner for his birthday. Everything was laid out, and I got the cake from the fridge to stick candles into and then I went to the drawer where I just knew I'd put the birthday candles and found his mobile lying in there. I picked it up and there was a message from

"Love". What would you think if you found *Love* in Jack's mobile address book? I opened it up thinking, well, hoping, that was what he called me, but no, the message was definitely not for me. It said, "So sorry about this evening. Longed for you to be here. Miss you. L."'

Mascara was running down her cheeks. I went to fetch some loo paper from the tiny bathroom. 'Shit,' I said to myself, flushing the loo.

'By the time I confronted him,' she continued as she blew her nose delicately on the pink loo paper, 'the first people were arriving at the door. For a while I pretended nothing was happening, and literally slugged back two glasses of vodka. Tom kept well out of my way. But then he came in to fetch some bottles of wine and I threw the cake at him and it spilt all over the floor and then he backed away and I screamed at him and Natasha came in and I broke down and it all just came out. Within a few minutes everyone knew that Tom was having an affair.'

'No!'

'Yes!' She was now talking in theatrical stage whispers. 'Everyone was gathered together in our sitting room, drinking and whispering, so I took refuge in the kitchen and most of the women were with me, while Tom remained in the sitting room. And in the middle of it, his mother telephoned. I heard myself saying, "I'll just get Tom – the adulterer."'

'No!' I laughed.

'Eventually, after what seemed like minutes but was in fact half an hour, Tom offered to leave. After he'd gone I spent the rest of the evening drinking and talking it over with his friends.' She removed the gum from her mouth, wrapped it in a napkin and took a sip of water from a plastic bottle.

'That must have been awful. Did you just carry on with the dinner?'

'Well, we did, in a very relaxed way, everyone just helped themselves and we sat around. His friend Simon said it was probably a meaningless fuck and he'd be home, begging to return soon.' She sighed and rubbed her eyes and shook her hair. 'It's such a shock. It just makes me wonder whether he's really been jogging and staying at his office or meeting *Love*.'

A shiver of guilty horror fizzled inside me – what would she think if she knew about Mark and me in New York?

A man came in wanting a takeaway coffee. I stood up and served him, while Tilda remained at the table, stirring her spoon round and round in the sugar.

'I just don't understand,' she said after the man had left, 'how a woman would choose a married man. Doesn't she realize that she is destroying a family? Three people – a husband, a wife and a child?'

'Do you think you've ever met this woman?' I asked, hoping to sound normal, hoping that I wasn't giving anything away because I was nervous and guilty and ashamed.

'No. Do you think you have?'

'Me? No, of course not, Tilda. Why would you think that?'

'After you've been betrayed,' she said, 'it just feels as though anyone could betray you, even in the smallest way.'

'No, no, of course I don't know her, I hardly know Tom.'

'Why would she go after a man who was married? What kind of woman does that?'

'I don't know,' I replied, beginning to blush. 'I don't know why. Maybe it was something that happened when they were drunk. Have you talked? Does he want to come back?'

'I'm too upset to talk to him.'

'It was probably a one-night stand.'

'I don't think so.' She burst into tears again.

Two women who worked in a nearby office came in for coffee, chatting about a film they had both seen on television the night before. Tilda swept her hands down the side of her jeans, pulled her hair back and ran behind the counter.

I went down to the kitchen to start chopping vegetables for onion soup. I chopped the onion and it made me cry. I wiped my eyes with the apron. My eyes were itching and burning, and I rubbed them again and they turned into real tears. Signs were coming at me from all directions. I had to give Mark up. I was a woman who loved other women. But, I consoled myself, as the tears ran down my cheeks, it was Lorrie who had left Mark. She had left a genuinely attractive man alone. Lorrie had left him, I repeated to myself, but that didn't excuse how terribly I had deceived Jack. If it ever got into the tabloids . . . it didn't bear thinking about.

We continued our conversation after the lunch-hour rush, still in our navy and white striped aprons. Tilda looked very tired, drawn and distressed. She had progressed from having one coffee a day to about six. She was so consumed with distress that she hadn't even asked me about my weekend in New York, which was a relief. While we were chatting, our most loyal customer came in. In the first few weeks after opening I'd been too busy to really notice the customers, they kind of merged into one big throng of people to keep happy. But now that we were into a routine, we began to get to know the names of the regulars. There was one man who came in every afternoon at about the same time. His name was Miles. If I had to guess I would have said he was about thirty-five. He wore glasses and was balding. He was stocky and dressed casually, usually in something like a dark blue sweatshirt and linen trousers. He always carried a battered briefcase with a leather strap and a black computer case. He was very polite and complimentary about the café. Once, just before we were closing, he told me it was a haven, a refuge from his study. Soon we had a joke: he would sit down and I would come over and say, 'That will be your usual, sir?'

'Thank you,' he would say. Or 'I love a bit of usual.' Sometimes, just to surprise me, he would say, 'Actually, you know what ... I think I'll have a toasted cheese today, but without the tomato and I'm going to be really strange and have an espresso rather than a cappuccino.'

He would come in with a laptop and sit at the corner table by the window for a couple of hours, drinking one, two or three coffees. He also talked on his mobile, but he was never joined by anyone. One afternoon a few weeks back, when it had just been the two of us upstairs, he'd told me that he was a journalist who wrote a daily problem page in one of the papers.

'Are they real problems?' I had asked. 'Do you use real problems?'

'Very occasionally if I have a bag of dud letters, I may use a friend's problem or make one up.'

'Are you trained in any kind of therapy?'

'I did actually train in psychotherapeutic counselling once, long ago.'

He came in that afternoon with his computer bag and briefcase and ordered his usual and said, 'Has somebody died in here? It feels like death.'

We laughed. 'Shall we tell him about your problem?' I said.

'No.'

'Go on, tell him.'

'OK, you tell him.'

'Miles,' I began jauntily, 'we have a real live problem over here: my friend has found out that her husband is having an affair. He's moved out.'

He looked at Tilda. 'Do you want him back?'

'Truthfully, I do,' she admitted, 'but at the moment I'm too angry to even look at him.'

'Remember though, anger is just covering up hurt,' he said.

'Yes.' She looked as though she might cry.

'I would say and do nothing. Be distant but polite, make no demands, no scenes. Just be cold, very cold indeed, detached. Then when you've recovered a little from the shock, you could try the tactic of the strong woman to jolt him to his senses. Have a good time, make him see that you can do without him. Flirt with someone, anyone really – it will be the last thing you feel like doing, but you must.'

'I can't really imagine doing that right now.' Tilda leant over the counter; she looked light and frail as though she might float away.

'Ah, but you will soon; you are more resilient than you think.'

'Am I?'

'Yes, definitely. Wait and see. If you want to practise on me, you can. Sorry, ladies, but this session is over. I've got work to do.'

He went back to his computer and we went back to serving other customers. Tilda tried really hard to get on with the job, but although she cheered up while Miles was in the café, as soon as he'd left she went back to moving very slowly and looking despondent and sad.

'Tilda, go for a swim or a walk, or just go and pray in a church. I'll be fine here.'

'Pray in a church?' She laughed, spluttering some water on to the table.

'Yes, you know, solace and all that. Churches are quiet and peaceful and restorative.'

'I can't see myself at church, but I don't want to go home,' she said. 'It just reminds me of Tom and that my marriage is ruined. Even seeing his shiny shoes and his whiter than white trainers upsets me right now. I bet he's never actually been jogging, he's just been shagging L.'

I laughed too, so relieved that Tilda could still laugh.

After splitting up with Hal all those years ago, I didn't laugh or smile for six long months.

'Do you want to stay with me? Jack and the children are away. You could take my key, go back to my house, walk round the labyrinth. Watch a movie, write a note to Tom telling him he's a shit.'

She laughed again. 'I would love to stay with you for a few days. Thank you. Are you sure?'

I nodded. 'Yes, couldn't be more sure.'

'I won't go now though, I'll go and get Frank as usual then come home with you.'

'Are you sure, Tilly?' I'd never called her Tilly, but it seemed appropriate at that moment. 'Sure you don't want to go and flop at my house?'

'No,' she said, 'I'll wait until we've finished.'

Tilda's news was a sure sign that a married woman, or any woman, should not fraternize with a married man, particularly a man with a baby, even if his wife had left him. As I swept the floor I became steelier and stronger, more determined not to let Mark disrupt my life. When I'd finished, before I'd lost my nerve, I walked round the corner to call Mark on his mobile. He wasn't answering, so I left a long, rambling message saying it would be really hard to see him again and then explaining that a friend was staying and it would be totally inappropriate to turn up at my door, but the machine didn't allow me to finish and I was promptly cut off. I sounded friendly and upbeat but I was desperate and sad and unnerved. *No one so much as you, ever again, ever.*

That evening I made frankfurters in buns for all of us, with a salad for Tilda and peas for Frank. After supper Frank went to play in Jed's room and Tilda and I had a glass of wine. We sat outside and watched the swifts and I desperately wanted to confide in her about Mark. I was relieved that she was there, plugging me to my house, not sure if I had enough will-power to stop myself going across to Mark's house and banging on the door.

She was making herself a fennel tea; she was bare-legged, wearing a short towelling dressing gown that had shrunk in the wash. Her legs were naturally brown and slender, unlike mine, which were unnaturally white and not that slender, although luckily my ankles were slim.

'Tilda, I need to ask you something.'

'What?' She was hugging her cup of fennel tea.

'I know it's asking a lot, but would you mind – I promised Jed and Maud that I would join them this weekend. I know our new girl, Arletta, will do Saturday and I will pay her.'

'That's fine, of course you must.'

'Thank you. And I was thinking – as it's August and we're busy, maybe we should pay Arletta to do Saturday all day for the rest of the month. I think she's going to be very good. She's got a wonderful smile and she seems really willing. What do you think? Do you mind about this weekend?'

'Really happy. I'll have to let Tom spend some time with Frankie next weekend ... I don't mind being at the café to help out. It will keep me busy. I'm going to miss

Frankie so much. It's going to be so strange without him.'

'It will be strange, but you could use the time to do something just for you. Go to a museum or a movie or for a walk.'

'I'm going to try.'

'And we should discuss the rest of the summer holidays. I want to take a week with the children in the country.'

'Good idea. I need to get away too. Mum and Dad have rented a house in Italy. I would like to take Frank for a week just as soon as we can arrange it. Maybe we could cover for each other and obviously take different weeks. And I think we should close over the August bank holiday weekend. Annie said the café was always dead over bank holidays.'

Frankie came to find us and asked where his father was. He was a sweet little boy, a year older than Maud. He had a side parting and was freckled, like a boy in an illustration in an Enid Blyton book. That evening he was brimming with questions. He asked why he didn't have Lego like Jed. And could ants fly? And how far was the sun? And was the sun a star or a planet?

Tilda ummed and half answered. She was distracted; she was in the kind of mood where she just wanted to chain-smoke and cry, but she pulled him on to her lap and rocked him like a baby. She didn't actually smoke, but she would have smoked if she'd been a smoker. I tried to answer some of Frank's questions, having read many knowledge books to Jed.

'The sun is the biggest star and it is many, many miles away.'

'How many miles?'

'I'm not sure about that.'

'About ninety-three million.' Tilda had sprung back to life and was ruffling Frank's hair.

'Very impressive.'

'Very good, Mummy.'

'What would I do without you, Frankie?'

'You'd be OK.'

'No, I would miss you.'

'I'd miss you too, Mummy. Really miss you.'

Tilda went and changed into a tea dress with a small flower print. She was the kind of woman who still looked glamorous in a crisis – wide-eyed and tearful, rather beautiful, like a war widow in the 1940s. I showed them Jed's herb garden that he'd planted in a big terra-cotta pot. Little patches of light green basil and mint. Tilda walked round the labyrinth while I was showing Frank the herbs and we met in the kitchen when it began to rain.

'I feel lighter.'

'Do you really? Or are you saying that because you think that's what you should say?'

'No, I really, really do – it's very strange. Walking around, emptying my mind, was very uplifting.'

'Light like a balloon?' Frank asked. 'Lifting up in the sky?'

'Yes, light like a balloon, just floating into the sky, drifting away.'

'Walk again in the morning – it's just a form of meditation, but easier than the more conventional way, and a labyrinth is such a beautiful thing to have in your garden. Don't you think? I think they should be built in public places; parks, playgrounds, even schools.'

'Yes, very beautiful. Something Tom would never agree to probably, too weird for him.'

Frank went to bed in Maud's room, because he liked the pink walls.

'Do you think he's gay?' Tilda asked as we settled down to bemoan our lives.

'No, I don't think he's gay. Would you mind if he was?'

'No. I just want him to be happy, to do something he really wants to do and to be confident. I want him to feel loved by me, but not smothered.'

I poured us some more Pimm's. 'When I was a little girl,' I confided to Tilda, 'I wanted to be somebody. I wanted to do something very well and be acknowledged for it – I wanted to be a showjumper, because my grand-mother kept horses, and then I wanted to act or be a poet. In my early twenties I remember the disappoint-ment I felt just knowing that I probably wasn't going to be that person, that person who I'd wanted to be.'

Tilda said she'd never wanted to be famous. 'I could never presume that I had a talent,' she said, 'nothing that really stood out. I just wanted to be normal, in a normal relationship. Not like my parents – not like my mother with all her lovers, or my father who lived abroad and seemed to be so lonely. I was one of those women who wanted to marry happily. I knew that Tom and I were not working that well, and that was why I was so eager to set up a business with you. Just driving around looking for property felt so empowering.'

'Do you think that you can just marry the wrong man? Do you think there is such a thing as a right man? One for you?'

'Well, the chances of meeting that right person seem very slim,' she said. 'I mean, it's just so unlikely. Your right man could be living in the suburbs of Paris or the centre of Manhattan. There are four and a half billion people in the world, how can we possibly know whether we have the right one?'

'What I'm trying to say is, is it possible just to be with the wrong man? Or are all relationships difficult and hard work, no matter who you are with?'

'I think it's possible to be with the right man at the wrong time.'

'Yes, I think that's possible,' I said, remembering Hal. 'I was so in love with Hal but he was more interested in his career than me. Do you know the perfect couple?'

Tilda leant back on her chair, so far I was afraid it was going to tip to the floor and crash.

'No.' She returned the chair to its normal position. 'I don't think I know the perfect couple. Well, there is Andy and Charlotte, they lead seemingly perfect lives – but who knows what really goes on?'

'You and Tom looked pretty perfect – I wouldn't have known you were having problems if I hadn't worked with you.'

'Well, I'd say the same about you and Jack. Beautiful house,' she looked around the room, 'lovely garden,' she pointed to the garden, 'happy, sorted children.'

I laughed. 'Maud isn't exactly happy, not all of the time. And Jed is sometimes so profound it worries me.'

'Maud is so cute, so sweet and so cheeky. She's absolutely adorable and Jed has marvellous manners.'

'Thank you. And can I say, Frank is heaven.'

'Frank *is* heaven,' she agreed.

'So will you be all right this weekend when I'm away? You can stay here, if you like.'

'I'll be fine. Frank is going to stay with Tom at our house and I'll stay here, if that's OK.'

'Of course you can. You must stay here and recharge.'

'I promise you, I'll kill Tom if he lets that woman into our house.'

'He won't,' I said, 'he wouldn't do that.'

'I'm not so sure any more. He's like a stranger to me. I feel that he is capable of anything.'

13

'Are you warm enough?' Ruth asked as soon as I'd stepped out of the taxi that had brought me from Southampton station. I'd spent the two hours on the train mostly looking out of the window, wondering why Mark had not responded to the message I'd left him. Probably because I'd said it couldn't go on, but still, of course, I was disappointed that he hadn't at least tried to make me change my mind.

Ruth glanced down at my small, hastily packed suitcase. 'You don't look as though you have enough for two nights.'

'I'm a very clever packer,' I assured her as the children screamed at me in welcome, hurling their small bodies at me, smothering me in hugs. I crouched down to hug them and kissed their faces. It was so good to see them and it seemed frivolous to have left them for a treacherous trip to New York. I covered them with guilty kisses until Maud pushed me away.

'I'll go and make tea. It's all prepared.' Ruth turned towards the kitchen. 'Mind you,' she glanced at her watch, 'it's five o'clock; we thought you'd be here sooner.' She looked immaculate as always, dressed for the seaside in navy slacks and a grey silk shirt. She wore a band of thick pearls round her neck.

'Hello, Petra,' I said as she sloped towards me, towering over Ruth.

'We've been down at the sea all day.'

'How lovely. Did you all go?'

'No, just the children and me.'

'What did Jack do?'

'I think he was reading,' she said in her Germanic, sing-song voice. A little twinge of fury crept through me – the same old gripe because Jack would not spend time with the children, even on holiday.

The children twirled around me. 'Where's my present?' Maud asked.

'Present? Was I meant to bring a present?'

'You always bring presents when you've been away.'

'Aha . . . well, I haven't been away. You've been away. Where's my present?'

'Don't trick me,' Maud said, 'stop tricking me, Mama.'

'I have a present for you,' Jed said, charging up the stairs. He returned a minute later, offering me a white seashell that he'd painted in coloured stripes. 'You lovely, lovely boy.' I kissed the top of his smooth, dark head. 'You angel. I'll treasure it forever.'

'Until you're really old and nearly dead?'

'Even then when I'm nearly dead.'

I gave Maud a beautiful doll from New York, that looked so unreal it was uncanny, and Jed a set of bow and arrows that he had been asking me for.

'Ah, the mother and wife has returned,' Jack shouted from the back door. 'Hip hooray. Come and have tea; we're going to sit in the garden room.'

The garden room was in fact a conservatory that looked across the lawn to the sea beyond. It was furnished in bamboo-style furniture – two armchairs and a small sofa. Magazines were strewn across the floor. One of Ruth's numerous pairs of reading glasses had been left alongside her crossword.

Jack was dressed in 'casual' wear, and casual wear doesn't really suit Jack. He wore jeans that were too new looking and too pressed and a Hawaiian shirt printed with mangoes and pineapples.

'Wow, Jack, that's a crazy shirt, man. I'll have the rum punch.'

'And nice to see you too.'

We embraced. Jack smelt salty and fresh, although combined with a faint aroma of tobacco.

'Here we go.' Petra came in with the tray of tea followed by Ruth who'd put a cardigan with gold buttons over her shirt.

'Weather turning,' Ruth said, although there was no evidence that it was at all.

'Ma, we must get someone to mow the lawn, it's a bit overgrown,' Jack said, tapping something into his new BlackBerry.

'You what?'

'Must get someone in to mow the lawn.'

'Well, you could mow the lawn, couldn't you, Jack?'

'Me?' Jack sneezed theatrically. 'I don't think so, you see, I've got terrible hayfever, can't move with sneezing, and also I've made a date with myself to go running.'

'The amount these people charge for mowing,' Ruth said, 'it's too much.'

'Maybe Petra would do it,' Jack said.

'That's not Petra's job.' I took the cup that Ruth offered me and a slice of pink and yellow Battenberg cake, even though I wasn't at all hungry. 'Anyway, Ruth, I'm sure you could get a boy in for a couple of hours, it's not going to break the bank.' Jack hadn't had hayfever for years — I looked at him and he winked at me as he stood up and left for his jog.

The children were doing a puzzle on the floor, while Ruth had a conversation with me about how well the other grandchildren were doing, particularly Simon, who had won a sports scholarship to a prep school.

'I'll make some more tea,' I said, not wanting to be left alone with Ruth for a minute longer, hearing about the success of my nephews and nieces. I was putting the kettle on when Petra sidled up to me.

'Ellie,' Petra was by my side, twirling her hair with her finger, 'can I go London for the night? Tonight?' She looked pinched and desperate and it was the weekend.

'Yes, of course, Petra, we should have thought of that. Of course you can. Maybe Jack will drive you to the station.'

'Thank you,' she sang out, following me into the low-ceilinged white room that Jack and I would share, which had a sideways view to the sea. 'It's been OK,' she said, 'but it would be good to go out in town.' She stood at the window, looking out.

I put my suitcase down on the bed and Jed came in,

saying he couldn't deal with Maud one minute longer and would I be able to take him to the beach. I sat down on the bed and called Jack on his mobile, interrupting his jog. He answered, breathing heavily into the mobile phone.

'Flying like the wind,' he gasped.

'Good, good – any chance you could take Petra to the station? She wants to go to London.'

'But she's only just got here.'

'Jack, she's been here all week.'

'Well, she can get a taxi. There's some cash in my wallet.'

I relayed what Jack had suggested to Petra and she went to pack a small bag, which obviously contained her size zero clothes.

'She's going in a taxi,' Ruth whispered to me in the kitchen. 'That will be at least thirty pounds.'

'Yes, well, it's Jack's suggestion.'

'Jack has always wasted money, always has.'

'He's a big earner. Well, he's just started earning again and will be a big earner. He can just about afford a taxi.'

'Yes, but he's not a hedge fund manager.'

'No. Thank goodness. I'd never see him.'

'He'd earn a lot more.'

'He does very nicely, Ruth. We're not exactly starving. You should be proud of him.' I switched on the kettle and reached up in the cupboard for two mugs.

'Well, he had a problem paying me back.'

'Yes, but that was a short bad patch. He's now employed fully again, as you know.'

'Oh yes,' she said, 'of course I know. Where is he?'

'He's out jogging.'

'Does she have to go?'

I put two tea bags into a brown functional teapot. 'Who?'

'What's her name? – Nanny. Nice girl, nice and tall.'

'*Petra*, she's been here for a week. Well, yes, she needs time off.'

'It's not as if she's doing much here.'

'Ruth! Who else is looking after the children? You and Jack don't appear to be taking them to the beach or giving them baths.'

'No, such a shame about my arthritis,' she said, 'otherwise I'd be able to look after them.'

'Well, no one expects you to.'

I gave her the tea and took a sip of mine. I'd managed to sit down and have two sips before the children found me and tried to drag me out.

'Mummy, can we go now?' Jed asked.

'Can I come?' Maud asked.

'No, I'm going on my own with Mummy.'

'I want to come.' Maud fell to the ground wailing, kicking her legs against the floor and scratching her hair.

'Jed, we'll all go, darling, and tomorrow I'll take you crabbing.'

'Goody, Mummy.'

'We'll find crabs, hooray,' said Maud.

I took their small hands and left the garden, already stifled by Ruth. Once down on the beach, though, I inhaled the salty, seaweed smell, and my spirits lifted. It was low tide and we ran all the way to where the water lapped. Ruth's house was up on the reddish cliffs surrounded by Monterey and Corsican pine trees; on a very hot day, it was like being in Greece. Terns were stalking along the shore searching for food, a cormorant rested on a blue buoy and a lone egret stood motionless but alert in the brackish waters. The children went off to search for dead crabs and seashells and I stood at the water's edge, thinking of Mark.

Ruth's house was just as a granny's house should be. After leaving London six years before, she'd first rented a very strange house that none of us had liked. Ostensibly it was a lovely Georgian house covered in roses, but really it was awful, surrounded by houses and with a view of a country station car park. She liked it because she'd picked it up for a bargain. There was also the problem of the traffic noise that could be heard from a busy road nearby.

She had moved to her present house just around the time of Jed's fourth birthday. It was a clapboard cottage that she rented off an estate. It was like a child's drawing of a granny cottage, with a white gate, little green grass lawn and a perfectly clean garage.

Ruth had a long-suffering woman called Ellen who came every morning to make her breakfast, put on her laundry, empty the dishwasher and do all the little chores that Ruth wasn't quite sure she could manage. Ruth had met a few other ladies in the area and they played bridge together and sometimes gave each other lunch or dinner. She should have been happy, but there emanated from her a strain of discontent and disappointment that, somehow, nothing was ever quite enough.

I lay down on the sand, which was peppered with tiny pebbles. The sound of the waves rolling back and forth lulled away any murderous feelings I had towards my mother-in-law and my husband. I closed my eyes, listened to the squawks of the gulls and drifted off for a five-minute sleep. I was woken by the sound of Maud barking in my ear like a dog.

On Sunday I suggested a picnic. It should have been easy, a lovely carefree picnic on the beach. A picnic on a gingham cloth laid out on the sand. I cooked eggs and potatoes for a potato salad. We had crisps, fruit and bottles of drink and Jack insisted on driving to the local garage to buy a throwaway barbecue. When he returned he set off with Jed to build the fire, whistling as he went, and I imagined that he felt rather like a Stone Age man going off to kill a bear.

Ruth, Maud and I left half an hour later, after Ruth insisted on changing from one pair of slacks to another and combing her hair, and putting on some make-up and a straw hat, covered by a scarf which she tied under her chin. Who she thought she was going to bump into, I don't know. She had to be helped down the forty or so steps that took us to the beach, which at her slow pace took about ten minutes. Having arrived we found that Jack was not visible through the immense wafts of smoke that engulfed him but we could hear his voice barking instructions at Jed. When we got nearer, we discovered the sausages burnt to hard black lumps on the barbecue.

'What's the smoke?' Ruth asked, waving her arms in front of her. 'There's something on fire.' Her tone was sharp and shrill.

'Something burning, something burning,' yelled Maud, impersonating the sound of a fire engine.

'Sausages are looking a little burnt,' I said.

'Won't harm you,' Jack insisted.

'They do look burnt.' Ruth was poking them.

'They won't kill you,' Jack yelled at his mother as she peered at them. 'We're at a bloody barbecue, not dining in a Michelin-starred restaurant.'

We sat down on the pebbly sand. Maud opened the box of hard-boiled eggs and promptly dropped it; all the peeled eggs fell on to the sand, rolling away like snowballs gathering grit. Jack shouted at her and she burst into tears, then I shouted at Jack for shouting at Maud and both the children burst into tears. I retrieved the eggs and poured precious mineral water over them, hoping to wash away the sand, but it was stuck stubbornly like glue. 'Shit,' Jack shouted as he burnt his hand on the barbecue. He wandered off down the beach, his body, his arms and his legs moving at a furious rate. Ruth tapped me on the shoulder and asked me two or three times what was wrong with him. The last disaster was that we'd for-gotten plates and knives, and a bottle opener for the cold bottles of beer that Jack wanted when he'd returned from his walk.

After the picnic I rushed in and out of the sea with the children, running away from the waves as they chased us on to the shore. They loved that game, particularly Maud, who made me do it again and again until I wanted to scream.

It was late afternoon when we returned to the house, laden down with plastic bags of rubbish, the disposable barbecue, sodden towels and sandy clothes. Jack grumbled and mumbled about how much more stuff there was to take home than there had been to take to the beach. He was tetchy when I used duck eggs for the children's supper and I accused him of being grumpy and depressing and we had another row in front of the children, which made Jed cry again.

'You're always rowing.' Jed got up from the table and ran out. I ran after him but he shrugged me off and shut the door to his bedroom.

'What's going on?' Ruth was watching television with the sound up very high.

'Nothing, don't you worry. Jed's a little upset, that's all. I have to go and see him.'

'Shall I go?' Ruth asked, rather sweetly.

'No.' I rushed up after Jed. He was sitting on his bed no longer crying. 'Jed, darling, I'm really sorry. Please don't be angry with us.'

'You and Dad don't see us very much and when you do see us you argue.'

'We won't argue any more. I promise you. Please come down.'

Jed followed me down the stairs and I sat next to him as he ate the rest of his food.

Later, as I was scraping plates into the rubbish, Jack

confided that he couldn't stand another minute with his mother and that he would be driving me up to London that evening. He said he could use a meeting with Eden and he had a couple of days free with no rehearsals. The children would stay with Granny for one night until Petra returned. Later in the week, Jack and the children and Petra would move to the rented house and I was going to join them for the following bank holiday weekend, go back to the café for two or three days and then spend the final week of the holidays in the country. The children were upset that I was leaving again, particularly Jed. I promised that I would telephone him in the morning and when I kissed the children goodbye Maud began to cry, which made me cry too.

We arrived home very late on Sunday night, leaving the piles of suitcases, crisp packets, water bottles and sandwich wrappers in the hall. It was strange to come home without the children, quiet and a little sad. I was stewing a herbal tea bag when I found the note from Tilda:

> Gone home – you are so kind, thank you very much. Took the problem man's advice and having a flirt. See you tomorrow.

Having a flirt? Who could she be having a flirt with? What could have happened? My immediate reaction was one of astonishment. It seemed a bit worrying that she had turned from desperate betrayed housewife to dynamic diva so fast.

Jack was settling in to watch one of his American dramas, shoes off, feet up, armed with a glass of wine and a cigarette. I said goodnight and went to bed, alone again. I undressed in the bathroom then went into my bedroom and peeked through the curtains. The lights in Mark's room were on. He was there. Just across the road. Probably climbing into bed, reading a book and turning off the light. Maybe, I mused wistfully, he was thinking of me.

Jack was on a new and very complicated diet. He had put on a little weight and wanted to lose it before filming began. The production company had put him in touch with a nutritionist who had written out a special meal plan. Breakfast included four tablespoons of porridge, two apricots, a handful of raisins, a spoonful of flax seeds, two vitamin B pills and a glass of freshly squeezed juice. He was also allowed one cup of tea with semi-skimmed milk and half a piece of granary toast with nut butter. So breakfast was now an event that took at least forty-five minutes instead of the usual five. Jack spread the newspaper over the entire table, so that with his food and his papers, my corner of the table was literally that, a tiny corner.

He showed me photographs of the house he had rented until the end of September with an option to keep it on if we moved away from London. It looked huge, though Jack said we would only have one wing of it. There was a swimming pool and a tennis court to share, and a garden of pine trees and hydrangeas. The master bedroom had a balcony and looked out to sea, the children would share a room and there was a small room for Petra.

'Well done, Jack, it looks wonderful,' I said, peering at the rather dubious carpet on the living-room floor, 'but don't you think I should look at it before you sign?'

'I have signed.'

'Jack!'

'You weren't here. You've been in New York, in the café, God knows where you've been.'

There was a tone in his voice that warned me not to go on. I didn't want him to ask me too many questions.

'Well done, darling.' I kissed the top of his head. 'You are brilliant.' Jack went out to the car on a hunt for his mobile.

Petra was by the door waiting to return to the country and I was on my way out when she said, 'That handsome man was here when I arrived on Saturday night.'

'Really?' I tensed and then, attempting to sound casual and nonchalant, asked, 'Which one?'

'Isn't he the neighbour?'

'Was he looking for me?'

'I don't know.' She was hovering by the door now, impatient to leave. 'He was having a drink with Tilda.'

'Having a drink with Tilda?' My heart rate quickened. 'What, in this house?'

'Yes, right here.' She swung her bag over her shoulder. Jack had arrived with his briefcase and was ready to take her to the station. I waved them goodbye in a carefree manner but a wave of shock cramped and tautened my chest and stomach.

I had not smoked for a few years but after they had left I scrambled through Jack's study searching for cigarettes. I opened and shut his drawers, looked in the boxes on his desk and finally found one in a jacket hanging in the hall cupboard. I lit the cigarette and on the way to work drove far too fast, and tapped the wheel as the traffic lights turned to red. I buzzed the windows up and down, desperately anxious and short of breath. At one point, unable to bear the tension, I nearly stopped the car to telephone Tilda.

I reached the café half an hour before it opened. The shut sign swung in the window. I unlocked the door; there was a lone fly buzzing at the window. I knew that Tilda would be down in the kitchen heating up the croissants and pastries because Andy was taking a short break in Spain. I walked down the narrow stairs to the hot basement kitchen.

'Hi, Tilda.' I kissed her. My voice sounded unnaturally high and a little strangled.

'Hello.' She came forward to greet me. 'Thank you so much for letting me stay. It was like being on holiday.'

I rummaged in the industrial-sized fridge, waiting for her to tell me about the note she'd left, saying she'd had a flirt with someone, but she was asking me about the weekend.

'I got your note. About flirting,' I said clumsily, after we had briefly discussed my visit to Ruth's.

'Note? Oh yes. A gorgeous man turned up at the door on Friday night after you'd gone. He looked so familiar, but I just couldn't think where I'd seen him. He wanted

300

to walk around the labyrinth.' Tilda was tipping out the croissants into a big basket.

'My neighbour?' My chest was banging; it was hard to breath.

'Yeah, the guy who lives across the road.' Tilda swept a clutch of warm croissants into a box. 'In retrospect, I shouldn't have let him in. He could have been anyone; but he was so charming.'

I twirled my hair round my finger. 'He's very charming and so good-looking.'

'So good-looking,' Tilda was whirling the salad around in a salad cleaner, 'so good-looking.'

We started to make the salads, washing the rocket and the lettuce, cutting up tomatoes, slicing the Parma ham and figs, washing fruit and making sandwiches.

'Did he walk round the labyrinth?' I was slicing some wholemeal baguettes, trying to keep my tone light and conversational, rather than panic-stricken and desperate.

'Well, we walked towards it, but he didn't actually walk round it.' Tilda was boiling some free-range eggs to make one of our popular sandwich fillings.

'Is he —' I hardly dared ask, but I had to — 'is he the man you had the flirtation with?'

She smiled. 'Yes. We had a drink together that evening.'

'Where?'

'At his house.'

'The house with the rustic kitchen and the photographs all over the walls? Number forty-six?'

'Yes, that's the one. Anyway, we drank vodka and ate a Lebanese takeaway on the floor of the sitting room. After supper we played backgammon. I went home quite late and the next morning he turned up for breakfast.'

'Just turned up?' He obviously had a thing about turning up at people's houses. I remembered when he'd turned up at mine, the day that Lorrie and Alice had left.

'Yes. I wanted to tell you about it. I tried to call you the night before, but the phone just went straight to answer machine.'

'Yes, there's no signal down there. I should have left you the landline.' I heaved the box of croissants to the bottom of the stairs.

'Anyway, he'd brought over some fruit and we sat in the garden.'

'Did he kiss you?'

'Well,' she blushed, 'I'm getting to that, well, yes he did.'

I let the warm tears flow down my face.

'Ellie! What's the matter?'

I sat down on the steps. 'Do you remember the day a man came into the café and I told you he was a colleague of Jack's?'

'I do remember vaguely.'

'It was Mark, my neighbour. I've been seeing him. It didn't amount to anything more than a weekend but, well, I know it sounds strange, but I fell for him. I left a message saying I didn't want to see him again, but only because I was afraid of hurting Jack and the children. He knew I had a friend staying, I told him, but he came over anyway.'

'*No!*' she exclaimed. 'You were seeing him? And he kissed me too?'

'Yes, but it's over. It's definitely over now. What a shit.'

'Ellie, I had no idea, I had no idea – I was over there last night. He said he was leaving today.'

'You were over there last night?'

'Yes.'

'Did you stay the night?'

'Nearly. But I didn't. I still feel married to Tom, even though he's having an affair.'

'I just don't believe it.' I wiped my eyes with a napkin.

'My God, Ellie, you listened to me going on about the bitch who was seeing my husband and you didn't say anything.'

'No. How could I? I'm married and your husband is having an affair. I just felt guilty and tainted. I thought you'd disapprove. Well, you do disapprove.'

She turned away from me and walked over to the fridge, where she took out a bottle of milk. She paused in the open door and for a moment I was afraid she would slam the door and walk out on me.

She switched the kettle on and reached for our stash of herbal teas.

'I know what can happen. Look at me, I kissed a stranger, but that's probably only because Miles suggested I flirt with a man to forget about Tom. But why did you do it?' She offered me a cup of tea and I accepted a ginger and lemon.

'It's really hard to explain. Jack is either so depressed

or so full of himself and there is nothing in between. I met Mark and he seduced me.'

'Do you think Jack suspects?' she whispered in one of her theatrical stage whispers and I knew then that she wasn't going to judge me too harshly.

'No, he doesn't.'

'Well, that's lucky,' she said. 'I'm sorry too. I had no idea. I knew I was being reckless, but when Miles said it would be therapeutic to flirt, I just went ahead with the first man who seemed interested. He was right. It seemed to take my mind off things. And I didn't know it was someone that you had been seeing. You never said anything.'

'No, I couldn't.'

'It sounds like we're both well out of it. Who needs a man like that?'

I wiped the salad bowl and then wiped it again. 'I just don't understand,' I said. 'He took me to New York. There was real passion between us, or at least I thought there was.'

Tilda gasped; with one hand on the salad spinner she turned to me, visibly shocked. 'When? That weekend you needed a break? When you told me you were going to a trade fair?'

'Yes. I'm sorry I lied. I was just madly swept up in it all. We were really taken with each other. That's why I just can't believe he would attempt to seduce a friend of mine. It doesn't ring true. I feel like such an idiot to have invested in him; even for a weekend.' We walked upstairs.

'Yes, but don't forget he's a married man with a six-month-old child and that didn't stop him having an affair.'

'True.'

At that moment a mother entered the café with three children in tow.

We trailed around each other for the rest of the day, too busy to have more than snatched conversations. There was part of me that resented Tilda for inviting a man she didn't know into my house. If, as she claimed, she didn't recognize him, then why had she let him in? He could have been a potential burglar, staking out my house, eyeing up our valuable art. And why didn't she recognize him as the man who practically stalked me at the café? After all, she had given me those knowing, curious looks. And maybe she would carry on seeing him secretly; maybe Mark had fallen for her.

As we were leaving that afternoon, she suggested that we should have a drink together. It seemed like a good idea, partly because I wanted to persuade her further that Mark had behaved really badly. We stopped in St John's Wood on the way home, at a restaurant that had a back bar and served dim sum snacks.

The staff were off-hand to a point of rudeness and the other clientele were mostly loud men, with rolled-up sleeves, already drinking quite hard. After my first drink I moved closer to Tilda. 'I almost loved him, you know. I thought there was something between us.'

She took a sip of her drink. 'You know what? He probably just used me to get at you, because he thought you were ending it.'

'Do you think so?' I was so happy that she'd said it, I could have kissed her.

'Maybe.'

I took a bite of a steamed scallop dim sum. 'The other thing is that he's not really officially separated from his wife. She only left a few weeks ago, but she wants to come back and work it out.'

'Really? God, he made it sound like he was separated, officially. What an operator. What a bastard.'

'Maybe he genuinely fancied both of us,' I suggested, cheered to hear her call him a bastard.

'Well, he hasn't telephoned me today,' Tilda said, 'and if he does, I won't respond. I feel like such a freak.'

Later that evening I parked near the house and walked home, head down, not wanting to bump into Mark. On the other hand, there was part of me that wanted to find him, just to ask what the hell he had been doing. I almost ran down the small slope of our street, looking straight ahead, but at the last minute, just before I opened the door, I furtively glanced up and down. The street was empty, except for a fat orange cat slinking along a wall.

Jack was cooking fish. He wore an apron and was flushed with the effort.

'Well, hello,' he greeted me, kissing me on the top of my head. 'Isn't it just great to be here without the children?'

'Yes,' I said, looking around vaguely as though everything might have changed. I paused for a minute to consider. 'Yes, I suppose it is.'

'You all right?'

'Yes – well, no. I didn't have a particularly good day at work.'

He took me by the hand, led me to the garden, sat me down in a chair and gave me a glass of water. 'There you go. You relax – I'm making dinner tonight.'

'What's the occasion?'

'Just that we're not going to be seeing each other much over the next week and I kind of wanted to say goodbye.'

'That's so kind of you, Jack, I appreciate that.'

I sat in the garden on the dirty deckchair and closed my eyes. I remembered making love to Mark in the shower with the water gushing over our heads, and waves of desire rolled through me. I saw us having breakfast at the café and recalled the thrill of sitting so close to him. I remembered his passionate speech at the charity dinner and the way he had found me with his eyes as he walked down the stairs of the platform.

'I was just thinking, Ellie –' Jack was pouring me a glass of wine – 'we haven't really been getting on for a while now, so why don't we just call a truce?' He looked so kindly and comical in his white apron. He took me in his arms and I began to cry.

He lifted my head away.

'What on earth is the matter?'

'It's just, I don't know …' I said, suddenly feeling so tired. 'I just … well, Jack, I have something to tell you.'

'I'll be right back, I just have to check my potatoes.'

He turned away from me and I wondered if he had an inkling of what I wanted to confess, but had decided that he didn't want to hear. It was probably best not to say anything to him. Maybe he knew, but didn't want me to say. I didn't want to hurt him and what was the point? We had everything to lose. I remembered lying by a pool at the Colombe d'Or near Nice, celebrating Jack's birthday just before he lost the part as Dr Granger. I was sunbathing after an exquisite lunch on their covered terrace and Jack had walked passed me and said, 'Ellie, you must get out of the sun now, you're going to get burnt.'

It was not a hugely interesting thing to say, but it was significant as it made me realize how lucky I was to be married. There was finally someone in my life who cared enough about me to tell me to get out of the sun. No one, not even my mother, had ever told me that I'd had enough sun.

'What's the matter?' He came back with a cheese biscuit covered in cod's roe. 'What did you want to tell me?'

The telephone rang and he went to pick up the receiver. He was talking to Eden; I could tell from the slightly confiding but slightly jokey way he spoke to her. 'That's marvellous,' he enthused in conclusion, 'absolutely bloody marvellous, you're so clever, well done.'

Jack got off the telephone and poured himself a glass of wine, muttering under his breath.

'What's up?' I asked. He told me that Eden had had lunch with the literary agent she was affiliated with and that she had been selling the idea of a biography about Jack.

'God knows what there is to say about me. Can you think?'

I had been on the verge of confessing my sin but didn't want to hurt him. He'd never admitted to me that he'd been adulterous, but I was sure he had been and kept it from me.

'Ready for dinner?' Jack beamed at me.

'Never been more ready, and can I say I'm really pleased that we're not going to have it on our laps in front of some film warped with blood and guts.'

'Me too.' He shook out a large linen napkin and placed it over his lap.

'Oh, Jack,' I said, 'this is delicious, really, really good.' I spooned a little salmon into my mouth and then a prawn. 'Thank you.'

We talked about what the children would do in the large house by the sea and reminisced about our childhood holidays. There was the time my parents had taken a holiday in a large windy house in Scotland, near Aberdeen. We had walked in the pine forests and played near a lake and been allowed to run wild. 'I'd like the children to feel free and be able to roam on to the beach with their bicycles,' I said, inspired by the memory.

'But Maud is only three; she doesn't ride a bicycle.'

'No, but she's a grown-up three. She's three going on five.'

'Life would be wonderful in the country,' Jack said. 'Why don't you come and live with me in Hampshire?' He had tucked the napkin into his shirt and looked like a pleading little boy.

'Oh, Jack.' I stabbed a piece of sea bream and oven-roasted potato with my fork. 'We've been through all of that. What would I do about the children's schools? It's all a bit late now.'

'Your marriage doesn't seem that important to you.' Jack finished eating. He poured himself another glass of wine and flung off his napkin. He sounded concerned rather than cross.

'It is important, of course it is. I love you and the children. But I can't give up the café; it's only just begun. We're starting to make money. We have another good review coming out in a local magazine. And, Jack, the children are staying with me. I couldn't bear to live apart from them; it would tear me to pieces.' Jack's face crumpled. 'I will look into schools down there. Just in case. OK?' I said, wanting to soothe him.

Jack paced around and lit a cigarette.

'Lots of other couples have weekend relationships; couldn't we? Hannah Cullwick and Arthur Munby didn't live with each other for twenty years but still managed to have a relationship. And Pauline advised me that it's a really good thing to have space from each other.'

'I don't give a toss about Arthur Munby and Hannah Cullwick, it's going to be so sodding lonely. And John and Pauline ... what's so good about them?'

'They have a great relationship. I think that living apart will invigorate our marriage. We won't be on top of each other.'

'Ah, but you may be on top of someone else.' Jack laughed wholeheartedly at his own joke. I didn't respond by saying, 'Actually, I was – ha ha.'

'I promise to talk to Tilda about the weekends. We've

got this girl Arletta now, we should be able to work something out.'

'Do you still love me?' he asked without a hint of humour. He had never asked this question before and it made me feel sorry for him.

'Yes, I do.' I went over and kissed the top of his head. He pulled me into his lap.

I stayed on his lap for a while, knowing that this was an important moment in our marriage. Jack was really trying to reach out to me, to talk to me, to somehow heal and move forward, but all I could think about was how fickle and untrue Mark was and how much that hurt. It had been stupid to drop everything and risk my marriage to go off to New York. I stretched and sat up.

'Jack, don't worry about us. We'll work everything out. I'm sorry for being distracted and preoccupied; there are just a few problems at the café.'

I went up to bed knowing that I should have stayed with Jack and talked more, reassured him, but I was just too fragile and upset, and somehow tainted and untrue. I needed time.

The next morning, after Jack had kept me up all night snoring, I thought about Mark again. It seemed so extraordinary that he would attempt to seduce my friend days after declaring love for me; it didn't seem right. He must have known how much that would hurt. While Jack was having his breakfast I cried in the shower and prayed that there was no chance I could be pregnant. Jack would never behave like that; for all Jack's faults he was a good man and, generally, I had a good marriage that deserved more love and attention.

But I wanted to see Mark and confront him. Just before I left for the café I crossed the road with a thumping heart. I tentatively stretched out my hand to push the bell and then quickly retrieved it. I stretched my hand out again and gently pushed the bell. Then I waited. And waited. No one came to the door. I peered through the shuttered windows – the sitting room was in darkness.

14

A few days later, just before the August bank holiday weekend, I was working in the café. Tilda had taken Frank to Italy. Tom had apparently begged to come with her but she had said that she needed time alone. The café was very quiet. It was ten o'clock and I'd only served two 'eat in' customers and three who had come in for takeaways. The door to the street was open as it was extremely hot and still. We had one fan blowing that seemed overwhelmed by the amount of heat it had to cool down and as a result only a small area of the room was cool. I fanned myself with a menu and fiddled with the layout of the sand-wiches, which were already wilting. The minutes ticked by so slowly that I kept watching the clock and yawning.

At about eleven, Miles, the problem letter man, arrived. I could have kissed him. He ordered a full English break-fast. My cooking skills had slightly improved but I still managed to burn the bacon and couldn't always get my fried eggs not to bubble and harden around the edges. After several minutes, I took the breakfast upstairs to him.

I nearly dropped the plate before I reached the table. There, sitting on his own at the table nearest the open door, was Mark. The sight of him still managed to make me tremble and ripple inside with fluttery nerves. He smiled at me. I delivered the plate to Miles, managed to smile when he made a joke about my cooking skills and then approached Mark's table.

'Hello, stranger!' He smiled up at me.

'What can I get you?' I asked coldly, but melting inside at the sight of him before me in a navy T-shirt.

'Just a coffee. I'm really here to talk to you.'

I edged away from the table and back behind the counter to make the coffee. We had a habit of putting homemade ginger biscuits on the saucers of the coffee cups, but rather spitefully I didn't put one on his. I placed the coffee on his table and then swiftly moved to Miles to clear away his cup.

'Thanks, doll,' Miles said, taking a last bite of egg and bacon. 'How much do I owe you?'

'Sure you don't want anything else? We've got a wonderful batch of almond cookies or some cheese and onion croissants?'

'No thanks, love, normally would stay, but I've got a meeting with my accountant in town.' He looked at his watch. 'Actually, I'm going to be late as it is.'

'OK.' I gave him the bill and he paid with a good tip. We said goodbye and I was left alone, secluded in my café with Mark.

'Sorry I haven't been in touch, I've been away.'

'Really?'

He pulled out a chair for me and – not wanting to be rude – I sat down.

'Yes. I picked up half a long message on my mobile and thought it best to leave you alone. Anyway, I had a short business trip to Brussels and Paris.'

'But you still had time to see my friend?'

'Friend?'

'Yes, my friend. One of my best friends; my business partner, Tilda.'

'Tilda?'

'Oh, don't play this stupid game with me.' A surge of anger was rising in my chest. 'In fact, I'd rather you left now.' I stood up. 'You don't need to pay.'

'But, hey ... Ellie, wait, I ...'

Two women came into the café – a rather beautiful, well-groomed woman in her sixties and her less well-groomed daughter – and a little boy wearing a Viking hat. The family sat down at a table and I brought the boy a colouring pad and a box of colours. I took their order and went off to fetch their sandwiches.

When I came back, thankfully, Mark was gone.

I had so desperately wanted to talk it through with him, but when it came to it, when he completely denied that he'd even heard of Tilda, my love for him waned. Soon after he'd gone, I found a note he'd left me, scribbled on the back of an envelope.

Don't know what you mean about friend, please
let's speak.
Love, Mark

'Oh, for God's sake,' I said out loud, ripping the message up and throwing it away.

I swept the floor and cleaned the kitchen with the help of Arletta. We were closing for the bank holiday weekend and I was due down in the country to see the children. I froze all the food that I was able to freeze and threw away the rest. I emptied the bins and secured the door.

Driving home that afternoon, I wondered how Mark could be so shallow and callous, and why lie? I was remorseful and ashamed at how I had even considered straying from my marriage. I was going to become the perfect wife, a super spouse, a domestic goddess. I would love Jack again. I had been in love with him once; surely I could be in love with him again? I would compromise and be more positive. Perhaps I would even move down to the country and commute to London.

We had invited Annie and Marco for the weekend and I was going to pick them up.

Annie was all ready, smock top over tight trousers, red handbag and green suitcase. Marco stood with his arm round her, waiting on the doorstep. They really were so damned happy, how did they manage it? What was the secret?

Marco decided that he would drive. I moved into the back.

'What is the secret to your relationship?' I asked them both after we had reached the motorway. 'You've been together how long?'

'Thirteen years.' Annie turned round.

'Can I just say,' Marco said, 'it's not all perfect.'

'Yes, of course that's true,' Annie said. 'And we have both made a decision not to have children so we don't have all the stress that goes with them. That's one thing.'

'Yes,' Marco agreed, 'I never wanted children.'

'Why?'

'It's hard to say. Maybe because I was quite an unhappy child. I was very short, much shorter than my friends, so I didn't like rough games and my parents never got on very well.'

'Oh God, that's like Jed. He's much smaller than his friends.'

'Ah, but hey, look at me now – handsome, creative, I'm OK.' He laughed.

Even though Annie was one of my best friends, someone I could really rely on, we had never sat down and had a proper discussion about why she had decided not to have children. I didn't want to touch on the subject too hard, because I just presumed, as a mother and wife, that most women, somewhere deep down, wanted to have children. But during the road trip, Annie just began to talk. She confided that she had really known that she hadn't wanted children from a very young age. 'I liked playing with dolls, elaborate games that involved dressing them in weird clothes that I would make for them, but I was also a bit of a tomboy and thought girls a bit wet.' She handed me a packet of crisps.

'I just knew that I would have children some day, but maybe I was conditioned from a really young age to believe that was true,' I said.

'The problem with me,' Annie said, 'is that I have a weirdly powerful memory. It drives me mad sometimes. I remember too much. I remember being a newborn child myself and being stuck in an incubator with this awful humming noise that hurt my ears. I just remember the frustration and pain of being a powerless baby. Wanting the noise to stop and not being able to make it stop.'

Marco laughed. 'You sound really crazy when you say that.'

'I know. I can't expect anyone to believe me but it's true.' She was filing her nails with a large pink emery board.

'Are you sure it's not just something that you imagine you remember?'

'No . . . I really remember it.' She passed me a bottle of water. 'When we first met we talked about having children and we decided that if we *did* have children, we wouldn't really want someone else taking care of them. And at the time, both our careers were taking off. Marco began to start travelling all over the place and I was just so busy designing two or three collections a year. There wasn't time to have children.'

As we drove along, I wondered if Jack and I would have survived without our children. Of course, there were marriages where people remained as couples without children, and Marco and Annie certainly seemed to have a strong relationship. But often, when I'd wanted to walk out of the house and disappear from Jack's life, the thought of our bewildered children had stopped me. It would be true to say though that our relationship had stopped being romantic after Jed was born. We bickered and bitched, and fought about who was going to get up in the night.

'Other women, mothers, can be quite hostile towards

me,' Annie said, as we stopped to look at a map. 'Either hostile or full of pity, it's very strange. Some people assume that I want children but for some tragic reason I am unable to. People think that women without children aren't whole.'

'God, I had no idea,' I said. 'How awful for you.'

'Then of course there is my father. Whenever we speak on the phone, he says, "Pregnant?" He truly believes that a woman will not be happy and fulfilled unless she is barefoot and pregnant.'

'But he is a banker,' Marco said. 'He wanted Annie to live in the country and marry someone like him and have three children and make porridge and pasta. He didn't want someone like me. A man who came from Rome and was a student until the age of twenty-eight.'

'Well, she's lucky to have you, Marco. And you are lucky to have her.'

We arrived quite late at the house that I had only seen in a brochure. It was a large, rambling Georgian house, flying a flag of St George from the roof. We drove through a gate and up a wide gravel driveway and parked next to a Land Rover that Jack had been using as part of the rental deal. As soon as we stepped out of the car some yapping, barking dogs – two Labradors and a large, black mongrel – gathered around us.

There was a hallway with corridors that led off in different directions. Annie, Marco and I clustered together, dumping our suitcases on the black and white large-tiled floor. There was a magnificent fireplace in the hallway, with a marble mantelpiece above. Paraded on the mantelpiece were a couple of lavender plants.

I had no idea where to go and called out Jack's name. No one came. I called again and my voice echoed.

Marco went to investigate and returned with a man who introduced himself as George, the caretaker of the house. George was about eighty and slightly stooped. He wore immaculate tweed trousers and braces over a checked shirt. He spoke with a slight country drawl but made no effort to charm us with a smile.

He led us to Jack, who was sitting in a large open-plan kitchen living-room area. 'They're here,' George announced.

'Hurray!' Jack said. 'Drinks all round.' Annie and Jack embraced. Marco shook his hand. I hugged Jack and kissed Ruth, who was standing by the oven.

'I've put a fish pie in the Aga. Well, Guy put it in; it's very heavy.'

'Thank you,' I said, stooping down to look at it. 'That's very good of you.'

'What was that?'

'Nothing.'

'It's been in forty minutes,' she said, 'five to go.'

'Great. Thank you.'

'Well, you've just arrived, you can't be expected to make dinner as well,' she laughed.

'No, I'm not a very good cook, as you know.'

'We know that. Although I have to say I'm not a good cook either. Don't know where Guy gets it from.'

'Maybe because you didn't like cooking, he decided to

master it. By the way, you weren't meant to agree that I was a really bad cook.'

'What was that, dear?'

'You weren't meant to agree that I wasn't a very good cook.'

'Yes, I like a good book.'

The effort of explaining seemed too hard and exhausting. I asked if her bedroom was all right and she replied that she felt there was something wrong with the heater. Nothing was ever good enough for Granny. I followed her to a downstairs bedroom, where there was a small double bed covered in a tartan rug. 'I just wanted a word with you,' she said, straightening the rug on the bed, 'about Guy.'

'Jack?'

'Yes, Guy.'

'Jack. I can't think of him as Guy. I've never known him as Guy.'

'Well, Guy is feeling a little sad about you both.'

The scenario that was playing out was already reminding me of when I was thirteen and my best friend's mother reprimanded me for no longer being friendly with her daughter. It had seemed too difficult at the time to explain that I had moved on from our friendship, which was about putting on plays of Cinderella and dressing up in our mothers' old clothes.

'We've had a few problems,' I said, walking towards a small and uncomfortable-looking chair and sitting down, 'but, you see, I think it's something we need to work out together.'

'I'm just talking as a mother here. I can see that Guy is upset. He feels you are neglecting the family and only interested in work. I know you love the children, I told him so.'

'But work is all he's interested in,' I protested, standing up again. 'He's only interested in work and cooking for friends.'

'But he's a man. So it's different.'

'Things have moved on. Women do work as hard or if not harder than men, but thank you for recognizing that I love the children. Of course I do.'

Ruth was patting her hair and putting on some lipstick. 'He's just sad, Ellie, sad and saddened. However modern life is now, men still like to feel that a woman can stay at home and support the family.'

'What exactly has he said to you?'

'Not very much; I am his mother though, I know what's going on.'

I walked towards the door. 'I'm really sorry if I've hurt your son in any way, but please believe me, it's not easy being married to Jack.'

'Marriage is not easy.' She followed me.

'You should know,' I muttered.

'What was that, dear?'

'Nothing . . . Thanks.'

'Promise to think about it,' she urged me. 'I must say, it's a bit cold in this house. Could you make sure the plates are hot at dinner?'

Jack was playing backgammon with Marco. Annie had gone down to the beach with Maud and Jed. I had planned to take Jack for a little walk and talk to him about us, about our future, and about how sorry I was that he'd felt neglected, but that evening the opportunity never arose. Annie went upstairs to bed, while Jack and Marco sat down together to watch a film on television. Ruth also went to bed with three books and three magazines.

'I don't get much sleep these days,' she told me. 'I nod off at about three and wake again at five. I don't like ageing, I can't bear growing old. Believe me, there are no benefits to getting older, none at all.'

'Sounds awful.'

'Yes, not much fun. Now if you don't mind, I'll just look for my brush and get myself ready.'

I left, closed the door behind me and sneezed into the torn tissue I had stuffed into my pocket. The corridors seemed very narrow, the house smelt musty. I opened the door to the small enclosed courtyard outside the wing of our section of the house.

Petra stood in the middle of the courtyard, smoking.

'Petra, how are you?' She looked as though she had been crying.

'Not so good,' she said. 'Happy to be with kids but still very sad about Felipe.'

'Has he been in touch with you?'

'Touch me?'

'Has he telephoned you? Sent you a card?'

'No. I really thought he loved me. It is very strange.' She stubbed her cigarette out, left it rolling under her foot. 'Well, I say goodnight to the children.'

'There will be many other men,' I said to her retreating back. 'Many others.'

She turned round. 'What?'

'Nothing, it doesn't matter. But if I looked like you, I wouldn't be worried. You'll find someone else.'

'Yes,' she shrugged, 'but not like him. He is special ... different.'

I walked out through the courtyard and across a drive and opened a door that led to a walled garden. There was a scarecrow with a painted plate for a head and yellow wool for hair, and a broomstick turned on its side for arms. It was darkly comic and a little eerie. I sat down on a wooden bench and gazed at the rows and rows of lettuce, tomato and other unidentifiable vegetables. Did I genuinely love Mark? Or was I looking for a distraction? Before I met Jack my height of excitement was walking out of the baggage hall at an airport into the arrival hall packed with waiting people, who all glanced at me for a mere second. My life was quite dull. After years of walking up red carpets with Jack and attending film premières, I had become weary, even blasé; glamour no longer excited me. The idea of someone real, someone good and worthy and handsome like Mark, was attractive. But he didn't want me.

I was asleep when Jack came to bed and up before he was in the morning to make breakfast for Annie and Marco. I was grateful when Marco decided that he would cook breakfast, mushrooms on toast. The mushrooms were cooked in butter and garlic, with a little lemon squeezed on top.

We had been invited to a local drinks party and Jack had accepted the invitation, having met the hostess at the farm shop. 'It's not so bad,' Jack said when he saw me pull a face, 'just next door. It will be fun, Ellie. You may have fun!'

'They only asked us because you're Jack Boore.'

'Oh, who cares.' He put his arm round me and squeezed me. 'It takes years to be accepted in the country. She told me that the weekenders from London are known as DFTs – Down From Town – and it sounded rather derogatory.' He was right, I supposed; sometimes in life, if you wanted to get on, get going, it was best to exploit your connections. Jack was my connection; the woman would not have invited me if she'd bumped into me at the farm shop.

After breakfast we played cricket with the children. Jed's white, thin legs were spindly under his large black shorts. He wore a football T-shirt and a baseball cap. He looked so small. He *was* so small. When he worried that he was the smallest in his class I tried to quell his fears by telling him he would definitely grow. He would grow suddenly as Jack had. Jack was a competitive dad and in no way made concessions for the fact that Jed was only six. He bowled him really fast balls and hit the bat really hard when Jed bowled to him. He only just managed to slow his bowl down for Maud and when she began to cry because she couldn't hit the ball, he ordered her off the pitch.

At twelve Jack went off to make a Bloody Mary and I followed, hoping to have a chat with him; but I was waylaid by Maud who said she was hungry and needed lunch. I took her by the hand to the kitchen and made her a sandwich.

'I want egg sandwich,' she demanded.

'Oh God, Maud, can't you have something simple like cucumber or Marmite?'

'No, I want egg.'

Jack came in to find a bottle of Worcester sauce. 'You indulge that child. It's guilt,' he said, 'for not spending the holiday with her.'

'Jack!' He was leaving the kitchen. 'We need to talk at some point before I have to go back to London.'

'When are you going back?' He turned round.

'Monday evening. In the bank holiday traffic.'

'Well, we've got time. We've got the rest of today and tomorrow and Monday, haven't we? We can talk at the party.'

There was a palpable distance between Jack and me; it had been building up and now it was setting. He seemed preoccupied and avoided my eye. I think he felt I had rejected him when he had reached out for me in London and wanted to talk. He was not affectionate towards me (I didn't count the squeeze as affection) and he only seemed to want to talk to me after he'd had a few drinks. We had never been quite so detached from each other and the situation was bleak and a little alarming.

We sat in the front of the house at a table between some pine trees and drank our Bloody Marys and ate some cheese and biscuits. Marco made some mini pizzas and we ate those too and then played frisbee and left

326

for the party far too late, leaving the children with Petra.

We walked down the beach to the party and found the guests milling around the garden, on a terrace in a large conservatory and in a pale-grey drawing room. We followed Jack to find the hostess, who greeted us and introduced me to a man, Ben de Venton, who was in the middle of a deep and earnest conversation. A crowd of women had surrounded Jack. I stood by Ben de Venton and his companion for a few minutes, but they made no attempt to draw me into their conversation, so I excused myself, saying that I was going to find a drink, and wound my way to the terrace where Ruth was sitting on her own at the table.

'Awful din,' she moaned. 'I find it so difficult to hear when there are so many people.' I sat down next to her and stretched out my legs. We drank our champagne and fresh orange juice and looked out to sea.

'There is something I must say.' She pulled the silk scarf that was tied under her chin. I fiddled with a bowl of peanuts, dreading the worst. 'I spoke to you yesterday because I'd like it to work out between you and Guy, or Jack as you call him. As you know, Guy's father and I separated when Guy was about the same age as Jed, and it was terrible. It's awful being alone with a small child and I really don't want you to be in the same position as I was.'

'Why?' I asked. 'Has Jack – Guy – said he wants to separate?'

'You must talk to him,' she said, wiping the sides of her mouth with a napkin. 'I'm in no position to be speaking for him. I don't think he's said as much, but he's sad, a bit despondent, and so are you.'

'Yes, maybe you're right. I've asked to talk to him, but he doesn't seem to want to talk to me.'

Ruth patted my hand, the nearest she had ever got to being affectionate towards me.

'Just persist,' she advised. 'A great friend of mine, Serena, lovely girl, once said to me, "If you can't feel something towards your husband, act as if you do, and after a while you will genuinely feel love again." And that included sex. You must have sex even if you don't feel like it.'

'Thanks, Ruth. I will try.' I shifted in my chair, trying to recover from the embarrassment of having my mother-in-law discussing sex with me.

'Go off and enjoy yourself,' she ordered. 'You don't want to sit around all day with your old mother-in-law.'

We laughed. In all the years that I'd known Ruth we'd never really shared a joke. So that afternoon, at the party, was a memorable first. I walked back into the conservatory, which was filled with a lone man's cigar smoke. I poked my head into the silvery-grey drawing room and headed over to Jack, who was talking to a tallish man who turned out to be our host.

'Lovely party.' I shook his hand.

'Thank you, my dear. We always have a party in August.'

He was like a caricature of a man who has been to public school, then graduated to the Grenadier Guards, followed by a stint in the city before retiring to the country, where he may have dabbled in stocks and shares. He was perfectly charming, but perfectly detached too, and probably shared Annie's father's view that women were only whole and happy when barefoot and looking after children.

'I'm going to take your mother home now, Jack. Do you know where Annie and Marco are?'

'I think they went home to check on the baby.'

'Right,' I nodded, thankfully not gauche enough to enquire, 'What baby?'

By Monday afternoon when it was time to pack up and leave, I still hadn't had a chance to talk to Jack properly. As we walked to the car in the tender evening light, I breathed in the salty sea smell and wished that I didn't have to go back to London and work at Café Blue. The children followed me to the car and Maud asked if she could come with me.

'You'll have much more fun here, Maudie.'

'I'll look after you,' Jed offered, trying to put an arm round her.

'I want Mummy.' She began to cry.

'Oh, Maudie.' I crouched down and picked her up. 'I'll be back in a few days for a long time.'

Jack took my suitcase to the car. I put my hands round his neck and whispered, 'I love you,' but wasn't sure if he'd heard, because Jed was climbing on to his back and Maud was clinging on to me like a monkey. It was awful leaving the children while they were on holiday but, I persuaded myself, other women worked in the holidays, I couldn't put my life on hold and I'd be back in a few days for the last week.

Petra, the children and Jack waved at the car as we drove away from the house and I had a rather dark premonition that everything was not as it should be. Things were unsettled and difficult and a little ominous. We didn't talk much on the way home, we'd all had too much to drink, too much food and too much sun. The traffic was, of course, terrible.

I walked through the front door to find a pile of post. I picked it up and took it through to the sitting room. I hadn't checked my mobile all weekend and didn't particularly want to. I turned on the television, opened the doors to the garden and wished very much that I could go back down to the sea. I checked on the small herb garden and went to lie in the middle of the labyrinth. Then I returned to the house and telephoned the landline at the rented house, knowing Jack didn't have a very good signal on his mobile. The phone rang on and on until I was just about to hang up, when it was finally answered.

'Lee House.'

'George, is that you?'

'Yes, speaking.'

'George, I'd like to speak to my husband, Jack.'

'Jack?'

'Yes, Mr Boore.'

'I'll have a look,' he said. 'It's rather late.'

'Yes, I'm sorry.'

He left the receiver dangling and I heard his footsteps

stamping across the stone floor. I waited for ages, more than ten minutes, and was about to hang up when I heard someone clearing their throat down the receiver.

'Jack, is that you?'

'It's George here. I can't find Mr Boore; his mother says he must be taking a bath.'

'Could you take a message?'

'Yes.' His tone remained flat and charmless.

'Could you say that his wife called to say goodnight?'

'To say goodnight.'

'Yes.'

'Right you are.'

He put the receiver down. The whole episode seemed to confirm how difficult it was to communicate with Jack. As my head touched the pillow, it occurred to me that I should stop trying for a while. Just before I turned off the light I went to the window and peeked through the curtain, like some twittering old pervert. Mark's light was on. He was there. I imagined him getting into bed, lying there alone. I wondered if he ever thought about me now.

15

I woke early but feeling quite rested. Downstairs I made myself a cup of tea and glanced at the pile of letters. There were two that had been posted by hand using the same handwriting. I tore open the top one with a quickening heart beat.

Darling Ellie,
Please please return my calls, give me a chance to talk to you.
M

I read it quickly then ripped open the second one:

Ellie,
We really need to speak. Must explain to you what happened the other day when your friend was here.
M

I pulled on a fawn-coloured linen dress and wedge sandals and wondered what he could say about attempting to seduce my friend – what was there to say that would make it any better? I poured myself a bowl of cereal, checked my watch and called Jack again. The telephone rang on and on, until finally I gave up. The café had been closed for three days and there was so much to do. I was obsessed with the idea that it would have to be aired, dusted and given a thoroughly good clean, even though it had had a thoroughly good clean before I'd left. I also had to go over the menus with Andy, write them up and print them and chalk up the specials on the board.

I opened the door, pushing my sunglasses up on to my head. Mark was leaning against the wall. 'Hi,' I said, sounding weirdly unsurprised.

'Ellie, I . . . did you get my notes?'

'I just got them. But, Mark, I've got to get to the café. Tilda's on holiday, but you probably know that.'

He was dressed in a well-cut grey suit. He was handsome, as men usually are in suits, though he was more handsome than most men.

'I'll be over at lunchtime, I have to explain. It's not what you think it is.'

'Not at lunch. It would be best if you could come either just before or just after lunch. But really it would be best if you didn't come at all. I mean, what is there to say?'

'Around eleven or around three?' He ignored my rebuff, exiting easily through the gate.

There was a small, orderly queue waiting for Café Blue to open. My spirits had lifted and I felt strangely, absurdly light – even happy. Andy was back from his holiday and was downstairs in the kitchen, cleaning the fridge. A box of salad and vegetables lay on the table.

'Hi, Andy.'

'Hello . . . have you seen the queue outside?'

'Amazing.'

'I think we should order a fan,' he suggested. 'Industrial size.'

'Don't they cost a fortune?' I sneezed.

'Well, I know someone who can get it for us cheap. He's a mate – he's got a kitchen wholesale shop down near Dagenham.'

'That would be great. Thanks, Andy. I owe you one.'

'That's all right. But I'll remember that – 'bout you owing me one.' He winked at me. 'Do you want to see my new tattoo?' He pulled up his sleeve and showed me the entwined initials A and B.

'What's B for?'

'Babe – I figured that if me and my bird don't make it, another babe will come along.'

After the breakfast rush I tied my hair back, put on an apron and began to dust, sneezing as I walked briskly round the café. A few lone stragglers came in for smoothies or coffees. By twelve I began to register the fact that I was disappointed; I worried that he had changed his mind about coming.

At four, after a table of schoolgirls had left, I realized he wasn't coming. I sighed and got down on my knees, sweeping up crumbs into a small dustpan. The door swung open. He smiled his wide, infectious smile, hesitating on the threshold.

'Hi, Mrs Mop.'

'Come in.' My heartbeat drummed against my ribs. I stood up and beckoned him over to a table and we sat down. 'Can I get you a coffee or something?' I fiddled with the strings of my long blue and white apron.

'I just want to speak to you. It won't take long.' God, he was attractive when he was serious.

'Go on then, I'm waiting, quick before someone comes in.'

'It wasn't me with Tilda.' He looked me directly in the eye.

I took a sip of water. 'Yeah, right. Tilda said she'd gone to your house. Petra saw you.'

'Petra! That girl is in such a bubble, one prick and she'd evaporate.'

'Well, if it wasn't you, who was it?'

'My younger brother.'

'Your younger brother!'

'Yes, he was staying at my house.'

'Who is this brother? Why didn't he tell Tilda that he was your younger brother?'

'I don't know, maybe he did and she's forgotten.' I looked at Mark. I wondered for a moment whether he was telling the truth but, intuitively, I believed him. I was shocked but relieved, because I had been so sure that we had had a real and true connection. Thank God the whole scenario hadn't been as humiliating and as awful as I had imagined.

The door to the café swung open. It was Candy, a regular who came in morning and afternoon for a chocolate croissant. She was one of those fat, sexy women: pale skin, dark hair, red lips and a swaggering confidence. I could see that a particular kind of man would find all that flesh irresistible, a cushion on which to bury their worries. We usually had a chat about the weather, and once she'd even shown me an underwired lacy bra that she'd bought at Selfridges.

'Hi, Candy . . . Usual?' I asked, standing up, walking towards the counter, reaching for the croissant.

'I'll have a coffee as well. Very strong. I had quite a night.'

I said nothing, not wanting to open up the conversation any further, while Mark – who was checking his mobile – sat waiting for me. 'Quite a night,' she muttered under her breath.

I handed her the bag with the croissant and while she waited for the coffee she stuffed it into her mouth in two quick, greedy gulps. Minutes ticked by as she fumbled around a black purse for the right change. She pulled out the coins, one by one; some of them were covered in hair and crumbs.

'One, two tens, and let me see.'

'Don't worry about the rest.'

'Well, I owe you.' She looked over at Mark. 'Is he your fancy man?' she whispered.

'Oh God, no . . .'

'The lady doth protest too much.'

'No really, Candy, he's just a friend.'

'What's your brother's name?' I asked as soon as she'd left.

'Matthew, Matt. He's lives in Cornwall and was up in town to see a few people. He also happens to be separated from his wife too, except he's been separated for a couple of years and they're about to get a divorce. He's the more sensitive, creative type. "The furniture maker."' He made quote signs in the air with his fingers. 'In fact, it's his way of not doing very much. I was always the apparent blue-eyed boy, so as a result we're not that close. He resents me and I feel guilty, and I'm still trying to make it up to him. We do look quite similar, it's true. But I'm better looking.' He laughed.

'How weird. If you were twins it could have been something out of a Shakespearean comedy. I'm not quite sure I believe it.'

A man walked in, long dreadlocks flowing down his back. 'One minute, Mark,' I said. I stood up, aware that Mark was watching me, and served the dreadlock man. I made him a cappuccino and handed him the cheese and home-made hummus baguette, longing to get back to Mark, who sat gazing at me. The man left. I returned to my seat, bringing a juice with me.

'Please believe it.' He was giggling. 'It's true. Sorry, I shouldn't laugh. But it's true. I promise. I left him a note to say that you were the only person I knew on the street. I mentioned the labyrinth. Anyway, I shouldn't have done it. I didn't realize he would actually go and knock on the door. Not unless the house was burning down or something.'

'But I left you a long message on your mobile, saying I wouldn't be there.'

'I only got half of your message, it was cut off halfway through. Anyway, it was a huge misunderstanding; you can speak to Matt if you want. I have his number on my mobile. If you ever come and visit me again, I'll show you his photograph. He's only eighteen months younger than I am. I don't know why he was flirting with your friend. Maybe he was lonely. I think he's written her a card.' He took my hand. 'You will come and see me again, won't you? Please.'

'OK,' I said rashly. 'This is all so mad, I . . .'

'There is always some madness in love, but there is always some reason in madness.'

I didn't ask him where the quote was from; I didn't want to sound too ignorant. I just nodded, aware that I was unravelling again. 'I'll come and visit you this evening for a drink, just so that I can see the photograph.'

'Great.' He left quickly, standing up in one swift, decisive moment, and then he was through the door without looking back.

As soon as he'd gone I called Petra on her mobile. The voicemail came on instantly. I tried the house, not expecting a reply, but after four or five rings Jed answered.

'Darling, it's Mummy. How are you?'

'Not that good. I've hurt my knee and cut my face and I've got a bruise on my thigh.'

'Poor darling. How did you cut your knee and your face?'

'I ran and fell on some stones.'

'Oh darling, poor boy. I wish I was there to kiss you. Has Petra put some arnica on your bruise? And some cut and sore cream on your cuts?'

'Yes, she has, but she wants to kiss it and it's soppy.'

'Let her kiss it. It may make it feel better.'

'Mum! NO!'

'I'm going to telephone you tonight, to see how you are. And I'm coming to join you for the last week of the holidays. So we'll have fun. Can you find Petra?'

'Yes, OK, Mummy.'

'Bye, darling.'

I could hear him running. I hadn't talked to him properly. I hadn't told him how much I loved him or blown him a kiss down the phone.

'Hello.' Petra's sing-song voice came down the line.

'Hi, Petra.'

'Hi, how are you?'

'I'm fine. How are you?'

'You know, OK. The country is a bit boring. Lots of fields, sea, birds. Nothing.'

I laughed. 'I just wanted to check about the other day. You know, you said you saw my neighbour, Mark. Are you sure it was Mark? Or could it have been his brother?' I heard her yawn.

'It looked like the handsome Mark, but it could have been his brother.'

'Thanks, Petra, that's great.'

'Why?'

'Oh, I can't explain. Are the children all right?'

'Yes, they're great.'

'I'm coming soon. Soon as Tilda's back; probably Thursday.'

After we'd said goodbye, I realized I hadn't bothered to find out what the children were eating or how they'd been sleeping or whether Jed had peed in his bed, which made me worry and wonder if I should call her back to ask.

After work that day, I went home and took a long shower. I washed my hair, blow-dried it, and put on a cream-coloured summer dress decorated with a small brown print. It was neatly ironed and I had been saving it up for a special occasion.

Jack sent me a text, which I read just before I left.

> **Hope you ok. Sending this as I**
> **go to buy wine in the short**
> **mile that there is a signal. X J**

I got back to him right away.

> **Fine will call you on landline**
> **in one hour. Love Ellie**

It was eight twenty when I rang Mark's door and I had almost decided not to come. What was the point? After the relief when he explained that it had been his brother and not him trying to seduce my friend, I had spent a sober few hours reminding myself that he was willing to give his marriage another go. In the end though, I had decided to meet him, just to see the photograph and put an end to it all. A minute or two passed before he came to the door. We kissed rather formally, mouth to cheek, as though we were friends greeting each other before the start of a dinner party.

He led me into their sitting room, so much more relaxed and informal than ours. There was a laptop on the sofa and several magazines spread over the floor. The door to the garden was open. The radio was playing music in the kitchen. He smiled at me and offered me a drink and showed me a white marble pestle and mortar that he had found in a junk shop. He poured me a glass of Pimm's and picked a sprig of mint from a pot to put in a green-coloured glass, along with a slice of apple and a strawberry. The drink was cool and sparkling and sweet.

'Come outside and let's sit down. My garden is half the size of yours.' I followed him to the threshold of the door, but couldn't relax enough to walk outside.

'Mark, just before we do anything, can I see the photograph of your brother?'

'You don't trust me.' He stood next to me and his hand touched mine, but not in the easy way it had touched me in New York. 'Yes, of course you can. Come,' he turned round to face me, 'follow me.'

We went back to the sitting room and he pulled out a heavy blue photograph album with thick, white, stiff pages. We flicked past photographs of Mark as a baby, a white-blond baby sitting on a white rug, Mark as a round toddler and, on the last page, a photograph of Mark and his brother, Matt, horse riding at about the ages of eight and nine.

'You're joking? What, I'm meant to believe that you have a brother from a photograph of an eight-year-old? Admittedly you do look quite alike, blond, blue-eyed, well-dressed, but he could have been a friend. A little friend from school.'

Mark was laughing. 'What are you like? Don't you believe a word I say?'

'Not really.' I smiled at him, a real genuine smile. 'Not really at all.'

'Look, it says Matt and Mark, written in my mother's own fair hand, but if you insist, I have a photograph of my wedding day and Matt was best man. He's in the picture.'

Wedding day. The wedding day photograph was the last thing I wanted to see. Why would I want to look at Lorrie and Mark on the happiest day of their lives? All dressed up in expensive clothes. Mark ran upstairs and came down waving a photograph. Lorrie wore a golden dress and they stood on some steps, with a grey building behind. Confetti floated in the air around them. Mark was laughing. Lorrie smiled up at him.

'We got married in a register office. That's Matt,' Mark said, pointing to a man at the end. He was smaller than Mark, his hair was a little longer, his nose a little wider, but they did look like brothers.

'All right, I believe you. What about Lorrie? Is she coming home to try again?'

'No news yet. She wanted to a few weeks ago, but hasn't committed. What about Jack?'

'Jack is off in his own world, being Jack. In fact, Jack should star in a reality show called *Being Jack*, or just *Jack*.'

'That leaves us then.' He smiled at me. 'Come here, beautiful, I want to take a closer look at you.'

'I was so upset,' I began to cry from relief, 'you've no idea.'

'It's like a farce,' he said, wiping my eyes gently with his fingers. 'Ellie, I don't make a habit of being disloyal to women. It was a big thing for me to invite you to New York.'

'It was a huge thing for me to do. I shouldn't have gone.'

'But you did, and we . . .' He looked sad and intense and we kissed just then, the longest, most profound kiss.

'But the point is,' I said as we hugged afterwards, 'the point is, we're both married and it can't go on.'

'Can't it go on just a little?'

I smiled but no words came.

It was ten thirty when we said goodbye. I always loved his mouth. He had large, lush lips, sweet breath, so tempting and so warm on mine. Once I'd got to the sanctuary of my hall, I remembered that I had forgotten about the telephone date I'd made with Jack, which reminded me that I didn't quite trust Mark; being with him made me reckless. I checked my mobile and Jack had left a message at nine or so, asking where I was. I tried calling, but again there was no answer. A few minutes later though, as I was relaxing into the huge white sofa, the landline rang.

'Did you just call?' It was Jack, not Mark as I had hoped.

'Yes, I did.'

'Where have you been?'

'I had a bath and fell asleep on the bed and just woke up.'

'Oh, I thought you were out dancing.' Jack laughed. He had a slightly sleepy, slurry voice. He had been drinking.

'No,' I yawned, waves of guilt and sorrow passing through me. 'I don't know. How could you possibly think that? I have no energy at all.'

'You better get to bed then.'

'How is everything? How are the children?'

'Maud is missing you, I think, but she denies it. Jed is definitely missing you. He's been asking why you can't put him to bed.'

'Oh God. I wish I could be with them. I'm sorry. Charming of Maud. Give them kisses for me tomorrow.'

'Yes, I will. Ellie?'

'Yes?'

'We all love and miss you.'

'I love and miss you.'

'Bye.'

'Bye.'

Oh God, what was I doing? I missed my children too and lying to Jack was appalling. I was spinning out of control, lurching into instability and treachery. Somehow I considered Mark a life force. Having Mark as my lover uplifted me and made me feel like a protagonist in a drama starring as the adulterous wife. But somewhere embedded in my psyche I knew that I had to stop seeing Mark. I had needed Mark, I persuaded myself, because being with him made me feel more vital than I had for many years. After seeing Mark my senses were heightened, everything was sharper, brighter and more vivid. But I knew it wouldn't be like that forever. It couldn't be.

Just before falling into sleep my body and brain clicked into sudden and unwelcome wakefulness. What would Alistair the vicar think if he knew I'd gone to New York? I was acting out one of the most tragic sins, lying to my spouse. What was I thinking? How could I be so selfish and so wanton? A few days before I had wanted to make the marriage work and had contemplated moving down to the country with Jack. I was awake for most of the night, worrying about the situation, swinging from one extreme resolution to another.

The next morning I woke feeling sluggish and tired but determined to telephone Alistair and talk him through the situation. In the middle of the night I had managed to convince myself that he would find my dilemma boring and unworthy of his time, but by nine, charged up with determination to see it through and a desperate need for someone else to haul me in, I dialled the number. After three brisk rings, an answering machine clicked on. There was a short, curt message stating that the Reverend Alistair was away until the 14th September, more than two weeks away. His part-time PA, Charlotte, would deal with urgent matters.

Was it considered urgent when a wife was unable to resist her neighbour? I considered leaving a message with Charlotte, but wisely decided against it. After much reflection I had realized that however much I wanted to,

I had to deny myself the pleasure of seeing Mark. I wouldn't be able to avoid seeing him, but I would not be intimate with him. And that was final.

I had been trying to telephone Tilda since finding out that Mark had a brother called Matt. Every time I telephoned her in Italy, the answering machine had come on. Once I had got through and we had been cut off before I'd told her the news. I tried again that morning. She telephoned back as I was sitting on the loo, but when I returned the call there was no reply.

'I think there is a romance blossoming,' Jack laughed down the telephone the next time I spoke to him.

'Between who?'

'My mother and George.'

'Really?'

'Yes.'

'But how do you know?'

'Well, he helps out the gardener twice a week and he took Ma to show her some olive trees. He gave her a lettuce, which she claims tastes of chemicals and then today they've gone off somewhere. To a local garden that's open to the public.'

'Wowww . . .'

'I've noticed that she's done her hair and is wearing her best shoes. And old man George even donned a tie. Rather sweet – he's like something out of Colonial India, like a minor civil servant, a policeman. Ma's all kind of giggly, but it hasn't stopped her complaining, you know how she likes a good moan. Well, she was moaning about the view today. Says she going to go home soon as there's not enough sea view from her room!'

I laughed. 'Can I speak to the children?'

'Maud,' I could hear Jack calling, 'Maudie, it's Mummy.'

'Daddy?'

'Maudie, it's Mummy – she wants to talk to you.'

'I don't want to talk to her.'

'Go on, Maud.'

'Sorry,' Jack came on the telephone, 'no, she's not up for it.'

'Jed?'

'Jed's made friends with a boy who's staying next door. He's over at their house.'

I came off the telephone feeling neglectful and longing to join my family, just as soon as Tilda was back. If I could see Maud and give her a hug, she would stop being cross with me for not being with her. And I worried about Jed, because sometimes Jack was a bit rough and insensitive with him.

That afternoon, just as I had closed the café, Tilda telephoned to say she wouldn't be back until Thursday evening, not Wednesday; she had made a mistake with her ticket.

'And what did you want to say to me? I got your message.'

'Well, I saw Mark, and it seems that you didn't see him, didn't even kiss him – you met his brother, Matt.'

'Matt?'

'Yes, Matt.'

'Matt is different from Mark?' She sounded very confused.

'Yes, did you call him Matt or Mark?'

'We only met about three times. Now I come to think of it, I suppose it could have been his brother. He did introduce himself when he knocked on the door, maybe he did say Matt and not Mark. How weird. I'm so sorry, Ellie. But I don't think you ever told me that your neighbour was called Mark.'

'Maybe I didn't tell you he was called Mark. I can't remember now. Didn't he say anything when he took you to the house?'

'Well, yes ... maybe he said he was staying there rather than living there. I presumed they were renting. It all happened so quickly. We didn't actually spend that much time together. Oh, it's all so creepy and unreal.'

'I know. I almost believe it, but there's part of me that doubts Mark.'

'No, he couldn't make something like that up. If I saw him his cover would be blown.'

'Yes, that's true.'

I sat down on one of our wooden chairs and picked at a piece of green plasticine that a child had wedged on to the corner of the seat.

'So you and Mark?' Tilda probed. 'What's going to happen?'

'I just wanted to see him once more to put my mind at rest but I'm not going to see him again.'

'Good. I think that's the right decision.'

'Have you heard from Tom?' I changed the subject because talking about never seeing Mark again made me sad and almost tearful.

'At least twice a day. He wants to come home. He swears it was all a dreadful mistake. The separation, short as it has been, has changed him. You will never believe this but he did a kind of five-day residential therapy course to sort himself out. This is a man who couldn't even admit he was ill, he was so fearful of sounding weak. He seems different anyway. He surprised me by taking us to the airport; he even looks different.'

'In what way?'

'Better looking. Less white and puffy, and he's lost weight.'

'Already.'

'Yes, well, he can't cook and presumably the woman can't cook either, but they must have gone out to dinner together. I mean that's what lovers do, isn't it?'

'Don't even go there.'

'No, I won't. But you know what?'

'What?'

'I imagined us being separated and sharing Frankie. Being naked in front of someone new, letting Frank go off on holiday with Tom's new woman and wondering whether Frank would grow to love her. I thought about what it would be like to have every other Christmas without Frank. Now that we are going to make a go of it together, I'm so relieved. Staying married just seems so much easier.'

'Yes, you've got a point. I'm sure if I went off with Mark, we'd be in love for a year and then he'd start to find my sneezing and dusting irritating.'

'Never!' Tilda laughed. 'Irritating, you? Hang on, Frank, I'm on the phone.'

'Just one second,' I said, 'there's something else.'

I told her the best news first, that for the first time we'd had a profitable month. We were making quite good money, and the property next door had come up for sale.

'Can you imagine? We could become an empire, with a Café Blue in every city.'

'God, that would be amazing.'

'We have to discuss the next phase of our business at a kind of crossover meeting on Friday morning before I go.'

'You could come over for supper on Thursday night – we could chat about it then.'

'OK, I'll see you then. Thanks.'

Tilda sounded stronger, more herself. I knew then that she and Tom would get back together.

16

I hadn't intended to see Mark again. I had planned to stay in London, work the following day, stay one more night at the house, have dinner with Tilda on the Thursday and then head off to Hampshire on the Friday for a week. My new mantra was to love and cherish Jack and the children, concentrate on building up the café, think about buying the property next door and discuss the idea of a part-time week with Tilda.

It was Wednesday morning. I was wearing a long, turquoise Marc Jacobs T-shirt with a print of a London bus on it and no pants. I was drinking my tea, half listening to a progamme on the radio about the habits of an ugly creature called a mole rat, when I saw the orange recycling lorry pull up outside. I put my cup of tea down, grabbed the orange bag stuffed full of wine bottles and old newspapers and leapt outside. The door slammed behind me. The men whistled at me and I blushed with shame. They drove off. I decided to rap on Pauline's door, as she always kept an extra key.

As I pressed the bell, I remembered that Pauline had gone off on holiday to a forest campsite in Denmark. 'Fuck,' I said out loud, 'fuck, fuck.' Our new cleaner was away too, back home in Poland. I crossed the road in my bare feet and rapped cautiously on Mark's door.

He was a long time coming. For one or two awful moments I wondered what to do if he was not in either. I planned to wait until the café was open, then limp up to the High Street, pulling my T-shirt over my bum. I would hail a taxi and take it to the café and get some money out of the petty-cash box.

When he did turn up he was wrapped in a towel. His hair was wet. In a porn movie I would have ripped off his towel there and then and we would have made out in the hall.

'What brings you here?' He smiled at me.

'I'm so sorry.'

'Don't apologize, I was fantasizing that you would turn up like this.'

'It's not how it seems.'

'Shame, cos it seems great.'

'It's ... I've been locked out.'

'Come in. I'm making coffee. We'll call a blacksmith, I mean a locksmith.'

We sat in his kitchen and after I'd called the locksmith and he'd lent me a pair of boxer shorts, we went out onto his patio and sat on some green chairs. We started to speak at the same time:

'I have something ...'

'We must talk ...'

'Lorrie is coming home on Saturday. I'm going to give it a go, really try and get the marriage back on track. She wants to. But please believe me, I'll always love you, Ellie. You're a special girl and you touched me.'

'You too,' I said, stretching out my legs, 'you touched

me, but I was going to say the same thing, I want to make my marriage work.' He looked relieved and then saddened. 'You have no idea how much I longed for you.'

'I do,' he said, 'I have an idea. I presume you have longed for me as I have longed for you.'

'The thing is,' I said, tucking my legs under the long T-shirt, 'it would be awful to split up my family, and quite honestly we'd probably be bored of each other in a couple of years.'

'Maybe.' He stood up, kissed the top of my head. 'But I doubt it.' He looked at his watch; my heart thudded and quickened and became heavy as I knew these were our last few minutes together. 'I have to go, sweetheart, but you can stay here till the locksmith comes.'

I stood up, biting my lip so that I wouldn't cry. We hugged and then we drew apart, holding hands as if we were about to dance. We stood for a while in silence and then we slowly let our hands slip from each other. 'Goodbye.'

'Goodbye.'

After he'd gone, I went back to the patio and slumped back into a deckchair. Everything was going to be all right. Neither of us had got hurt and our marriages were intact. After a few months the ache of wanting him would diminish. I sat weighed down in my chair, too sodden with grief to move.

The locksmith turned up an hour later, a stout middle-aged man with a protruding stomach and an easy smile.

'Can't be that bad? Can it?' he asked, studying me.

'No, not that bad.'

'You'll be back at home soon. Safe and sound.'
'Yes.'

I was on my way to Tilda's for a drink on the Thursday night, when Jack telephoned. I knew immediately that something was wrong: his voice was subdued and grave but tinged also with a weird and strange tone of panic.

'What?' I demanded. 'What?'

'You better come down at once. Jed is missing.'

'What ... what do you mean?' A police siren wailed somewhere near me. 'Jack, I'm going to stop the car and ring you back. Are you by the landline?'

'Yes,' his voice was breaking, 'my boy ... where is my boy? Ellie, we need you. You can't be away all the time.'

When I called back he answered immediately and then he began to cry, great hulking sobs and big rasping breaths, as though he'd been bottling up his fear and misery while waiting to talk to me.

'How long has he been missing?' I asked when he'd recovered slightly, regretting the days that I had been away from my family.

'Since lunchtime. He's with this boy, this older boy, Francis, who's staying in one of the cottages up the road. Francis came over this morning. I said they could make a den near the copse. I went to check up on them about half an hour after Francis arrived. They were gone. I should have checked after twenty minutes of course. We've been looking ever since. Up and down the beach, through the woods, up the lane. I was in the study most of the morning learning lines for the first couple of episodes. The most awful part of it is that I can't remember what he was wearing.' He broke down again in tears.

'Was he wearing the dinosaur T-shirt?'

'I'm not sure.'

'Where's Petra?'

'Petra went to stay with her friend in Bournemouth. She said she needed a break.'

'Why? Why didn't you call me?'

'I didn't want to alarm you unnecessarily, darling.'

'Oh my God, Jack, how am I going to get to you? I'm shaking. My body is shaking all over.'

'Drive now. You must. The police have been and now they are sending out a team with dogs. I've been down the beach with Francis's parents, nice couple, into the wood. We're going out again. Oh yes, the police need a photograph.'

'A photograph? I've got one on my phone.' I scrolled to the picture of Jed, naked from the waist up, arms stretched out in a wide V. He was smiling. 'I can't live my life without Jed. My life isn't worth living without Jed.'

'Darling, don't dread the worst, not yet, please, he's probably wandered off and they got lost. You better send the photograph to my mobile.'

'I will . . . bye.'

I sat in the car for twenty minutes pleading with God to make it all right, to bring him home. I'll do anything, I bargained with God, if you bring Jed back to me. If I'd been there, I convinced myself, it wouldn't have happened. If I hadn't stayed in London to work but had gone to the country for a holiday with my husband and children, it wouldn't have happened. Jed missing was some dark retribution.

I telephoned Tilda, starting off with a calm hello and descending into a howl.

'Jed's missing. I'm driving down now. I can't make dinner.'

She offered to drive me, but I declined, wanting to be alone in my madness and get there as quickly as possible. I drove as fast as I could, believing in some strange way that the sooner I got there the sooner he would return.

While I was in the car, I spoke out loud to Jed, willing him to be all right. *Jed come home, Jed come home.* My mobile lay on the passenger seat, and I longed for it to ring and everything to be normal again. It would be Jack saying that he'd been found. When I reached the M3 it began to rain, great torrents of water slashing against my windows. I thought then of Jed, sodden by some roadside, lying injured, the other boy next to him. Jed. I had a picture in my head of him as a small baby. I had one hand under his head and the other holding his back and he floated in the bath, his tiny face looking up at me.

When I arrived at the house, Ruth came to meet me. She watched me stagger out of the car and steered me carefully and a little too slowly towards the house. She sat me down and even brought me a cup of far too weak, sugary tea.

'I'm sure it's just a boy thing,' she said, 'he'll be back soon.'

'But Jed isn't like that. He's such a good boy.'

Maud was still up. I pulled her on to my lap and for once she didn't resist. 'Maudie, what happened?'

'I don't know,' she said, sticking her thumb in her mouth. 'I don't know, Mummy. But Jed hates it when you and Daddy arguing.'

'Where is Daddy?'

'He's looking for Jed.'

A few minutes after Maud had gone to bed, a police-woman came to the house and asked me if she could speak to Maud. I woke Maud, and asked her if she wanted a cup of warm milk. She loved warm milk and I knew she would follow me into the kitchen. The policewoman took off her hat, sat down and, after warming the milk, I made her tea. She was pretty, blonde, quite plump, aged about thirty, with a shiny face. She asked to see Maud's teddy that was in fact a dog.

'Maud,' she probed gently, 'do you know where your brother went? Did he tell you he was going to go and hide?'

'No, he didn't. I don't know.'

'Are you sure? It's very important that you tell us because then we can go and find him.'

'I don't know,' she said again. She climbed on to my lap, which was very unlike her and I hoped she wouldn't tell the policewoman that Jed ran away because his parents rowed.

'Mummy, will you tell me a story?'

'Yes, in a minute.'

'Will you tell me a story about me and Lola? The one about the party and us dancing like fairies?'

'Yes, I will. In a minute, I will.'

PC Michelle asked if she could look in his bedroom and followed us up the stairs. The children were sharing a small room at the corner of the house that had a view of a yard and the front gate. Jed should have been on the top bunk, while Maud slept at the bottom.

'Where is Jed?' Maud asked.

'I don't know.' I bit my lip, not wanting to cry in front of her. 'I think he'll be back soon. I think he's playing somewhere with his friend.'

'I want to see Jed,' she said.

'Me too, darling, but we'll see him tomorrow.'

The policewoman climbed up the bunk ladder and then came down again, and I turned off Maud's light. I said a little prayer to myself as I walked down the stairs: 'If someone has Jed, please don't scare him. Please don't let Jed be frightened.'

Back in the kitchen Michelle sat down again; she looked tired and her hair was a little greasy under the hat.

'Mrs Boore, were you aware that his duvet cover is missing?'

'No,' I said. 'I wasn't aware.'

She was writing something in a notebook. 'Do you know the pattern of the cover?'

'Well, at home he has a dinosaur one and a kind of monster one. But, well, this is a holiday home. We don't actually live here. I haven't spent much time here,' I confessed. 'To be honest, I feel terrible that I haven't been here.' A few hot tears trickled down my cheeks.

'Would your husband know?'

'I'm not sure, but we have an au pair. Her name is Petra and she's gone away. She knows that Jed is missing and she's in a terrible state about it, but I'll call her now about the duvet cover. She's coming back tomorrow in the morning.'

'If you could call her. Thank you.'

I spoke briefly to Petra on a mobile phone that kept cutting out.

'Oh Gods, it's so terrible, oh gods, it's so terrible. Tomorrow morning I will be there.' I asked her about the duvet and she remembered that the duvet cover was blue gingham.

PC Michelle wrote more notes in her book and then questioned me about Jed: Was he happy at school? Had he had a row with his father? Did he get on with Petra? Was he the kind of child to wander off? What was his hair-cut like? When she asked me the question about his hair, I put my head on the table and sobbed without shame.

After the policewoman left I found a bottle of brandy and poured myself a glass. The liquid burnt down my throat and made me shudder.

I couldn't sleep. I was so worried and so plagued with guilt, sure that Jed had run away because of his rowing parents. I finally collapsed on the bed and dozed off for a few minutes as it began to get light and dreamt that I was falling from a great height. Jack appeared and lay down next to me. We clung to each other like drowning rats on a raft adrift on a big sea and I realized how far apart we had been from each other for so long and how much I wanted to be close to him again.

'Where is he?' Jack asked. 'They were playing in their den at the copse at the end of the garden and when I went to find them, they had gone. We've looked and we've looked, I can't think where they could be. I should have checked, I should have checked.'

'Don't blame yourself, Jack.' I stroked his hair as I had done when we first met. 'Don't blame yourself,' I said again, though I knew I would have if I had been in charge.

I slept for an hour or two and then for a split second when I woke, everything was normal. With the realization that Jed was missing my body shook with grief and waves of despair folded through me. My chest felt tight, and there was a profound heaviness about me as I climbed out of bed and made my way down to the kitchen. Jack slumbered on; he was always good at sleeping through anything. I had begun to fear the worst, but living my life without Jed seemed unfathomable. I boiled an egg for Maud and knew that I couldn't live apart from Jack. I made myself a cup of tea, but couldn't drink it.

I was out at seven fifteen, searching the beach, calling their names, calling and calling until my voice was hoarse, with Maud trailing behind me. Then at eight, as I was returning to the house, I saw the parents of the other missing boy walking up the drive. Jane and Luke were a London couple like us, staying with her sister in one of the coastguard cottages. Their only son, Francis, was a year older than Jed. Jane was a highlighted blonde with a sloppy, hippy appearance and a husky, sexy voice. He was dark and quiet, and very polite. Their son had taken his duvet and they had also discovered that some tins of food were missing. We wandered out to the terrace at the back of the house, which had a view of the sea.

'I have to say, I'm relieved,' I said. 'It sounds like they had a plan to run away. My biggest fear was that they had been snatched by someone.'

'Yes,' Jane agreed, 'but why haven't they come home?'

'I think they will be just fine,' Luke said. 'Of course, we're all emotional and physical wrecks, but little boys are robust creatures.'

Jack joined us and made everyone a cup of tea. In normal life he only made tea for himself. He also took the trouble to make me a bacon sandwich, on white bread, with tomato ketchup, which I couldn't eat. Maud climbed on top of me, wrapping herself around me, clinging like a monkey. She smelt of coconut and sun. Jack urged me to eat, but I couldn't, not even a bite.

At nine, Jack went to fetch Ruth, and Maud and I went down to the beach again, but this time walking the other way. I waited until Maud had gone to look for shells and then telephoned my parents. Dad answered the phone, saying hello in his languid drawl.

'Dad, Daddy, Jed is missing. He's gone missing. Dad, I don't know what to do.'

'We're on our way. Just give me directions. We'll be there. I'll call you back when we're in the car.'

'Thank you.'

'Your mother will want to be with you too. Shall I call your sister?'

'No, don't worry her yet, Daddy.' I hadn't called him Daddy since I was six years old.

Petra arrived about half an hour after Maud and I returned from our walk. I was pleased, really pleased, that she wasn't wearing a bikini bottom and oversized bra or a skirt the size of a belt. She wore a pair of jeans and a man's shirt, totally befitting the austere gravity of the situation. Her hair was in plaits and she wore no make-up. She looked like a very tall twelve-year-old.

She blamed herself for taking a day off, as we all blamed ourselves in our different ways. I hugged her and reassured her that it was not her fault. She said she wanted to go and look for the boys. She changed from flip-flops into sturdy boots, put on some sunglasses and set off. While she was gone, Maud and I played with a tea set and two teddy bears, one of whom, apparently, had broken his arm and leg. My ears strained for any noise – a telephone ringing, the sound of Jed's voice, a cry, a shout. Jack chain-smoked in his study, made cups of coffee and tried to learn his lines, but gave up and sat down to listen to the soothing, easy sounds of Neil Young, which he played very loudly.

Petra was still gone at lunchtime and there was no signal on her mobile to call her. Jack and Maud ate pitta bread filled with banana and bacon but I could only manage one tiny corner that made me feel nauseous. Ruth said she'd never heard of a banana and bacon sandwich and could I find her some cheese; I snapped at her and asked her how she could be so demanding at such a desperate time. We were wretched and taut with worry and Jack said we had to go searching in the car, but we were afraid to go too far without signals on our mobiles.

We drove back to the house and a few minutes later, sometime in the afternoon, Petra returned.

'We're here!' she called out from the pentagon-shaped hall. 'I found them!' We ran from all directions of the house. I flung myself on Jed, kissing him all over, while Jack hugged Francis.

'I'm sorry, Mum. Sorry, Dad.' Jed was crying.

'Sorry,' Francis mumbled.

'Sorry doesn't quite do it for me,' Jack said. 'I'll need something more than that.'

'Where were they?' I was weeping with relief, dizzy with gratitude and shaken because now that the boys were back, anger was surfacing. 'Jed! How could you disappear? We have been mad with worry.'

Petra went to the kitchen, took off her boots and stood barefoot, drinking a glass of water. She seemed to have regained her *joie de vivre*.

'I went to the place where we climbed the cliffs a few days ago. The boys loved it there. I climbed to the top and shouted to them. They had climbed through the wire and made a kind of camp at the bottom of a garden. It was that big house very, very far down the beach with the swimming pool. You know?'

'Thank you, Petra, thank you. Thank you.'

'You're a good girl.' Jack came over and gave her a kiss. 'Words don't convey how grateful we are that you found them. I'm still not sure how we missed them.'

'Why did you do it?' I asked Jed, who was sitting on a kitchen chair, swinging his legs back and forth.

'We wanted to have an adventure. I didn't even think

anyone would notice. You weren't here, Petra wasn't here and Dad is always busy.'

'Sorry,' Francis repeated. Francis was about a head taller than Jed, with short dark hair and olive skin like his father. 'It was my idea,' he said bravely. 'It was my idea to camp.'

'I'm so sorry, boys, that I didn't keep a better eye on you.' Jack grimaced.

'They made a tent,' Petra said, 'with a duvet cover and a stick. They had another duvet on the floor and they had eaten crisps and bread but they had no tin-opener.'

'I missed you, Mum,' Jed said, 'I really did. And we were hungry. Can we have something to eat?'

'Thank God,' Jack said, as we sat watching Jed and Francis eat, waiting for Francis's parents to arrive. 'Thank God you boys are home.'

'I prayed,' I murmured to Jack, falling back into his arms, 'all night. I prayed for you and me and the children. I love you, Jack. Always.'

'I love me too,' Jack joked.

'Jack! Really.'

'I've never been in any doubt about how much I love you all,' Jack said.

'Mum! Dad!' Jed made a face.

'Well, it's better than arguing, isn't it?' Jack said.

'Only a little bit,' Jed laughed.

The sun shone through racing clouds that afternoon and in the early evening, sitting outside with my family, I was so thankful and pleased that there was still love and hope for our lives together. My parents had arrived twenty minutes after Jed and his friend Francis came home and we had all helped to prepare a picnic of marinated chicken thighs, tomato salad and hot dogs, which we ate on a trestle table outside the house. My mother had brought a crystal on a string which she had planned to use to locate Jed and which the children were now using to find hidden treasure.

'I'm very glad we found the boys before you had to go out touting that hocus-pocus crystal thing,' Jack laughed. My mother giggled, even though she took her alternative life very seriously; she even made decisions according to whether the moon was waxing or waning.

We toasted Petra for being the one to find the boys, and then Jack stood up to make a speech.

'Any excuse to hear the sound of my own voice . . .' he began. Lovely Jack, I thought, as he stood there in his sailing shoes. 'Can I also say, Jed, that your running away prank was the prank to outdo all other pranks. A story you will be telling your own children. But please don't run away again. Your mother and I were white with worry.'

We clapped and shouted *encore!* and *bravo!* Petra whistled through her fingers.

That strange day, the day that Jed was lost and then returned, should have marked the beginning of a new era in our marriage and our lives. Jack and I should have been happy ever after, loving and cherishing our two adorable children and each other as we did that summer evening, but sometimes life doesn't work like that.

I had decided quite definitely that I would move to Hampshire to be with Jack, and had found the children schools. I was resigned and, in my more positive moments, even happy to do so. I could see myself living part time in the country, with a healthy glow to my skin and frizzy hair from the salty sea air. I had grown fond of my beach walks and the wing of the house that we would be able to carry on renting, and I could imagine running up the beach with the children and a dog – yes, I could see a black and white sheepdog – whooping and whirling around us. I loved our country bedroom with its white shutters and view of the pine trees and the swirling sea, and the children seemed to thrive with so much space to run in. My plan was to be in London three days a week, staying in Tilda's spare room for two nights. Jack and I went for a long walk, hours before packing up for London, and he admitted how happy he was that I had decided to move down to be with him. He took my hand and we walked along entwined like the couples I had been so envious of a few months before.

Then in the days following our return, we walked around our house in Hampstead, deciding what to put in storage and what to take with us. We were going to rent our house out partly furnished. We packed up the paintings, which we were lending to my sister, and wrapped up wine and champagne glasses to take with us. I went through all the children's clothes, bundling up piles and piles of bottomless pyjamas and too-small swimming suits, and then went through my desk, stuffing piles of paper in recycling bags. It definitely seemed like the end of one era and the beginning of another, more hopeful, one. But during those still hot days in September, just before the children started their new schools in the country, just two days before we were due to move, events unfolded and changed the course of our lives. Mark rang me in hushed whispers:

'The worst has happened, the absolute worst. Lorrie is locked in the bathroom and refusing to come out.'

'Why?' I was buzzing up the electric window in my car, having just pulled up outside my house.

'She's found the parcel with the boxer shorts you borrowed.'

'She opened the parcel?' I had posted a parcel with his boxer shorts and a note saying:

Thank you so much for lending these to me. xxx Ellie

'Yes. I'd forgotten to open it. I didn't realize it was from you. It was lying on a chair in the hall.'

'Just tell her what happened; tell her that I was locked out.'

'I have. But she just won't believe me. She's threatened to tell Jack.'

'Oh *no*.' I leant against the car, finding it hard to breath. 'Why doesn't she believe you?'

'One of her friends saw me leaving with a woman who obviously looked like you at that charity benefit. She thinks I'm having an affair. She's convinced it's you.'

'It *was* me,' I said, looking up at their window, wondering if she was watching me, cursing me, making a voodoo doll of me and sticking pins in it. 'I better go in,' I said.

When Jack returned a few hours later, I searched his face to see if he suspected anything. But he was in a jovial mood and went off whistling to tidy the small shed in the garden. I managed to call Mark on his mobile for an update on events and he told me that she definitely did not believe that I had been locked out. He said his marriage was almost certainly over and advised me not to telephone again. He sounded distant, even cool, though at the end of the conversation, he said, 'Goodbye, my love.'

That evening I asked Jack if we could leave for Hampshire a day earlier than we had planned. 'What's the rush?' he asked me. 'Can't take the heat?'

'You know what it's like when you're going, and you're just waiting for it to happen. I'm exhausted by the knowledge that we're leaving. I just want to go.'

'The moving lorry is booked; we can't change everything now. One more day. Are you OK?' He came to where I was sitting, hunched, on a white chair and massaged my shoulders. I recoiled and squealed with pain and wondered whether he intended to hurt me. 'You're tense,' he said, rubbing my shoulders, 'really tense. Relax, darling.'

'I'm stressed; haven't you heard? Moving is as stressful as divorce.'

'Is it? I don't feel it, not yet, although I'm not going to clear out my desk until the last possible moment. There are so many papers to go through.'

We sat through a tuna pasta dinner, but I only ate a

couple of mouthfuls. Jack fussed around me, urging me to eat more, asking what was wrong. The telephone rang out twice and both times I jumped with fear, panic rising in my chest. After dinner we moved to the one remaining sofa – the other was tipped on its side, covered with plastic wrap, ready to go. I was suddenly afraid. Very afraid. I sat as close as I could to Jack, wanting to be near him, wanting to somehow lap him up.

I didn't sleep that night. Every half an hour or so I would tiptoe to the bathroom and check my mobile, to see if there was a message from Mark. What was I hoping for? A message to say that Lorrie had changed her mind and no longer suspected me of having a liaison with her husband? At around three in the morning I almost sent him a text message, but decided against leaving any more incriminating evidence. I thought about waking Jack and begging him to move first thing in the morning, but I was still sane enough to know it would seem mad.

We ate breakfast with the children on the battered old garden table. At eight thirty the postman rang the bell and for a few terrible moments I imagined it was Lorrie. She would scream at me and call me a marriage-wrecking bitch. She would be holding out Mark's mobile with the video clip of me swaggering and pouting towards him in the bar in New York, like some low-grade tart.

After the postman left, Jack and I packed up the rest of the kitchen; I knew I just had to get to lunchtime and then Jack would leave for an appointment with his accountant. Jed and Maud were going out for the after-noon with my mother. At least when I was in the house alone, I could monitor the front door and the telephone. We didn't talk much as we packed, partly because Jack was listening to a play on Radio 4, which I could not digest or even hear; my mind was in such turmoil.

'So,' Jack said, after we had finally finished the kitchen, 'now I'll have a shave. When I get back from lunch, I've just got my desk to do.'

As he was about to leave, I hugged and kissed him. 'You know I love you always.'

He kissed me. 'And I love you,' he said, opening the door. After he was gone, I wandered around the house and tried to concentrate on picking up the children's toys. The house was very silent and empty and still. I packed up our bathroom and when I stood in the bedroom taking down our curtains I was sure I heard a woman screaming in the street.

In the late afternoon, before the children were back from Kew Gardens, I heard Jack slamming the front door.

'Jack?' I called out.

He didn't come into the kitchen and say hello as he usually would. I went into the hall as he was going up the stairs. 'What is it?' My heart thumped with fear.

He didn't reply; he didn't even turn round to look at me and I couldn't follow him up the stairs because at that moment my mother and the children returned from Kew. The children were tired and excited and my mother needed a cup of tea. She wanted to chat about a holiday she was planning to Sri Lanka, but I was preoccupied and couldn't concentrate, so she put it down to moving nerves and joined the children for a game of matching pairs. Finally she kissed me goodbye and shouted up the stairs to Jack. He appeared for a moment and greeted her with a courteous but curt hello. My mother raised her eyebrows after he'd disappeared and I had to make up an excuse for him. After she'd gone, I bathed the children, far too roughly and quickly, and finally when they were watching a film I was able to go and search for Jack.

He was listening to some classical music in his study. I knocked and he didn't reply, so I gently pushed the door open.

'Jack.' I stood in the threshold.

'What is this?' He turned round. He was holding a small, yellow Post-it note, the one where I had drawn a silly heart, punctured with a childish arrow and the initials M and E at either end a few weeks before. He held it between his forefinger and thumb, dangling it like something dead and rancid.

'It's just a doodle, something I did ages ago. Did you find it in the bin?' I couldn't believe he had found the note; evidence of my adultery. I wondered what to say, how to explain. My eyes darted to the wicker basket on the floor and then to the blu-tack marks on the wall where he'd taken down the film posters and photographs of the children and me.

'So who is M?' He studied me, scrutinized my face, locked me in a stare, until I almost wanted to giggle to set myself free.

'M?'

'M – it's written right here in your writing. With an

E the other end. That's obviously you. I kept that note when I found it, I meant to ask you about it. Don't smirk, Ellie. It doesn't suit you.'

'I don't know, Jack.'

'Well, I do. I've just had a conversation with our neighbour Lorrie. She certainly didn't hold back when she told me all about you and Mark. M for Mark. Always thought the bastard was slimy.'

'But, Jack . . .'

'Don't but me. I remember you calling me from the airport to tell me that you'd bumped into Mark. Eden saw you together at the airport as well. Remember? You obviously went to New York together and had some kind of sordid sex fest. How could you?'

'Jack, this is silly. It's all coincidence . . .' I pleaded desperately, knowing how feeble I sounded, and frightened of his cool anger, not sure what he would do next.

'Don't lie. M is for Mark. There is no doubt in my mind.' Jack went to the window and stood looking out with his back to me. 'I never imagined you could be so low, Ellie.' He sounded disgusted, as though he pitied me.

'Jack . . . I . . . It's all . . .' I began to cry then, because I could see that he was right to loathe me. 'Nothing much happened, not really, I don't love him . . . I never loved him. He's not like you, not in any way. I love you.'

'Ellie, give up protecting me, will you?' he suggested, not unkindly, turning round to face me.

Lorrie went back to America. Mark put the house on the market, as he said there wasn't much point living without a family in a family house. Jack decided to leave me. I begged him to stay with me, beseeched him to listen to me, swore that the whole sorry escapade had been a cry for help, a need for attention, a folly. I repeated over and over again how much I wanted the marriage to work but he had made up his mind and nothing I could say or do would deter him from his decision. I reminded him how happy we had been in the country after Jed was found and how I'd planned to live with him, but he had hardened towards me and was not interested in what I had to say. When I desperately accused him of straying from our marriage and sleeping with the actress from Birmingham, he harshly denied it.

I saw Mark once more after Jack left. We met in a café at the park but the connection between us was stilted, probably because Lorrie had moved back to London and they were doing couple therapy and really trying to get the marriage back on track.

'Things are looking bad for you right now, but life has a strange way of working itself out,' he said, as he brought me a hot chocolate. 'Just you wait and see.'

What he said sounded trite and dismissive and for a moment I hated him.

I often think of that afternoon that turned into a balmy evening, when I sat with my family in the garden by the sea, so relieved that Jed was home. Some days, well, most days, I want to rewind history and pause at that particular point, jump into that scene and stay there forever, laughing with Jack and Maud and Jed.

Acknowledgements

Great heartfelt thank you in no particular order to: Starling Gifford, Peter Evans, Peter Straus, Clare Ledingham, Alexis Sinclair, Natalie Briscow, Maderlane Naylor, Karen Whitlock, Gillian Greenwood, Josa Young, Deborah Susman, and most of all to my husband, Luke White.

JULIA LLEWELLYN

THE MODEL WIFE

How to be The Model Wife

Cook Him a gourmet meal every night.

Never ask Him where He's been.

Make sure He is happy.

Oh, and if He has a first wife . . . humour Her.

PAH!

Twentysomething Poppy became a cliché when an accidental pregnancy presented her with a forty-nine year-old husband. But Luke Norton isn't any old husband – he's the anchorman for television's Seven Thirty News and his ruggedly handsome face is beloved by the nation.

Life isn't coming up roses thanks to the first Mrs Norton's popular column, 'Diary of a Divorce', about her ex, 'the Cad', and his new wife, 'the Bimbo'. Luke's having a midlife crisis and spending more time with his plastic surgeon than his daughter, former lovers are circling like sharks and Poppy's left holding the baby, her modelling career a distant memory. It's time for 'the Bimbo' to fight back and show the world exactly what she's made of . . .

'A perfect beach read' *Elle*

Calling all girls!

It's the invitation of the season.

Penguin books would like to invite you to become a member of Bijoux – the exclusive club for anyone who loves to curl up with the hottest reads in fiction for women.

You'll get all the inside gossip on your favourite authors – what they're doing, where and when; we'll send you early copies of the latest reads months before they're on the High Street and you'll get the chance to attend fabulous launch parties!

And, of course, we realise that even while she's reading every girl wants to look her best, so we have heaps of beauty goodies to pamper you with too.

If you'd like to become a part of the exclusive world of Bijoux, email
bijoux@penguin.co.uk

Bijoux books for Bijoux girls

He just wanted a decent book to read ...

Not too much to ask, is it? It was in 1935 when Allen Lane, Managing Director of Bodley Head Publishers, stood on a platform at Exeter railway station looking for something good to read on his journey back to London. His choice was limited to popular magazines and poor-quality paperbacks – the same choice faced every day by the vast majority of readers, few of whom could afford hardbacks. Lane's disappointment and subsequent anger at the range of books generally available led him to found a company – and change the world.

'We believed in the existence in this country of a vast reading public for intelligent books at a low price, and staked everything on it'
Sir Allen Lane, 1902–1970, founder of Penguin Books

The quality paperback had arrived – and not just in bookshops. Lane was adamant that his Penguins should appear in chain stores and tobacconists, and should cost no more than a packet of cigarettes.

Reading habits (and cigarette prices) have changed since 1935, but Penguin still believes in publishing the best books for everybody to enjoy. We still believe that good design costs no more than bad design, and we still believe that quality books published passionately and responsibly make the world a better place.

So wherever you see the little bird – whether it's on a piece of prize-winning literary fiction or a celebrity autobiography, political tour de force or historical masterpiece, a serial-killer thriller, reference book, world classic or a piece of pure escapism – you can bet that it represents the very best that the genre has to offer.

Whatever you like to read – trust Penguin.